FINDING HOME

A Journey from Ireland to the Texas Badlands

Joel Beeson

Copyright © 2022 by Joel Beeson

All rights reserved. No portion of this book may be reproduced in any form without permission from the publisher, except as permitted by U.S. copyright law.

Cover Design by Robin Locke Monda

Book Design by Robert Henry at Right Hand Publishing

Published by Hawley House Publishing

ISBN: 979-8-9864057-0-4

This book is dedicated
to the many courageous
immigrants who defied all
odds to help build this
great nation.

CONTENTS

CONTENTS

CHAPTER 1

New York

John fought back tears as he held his mother's hand. She was still now and getting colder by the minute. As the sun set, the temperature of the room dropped too. Molly Delaney was gone.

It was late April 1858, and spring in New York was behind schedule. His mother had taken her last breath shortly after his younger sister Nelly left to get the priest. John was not a religious person but his mother had been a good Catholic and he knew she'd have wanted the priest there doing what priests did when people died. Nelly was also fond of all the church business so she would know what to say to the priest. John wondered if the man would come since they were Irish peasants. If Nelly wasn't back soon, he'd need to go find her. This part of New York was no place for a girl of fifteen. He didn't like her being out alone after dark.

It had been just the three of them, living in a one-room apartment above a saloon. They had arrived in New York from Ireland less than a year before. There had been nothing for them there, not after his father died. What family they had left had boarded two different ships for America. His sister Elizabeth, the baby, had died in a tragic accident on the ship and was buried at sea.

The oldest brothers, Daniel and Patrick, had left Ireland first and were living with relatives in Massachusetts. They had both found work though the family had not heard from them since Christmas. Molly wrote to the boys often but they rarely wrote back. John himself could not read. He knew his letters but that was all. He knew Patrick could read and maybe Daniel could but John figured they were too busy.

The loss of baby Elizabeth had been hard on Molly. John did not think she would ever get over her sorrow but somehow she had managed. Molly was a remarkable woman. Tears coursed down John's face as he thought about all his poor mother had gone through. John's father, Michael Flannery Delaney, had died in a British jail, beaten to death by the guards. In June of 1857, there had been a riot in Belfast that lasted ten days. It was the usual Protestants against Catholics. The police, and later the soldiers, mostly Protestants, rounded up the men they thought were the leaders. By chance, they ran across Michael Delaney, who had just arrived in Belfast. They were happy to find him. For years he had led bands of Irish thugs, fomenting no end of chaos for the crown. During that time the British had killed two of his sons and there were arrest warrants out for all the Delaneys.

They locked Michael Delaney up but he died before he could be tried. When word got out that he was dead, the riots began anew. Molly Delaney sold what she had before the British could confiscate it. She booked passage to America, escaping Ireland with what remained of her family.

Though the Delaney family had fought bravely for generations against the English, the war was over now. They had nothing left to fight for. Their land was gone, taken legally by a corrupt English court. Proud Irishmen fought to the death against the British as their Celtic forefathers had done, with the same result. Molly was not going to let them take her remaining children as they had taken everything else. She was not going to let the proud Delaney name die.

She could not have known that America would not be much better. Within a year she would die in a strange new land that didn't want her, chased from her home by a hostile English government happy to see her gone.

Once in America, she had found employment sewing leather for a cobbler in a shoe shop. Jonas Blackman, a local fixer and blackguard, had rented them a room above the saloon. Just when it looked like things might be settling down, Molly took sick. She worked as long as she could with the fever but now she was gone.

John listened as he waited for Nelly. He half expected to hear Blackie clomping up the old stairway from the alley down below. The man had a talent for showing up at the wrong time. Rent was paid until the end of the week but John would need to do something soon. At seventeen he was full-grown, six feet tall, with broad shoulders, and he was strong. He could always get work. But he worried about Nelly. They had no family in New York and as he closed his mother's eyes, he wondered how he would take care of his sister.

The last shadows were closing the door on this sad day as he heard Nelly coming up the stairs with another person. If it was the priest, then good. If it was Blackie, trouble was brewing. John had done quite a bit of fighting in his life and didn't mind doing a little more to protect his sister. He left his mother's side and opened the door just as Nelly reached the landing. Several steps behind her was a nice-looking priest smiling at John as he tried to keep up with Nelly. She flew past her brother to their mother's side.

"I'm too late. I did my best. Oh, my dear sweet mum is gone," Nelly wept.

The priest shook John's hand, then went to Molly's bed. He went to work chanting and waving over his mother. It seemed to help Nelly, so John didn't mind, though it all seemed meaningless now with Molly gone. Before the priest could finish his duties, the door swung open without a knock. There stood Blackie in the doorway, glaring at the bed.

Blackie worked for a man who owned all the buildings on their block as well as most of the buildings in the area. John had never seen the owner and never would. Blackie made his rounds collecting rent and evicting tenants when necessary. He was good at his job and he enjoyed it. His collecting duties took little time so he spent most of his day visiting the local saloons, keeping up on all the latest gossip. Blackie was a huge man with hands like ham hocks, dark eyes, a round face, and a bad temper.

"I thought this might be the case, yes sir," he said. "When she hadn't been out in a couple days, I figured this was next. I ought to start reading futures on the corner with those Gypsies. Rent is due at the end of next week. We don't operate no charity round here."

"We'd never ask for anything from you," John shot back before Blackie knew he was through talking.

"Why, you, insolent little Irish cur. I ought to give you a good licking."

"That will be enough, sir," the priest said as he moved between John and Blackie. "I'll thank you to leave this family while they mourn their loss."

Blackie grinned at John and looked around the room, appraising everything, trying to figure out if anything was worth taking. Then he stepped toward the door as if he might leave. Instead, he turned around and pointed at Nelly.

"We might be able to work out a trade for the pretty little filly."

John didn't wait for another insult. His father had taught him it was best to get in the first lick. He had also taught him to fight to win, which meant the other man could not even get in the fight if you were fast. And John was fast. The first blow was from his right fist. It landed square on old Blackie's neck, right in the windpipe. It had the full force of John's weight moving fast over several feet. Blackie stumbled out the door and onto the landing. He was still on his feet as John kicked him hard, just below the knees. It was a slight miss. Had it landed square, Blackie would have been finished for the night. It was enough sudden pain to make him look down. This was a mistake, as he was greeted with another right. This uppercut had not been well-aimed but John put all he had into the punch as it landed at the bridge of Blackie's nose. The man's eyes rolled back and he passed out, hitting the landing rail which, by some miracle, held his weight. Then he went to his knees. John threw a flurry of left and right hooks to the sides of his head before he felt his legs lift off the ground. The priest was carrying him back inside. Blackie fell over and tumbled down the stairs. John tried to go after him but the young priest held him fast.

"I believe Mr. Blackman understands you don't appreciate his forward ways," the priest said, with a smile. "I'm Father Matthew. Now if you would come and sit by your lovely sister we can continue."

John was still too high on adrenaline to sit. He marched back to the door and saw Blackie still at the bottom of the stairs. The man was moving around but had not been able to gather himself up completely. John finally did as the priest asked. Father Matthew was calm and compassionate. He told them about what had to happen. He would take care of as much as he could since he knew they had no funds. He turned to Nelly and assured her that her mother would be properly cared for. He himself would arrange for the undertaker who would arrive soon.

A few hours later John and his sister were alone in the small, cold apartment. Neither one of them wanted to be there.

Blackie was gone but John knew it was not over. When the man recovered, he'd be back and he'd have friends—or weapons. John had been trained since he was a lad to deal with types like Blackie. His father died fighting bullies and if John had to do that now, that was just how it had to be. First, though, he had to take care of Nelly. She cried herself to sleep that night and was still asleep several hours later when John went out looking for Blackie. The man was nowhere to be found. Troubled, John stayed awake all night watching for the old scoundrel.

In the morning, John took Nelly to St. Patrick's in search of the kind young priest. They were told he was at his morning prayers and they were asked to wait in a little garden outside the church. They were given warm bread and hot tea with a plate of fresh fruit. They were ravenous. John could not remember the last time they had eaten.

Just being near the church seemed to cheer Nelly. A short while later, an older nun came out and silently led them down a long hallway. They finally arrived at a large room filled with priests and nuns. They were seated in some sort of semicircle with an old priest dressed in a fancy robe at the front of the room. The nun led them into the center of the group, then bowed and left them with the priests. The old priest in the fancy robe seemed to be their leader.

"Good morning my children," the priest said, with a gentle and kind voice. It was a mellow voice and soothing to hear. "Father Matthew has told us your story—as much as he knows. But now we'd like to hear it from you if we could."

He nodded and a couple of nuns appeared with chairs for them. John looked at Nelly because she knew how to talk to these church people. He might be a bit too vulgar for their taste. This was a good plan, as it turned out, because Nelly was ready to talk.

"Your Excellency," she began.

John would never have thought of that.

"We arrived in New York from Ireland last fall. Twas on All Saint's Day so our mum took this to be a good sign. Our baby sister had died on the voyage over and was buried at sea, so as soon as we landed, we came to this very church to pray for her soul and that's when we met Father Matthew. A kinder soul has yet to be found than this one."

Nelly motioned toward the young priest. He smiled at her and winked.

"Mum and I never missed a mass except when she was forced to work on the Sabbath," Nelly said.

John had no idea what a Sabbath was but he kept quiet. The old priest just smiled and nodded, encouraging her to continue. She did and by the time she was finished, all the priests were nodding earnestly. Every eye was fixed on the old priest as a moment later, he stood.

"Father Matthew I'd like for you to join the council in my chambers. We have some things to discuss. I'm sure we will have an appropriate solution when we return. After our noon meal, we shall announce what the Lord's will is in this matter."

He turned and a few of the priests followed him. The rest began to prepare the room for a feast. It seemed the old man loved to have a good meal after one of his proclamations. John had no idea how the fellow was going to determine the Lord's will. He wasn't even sure if he approved of the Lord's will. He was not going to be ordered around by some old man in a fancy robe. John was not comfortable with someone else deciding what was best for them, especially after a lifetime of bowing to the British. Nelly knew he was having a problem with this so she hurried him off, away from the others.

"Now don't you say a word until I'm finished talking," she warned him. "These people are not the English. They do not want to take anything we have. So you just swallow that Irish pride and don't say a word."

"I'll hear what they have to say but I'm not going to be told what is best for me," John said.

"What about what I want?" Nelly interrupted.

John didn't want to argue with his sister. The hurt was too raw. He simply shook his head in agreement as they wandered back out to the garden for a few moments. They talked quietly, reliving old memories in Ireland. For a moment they forgot their troubles.

When everything was ready the old priest arrived with his crew. Everyone stood as he walked in. He lifted his hand and began chanting in Latin. Nelly seemed to know what was going on but John was baffled. The whole thing was making him nervous. Had it not been for the wonderful smells of fresh bread and roast lamb, John would have walked out but the aroma kept him there.

After a while, the old priest had said enough and they all took their seats. Within moments they were served the best meal they had seen since their arrival in America. Afterward, a couple of young priests got up and sang a few tunes that John thought were pleasant. Then the old priest nodded and everyone fell silent, waiting with great anticipation.

"I feel certain we have come up with a solution to the children's immediate needs," he said.

He looked at John with a kind and understanding countenance.

"Son, I know you have had a difficult road thus far and I suspect you will have your share of trouble in the future. This is a hard land but it offers promise to those who behave themselves, work hard, and take advantage of what they are given.

Now you are about to be given something and I hope you will take advantage of it. I'm going to give you something more valuable than you can imagine. I'm going to give some advice as well as some charity. I hope your pride doesn't jump in and cause you to reject such a gift."

John didn't have to look at Nelly. He knew she was glaring at him. John nodded.

"My Paw and Mum taught me to respect my elders, and if what you say is good for me then I'd kindly accept it."

He was hoping this would please the old man. He couldn't tell. The old priest paused for a moment, his gaze fixed on John. John felt he should not interrupt the man again.

"As I was saying, Father Matthew has spoken highly of you and we will surely come to your aid. First, there is the immediate matter of your mother's funeral. The church will handle all the arrangements and the service will be held in the east chapel. Please accept our condolences on your loss.

Now, for the child. New York is no place for a young lady. There are far too many ruffians about. Father Matthew has family in New Jersey with a farm. He tells me it's a fine place for a young lady and that his mother will look after her properly. They are good Catholics and will do right by her.

John, you may do as you please, I hear you can handle yourself well enough, though I may not entirely approve of your methods. There is work in the city and Father Matthew will look in on you from time to time. After your mother is properly buried, he will take you both to meet his family. As I said earlier, and I hope you see it, this is your best option. Please consider it."

When John was sure he was finished he said, "I will, sir."

John said this without thinking. As soon as the words were out of his mouth, he wondered what he had done. He didn't know these people. They weren't even Irish. Then he looked at Nelly. She was glowing. He had never seen her look at him with such admiration before. So he let it ride. They would go to New Jersey and meet these people. What would it hurt? He hated New York so New Jersey might be better.

Father Matthew led them out of the dining room and down a hall with doors every few steps. He showed them to two small rooms. Each had a small bed and a desk in the corner. There were no windows or decorations of any kind. John didn't care, though, and Nelly seemed pleased just to be around all the religious folks.

"We still need to get our things before Blackie decides they are his—and what is left of mum's things too," John said when he and Nelly were alone.

"John, can you do it without me? I can't bear to go back. I never want to step foot in that place again."

"It's probably best if you don't go back," John agreed.

He was trying to be strong about this but the truth was he didn't want to go either. But he did want to see Blackie again. He knew there was unfinished business between them. He didn't want to be always looking over his shoulder because he knew Blackie was not going to accept defeat so easily. John leaned down, kissed her on the forehead, then left.

He circled around and came into the neighborhood from the east. He didn't go to their rooms at first because he needed to locate Blackie. This time he was easier to find. He was sitting at his favorite table talking to a local policeman John recognized as one of his buddies. Blackie knew how to stay just inside the law by buying whiskey for the right authorities and giving them easy work when they needed to make an arrest or two. John slipped into the bar and merged with a group of young Irishmen. Blackie was nursing a few wounds from the night before. His left eye was swollen almost shut and he was limping rather badly. John inquired from the lads at his table if any of them knew what had happened to old Blackie. They knew nothing but reported he was being very tight-lipped about whatever it was. John felt sure the man did not want anyone learning that a young immigrant had gotten the best of him.

After a while, the policeman finished his drink and went back outside to walk his beat. Blackie was alone now, working on a whiskey that was doing a fair job of dulling the pain. He looked up from his glass only to see John sitting directly across the table from him, looking straight into his good eye. The young brat had the nerve to show up here. Good, Blackie thought. It saved him the trouble of having to look for him.

"You have your nerve," he said as he slid his hand off the table to fetch the pistol from his pants pocket.

John never took his eye off Blackie but quick as a cat, he pushed the table into Blackie's stomach so fast and hard it took away his wind. Then John reached under the table and tore the front pocket of Blackie's pants open, spilling its contents onto the floor. The gun and several coins hit the floor and John kicked the gun across the room away from Blackie. By now the entire saloon was paying close attention. Before Blackie could catch his breath, John slapped him open-handed across the face. Blood began to trickle from his lip.

"I'm losing my patience with you, old man," John leaned in and spoke softly to him. "If you give me cause again, I'll beat you worse than last night, and there isn't a priest here to pull me off you. Now can you behave yourself?"

Blackie didn't say a word. He looked around the bar only to see what he was most afraid of. Everybody was witnessing his disgrace and his compadres were nowhere to be found. His gun was out of reach and his paints were ruined. He glared at the young Irishman as he gathered himself. He took out a handkerchief from his breast pocket and dabbed his lip, then rubbed his eye tenderly.

"I need do nothing, my fine lad," he said in a mocking Irish accent. "As it turns out there is a warrant for your arrest. I need only sit back and watch as the authorities do their work. You'll make a fine addition to the city jail."

He laughed and leaned back in his chair. What few teeth Blackie had left were rotten so the sight of him laughing was as disgusting as his rude comments about Nelly had been. John raised his hand as if to slap him again. Blackie jerked back, causing his chair to topple over and the big man landed hard. John was on his feet in a second looking down at him. The smile was gone from Blackie's face.

"I spent most of my life dodging Bobbies and I'll be just fine. But I'll make you a promise. If I ever see you near me or my sister again I'll finish what I started. We have plans to leave this hell hole of a city but until then, you'd do well to stay out of my sight."

John walked over and picked up the pistol. He examined it, grinned, and put it in his pocket.

"I'll keep this for my troubles, thank you."

John bowed to the fat man lying on the ground, turned and winked at the young Irishmen, then strolled across the room like he owned the place. He departed to the sound of laughter.

John spent most of the afternoon and evening carrying their things to the church. He could have wept over how little they had. But he was ready to move on. New York had meant nothing but sorrow.

The day for them to leave finally arrived, less than a week after they buried their mother. The funeral had been nice but it was very different from what John was used to. Funerals in Ireland started out with everyone crying and telling sad stories about how life was hard and ended with everyone drinking and laughing when the stories became more humorous. Mum's funeral had been very formal. Nelly kept saying how she would be pleased, that everything was just so perfect. John was satisfied if not entirely convinced.

Spring had finally arrived and the sun felt good as they loaded all their belongings into the wagon. As was his custom, he had scouted out the area around the church prior to them loading the wagon. Blackie was nowhere to be found so perhaps they would get out without seeing him again. This was not to be, however. As they were loading, a couple of policemen arrived with orders to arrest John. Father Matthew looked at the warrant, then called for a nun. He wrote something on a note and handed it to her.

"Please take this to Margaret Murphy at once," the priest said.

Then he turned to the policemen.

"If you gentlemen would like to wait inside, I've sent a note to the Police Commissioner's wife. She is the head of our benevolence committee. These children are directly under her care and I'm sure she will be most interested in what you are doing here."

The two policemen looked at each other and it was clear they wanted none of what was about to come down. One took the warrant back and they left without another word.

They didn't leave alone, though. John followed them. He knew who was behind this. They stopped at a tenant dwelling a few blocks away and knocked. Blackie opened the door and he didn't look happy during the discussion that ensued.

After the policemen left, John went to the door himself and knocked on it. As soon as Blackie opened the door, John pushed him inside. Blackie was caught off guard. Once again, John had the advantage. Before John could do anything they heard a voice.

"Who is it, my love?"

An elderly lady stepped through a doorway from the back. John and Blackie both turned to look at her.

"Oh, we have company," she said. "I'll make us some tea."

"Don't bother, mother. He is leaving."

"Nonsense! We can all have a spot of tea. I've just baked sweet biscuits."

John could not believe what he was seeing. He had never imagined Blackie having a mother, much less that he'd be here visiting with her. The desire to do further damage to Blackie had evaporated the minute she appeared.

"Madam I really can't stay," John nodded politely. "I just came by to tell your son goodbye."

John stuck out his hand and Blackie took it. They shook hands firmly like old friends and John walked away. John then hurried back to the church to find the wagon loaded and Nelly and the priest waiting for him.

"We need to get going if we plan to make it there by dark," Father Matthew said.

John looked over the wagon, then jumped up on the seat next to Nelly as they headed out of town. The day was nice and they chatted easily as they moved through town. They told Father Matthew their story and he told them his.

CHAPTER 2

Rio Grande Valley

Somewhere in South Texas, in an area claimed by both the United States and Mexico, Josephina dropped the last bit of dirt on her father's grave. She was barely fifteen years old but there were two younger brothers and now she was all they had. Felix was ten and tall for his age. Aldo was small. He had been sick as a baby and although he was nearly nine, he was half Felix's size. The four of them had been headed to the coast so Papa could get work on the docks. A violent storm had blown through two nights before and their horse had been spooked by lightning. He broke loose, trampling Papa to death while he slept. They never saw the horse again. They were left only with a small burro they called Chico.

They were miles from any settlement. Josephina and the boys wept for Papa, then buried him as deep as they could. Felix set out looking for the horse but the trail was cold. They had no choice but to load Chico with everything they had and set off toward the northeast. They had no idea what they would find or what they would do when they got there. The main thing Josephina wanted was to steer clear of two banditos who had been stalking them. Papa had chased them away but Papa was in the ground now. The children didn't know it then but outlaws had little fear from any authority since the Texas Rangers rarely came this far south. What little law there was in Mexico

15

was concerned with things other than this forgotten piece of worthless land.

"I did my best to find that horse, Josie," Felix said for about the tenth time since returning last night.

"I know you did. We don't need that crazy beast. I would probably have used Papa's pistol on him anyway. I see you have it stuck in your belt, Felix."

"In case we have trouble," her brother said quickly. He had been practicing that response, waiting for her to notice he was carrying the gun.

"I guess that's smart but make sure it is not cocked."

"I know how to use it."

"I know you do. I just don't want to have to bury anyone else. It has only been a few months since we buried mama, and now Papa is gone too."

"I can shoot too," Aldo chimed in. He did not like being left out of the planning. He was small but saw himself as their equal in every way.

"Forget about the gun," Josephina said, mopping her brow. "We need to find water. Give Chico his head. He may smell some and lead us to a stream or something. We haven't had a drink since yesterday and it's going to be hot today."

They followed Chico and were pleased when he took a hard left and picked up his pace. Even their empty bellies could not compete with their powerful and growing thirst. They almost stumbled on an ancient Indian woman picking wild herbs. She seemed puzzled by their language. Through hand motions they made her understand they were thirsty. She led them to a small gully where she moved a few rocks and began to dig in the loose sand. After a few minutes, water bubbled up. They drank to their hearts' content, then captured enough fresh water to fill their bottles and give Chico his fill. The little pond created by the old woman soon vanished back into the sand. The woman bowed her head slightly, mumbled something, and walked off.

The strangeness of this encounter puzzled them but they were too tired and too grateful for the water to question it. They found a place in the shade to rest for a few hours, then took off again, walking as the desert cooled with the setting sun.

They would walk late into the night since it was safer and cooler, covering as much ground as they could. Around midnight they stopped, unloaded Chico and they all lay down together, hoping nobody would find them. They slept fitfully.

They were still asleep as the day dawned. Aldo was using Chico as a pillow. The burro was more of a pet than a beast of burden but he was what the children needed. He raised his head and snorted. His ears rolled forward as an old man eased up on them ever so gently. Felix saw him and had the gun out, pointing it directly at the intruder.

The man stopped, smiled at the children, and held his hands up in a gesture of surrender. He seemed to be alone and unarmed. He spoke gently to the children but they could not understand him. Josephina thought it might be English but she was not sure. His words were lost on them but his tone was soft and even and very gentle. They were all on their feet now, with Chico out in front as if to protect them.

"My Spanish is a bit rusty and not very good, I'm afraid. I will do my best," the man said clearly in Spanish which was quite good although heavily accented in a language they had never heard before.

"Now young man, I mean you no harm so please lower the pistol."

Felix looked at Josephina, then did as the man asked.

"I know you meant nothing by that. The gun wasn't even cocked but I'd rather visit without firearms being brandished about," the fellow said politely.

Felix felt foolish for not cocking the gun. Without knowing it, he hung his head.

"It's all right, sport," the old boy laughed. "If it makes you feel better you can hold it on me. I mean you no harm."

"Can we help you?" Josephina asked, as politely as if she were welcoming an honored guest.

He smiled, showing a mouth with few teeth. He was a strange little man, with the trunk of his body shorter than it should have been. His legs were bowed, which reduced his height further, and he had a hump on his back, high up near his left shoulder. His hands were large for a man his size and his arms were too long for his body. His head dominated his body and it was covered with thick, rust-colored curly hair. He wore no shoes and his pants were frayed and held up by a rope. His shirt was made from a strange material they had never seen before with an odd pattern of squares. Every inch of him was odd, though not threatening.

"I came not to ask for your help, my lady," he said with a bow. "Rather, I come to offer my assistance."

His accent was strong yet his Spanish was that of a learned man.

"Broken Wing has told me of your plight. This is dangerous country for young people. She asked me to guide you to the Nueces, and then down to the coast. She believes you were headed there before you lost your father."

"Is Broken Wing the Indian lady?" Aldo asked.

"How does she know where we are going? Felix added.

"Yes, that's her. She has been watching you for several weeks," the old gentleman replied. "I believe she has grown fond of you. She was sad when your father died. She killed the horse herself—she said it had a bad spirit. Not so bad as to not be good to eat, though. It will feed her for several more weeks."

"We never saw her until yesterday," Aldo said.

"If she doesn't want to be seen, you won't see her. She's a peculiar old witch but she took a shine to you right off. She said your father was kind and you children honored him well at his death. That means a lot to her."

Without another word, he turned and whistled. Soon a large gray mule came over the bluff. Chico let out a welcoming bray. The mule walked up behind the old man and stopped.

"Now I think proper introductions are in order. This is Sally, the smartest and most stubborn creature in this wide land," he said, "and I am Bartholomew Donnally McGentry, a Scotsman by birth and a Christian by choice. My friends call me Mac although I was known as Bart in another time. Mac is good, though. I've grown rather fond of it."

He bowed to them and waited for them to speak.

"I am Josephina Lopez de la Garza. These are my brothers Felix and Aldo Lopez de la Garza," she said after a long and uncomfortable pause. She pointed to each of them as she said their names.

The boys stepped forward politely and shook the man's hand. The gun was back in Felix's belt. Chico also walked over and greeted Sally, then the old man. This made the children even more comfortable because Chico was as good a judge of character as they had ever known.

After a few short stories from Mac and a few bites of jerky he shared with them, they were off again, trusting this new stranger to lead them in the right direction.

As the days passed, Josephina began to notice a difference in her brothers. They seemed more at ease as they made their way toward what she thought was due north with this strange little man. They settled into a natural order as Sally took the lead, carrying all their earthly belongings. The big mule moved as though she had no load at all and Chico did his best to stay close to her. Felix was next in their parade line, marching like a trained soldier with his chest poked out, doing his best to assert his dominance. Mac seemed amused by this. It did not threaten him in the least that a boy considered himself an equal. Behind Felix, Aldo and Mac walked side by side. The two of them talked continually with Aldo questioning him for more details on his stories.

"When you were my age what were you like?" Aldo asked.

"That is a great question. My life was quite different from most boys' because of my deformity. I was sent to an orphanage since my folks were not sure what to do with me. I never knew them in fact. I did have a kindly old maid aunt who made sure I was cared for. Later she paid for the finest education available. I studied in France and Spain at some of the most prestigious schools. My aunt was well-to-do and she provided for me until I could take care of myself. She died shortly after I came of age. So I did what I could. My education helped me greatly."

Mac went from story to story, switching effortlessly from his personal saga to world events in a manner that seemed to project him as a part of the history of the world. The stories made the long, hot journey less arduous than it might have been if they were only thinking about being tired, hungry, and thirsty.

"How did you get to Texas? You said you were from across the ocean," Aldo said.

Mac laughed. "Now that is another fine question. You, my boy, would make a very fine attorney."

Aldo didn't know what that was but he took it as a compliment.

"My aunt left me with enough funds to book passage from France to Tampico, Mexico," Mac continued. "I learned a valuable lesson when I arrived. You can never run from your problems. The people I found there were just like they were in Europe. Although they appreciated my education, my personal deformity was not accepted there either. I did not fit in but I eventually made a life for myself trading with the Coahuiltecan Indians. I found them to be welcoming and it didn't seem to matter to them what I looked like.

"The Coahuiltecans were not a single tribe as the Spanish thought but a large collection of family groups that shared a common goal. That goal was to survive. They developed a language that combined several tribal dialects with some Spanish. These family groups never organized into a single group as the Apaches had. They were nomadic, like the Comanches and the Apaches but peaceful. They chose to move out of the reach of the white men rather than fight.

"It was somewhere close to Monterrey that I met Broken Wing. It was almost ten years ago. She was headed north in search of what she called the "sparrow spirit," he said. "We have traveled together ever since."

Mac was good with stories and could get a smile or laugh out of them anytime he pleased. Even Felix, who tried to remain serious as he played the part of royal guard, laughed at Mac's stories.

When the sun was at its hottest, Sally always found them a cool place to rest under scrub oaks or other vegetation. One afternoon, Mac noticed Aldo looking at his hump in a curious way.

"Come here, Aldo. You may touch it. I was born this way. It's all I know."

Aldo reached over and patted Mac's hump gently.

"You can't hurt it," Mac said. "It's all gristle and as hard as a rock. Hit It. Go ahead, hit it."

Aldo did. Then they both laughed.

"Does it hurt?" Aldo asked.

"Not usually. When you get to be my age, everything hurts sometimes but my hump is just my hump. Would you like to touch it, Felix?" Mac asked.

He had noticed Felix was watching. Felix shook his head no, although he was as curious as Aldo about the hump.

That evening they sat in the cool and chewed on jerky, then one by one, they dropped off to sleep. Mac was first to be overcome by drowsiness. He was in the middle of a story about a Spanish knight tracking a band of Moors when his head sagged and he began to snore in a deep, raspy voice that delighted the children. Felix eased over close to Josephina and whispered in her ear.

"What do you think? I mean can we trust him?"

"I guess we'll see. We have nothing else to do."

"I could shoot him in his sleep."

"He has done nothing to cause you to shoot him. All he's done is feed us and keep us company."

"He might be leading us into a trap," Felix said, reaching for the handle of his pistol.

Josephina chuckled to herself, then pushed him away and closed her eyes.

"Felix, we were in a trap before he showed up. This entire place is a trap without Papa. He seems to be the first good thing to happen to us in a while."

"I guess you're right. He has done nothing yet but I'll be watching him. Besides, I really rather like him."

"Of course you do, you are already starting to talk like him," she said. "Listen to yourself—*'I rather like him'*."

She giggled. Josephina was starting to like Mac too. His stories as well as his charming manners had gone a long way toward winning her over. She was thinking he must be a kind man to go out of his way just to help them. She thought about all he had said that day as she drifted off to sleep. He had been born in Scotland, a place he referred to as "The Highlands". She tried to imagine this strange and wonderful place.

Later, Josephina woke when she heard Sally get up. The big mule eased to her feet and shook. Then she strolled over to a small bush and stood still, watching it. Chico was awake now and he was watching her closely. After a minute or two, Sally kicked some dirt forward with her foreleg. Then she reared up on her hind legs and came down hard on the small bush. By now they were all awake. Felix jumped up and ran over to see what had happened. He reached down and came up with a rattlesnake as long as he was tall. The snake's head was a mess.

"Sally never did like snakes," Mac observed. "Let's load up. Like many creatures, snakes find comfort in one another so there may be more around."

As they loaded up, he told several stories about snakes and other reptiles. They were fascinated to hear about an animal he called an alligator. They wondered if there really were such creatures.

They walked the rest of the day and into the night before they came to a little hut near a creek. Mac told them the creek emptied into a river a few miles south of there. He said the river would lead them to the coast. Broken Wing was sitting out in front of the hut with a small fire. She got up to tend to Sally and Chico. Mac greeted her with a smile but no words were exchanged. They learned later that Broken Wing was not much of a talker. Mac, however, seemed to talk enough for several people. Inside the hut there was enough room for several pallets. Mac slept outside by the fire but the children couldn't have said where, or if, Broken Wing slept. After the animals were cared for, she just faded away into the night.

That night Mac had told them stories of Europe, a faraway place, and of Africa. Josephina thought it all must be make-believe. There could not be that many places in the world.

While Mac was telling stories and the children, with full bellies, were finally able to relax, Broken Wing had located the two banditos tracking them. As the shadows deepened and the children slept, she watched the men move in the direction of the camp. As they neared the sleeping party, she moved in among them as if a ghost. They tied up their horses and crept quietly down to the water's edge, completely unaware of her presence. Mac was snoring loudly. The first man heard the snores, then he heard something else. It was a gurgling noise from behind him. He froze and listened but could not have known that the noise was Broken Wing cutting his companion's throat. He waited a few minutes for his partner but the man never came. He then turned, just as a large knife blade slid through his ribs and found his heart. Broken Wing slew him as quickly and quietly as she had dispatched his friend.

Broken Wing woke Mac noiselessly. They spoke quietly in her language, then went to work ridding the camp of the vermin. Broken Wing went for their horses as Mac buried the two in a shallow grave. The children never heard a thing. By the time they awoke, the horses were tended to properly and the men were gone. As they traveled that day, when the children asked Mac about the horses, the guns, and the supplies, Mac told them the story. There was nothing Mac liked better than telling a good story.

Mac gathered the children together the next day to discuss a matter which had long been on his mind.

"One thing I know for certain is that life will be much better for you in the towns if you all learn English."

"We will, eventually," Felix said.

"Texans love their English," Mac continued. "Many Texans speak both Spanish and English but if you want to work you need to learn English," he said.

"Yes, then. We will," Josephina said, answering for her brothers as well as herself.

"Wonderful! And you are in luck because I am a very accomplished teacher. There is nothing I know better than my own native tongue. I shall be your instructor," Mac said, with a courtly bow.

Thus they stayed with Mac and Broken Wing on the little creek and learned to converse in English. Broken Wing liked them being there. She taught them valuable secret skills about living on the land. As the months passed, the children grew resilient and resourceful and they grew to love both Mac and Broken Wing.

CHAPTER 3

New Jersey

It was late afternoon when one of Father Matthew's brothers rode up to the wagon on a giant plow horse. The young man had curly brown hair and a smile that covered his face. His blue eyes sparkled. He was nearly fifteen and it was clear he was glad to see his big brother. The priest introduced him to John and Nelly, then the boy rode on ahead to announce their arrival. About an hour later, they pulled up to a well-kept farmhouse surrounded by a copse of ancient oak trees. Under the massive canopy, a crowd of family and friends waited on the porch and lawn. A middle-aged lady, five feet tall and almost as wide, was obviously in charge. She hurried down the steps of the porch and the others followed. As soon as Father Matthew jumped off the wagon, she assaulted him with hugs and kisses. Mildred giggled like a young girl as she greeted her son.

"I swear Pudge, you keep getting thinner. Ain't they feeding you at the church?"

She then pushed him aside and went straight for Nelly.

"Would you look at this little angel? Look at those gorgeous green eyes and that auburn hair. Honey, you are a living doll."

Nelly was blushing but she was also grinning from ear to ear. Mildred folded her up in hugs and patted her as she spoke. She went on and on about how honored they were to have the children visit.

By now the crowd had gathered around the wagon. John sat on the bench seat, taking it all in. It made him feel strange to be so welcomed by strangers but not in a bad way. It also made him feel comfortable. A rare feeling. A few minutes later he was invited to get down by the lady of the house. He stuck out his hand in hopes that this would keep her from attacking him as she had the other two passengers. She took his hand and formally shook it, then pulled him into her large bosom and hugged him, too.

"You must be Master John Delaney. I've heard a good bit about you from Pudge."

"Pudge?" John had meant to say happy to meet you but all that came out was "Pudge".

The Padre laughed. "A prophet is not known in his own land."

John thought this must be a quote from the Bible. Mildred let go of John and swatted at her son lovingly.

"My name from birth is George Swenson," said the priest, "but the family always called me Pudge. Matthew was given to me by the church."

By now John had lost track of what was being said because the family was hugging them and talking all at once. They began unloading the wagon and the entire group made its way up the porch and into the house.

"We couldn't wait to eat but we saved you something," a tall gentleman said.

This must be Father Matthew's father, thought John. The man was tall and strong-looking with wide shoulders and a barrel chest. He was groomed rather nicely for a farmer. John thought they must have all cleaned up for their arrival, which was a kind gesture. The three of them sat at a long table and waited for Father Matthew, or George, or Pudge, to bless the food. After his prayer, one John thought lasted far too long, they all said amen.

The food was set before them. There was more than they could eat. John first went for a plate of smoked ham, as Nelly filled her plate with cabbage, peas, and candied carrots. John put as much as he could on his plate, then looked up to see Father Matthew smiling at him. John paused for a moment wondering if he had done something wrong.

"Take all you want," the priest said. "If we eat all of this she will just bring more."

Mildred sliced a loaf of bread for them, still warm from the oven. She buttered each slice and served it with more than a little pride. Nelly could tell Mildred was proud of her baking skills and she commented on how good the bread was. John and Nelly thought everything was delicious. Meanwhile, the entire family sat at the table, watching them eat. It was obvious they were glad the guests had arrived.

After dinner, the party adjourned to the porch where the laughing and storytelling continued until Malcolm—that was the name of Father Matthew's father—announced it was bedtime.

Malcolm and Mildred Swenson had a fine family indeed. Included in that group was their uncle, Malcolm's older brother. Uncle J.D. was considerably older than Malcolm. He didn't talk much but he grinned a lot as he listened closely to everything that was said. Malcolm and Mildred also had five boys and one girl. Three of them were grown and gone while the other three lived and worked on the farm.

Rebecca was older than Father Matthew. She was married and expecting her first child soon. Then there was a brother named Lemuel who also seemed to live elsewhere. No one explained where he was or what he did. John figured that his chosen career might not be one they were proud of.

The remaining three children were all younger than Father Matthew. Their names were David, Peter, and Samuel. Samuel was the youngest—the smiling young boy who had met them on the road. John noticed that he continued to smile as he joked and played with his brothers.

When it was time to sleep, John learned he would share a room with Peter and Samuel. Father Matthew, David, and J.D. shared another room. Nelly had her own room, and Mildred had placed fresh flowers on the bureau to welcome her. The entire family was friendly and kind to both of them. John slept well that night as he dreamed of his home in Ireland.

Everyone in the household was up early the next morning. They ate a quick breakfast then all went off in different directions, tending to their animals and performing various chores. There were cows to milk, chickens and geese to feed, and hogs to slop. A huge plow horse was working with Uncle J.D. as he plowed for a vegetable garden. Nelly, John, and Father Matthew sat on the porch, swinging and chatting.

"How do you like it here?" the priest asked.

"I love it," Nelly chirped.

John felt he was just waiting for something to happen. He couldn't explain what he was feeling. His whole life seemed to follow a familiar pattern. Just as things seemed to be going well, something always went wrong—and wrong in a big way. He was afraid to hope for a good life as he waited to see what would come next. Hope had not been his friend.

"It was great growing up here but I have to admit I couldn't wait to leave," Father Matthew said.

"May I ask you a question, George?" John inquired.

"His name is Father Matthew," Nelly scolded. "Don't be so common, John. You make me so furious."

"It's fine," the priest laughed. "There is no sin in calling me George. While we are here you may call me George or even Pudge if you'd like. They all will. And you may ask me anything you like."

"I have a lot of questions," John said, then glanced over at his sister. "Maybe later, though. For now, do you mind if I go for a walk down by that pond? I have some thinking to do."

"John, you have the run of this place," said Father Matthew, "and I'm certain you have plenty to ponder. Just try to be back by noon. You don't want to miss lunch. Mama doesn't like to feed but once and I think she is making cobbler."

John left the porch and walked down to the pond. He sat under a tree and let his mind wander. He didn't have anything specific to think about. He just felt the need to be alone. After a while, he dropped off to sleep. Meanwhile, Nelly made herself useful in the kitchen. She and Mildred were becoming fast friends as they worked together making lunch. They chatted continually as only women can do. It was as if they had known each other for years. Nelly was truly happy for the first time since arriving in America. Hope seemed to come back to her and with it, a fresh chance at life.

"You sift the flour just like my mother did. She was a good cook, too. She taught me..."

Nelly caught her breath.

"I wish mum was here. She would love this kitchen."

Tears filled her eyes as she spoke of Molly.

"I do too, honey. I wish I had known her," Mildred said as she stopped what she was doing to hug Nelly. "I know you miss her. I never met her but she must have been something special. She did a wonderful job raising you both."

"I don't know what I'm going to do," Nelly wept as Mildred held her.

"We will figure that out. Just trust me. We will figure it all out. Now let's get those tomatoes blanched. And I need to get the cornbread in the oven."

Down by the pond, John awoke from his nap. When he opened his eyes, David was sitting there, watching him sleep.

"You move quietly, I never heard you," John said.

"I'm a fair hunter," said the young man, who was about John's age. "Not nearly as good as Uncle J.D. though. Now that man could sneak up on a ghost. Best woodsman you'll ever meet."

David and John sat under the shade of an oak tree talking about hunting and fishing and life on the farm. It was comfortable and the time seemed to fly by. They strolled up to the house for lunch and John was surprised that it was every bit as good as the meal they had the night before.

After lunch, David talked his father into letting him off work the rest of the day so he and John could fish. They walked to the far side of the pond to where a little creek emptied into it. They sat on an old log and fished for a few hours.

While John was fishing, Nelly helped Mildred with the laundry. Doing the laundry for that many working people was a chore but Nelly enjoyed her time with Mildred.

Mildred knew how to get information and she learned much of what there was to know about the Delaney clan in that one afternoon. It felt surprisingly good to Nelly to talk it all through. She loved her brother John but he was not much of a conversationalist and he was a male. Even at fifteen, Nelly knew men were not good at talking about important things like feelings and dreams and love. Men might know about these but they did not know how to talk about them.

She had a few minutes to think while she was hanging up the clothes to dry on the line. She felt selfish about wanting to stay here. She knew it wasn't her home but she realized she never wanted to leave the place. This made her both happy and sad. Happy because it was a wonderful place and sad because it wasn't hers. She had no right to think that she could be a part of this life.

Just as she felt a familiar melancholy spirit come on her, she heard Mildred with that wonderful belly laugh that made you happy just to hear it. She turned around and saw what was making her laugh. Samuel was trying to corral a litter of puppies that had gotten out of their pen. There were six or seven of them still loose and they were in the garden. Nelly joined in laughing with Mildred as she finished hanging the clothes. Nelly stayed close to Mildred the rest of the day. The sadness couldn't return when she was around her. The woman was too full of joy.

John and David fished all afternoon. John had never fished like this in Ireland, so his new friend David showed him how it was done. John learned fast and he caught three good-sized perch while David caught five. John liked David. He was easy to talk to and he didn't ask too many questions.

Later they cleaned the fish and the women fried them for supper. Afterward, John and David sat on the porch again, laughing and telling stories. John was finally letting himself remember how much he missed his brothers. Malcolm sent everyone to bed earlier this time but all seemed ready to retire except Uncle J.D. He stayed on the porch by himself smoking his pipe as he looked longingly into the starry night sky.

The next morning was different. It was Sunday. There was no big breakfast—just a biscuit and a cup of black coffee before they went to work tending to the animals. When everyone was finished with chores, they came in, cleaned up, put on their best clothes, and loaded up to go to town for mass.

Mildred was as happy as she could be because she was about to show off her son the priest. She would be referring to him as Father Matthew today. She could hardly wait for her friends to see him dressed in his priestly robes.

This mass would be special with a visiting priest from their own parish. Mildred had made sure her family looked their best. They arrived in time for her to ensure her son the priest was in plain view of all her lady friends. Nelly was right in the mix of things, while John did his best to stay in the shadows. Periodically, however, Mildred would drag him forward to show him off to certain people. Mildred wanted all her friends to meet the children.

Father Matthew was not enjoying all the attention but he'd known it was coming so he was prepared to tolerate the pageant. When it was time for the mass to start, Mildred gathered her group. Everyone had already seen them all. It was not a big church—perhaps fifty people at most. The majority of them were Swensons. John tried to sit in the back but David was sent to fetch him up front with the rest of the family.

The mass was short and John didn't understand what was happening. The priest would say something in Latin, then they all would stand or sit or kneel. John could not understand what all the movement was about. But it seemed to make sense to them. At the end, Father Matthew joined the priest at the front, where they held out bread and wine that everyone lined up to eat and drink. This time John was allowed to hold back. And he was glad. He was getting hungry but since each person only got a crumb of bread and a sip of wine from the same cup, he didn't see the point. They all seemed rather pleased with the ritual. John could not imagine why this was so meaningful to them but he figured it must be.

After the service, they said their goodbyes, then loaded up and went a few miles down the road to a cousin's house. A huge table sat out in the yard in the shade of several massive oak trees. It was filled with more food than John thought he had ever seen. People had gathered from several different farms in the area. David told John these were family from his dad's side. They were Protestants but good folks. John had never seen Catholics and Protestants get along as they did that day. Back in Ireland, they seemed to fight about everything. This was a different world.

There was no porch sitting that night, except for uncle J.D. and his pipe. Tomorrow was a work day and they all knew Malcolm would be pushing hard to make up for time lost today. John walked down by the pond. When he came back to the house, he saw David and Nelly sitting in the kitchen having a glass of buttermilk. He thought about joining them but decided to go to bed instead.

Early the next morning, Father Matthew, who was back to being Pudge, or George, asked John to walk with him. They went out back and sat on a couple of stumps and watched the chickens scratch around the yard.

"John, I want to discuss something with you. It's about Nelly. New York is no place for her, and my mother wants her to stay here. She will be a big help and I know she would feel safe here. I think your mother would have agreed."

"She does seem to have taken to this life," John said.

"Yes," Father Matthew agreed, "and this life seems to have taken to her if you know what I mean. The fresh air will do her good. She and I have already talked about this."

Father Matthew studied John's reaction for a moment, then continued.

"She wants to stay but she is afraid you won't approve. She will do whatever you say. She loves you dearly," the priest added.

"I don't know what to say," John said.

"Well at least think about it. You could come and visit her as often as you like. Mother would love it."

John nodded as if to say he'd think on it. He didn't want to talk. He was afraid his voice would crack and he'd start tearing up. He was not going to let Father Matthew see him cry but he had a lump in his throat the minute he heard the priest say that Nelly loved him. Because he loved her too. He got up and walked over to the barn. He knew Nelly belonged here. He knew the priest was right. But she was the only family he had left. Could he just give her up? He knew he could not give her the life she would have here.

On the verge of tears, he looked over at a little pen beside the barn. It held the litter of pups and their mother, who watched him for a while, then came over to the fence and raised up on her back legs. With her paws on the fence, she was almost as tall as he was. Her brown eyes sized him up. He patted her on the head and her tail began to wag. After a couple of minutes, she took a few steps back, gathered herself, and jumped out of the pen. John found a place in the shade and she lay down at his side. She was needing some attention and so was John. He threw a stick and she ran after it and brought it back to him. The game of fetch turned into a wrestling match with them both rolling in the tall grass.

John looked up to see David standing beside the barn with a pitchfork in his hand and a grin on his face. He had been cleaning the barn but had stopped to watch his dog wrestle with John. John started toward David when the mother dog jumped him from behind and they both went rolling down the hill toward David. David's grin turned into a full belly laugh.

"Lucy, heel girl," David said in a commanding voice.

The dog stopped fighting and ran to David's side and stood there looking up at him. John was astonished at the dog's obedience.

"I see you and Lucy have met and become good friends. I'm surprised. She usually doesn't take to strangers."

"I was just looking at the puppies and she suddenly decided we were best friends," John said.

"She is a good judge of character," laughed David. "Purebred Mastiff. Her father will compete in the first-ever dog show in Tyne, England. I expect him to win the show," he added.

John had no idea what a dog show was. He hated to reveal his ignorance, so he just nodded.

"The show is next June. The dogs are judged on how they look and how they behave. It won't be long before we have dog shows here in America too. l will enter one of Lucy's pups if they prove to be what I think they are. Lucy was bred with a handsome Mastiff from Hartford. I suspect the pups will be of high quality."

David continued on about the origins of the breed, and how they were used by the Romans as war dogs and later turned into popular guard dogs for castles across Europe.

They walked back to the pen and David pointed to one of the pups.

"See that blond-colored one?"

"I do."

"He will be a fine dog. He's smart and he'll dominate. He stands out above the rest—I can see it already. If trained properly he will make a fine companion. I want you to have him."

John froze. "I can't, I mean I don't know anything about training a dog. And you need him if he's the best."

"Oh, he's the best all right," David said. "Lucy will have more pups later and who knows? One might be even better. I want you to take him. I'll teach you how to train him. It's not hard. You just have to be consistent. I can see you have a way with dogs and since the pups are weaned already and ready to leave her, the timing is perfect," said David.

He picked up the blond puppy for John to hold.

Nelly and Father Matthew had been talking on the porch for a while and when David and John walked up she was grinning. She ran to John. "Thank you for being so kind. Father Matthew said you thought it was a good idea. Oh, I love you so much and will miss you but you can come visit me here often. I'm so happy."

She kissed him over and over as she danced around him. John wondered if his life would be like this forever—one decision after another but none of them made by him. His last decision had concerned how best to handle Blackie. Since then, it had been the priests and the Swensons making the decisions. But he had to admit they were doing a better job at it than he had, so he guessed the best thing was to go along with it. What choice did he have?

Maybe this was what it meant to be an adult. He didn't know. His father was gone. He had to figure out how to be a man on his own. He had lost his mother, lost his home, and it was looking now like he would lose his sister. He had no place to go. But he had made friends with these folks and he had gained a good dog. Maybe all would be well.

A few days later, Malcolm asked John to work with him. John figured he had something to say. He might ask for room and board, or he might ask him to leave. They worked all day fixing fences and talking about nothing important. The weather seemed to be important to Malcolm. He loved to talk about it. They worked hard and John had a good day. Malcolm was a good man. He was serious about the farm and he made sure the boys all put in a good hard day's work every day but he was kind, and it was obvious he loved his family.

The following day Mildred requested John's help as she began to rearrange the pantry. There were high shelves that required a ladder and Mildred's body style was not conducive to ladders. While Malcolm rarely spoke, Mildred never stopped talking. She had one question after another, each requiring much more than just a yes or no answer. John had no idea that so much conversation could take place in such a short time. Her questions were things like "What do you plan to do with your life?" How could John know that? It seemed whatever he said just led to another question. When they finished the pantry, she began to prepare dinner. John was worn out. Taking to Mildred was harder than working all day with the men. Somehow, however, Nelly seemed to gain strength from these talks. Women were just different, he guessed. He was happy when she released him. Mildred was a sweet lady and John felt bad about wanting to get away from her but he'd had all he could bear. He hoped he didn't have to speak again for several days.

The day finally came for John and Father Matthew to return to New York. As he and David walked down to the dog pen, David seemed nervous. He finally got the words out.

"John, I need to ask you a question. I've grown fond of Nelly over the last few weeks and with your permission I'd like to court her. If you approve and she agrees I'd like to…"

He stopped talking as he looked at John's face.

"I'll ask her if she wants to. If she does it's fine with me," John replied, without enthusiasm.

What in the world had he just said? Yet another major decision and all he could do was agree before he even thought about it. He wasn't too surprised, though, since he'd seen them talking and they seemed to like each other.

"Thank you," David said, smiling at his new friend.

David put a collar around the blond pup's neck as they led him away from his litter mates.

"A fine dog like this needs a good name. What will it be?"

"His name is Hank," John said. "I've been calling him Hank."

"Hank is a fine name. Hank it is," David agreed.

John, Father Matthew, and Hank loaded up as the Swensons and his sister waved goodbye until they were out of sight

CHAPTER 4

The Nueces River

The children had been living with Mac and Broken Wing for a few months. They had settled into a routine they'd all grown to enjoy. Most of the day was spent with Mac, who took his task as an English tutor seriously. He insisted that the Lopez children learn proper English. Mac's method was effective. He used everything they saw as an opportunity to create a story. He started simply, by showing them a noun, like a bird or a rat. Then he would make them use this noun in various ways, teaching them how to invert the sentences as the English did. It seemed strange at first but they caught on. This conversational method made learning easy and fun. The children competed, trying to get it right. Aldo, even though he was the youngest, had a particularly good ear for this and he learned quickly. His English was better than Josephina's or Felix's. This irritated Felix more than a little. He was older so he thought he should be the best. Josephina could see that this was good because it made him work harder. Mac wanted to teach them to speak properly, as an educated person might.

"May I have another slice of bread please," or "Would you prefer more cream in your coffee?" he would say.

The children loved pretending to be nobility and Mac knew just how these people spoke and acted because he had lived among them. Day by day, the children's opinion of Mac was growing. He seemed less grotesque than when they had first met him and his odd manners were becoming something they enjoyed. They also loved how he mixed in stories with the lessons. He would begin his tales in English, only switching to Spanish when he felt they were not yet ready to move on. He made them work hard on this new language, often telling them how important it was. And they believed him.

Broken Wing watched it all without saying a word. She busied herself gathering food. Though Mac told them that she liked them, they could not tell by her actions. She had no interaction with them other than to observe them with a strange, inquisitive look on her face.

One day Broken Wing disappeared. Mac told them not to worry since this was her way. But they worried anyway. It seemed empty in camp without her creeping around, monitoring their every move. Mac provided for them in her absence, though it took him longer than it did Broken Wing. Mac used this as an opportunity to teach them more than just English. He was also teaching them to live off the land. Even in South Texas, if you knew what you were doing, you could find plenty to eat. By now they were in the hottest part of summer and the creek they were living on began to dry up. It was just a thin trickle of water, barely enough for survival.

Just as things began to look bleak, Broken Wing returned. She and Mac spoke in some language foreign to the children. Mac told them they would be moving north to a spot on the Nueces River. She was already gathering and packing their things.

Mac amazed the children as he removed a few pegs and took down the shack in four equal pieces. He stacked them neatly and made a sled out of them. The roof was made of skins so he used it as a mat and lashed it to Sally. A few long poles were attached to the sled and a blanket was fashioned to hold the poles and attach them so Sally could pull them. Chico, too, was loaded with all he could hold, and soon they were headed north, Sally leading the way with Chico at her side. Josephina thought she saw Broken Wing smile as they moved out though she couldn't be sure.

They walked until dark, then Mac built a little fire and they ate a few bites of dried horse meat. Soon Mac was snoring and before long the boys followed. For a while, Josephina watched Broken Wing, who stayed awake most of the night just looking into the sky as if she alone could gather meaning from the stars.

In the morning light, they found that Broken Wing had a hole dug not far from them with enough brown water in it for the animals. Then they loaded up again and headed north. Mac continued the lessons as they moved. He seemed to feel an urgency about completing his task. The land was harsh and the traveling was tough. The children and animals were spent by noon, so they stopped to let everyone rest. Sally found a patch of dirt not far from them and had herself a good roll in the sand. Chico was at her side. He seemed to find comfort in being near Sally.

Broken Wing was ready to move. She wanted to get to the river. Mac persuaded her to let them linger the rest of the afternoon as he knew the children needed to rest. They walked a bit more in the late evening. Sally could see well in the dark and they stayed close to her. She continued to lead the caravan until Mac stopped the parade after the boys stumbled and fell several times and Josephina could hardly stay upright. Though Broken Wing could have continued, Mac decided it was time to stop. They had found no water since morning so they slept fitfully, often awakened by their thirst.

The next day was no better. The heat seemed to come from every direction. There was no breeze. Despite her best efforts to find water, Broken Wing was unsuccessful. Mac pointed to the east and said something in their strange language to Broken Wing. She nodded in agreement.

"We are going to get a rain this afternoon," Mac said with certainty.

And rain it did. Mac put out skins to catch as much water as he could. They let the animals rest while it rained. Later, after the rain let up, they made camp where they were. They slept better that night, but by morning, Broken Wing had disappeared again. She had slipped away in the night. They were out of dried horse meat and they had drunk all the water Mac had caught in skins. They had to move on, though. While they walked, Mac kept the English lesson going, requiring that only English be spoken. This day was the hottest yet and the land seemed harsher with each step. They walked until dark but there was still no sign of Broken Wing.

That evening, as the animals lay down, Mac was afraid he had pushed Sally too hard. She was a noble beast and it was not like her to complain about anything but Mac could see she was exhausted. Little Chico was somewhat less so but he hadn't had the burden Sally had. Mac rubbed her down, then went to sleep beside her. Josephina was moved by his love for the animal.

That night, no one talked. Josephina was afraid to say what was on her mind and she was sure her brothers were in an even worse state. The entire band was suffering from severe dehydration. It was becoming difficult to think clearly. Their feet were swollen and they were all badly sunburned. The hot, dry weather had turned the mesquite and scrub oaks into thorny enemies. Their flesh wounds from the thorns were a problem but even this could not compare with their thirst. They had reached their limit. Body, soul, and mind, they were spent. Josephina was sure that by the morning one, if not all of them, would be dead. She was in such a bad condition that she found herself hoping she would go first. She had always been the hardiest of the children, though. It would probably be one of the boys. That made her even sadder, as did the thought that Mac might pass in the night. She wondered what they would do.

That night, she dreamed of being stuck in a dry well with no way out. The villagers from her home strolled by and looked at her. No one tried to help her. All the familiar faces from her childhood passed by without a word. She tried to cry out to them but could make no sound. She wept as she watched them pass.

Light was trying to push the darkness away when she woke early the next morning. She stared into the eastern sky but she found it hard to focus. She finally understood what she was seeing. Sally and Chico were walking away. They were almost out of sight. She thought *good, they are saving themselves*. She closed her eyes. She would not have known whether she was still alive were it not for the aches and pains from the previous day's march. The others were not moving though and she hesitated to check on them for fear of what she might find. She closed her eyes and passed out again.

The sun was high in the sky when Josephina heard Aldo's voice. He was on his knees, weeping. Josephina mustered all the strength she had and crawled over to him.

"What's wrong?" she asked.

She wondered at her own words as she realized that everything possible was wrong.

"I can't remember how to say it in English," he said softly in Spanish. "It's her, it's Broken Wing. We are saved. She has come back for us."

Josephina looked at the rising sun and saw Broken Wing moving steadily toward them. The animals were small dots on the horizon as they continued to walk away from them. Mac sat up, gathered himself, then limped toward her. The old hunchback Scotsman looked more like a troll than a human as he made his way toward their Indian savior. Felix could only turn his head to try to see. He was too weak to move.

Mac moved slowly as Broken Wing approached. They met and exchanged a few words and signs in their weird-sounding tongue. Then Mac turned and followed the animals.

"They are leaving us," Felix croaked.

"Hush," his sister scolded.

A few minutes later Broken Wing was with them. She gave them each a piece of root to chew on. It was full of juice, bitter but wet. The cracks at the corners of their mouths burned for a moment then went numb. She helped them up and they began to follow Mac. Josephina and Broken Wing were having to help Felix walk and they had gone only a short distance before Felix dropped to the ground. He could move no more. Aldo sat beside him. Then their sister joined them. They would all die together. They couldn't move another step. Broken Wing gave them more root, then hurried off toward Mac, moving faster than before. The boys thought she had left them but Josephina had a calm peace about what the old woman was up to. They all lay there on the sandy ground, watching her disappear.

Later that day, Broken Wing returned with Sally and Chico. It was impossible to know how long they had been there but the sun was deep in the western sky. The animals appeared refreshed and rested. Then Sally did the most remarkable thing Josephina had ever seen a mule do. She got down in a crawling position so Broken Wing and Josephina could get Felix on her back. Josephina crawled on behind him, both arms wrapped tightly around her brother. Sally rose to her feet carefully without shaking them off. Aldo was able to get onto Chico with the help of Broken Wing and they marched on. Sitting high up on Sally, Josephina could see what looked like a line of green. It had to be the river. It was the most beautiful sight she had ever seen. She pointed for Aldo to look. Aldo nodded and grinned.

When they finally reached the river, they saw Mac sitting in the water. It was as if life had returned to the old man. As they drank the sweet cool water, they also felt life and hope returning. Felix was in a bad way, though, passing in and out of consciousness. Josephina was worried about him. Soon, Broken Wing came back carrying a couple of rabbits. Mac made a fire while she skinned them. They roasted them and ate well that evening, except for Felix. He threw up the few bits he ate.

Aldo and Josephina had recovered by noon the next day, though Felix was still the same. He had always been lean but now he was skin and bones. Broken Wing spent the morning preparing a restorative broth with roots and medicinal herbs. She fed it to Felix a bite at a time while she chanted a strange song. Mac and Sally went to get the sled and Chico tagged along. Aldo and Josephina sat in the shade all day resting. They were worried about Felix but were happy to be alive and with their new family. Josephina thought it a strange family indeed but wouldn't have traded it for any other as she watched the old Indian woman nurse her brother. To everyone's surprise, Felix was able to hold down the broth they had given him. He was still too weak to sit up but he was able to stay awake for longer periods of time now. Mac returned by dark and they all settled in early, except Broken Wing. She stayed by Felix's side all night, forcing the broth down him when she could.

By the next morning, Felix was better, though it would take him several weeks to recover fully. Mac had already pronounced them proper English-speaking Texans. He said he was sad that he didn't have diplomas for them. They didn't know what he was talking about. This worried Aldo until Mac explained. Josephina thought to herself a diploma was not all they didn't have.

Broken Wing seemed worried now, despite Felix's improvement. She would go off for days at a time. Mac said she was looking for a place to winter. The river was far too densely populated for her. This was surprising to the children, who saw only a few barges and one other party during the month they were camped there. Mac explained that even those few were far more people than Broken Wing wanted to see.

"I think we will pack up and head toward the coast tomorrow," Mac said.

They breakfasted on a couple of squirrels he had shot. He was a pretty fair shot with his scattergun and he had also worked with Felix showing him how to properly handle his pistol.

"I'm thinking we have a couple of weeks' walk to get there," Mac said.

"What will we do when we get there?" Aldo asked.

"It's up to you," Mac said, smiling. "My guess is there will be a wealthy family or two, looking for help. Josephina will make a fine ladies' maid while you two fine lads should have no trouble gaining employment as stable hands or maybe couriers."

"What's a courier?" Felix asked.

Mac just laughed.

"Will I need my pistol as a courier?"

Mac laughed harder.

"I suppose you might."

"Do you know anyone where we are going?" Josephina asked.

"Corpus Christi is our best bet. It's settled and the people there are used to speaking Spanish and English for the most part."

"Then why did we have to learn English?" Aldo asked.

"You always ask the best questions," said Mac. "I'll tell you why. If you ever want to be more than a common worker, you must speak English. That's the language people use for doing business."

"Is Broken Wing going with us?" Felix wanted to know.

He had grown fond of her since they'd arrived on the Nueces. She had taken him out with her several times showing him how to find food and gather wild herbs. He knew what to do with the creatures they killed because she had taught him how to properly dress them. He had no idea what the herbs were for but he learned what they looked like and where to find them.

"No," Mac said. "She is already closer to civilization than she wanted to be. I'll take you into Corpus Christi and make sure you are settled. Then I'll find her."

"How will you find her?" Aldo wondered.

"It's more like she will find me. If I go looking for her, she'll know it and she'll come for me. I have no idea how she does it."

Mac was not finished educating the children, though. As he considered the waning time they had left together, he wanted to equip them for their new life. He pointed to the river and began to discuss a party of settlers he had seen that morning.

"I'm a decent tracker and I know if somebody is in the area," he began. "I watched them all morning and have concluded they are no threat to us. They must know we are here since we have a fire. The fact that they haven't come around tells me what I thought was probably correct."

"How can you be sure?" Felix asked.

"We can't really know, and that's why we stay alert. They are not a family group but you can tell they are not evil folks by the way they act."

The children looked puzzled.

"Bad men don't treat each other with courtesy and they have no manners, as a rule. These people seemed rather civil to each other. Their weapons were stored and their horses looked more like farm stock than saddle horses. I suspect Broken Wing has been watching them for a couple of days as well. If she didn't like the looks of them she would have come back here by now."

The wanderers never came around so the next morning, Mac loaded up Sally and Chico. They took enough supplies for a few days, though he said they would find plenty to eat along the way. Before noon that day, they were on their way to Corpus Christi. The name sounded exotic and the children were both excited and afraid of what the trip would bring. Felix was more worried than the other two. Their last trip had almost cost him his life, and the trip before that they had buried their father. However, he was calmed more than a little by Mac's presence. The old Scotsman had proven himself capable of tackling whatever came their way. So he kept quiet. After all, he was the oldest male in the family. He figured that put him in charge. But he knew he really wasn't. Josephina would always be in charge. She was by nature the more dominant. As they moved along, he found himself reaching down to touch the pistol. It seemed to help as they moved down the river toward Corpus Christi.

CHAPTER 5

New York

In the 1850s, New York, like most of the cities on the east coast, was growing. Manhattan was a boomtown. There were the wealthy and the poor, most of them immigrants, all living together on a small island. Those with money lived around 5th Avenue. Those without means lived wherever they could.

One of the poorer areas was just north of 59th Street. It was an irregular terrain of swamps and bluffs, punctuated by rocky outcroppings. The land was not suited for building. It was inhabited by those who could not afford anything better. German stonemasons, Irish pig farmers, and sheep farmers lived there. It was also home to Seneca Village, a thriving community of freed slaves. Founded in 1825, it was the largest community of free black people in New York. It boasted a population of 264. There were three churches, a school, and three cemeteries.

New Yorkers at the time were frustrated that their city was not as cosmopolitan as the large cities in Europe. London and Paris had luxurious parks for the wealthy to enjoy. New York did not. The elite citizens of New York were forced to leave the city to enjoy the scenic life they needed. To remedy this problem, the state legislature passed a law creating a park on Manhattan Island. This law authorized the City of New York to acquire 700 acres via eminent domain to create the park.

At the time the project began, there were approximately 1,600 residents occupying this land. Many of these displaced Germans, African Americans, and Irishmen were pressed into service to complete the massive public project. It was on this project that Father Matthews was able to find John a job and a place to live.

A stonemason named William Roberts was employed building walls, stone houses, and walkways for the park. John was working as a mason's helper, which meant he spent the day carrying stones or bricks and mixing mortar. Father Matthew preferred that John stay away from his previous haunts since he didn't want John to encounter Blackie again.

John liked the work he did. It was hard but he was used to hard work. The pay was fair and he worked around men who seemed of higher character than the dock workers he'd become accustomed to. William Roberts, known as "Billy Brick", was a decent man. Though he was English, John felt comfortable with him. John was not sure how the name "Billy Brick" got started but maybe because he was a mason, or maybe because he was a little slow-witted. Billy had plenty of work but he was a poor businessman so he never got ahead like so many of his fellow builders who were getting rich off the Central Park project. Billy had a big heart and he was a gentle man. He let Hank hang around the job so John was able to spend the day making money while enjoying time with his best friend. Hank was only half-grown but he was already over a hundred pounds.

The priest had also found a boarding house nearby. Miss Irma ran her house like a general would run a military camp. The small lady with the thick, German accent kept everything on a tight schedule. She served three meals a day and the men knew you could bet your last dollar that the meals would be on the table at exactly the time she planned to serve them—six in the morning, straight-up noon, and six in the evening. No exceptions. Ever. Eight to ten men rented rooms in her multi-storied row house. Most of them were workers who had no family or were there temporarily. John's room was just off the kitchen on the first floor. It occupied a small, narrow space she had converted into a room by enclosing an outdoor porch. Miss Irma was not one to be sitting on a porch knitting like most women her age. She was far more industrious and when she devised a plan to convert the porch into another room, she did so because this meant room for another tenant. When it rained, it leaked, and most nights John heard the wind whipping through the cracks in the walls.

The room was small, just big enough for a bed, a small chest that held his things, and a lamp on the chest. But it was good enough for John. Hank was allowed in John's room since it was technically a porch. This allowed Miss Irma to save face because one of her many rules was "no dogs in the house", and rules with Miss Irma were to be followed. Secretly she liked Hank. She fed him scraps and she liked that he was obedient. Each evening after supper, John and Hank romped in the backyard. Hank lived to please John and he was learning quite a few commands. Miss Irma would watch them through the kitchen window as she washed the dishes. Often in the evening, John would help her put things away. Miss Irma was becoming rather attached to both John and Hank.

One Sunday afternoon as John was sitting out back, Hank's ears perked up and he ran around toward the front of the house. John followed just in time to see Hank as he greeted Father Matthew.

"He has grown rather large since last I saw him. He is a beautiful dog," said the priest.

"Pudge," John said with a worried look on his face. "We didn't expect you. Is something wrong?"

"Not at all. I have a letter Nelly posted to you in care of the church. I thought I might bring it in person."

"For me?" John had never had a letter. This was a first. He started to reach out and get it when he remembered that he couldn't read. He drew his hand back.

"If you like I can read it to you. We priests have a way of keeping things to ourselves. So your secrets will remain just between you both, if there are any."

He said this with a jolly laugh.

"Let's go see if we can talk Miss Irma out of a piece of pie while I read this to you."

He put his arm around John's shoulder as they marched up the front porch and into the kitchen. Miss Irma was happy to see the young priest and she bowed to him properly and kissed his hand. Then they sat down at the table and she served them. Hank waited patiently at the back door. After a cup of tea and a piece of pie, Miss Irma excused herself and Father Matthew took out the letter and opened it.

My beloved brother,

Oh, how I have missed you. I wish you could come visit. I know it's a great distance and Father Matthew told me how busy you are at your new trade. I bet it won't be any time until you are building fine buildings all on your own."

John grunted to himself. He was not overly fond of the work he was doing and he could not imagine doing it for the rest of his life. The priest grinned at John's reaction, then continued reading.

"Maybe soon you can take a holiday and come for a visit. I hope you are as happy as I am. I miss you so much but I'm so happy here, and I have the most wonderful news. I want to tell you in person but I can't hold it any longer. You know how I am. I guess there is no

other way to do this but to come right out and say it, John. I want to get married. David and I have become very fond of each other and he wants to marry me if he has your blessing. I know you might think this is too modern but I understand in America it's done this way. I so want you to be happy for me. You mean the world to me. Please say yes. When we hear back from you we will set a date. I hope it is soon. David is such a fine man and he thinks the world of you. All the family here treat me so well. It is a dream come true. Oh, please say yes. I love you.

Your Loving Sister,
Nelly

The priest folded up the letter and waited for a response. John said nothing. After a long pause, Father Matthew took out a clean sheet of paper from his coat pocket and asked John what he should write.

"No, I mean this can't be happening. I should have never agreed to let her go. Now she's gone. Now I have nobody. What can I say?"

John was shaking his head. He had to stop talking. The emotions were too much. He had lost his mother and now he was losing his sister.

"Before you go any farther I need to say something," the young priest said. "My brother David is not a rash man. He would not do this unless he was serious about making her happy. I trust his judgment and I trust Nelly's as well. She is young but she is wise beyond her years. Please don't make her choose between you two. She loves you both. If you say no, David will go no further. It will be over. Nelly may resent this the rest of her life. So please think about it. You don't want to lose your sister but think about it this way. You are gaining a brother."

John remained quiet. Father Matthew was patient.

Finally, John spoke. "Can you write for me?"

The priest smiled. Together they wrote a reply giving David and Nelly his blessing. He told them all about his job, where he was living, and Hank. He said quite a bit about Hank. When the letter was finished, Father Matthew folded it, put it into his coat pocket, and stood up to leave.

"I'd like to see you at mass sometime. You could come with Miss Irma."

"Maybe," John said, knowing it would not happen.

The next Sunday, Father Matthew returned, this time with David. Father Matthew greeted everyone, then left David with John.

David played with Hank for a few minutes, then hesitated.

"I suppose you know why I'm here. Nelly said you approve but I need to hear it from you. I have grown fond of you and the very last thing I want to do is impose upon you. I want—*no, I need*—your blessing. Not just that you agree, I want you to be as happy as Nelly and I are."

"Your brother said you'll make a fine husband," John said.

"I want to hear it from you," David pressed him further.

John looked at Hank as though he would have the answer and it seemed he did. He raised up, put both front paws on David's shoulders, and began licking his face.

"I guess if Pudge and Hank think you are acceptable, who am I to argue?" said John.

John pushed Hank down, put his hands on David's shoulders, and pulled him forward. The men hugged.

"You have my blessing. I would be honored to have you as my brother. I want Nelly to be happy. Please make her happy," John said, with tears in his eyes.

"I will. I promise I will."

"David, I think it is good that you have each other. It is just that I never planned any of this. Things just seem to happen, and I can't control any of it."

"None of us can. It's the way life is. We just need to make the best of what we get. And I'm sure this is the best," David said.

David told John about the house he was building and the plans they were making. John was getting used to the idea and it no longer seemed so strange. They spent the afternoon talking about life on the farm, raising dogs, raising kids, and just about everything. David spent the night at the boarding house. Miss Irma had a spare room and she didn't even charge him. In the morning Miss Irma packed a lunch for David and he caught the train back to Jersey. John and Hank went to work where they found Billy Brick waiting for them with a soup bone for Hank and a load of bricks for John.

Over the next few months, Father Matthew showed up occasionally with a letter from Nelly or David. John felt he was getting to know her better than when he lived with her. It made him want to learn to read. Yet every day, John grew more restless. There were many days in the winter when they couldn't work. It was either too cold or there was too much snow. John spent the days he could not work wandering around, trying to find something better to do. He had begun to frequent several taverns in the neighborhood. One day, he entered a local tavern run by a Frenchman named Lemieux. As he walked in, a man with a patch over his eye walked across the bar and said, in a strange accent, "I know you."

John looked at him and shook his head. He would have remembered a tall scruffy-headed man with a patch on his eye.

"Maybe not," John said. "I'm sure we have never met."

"No, I know you. I'm sure I know you. Old One-Eyed Joe has seen you 'afore."

So his name is One-Eyed Joe, John thought. *I guess that fits.* John stepped around him, ordered a beer, and sat at a table with several local workers he knew. One-Eyed Joe followed him over to the table and continued to stare at him. John was getting up to leave when the man spoke again.

"I know. I know. You are the young pup who boxed old Blackie's ears. Ha, I knew it was you. Old One-Eyed Joe ain't crazy."

John walked over to an empty table in the corner and sat down. The gentleman followed him.

"My name is Jamal Darvish. My friends call me Joe."

"I don't recall ever meeting you but my name is John Delaney."

"I was in the establishment the day you slapped that old devil around. It did my heart good."

"He had it coming."

"I have no doubt of that. No doubt at all. I'd be honored if you allowed me to buy you a drink."

"I have a beer, thanks."

"Oh, that will run dry soon enough," said Joe. "I'll get us a real drink."

He got up, dug deep into his pocket, and brought up an entire bottle of whiskey. This impressed the small crowd that had gathered around to listen. John was mildly curious and he sipped his beer as he listened to the man spin his tale. A Turkish merchant, Jamal was working on a cargo ship docked in the New York harbor.

He said he was here recruiting for a passage leaving in a few days. They would sail to Jamaica and back several times over the next few months. Jamal was a good storyteller and he talked about wonderful mysterious places—islands where beautiful, brown women went around unclothed and ate coconuts and pineapple on the beaches. There were ancient lands where people had lived in the exact same way for thousands of years.

The whiskey was good and after a few glasses, John was enjoying himself. Jamal had coaxed him into telling a few stories of his own. He wanted to know about the trouble with Blackie. John also told him about a few fights he and his brothers and his father had fought with the English. It was after midnight before the bottle was empty. It was a good thing Hank was there to lead John home. He was hoping the storm held out another day. He was not sure he could work the following morning.

Letters from Nelly kept coming. The building business was getting old. Billy Brick had no time to teach him anything. He just wanted him for mixing grout and hauling bricks. Near the end of January, Nelly sent the date they were to be married. It was to be on May 23rd. John wished it were sooner. He was ready to quit his job and he needed a good reason. Living at Miss Irma's was pleasant enough but it was not what he wanted.

Another ice storm hit a few days later and John again found himself killing time at the Frenchman's tavern. He was getting ready to head home when once again he encountered Jamal Darvish, the one-eyed seaman.

"It's a stroke of luck for sure," the man bellowed. "Now I don't need to go looking for you."

"I'm not too hard to find. Ask anyone around here where to find the boy with the giant dog. They'll tell you."

It was true, Hank had become a familiar sight in the area.

"Sit back down. We need to talk," Jamal said.

John sat down and Jamal waved for the barkeeper.

"None for me," John said.

"Then I'll just have a shot of your finest rum," said Jamal.

"You'll have beer or whiskey," Lemieux said.

"Whiskey it is. Now, my boy, I have a business proposal for you. This Saturday night you can earn some easy money for a few hours' work. Are you interested? It's completely legal, I assure you. Well?"

the Turk asked.

"I'm listening."

"Good. The lightweight champion is putting on an exhibition. He is in training and his manager will pay $20 a round for anyone who will get in the ring with him. If you can go three or four rounds with him you can earn some good money."

"And if I win?"

"Ha! I'll need to cut a deal on that one. Anyway, I stand to make some good money on side bets. I'd bet on you going several rounds."

"How big is he?"

"He's about your size but he's a professional."

"I'll do it," John said.

"Great. I'll come by for you around noon on Saturday."

John got up and walked out without saying another word. He knew how to fight. It's about all he really did know. He was getting stronger from all the brick hauling and he was ready to do anything else. The next day he told Billy Brick he would not be working Saturday. Billy didn't like it much but he didn't fire John. He just grumbled to himself as he did most of the day.

Jamal showed up at Miss Irma's at noon on the dot on Saturday. He and John walked down Broadway into the heart of Manhattan. For the first time, John was without Hank. Jamal had said Hank would not be welcome where they were going, so Hank was forced to stay behind with Miss Irma. They caught a carriage that took them into the garment district.

John was not familiar with this part of New York. They entered an old warehouse that had been converted into an arena. John and Jamal were ushered into a small dressing room.

"I got you in first. It pays an extra $2 a round because the champ is fresh."

Jamal was excited about this.

John didn't care. They put some cloth gloves on him, then some larger leather gloves. Then they wrapped the gloves tightly with more cloth. Jamal left the room to work the crowd, gathering as many bets as he could.

John sat on a bench, wondering what Nelly was doing. He imagined she and David sitting on the porch swing. He was wondering what their house looked like. He was happy for them. John had grown used to the idea of Nelly living on the farm. It didn't seem so bad.

When Jamal came back, he was grinning from ear to ear. He was pleased with the result of his wagering. He and John walked out to the ring. The crowd had grown to over a hundred. Chairs encircled the ring for seven or eight rows with more people standing in the back. The first few rows were filled with dandies—businessmen in dark suits. Jamal was growing more excited by the minute.

"Try to stay away from him. I need you to get into the third round. Go to the third round and I'll give you another $50."

"What if I win?"

"Just stay away from his right," said the Turk, laughing.

John entered the ring, then looked around at all the people. The cheering started when a curtain was pulled back and a man wearing tight pants and no shirt started bouncing on his toes as he neared the ring. He was punching the air and whirling around. John stepped to the middle and waited, ignoring the champ's theatrics. He looked at Jamal and nodded.

The champ stepped into the ring with five or six other men. A little man with a big voice raised a megaphone and the crowd roared. John just stood there, looking around the arena. He was not going to look at his opponent. A hush grew over the crowd as the fighters went to their corners.

"In this corner," said the big voice, looking at a card, "We have from Ireland, Johnny Delaney." A few people clapped. John figured they were mostly Irish.

"And in the opposite corner, the reigning lightweight champion of New York! Your very own Barney Aaron!"

The crowd cheered. This is what they'd been waiting for. Barney stepped forward, kissed his hands, and blew kisses to the crowd. John looked over at Jamal and grinned. While Barney was circling the ring, playing to the crowd, John walked over and whispered something to Jamal. One-eyed Joe looked back at him and shook his head. He was not going to double the bets.

After Barney was through working the crowd, he went back to his corner. At the bell, John walked to the middle of the ring with his hands at his side. The champ danced out to meet him, then darted in toward John and threw a left jab that was close. It had been a feint, meant to fool John. A right cross was headed to where John should have dodged. Rather than move back, however, John leaned in and threw a hard left that landed square in Barney's stomach, then a right hook that landed in his ribs. The blows stopped Barney's forward movement. John looked him in the eye for the first time, then stepped back. His hands were at his side again. Barney threw a flurry of jabs at John that were mostly blocked. John then went after him, absorbing some of the punches and landing some hard blows to the champ's middle section. The crowd was cheering wildly as John kept coming after him. Blow after blow landed on the champion's body. John had taken some blows but he had learned to not give in to pain until it was over. Pain was for later. He ducked his chin and kept swinging. When the bell rang, it was just in time because Barney was about to go down. John went to his corner and waited for the stool as Barney wobbled back across the ring. His corner was busy giving advice and caring for the champ. John had a cut lip and a mouse under his left eye. He spat blood and looked at Jamal.

"How am I doing?"

Jamal grinned.

"How much longer do you want me to string it along?"

The bell rang for round two and John stood up. He walked to the middle of the ring where he and the champ touched gloves. Barney was using a side-to-side tactic now, a bob and weave maneuver that he was famous for. John didn't play along, quickly going to work on the champ's middle again. The damage was done, and with probable broken ribs, Barney covered up low. As soon as he did, John clipped him hard on the chin. His head snapped back just as a solid right fell on the bridge of his nose. It was lights out for the champ. He dropped like a sack of potatoes. John stood over him for a few seconds, then walked back to his corner. The fight was over.

John was sore by the time they got back to the neighborhood but the $235 in his pocket made it worthwhile. Jamal probably had more but John didn't care. They went to the tavern and Jamal bought a round for everybody. Jamal was talking a mile a minute, giving all the locals a blow-by-blow account of how Fighting Johnny Delaney had beaten the champ. It was not a sanctioned fight, so of course, Barney was still the champ. But when they'd left the arena, the champ was still out cold.

The whiskey they drank seemed to ease John's pain. His left eye was swollen and he had a fat lower lip with a couple of loose lower teeth. His right hand was swelling too but he didn't think it was broken. While he could still walk, he started for Miss Irma's. He was worried about Hank. By the time he left, he was a hero. All the men in the tavern were patting him on the back, each claiming to be his best friend.

John found Hank sitting on the front porch waiting. Hank was not just glad to see him. He seemed concerned about John. John rolled into bed in his clothes and slept until after noon the next day. Hank never left his side.

When John woke that afternoon, he wandered into the kitchen, hoping to get a cup of black coffee. He found Father Matthew sitting at the table waiting for him.

"Well, I have to say I've seen you looking better," said the priest. "Miss Irma, would you be kind enough to put on a pot of coffee?"

The priest got up and looked closely at John's eye and lip. Then he sat down.

"Are you going to tell me what happened?"

"I'd rather not."

"Are you in some sort of trouble?"

"No sir, nothing like that."

"You had better not be lying to a priest," Miss Irma said. "Not here in my kitchen."

"No trouble with the law, I promise. In fact, there were a number of policemen watching," John said, suddenly realizing he might have said too much.

"Then I guess I'll just read you the letter and be on my way," Father Matthew said, his tone cool.

"John, you apologize to that man of God right now," Miss Irma demanded. "I'll not have a man of the cloth offended in my house, no sir."

"I didn't mean anything by it. I'm fine, I just don't want to talk about it."

"When you are ready to talk, will you talk to me?"

"Yes sir, I will."

"Now, you can't be breaking a promise to a priest," Miss Irma said. "There is no telling what kind of evil that is. You are treading on thin ice, John."

"Miss Irma if you don't mind, I'd like to speak with John alone. Thank you for the coffee. I can take care of it from here," said Father Matthew.

He walked her out of the kitchen and watched her climb the stairs. He came back in and poured two cups of coffee and sat down to read the letter. They didn't talk anymore about John's wounds. The letter was like the others—warm, tender words filled with love. As Father Matthew was getting up to leave, John finally spoke.

"It was an arranged fight downtown, for money."

He hung his head.

"Are you sure you are all right?"

"I'm fine. It was just a one-time thing for some quick cash. I'm through with it."

"Good. This is not the kind of life you want."

The priest looked at his face once more, then walked away without another word. John wondered if the priest believed him. He thought he probably didn't. After he was gone, John and Hank spent the day resting. John was completely exhausted after the fight. As short as it was, it had taken a lot out of him. And Hank seemed worried. He never left John's side.

CHAPTER 6

Corpus Christi

It had taken them six days to reach Corpus Christi. The traveling was easier as they stayed near the river. Mac shot a young doe so they had meat. They met several other parties on the journey. Some were going to Corpus, others were moving west into the heart of Texas. All appeared to be pleasant people. The children were amazed at how easy it was for Mac to relate to everyone he met. It seemed he never encountered a stranger. After conversing for a few minutes, Mac could always find something in common to bond over. Josephina wondered if Mac invented it all to impress them or if his stories were real. A family heading west needed meat so Mac traded the rest of the deer for supplies. This journey was not like the one before. The previous trip had been simply to survive, with little hope. This time it was different. With Mac, they had a purpose. They enjoyed this trip as they practiced their English and spent more time laughing than worrying.

They camped a few miles out of town and Mac told the children he would go into Corpus alone. He explained to them that every town was different. Some were friendly and some not. Mac spent the evening teaching them about all the different towns he had experienced. He had an opinion as to why they varied. His theory was that each city had its own individual style or personality, as a person would. The children had discovered that Mac loved his theories and they loved to hear him talk. They were beginning to love everything about the odd little man.

In the morning Mac rose early. He bathed, then he and Sally prepared to ride into town. It was the first time the children had seen him ride her. She looked comfortable with Mac on her back, even though with his deformities, the overall appearance of the two was odd. Sally was a huge animal and because of Mac's compressed torso, he had a difficult time seeing over her head.

"While I'm away, you are in charge, Felix," Mac said, craning his neck to see. "I know you will take care of everything while I'm gone. I have no doubt your brother and sister are safe in your care."

Felix tried to keep from smiling. He wanted it to seem normal for him to be in charge. It was about time, he thought. He looked over at Aldo and stuck out his chest, or at least he attempted to do this. He was still weak from his recent heatstroke.

"If someone comes around," Mac continued, "act neighborly and at the same time let them know you are armed. Keep that scattergun close."

Mac winked at Josephina as he and Sally rode away at an easy trot. As Mac bumped up and down on the big mule, the children were afraid she might bounce him off. Somehow, though, he stayed on.

It wasn't long before Sally and Mac arrived in Corpus. Sally slowed to a walk which drew less attention. It was not every day the citizens of Corpus saw an old hunchback Scotsman riding into town bareback on a mule. Mac rode around for a while, up one street and down another. When Mac had a feel for the town, he found a livery stable and paid the man with a gold piece he had taken from the banditos. He paid for Sally to be brushed and given a bag of oats. She approved of the attention and she enjoyed her leisurely afternoon.

Mack spent a few hours talking with different people. When he had learned what he wanted to know, he walked over to the General

Store and bought a few items, then went straight to the newspaper office. There he talked the clerk into letting him do some research. He stayed there all afternoon until it closed. Then he and Sally rode back to camp.

Mac arrived in camp in the best of spirits. He was singing to himself and laughing. He refused to tell the children what had happened, teasing them and creating a sense of wonder about what they would find out. He told them that if tomorrow went well, the future looked very bright indeed. He and Sally would return to town the following morning. He instructed the children to break camp at noon and walk into town, where he would meet them at the first church they come to.

The next morning, Mac was up early preparing for the day. Aldo and Felix had to hold Chico back. He did not want Sally to leave him two days in a row. He tried his best to follow her. Long after they were gone, Chico was still braying for her.

Sally went straight to the livery stable where she would again spend the day in the shade, enjoying another bag of oats. She was liking these visits to Corpus Christi. Mac went back to the General Store and bought the finest paper he could find as well as some ink and a quill. He then went to the McGregor Hotel where he inquired about a guest he thought might be staying there. He went into the dining room, ordered a cup of coffee, and began writing a letter. He was there most of the morning working on it. He ordered lunch and ate as he finished his work. When he was pleased with his correspondence, he folded the paper and addressed it to Henrietta King. He left it at the front desk with orders that it be delivered by hand. He then tipped the clerk with a smaller gold coin.

Industrialist and rancher Richard King was due in today and he had planned to meet his wife for lunch. Mrs. King was coming down the stairs to meet her husband when she saw the strange little man hobbling through the front door of the hotel. She noticed that everyone in the lobby was shaming the gentleman as he left. She could hear the whispers as they ridiculed him.

"Who does he think he is?" one well-dressed man asked.

"Have you ever seen anything so outrageous?" another one whispered.

"Doesn't this hotel have rules against this type of thing?" asked an elegant lady.

Mac exited the finest hotel Corpus had to offer without looking back. He knew what was being said about him. He had heard it all before.

Henrietta King was moved with compassion as she saw every eye in the place fixed on the stranger. Her compassion quickly turned to anger against the rude hotel guests. She swept through the lobby toward the dining room, glaring at the people who had just spoken ill of this man who had done them no wrong.

Just then, the desk clerk called her name. He handed her a note, then ducked his head and returned to his desk. He had seen the way she responded to the lobby chatter and he wanted to stay clear of her if he could. She selected a table near the window, ordered their food, and read the note.

To Lady Henrietta Maria Chamberlain King:

It is with the utmost pleasure that I have the privilege of communicating with you about an urgent matter that only our LORD and Savior would have the ability to orchestrate. I was completely unaware that this small coastal town would have such an eminent visitor as yourself at just the opportune time. Both your benevolence and your abilities are well known to those who take the time to look for such qualities.

Let me introduce myself. It is not that I matter in this but you should know with whom you might have future dealings. My name is Bartholomew Donnally McGentry of the House of Lord Kilgore. All my credentials are easily verified, even in this small Texas town. At any rate, I find myself in this particular set of circumstances through a number of adventures—some glorious and some disastrous. If time permits at a later time it would be my pleasure to share with you a few of my tales. But for now, if I may, I'd like to make a proposal to you—a proposal that if given a fair chance might bring you a type of fortune and solace that only a saintly woman like you would understand.

Fortune has placed me in a position of being the benefactor of three wonderful and talented orphans, though not through legal means. As you know, courts are few in this place. These young souls with whom I have traveled through dire circumstances are in need of three vital necessities which I am unable to provide. These are, in no certain order, education, Christian values, and employment. And as fate would have it, you are perhaps the only person in this part of the world equipped to meet and surpass all these immediate needs.

If you can make time for us in your schedule I'd like for you to meet these fine children. I'll have them in the lobby of the hotel this very day at 5 pm.

Yours truly,
Bartholomew McGentry

She folded the letter, put it into her pocketbook, and waited for her husband. She knew there was more than just a little puffery in the letter, and she'd had experience with con men who had tried to manipulate her before but there was a certain curiosity and compassion that was driving her to meet this man. She had to see him.

Mac and Sally got to the little Presbyterian church before the children arrived. He spread a blanket in the shade of a pecan tree on the side of the little church and laid out the food he had obtained in town.

As the children arrived, Chico was the first to see his friend Sally. He took off in what was his best attempt at a gallop. He was loaded with all their things but realizing Sally was close gave him enough strength to easily bear the burden. Sally saw him and walked out to meet him. They greeted each other as Sally led him to a small ditch behind the church where they both drank.

Mac was unloading Chico when the children arrived. Josephina and Aldo hugged Mac while Felix shook hands and returned his scattergun. It was the first time the gun had been out of his hands since Mac had entrusted it to him two days before.

Mac had brought another bag of oats for Chico and Sally to share. They enjoyed the oats while Mac and the young ones lunched on sausage, bread, and cheese.

"Sit back and listen, I have a lot to share with you. As fate would have it, Mr. Richard King is in town this very day to meet his wife," Mac said as he made himself comfortable against a tree. "Mr. King is perhaps the richest man in this part of Texas. His story is interesting and worth hearing, even if nothing comes of this. However, I think it may result in something more than just interesting if my plan is successful. Richard King comes from a poor Irish family that lived in New York. At the age of ten, he stowed away on a ship and ended up in Mobile, Alabama."

The children had never heard of any of these places but it all sounded so exotic and they listened intently, not knowing where the story was leading or how it would affect them.

"Because he was a good worker and fate was on his side, he ended up learning, then mastering a trade. He worked on steamships which were becoming the fashionable way of transportation along the rivers and shallow waters of the Gulf coastline. These boats could navigate shallow waters that larger vessels could not. Large ships could only use deepwater ports, so the steamships were vital for taking people and goods to places the large ships could not enter.

He saved his money and bought his own steamboat, transporting goods from Florida all the way to Veracruz. He was able to partner with men who had the means to build a fleet of steamboats. Currently, he has a monopoly on all trade up and down the coast. A few years back he started buying up land and he is now building a cattle ranch.

While running cotton up and down the Rio Grande River, he met a beautiful young lady who was teaching school in Brownsville, Texas. Henrietta Maria Chamberlain is the daughter of a Presbyterian minister, Hiram Chamberlain, previously from Missouri. She received her education from a prestigious girl's school in Mississippi and now devotes her life to both the Gospel and education.

"They fell in love and were married four years ago. She is in Corpus today, waiting for her husband to arrive."

"How do you know all of this?" Aldo asked.

"There is no limit to what you can learn if you ask the right people and can read. After hearing about King's arrival today, I went to the local newspaper and read all I could about him. After discovering Mrs. King's passion for education, and considering your needs for the same, it appeared to be a fine fit. I left her a note asking for a meeting this afternoon. We will go to the lobby of the hotel soon and perhaps we can speak with her.

If she is too busy or doesn't show up, we will return here and wait for her. She will pass this way as she proceeds to the ranch she is having built. The ship Mr. King arrived on is full of lumber that will be hauled to the ranch. He is hiring men today to transport the material. Mrs. King will supervise the construction of their new house."

"What if they say no?" Josephina asked.

"How could she say no to such a pretty face," Mac said as he patted her cheek. "And every ranch owner needs an experienced hand that can handle a pistol as well as Felix can. And with a little training, Aldo here will make a fine linguist. I will bet he speaks 17 languages before long. Texas can always use a young man with his abilities."

Mac rubbed Aldo's shaggy head. They all needed grooming.

"Mac what do we do if they say no?" Josephina asked the same question again.

"We'll think of something. I won't let anything happen to you. Sally would never forgive me, nor would Broken Wing."

They finished their meal and walked into town, using a back road. Chico and Sally visited the livery stable while the three children bathed at a boarding house Mac had found. Then they put on the new clothes Mac had bought for them at the General Store. Josephina knew Mac was probably almost out of gold coins but she was glad they had something nice to wear.

It was late afternoon by the time they reached the hotel. Mac hoped they were not too late. He was second-guessing his plan now but it was too late to change anything. The children sat on a sofa in the lobby and Mac went up to the front desk. Before he could say anything, a man in a dark suit tapped him on the shoulder.

"Sir I need you to follow me," the man said in a deep voice.

Mac turned to look at the children.

"They will be fine," said the man. "Now sir if you would please… right this way."

He motioned toward a closed door and they went in. At a table in the middle of the room sat another man in an elegant suit. He was a striking gentleman with curly black hair and a perfectly trimmed goatee. He appeared to be in his late thirties. Mac recognized him from the photos in the newspaper.

"Mr. King, it is my pleasure."

"Not at all, Mr. McGentry, the pleasure is mine."

The two men shook hands.

"Please have a seat."

King motioned toward a couple of upholstered chairs and a sofa on an ornate Turkish rug. Mac sat in one of the chairs and though his hump restricted him from sitting up straight as a normal man would, he still looked completely at ease.

"May I begin?" King asked.

"Please do."

"You have me at a disadvantage, sir. I typically know the people with whom I do business, or I don't do it. But my wife is set on meeting with you this afternoon, and once her mind is set, I have little chance of changing it. I'll ask you to be straightforward with me. I have read your note and I must be honest. I am not sure I understand your intent. Without the ability to investigate your past I must trust my gut feeling about you. This has always served me well. You see, McGentry, I know a liar when I see one."

"I fully understand," Mac replied. "As to any personal advantage I might achieve, I assure you there is none. My only concern is for the children for whom I have been caring these last several months. My nomadic existence is not an appropriate life for them. They need education, training, and jobs, and these things I can not provide."

Mac went on to tell him their story as honestly and completely as he could. After he finished all that he intended to say, he waited for King to respond. King nodded at the man standing by the door who stepped out, leaving them alone.

"Mr. McGentry, I am satisfied. You are free to speak with my wife and I will trust you to do as you said but please remember I am not a man to be trifled with."

The men stood and shook hands. When Mac walked back out into the lobby, he saw Henrietta King sitting with the children. They were laughing and talking like old friends.

"So happy to meet you, Mr. McGentry," she said. "I have made arrangements for a meal to be brought to our suite. I trust you will all join us?"

"Mrs. King, it would be our pleasure," Mac answered.

They followed her up the stairs where they found a table set with fine linen and beautiful china. Henrietta sat at the head of the table and gestured to Mac and the children to be seated.

"Mr. King will not be able to join us tonight, Mr. McGentry. Would you be kind enough to say grace?" She asked as she held her hand up for the waiters to pause.

Mac stood up and bowed his head.

"Our Lord and Savior, it is with great thankfulness and humility that we approach your throne asking your blessings on this meal that you have provided. Please bless our time together this evening. As I was telling you earlier today, I intend to turn this entire matter over to you and trust your hand will be on everyone here. Amen."

"Thank you, Mr. McGentry," Henrietta said as the waiters resumed their work. "If you don't mind, we will talk business as we eat."

"Yes, we can, and if I may ask, will you do me the honor of calling me Mac?"

"Thank you, I will, and you may call me Henrietta," she said.

"Call me Aldo," Aldo said, imitating the adults in his most earnest manner. They all laughed.

"Then it is only given names for us all," Henrietta said.

"I trust you will ask anything you like of us and we shall answer you as honestly and forthrightly as I answered your husband," Mac began.

"Don't be worried about him. He may seem harsh but he has a good heart. I would never have been able to establish the orphanages had he not been one hundred percent for them. He loves children as much as I do. He just wants everybody to know he's in charge. And I allow that. It is important to him."

Mac nodded and she continued.

"I was very moved by your letter and I wish to hear all about this situation."

Mac then repeated the story exactly as he had relayed it to Mr. King. Regardless of what she said, he did not want Mr. King to find any discrepancy in his story. After he was finished, she had a few questions about the journey. She seemed astonished at how well the children had handled adversity.

She then questioned the children themselves. She was surprised and pleased at the English they had learned. When dinner was over and their stories had been told, she gathered her things and excused herself. The children liked her but were afraid to say so since there had been no decision yet. After a brief delay, she returned.

Henrietta smiled and said she had made arrangements for the night with rooms for all of them.

"Felix and Aldo will share a room with Mac down the hall," she said. "Josephina will be in the room next to us. Mr. King and I will discuss everything tonight. I cannot imagine that we will find ourselves in anything but full agreement but it is our custom to talk through all major decisions affecting our home or family."

"We completely understand, Henrietta," Mac replied.

"In the morning we shall have breakfast here together and I am sure we can come up with an arrangement that will be agreeable to all," she said.

Henrietta supervised the staff as they prepared the rooms. When everything was in order, they settled in. The children had never slept in beds so luxurious. In fact, it had been a long time since any of them had slept in a bed at all. And never had they felt softer mattress or finer linens.

Josephina's room had a small balcony overlooking the river. That night, there was a pleasant breeze blowing warm moist air from the Gulf. Josephina curled up in a chair by the window, thinking about all that had transpired over the past few months. She felt hopeful for the first time in a very long time. Perhaps it was the nice room or perhaps it was the kindness Mrs. King had shown them. She pulled a blanket up over her shoulders and fell fast asleep in the chair.

She had been asleep a few hours when she was awakened by familiar voices. At first, she thought she might be dreaming. One voice she heard was Broken Wing's, the other was Mac's. She looked down and saw the two of them in the courtyard below. The minute she looked down, Broken Wing sensed her looking and looked straight up at her. The Indian woman nodded at her and went right back to speaking with Mac in their strange language. After a few minutes, Broken Wing eased away. She was at one with the night and she moved soundlessly. Not even the local dogs barked. Josephina watched her disappear. A few minutes later there was a light tap on the door. Josephina opened the door to find Mac standing there.

"How did she know where we were?" Josephina asked

"Broken Wing knows what she wants to know. She has been watching us the entire way. She is fond of you and your brothers. It took a while to convince her that you would be safe in town. She would feel better if you were sleeping out under the stars where she could keep watch over you."

"I never saw her," Josephina said. "I was looking for her the entire journey."

"You do not see her until she is ready to be seen," Mac reminded her. "I've gotten used to her ways over the years. I admit it took some time."

"Are the boys asleep?" Josephina asked.

"Yes, they were sleeping soundly when I left them. It's time we were all in bed, I think. We have a big day ahead of us."

"Tell me what you think Mac," Josephina begged.

"It doesn't matter what I think at this point. I've done all I can. I have turned it over to the Lord and it is up to him. Besides what matters is what Mrs. King thinks. Don't worry if this doesn't work out. Ol' Mac may have another trick or two left. I'll make sure you are all taken care of. I fear Broken Wing too much to let harm come to you."

He said this with a smile as he put his big rough hand on her shoulder. She leaned over and kissed him on the cheek.

In the morning they all gathered for breakfast. Mr. King was now sitting at the head of the table. He appeared to be in good spirits. After the dishes were cleared away, he excused himself and wished them all a fine day.

Once he had taken his leave, Henrietta invited them into the parlor.

"Mac, Mr. King and I have conferred and we would like to offer a proposal if we may," she said.

The children were hanging on to her every word but Mac merely nodded.

"Please do."

"I am in need of a ladies' maid and Josephina would be excellent. She would travel with me, taking care of any and all duties as they arise. She would be paid a fair wage. The job includes training, which I personally will oversee. This means she would learn to read and write—skills of which I know you approve.

Felix would be employed as a stable hand until he is able to ride and rope. Then he would be trained as a cowboy. He would also learn to read and write. His pay would be commensurate with the level he obtains as a ranch hand. Aldo would not work as he is too young. However I believe families should stay together, so he would live with us at the ranch doing whatever chores are needed as he continues this education.

If the children are in agreement, and if you approve, they will travel with us to the ranch as soon as we leave Corpus."

"It is most generous. It is even more than I had hoped for, thank you."

Mac was pleased.

"As you know Mac, when you turn things over to the Lord, they often have a way of working out for the better. Now as for you Mac, we could use a well-educated man..."

"I must graciously refuse," Mac interrupted. "Broken Wing needs me. And having lived in towns before, I don't miss them. I like it better in the wild with just my Indian companion. After decades of watching small-minded people enjoy ridiculing my maladies, I have found a certain solace that the wild provides."

"As you wish but I assure you that you would be treated with respect in my presence."

"That I'm sure of but I can't be forever in your presence. And as I said, Broken Wing needs me. Not to survive, for she is completely capable of caring for herself. She was abandoned by her people, as was I, so we have that in common. I assure you the relationship is quite platonic. We are both too old to be worrying about that sort of thing."

He winked at her and she blushed.

CHAPTER 7

New York

The week after the fight, John was met at his job site by a few men in business suits. They had approached Billy Brick and asked for John Delaney. The men arrived in a carriage pulled by two fine black horses. John was given leave of his duties and he and Hank followed the men to a local cafe. Hank waited outside. The men smiled at John and presented themselves as if they were his friends. After coffee was served, the first man spoke.

"May we be straightforward, sir?"

"Please do," John said.

He was not normally impressed by dandies but these two seemed friendly enough.

The other man then spoke.

"I saw you fight last week."

John nodded and held his gaze on the man speaking.

"My name is Jacob Underhill and this is my brother Francis. We are investors and we have a business proposal for you."

John nodded again without changing his expression.

His father had taught him about fancy men. They fought with words, not fists. John heard warning bells go off. These men were takers, not givers. Father Matthew was a giver, the old bald priest was a giver, and the Swensons were givers but these men wanted something.

"We would like to manage your career," Underhill continued.

John knew what they meant but he feigned ignorance. He knew when it came to words these men were far his superior. However, he wanted to see what they would propose.

"I think I can manage being a mason's helper on my own. But if Billy Brick becomes too hard to deal with, then I'll be sure to look you up and see if you can broker a better deal."

The two men saw no humor in this. The displeasure on their faces told John he had scored. They continued, ignoring his insolence.

"We are talking about your fighting career."

"I have no fighting career," John said.

"That is exactly our point. You could be rich. With your skills, proper training, and the type of promotion we are prepared to provide, you could do very well, young man."

Jacob handed John a business card. John looked at it, pretending to understand what it said. Then he stuck it in his pocket. Now it was the other brother's turn to speak.

"We are prepared to offer you a lucrative contract. This document details all of your benefits as well as your immediate compensation, which is, I might add, very generous."

He reached into a satchel and pulled out a stack of papers.

John liked this man even less than Jacob. He took the papers but did not look at them.

"All you need to do is sign this last page."

Francis took the papers back from John and began shuffling through the pages.

"I'm not a fighter," John said.

"Not yet but you could be with our help," Francis said.

"I don't like to fight."

"But I saw you, son. You are a natural. Quick hands with a heavy punch. You are a fighter," Jacob said.

"Yes I can fight but I don't like to fight," John replied.

"Then why were you there?" Francis asked.

"I needed money and I wanted to see what it was all about. Curious, I suppose is why. Now I know what prizefighting is and I don't like it."

"We are prepared to…"

John got up to leave and Francis stopped talking. As he walked toward the door, he remembered himself telling Father Matthew he was done with it. He knew that moment that he meant what he said. His promise to Father Matthew meant something. These two meant nothing to him.

"Good day, sirs. Please never bother me again about fighting. I'm through with it. The entire thing turns my stomach. A room full of men, cheering for one man to hurt another, even wagering on who will win. That, sir, is no sport. I never want to be involved with it again."

John returned to work, hoping he was through talking about the fight. He could not go anywhere in the neighborhood without someone stopping him to ask him about it. It troubled him that the only person here he admired was Father Matthew and the priest was disgusted by this business.

A few days later, a couple of other men showed up. His friend Jamal had convinced John to have one drink with him after supper. When they got to the tavern, the two men were waiting. Both were well-dressed, about the same age but that's where the similarity ended. One was so fat he could hardly walk. The other gentleman was small, with thin features. He looked more like a rat than he did a man. John thought they looked like predators, waiting to pounce. They started out the same way as the others had but when John told them he didn't want to fight, they switched to threats.

They said they were powerful men and could see to it that John never worked in any trade union along the east coast. If he didn't fight for them, he would remain penniless the rest of his life. John listened, betraying neither fear nor interest.

"What you're saying is that if I don't work for you I'll have to leave New York?" John asked.

"Yes, you understand us clearly," Rat Face said, "but if you sign this contract…"

He began pulling paper out of his coat pocket and the fat man grinned, letting John know he was in control.

"I have looked over the papers, John," Jamal said, finally speaking up. "This is a good deal for everybody."

"So you will also be making money on this, Jamal?" John asked.

"Just the customary fees for my services," said the Turk.

"How long do I have to decide?" John asked.

He felt betrayed by his friend and he was becoming angrier by the moment.

"We were hoping to get the papers signed tonight," said Rat Face. "The details can be dealt with at another time. Let's celebrate with a drink."

"You mean I have to give you an answer now?" John asked.

"It's best for everybody if we move along with this," said the fat man, pushing the paper forward.

Jamal was shaking his head in agreement.

"OK if I look over it first?" John asked.

The fat man nodded.

John took it, rolled it up, and stuck it in his back pocket, then walked out of the room. The bar broke out in laughter. The fat man cursed as the bar door closed. Rat Face scurried to the window in time to see John and a big dog walk away.

John decided he would need to find another tavern. He was still angry at Jamal for staging the meeting. A few blocks away, he dropped the papers into a burn barrel. The men warming themselves there welcomed the heat the papers produced. As he watched the contract burn, John made up his mind that he would get out of town as soon as he could. In fact, he would never again live in any city. He didn't know where he would live but he knew it would not be a city.

The next day it snowed and there was no work. He used the time to purchase several new shirts and tailored trousers. He also bought a suit he would need for the wedding. It was not far off now. He bought a hat, too. Not a fancy hat like the bankers wore but a broad-brimmed hat like they wore out west. He also bought a valise that would hold all his belongings. He was planning to go but he didn't know where.

The third and final attempt to get John into the fighting business came the next afternoon, as John and Hank were walking home from work. From down the street, John could see he had visitors. Jamal, Rat Face, and the fat man were seated on Miss Irma's porch. John sent Hank around back and told him to wait there. Hank didn't want to go but he did as John commanded. When John reached the porch the fat man stood up.

"We have come for the signed contract," he said.

He put out his hand aggressively.

"You are in the wrong place. There is no signed contract here. Nor will there be," John replied. "I do not want to fight. And I'm tired of talking about it."

"I suppose you do not understand who you are talking to."

John said nothing but looked the big man in the eye.

"My name is William Tweed," he said.

"Most people call him Boss Tweed," Rat Face said. "He has represented the great state of New York as a congressman and has recently been appointed head of the governing body of New York City. Nothing gets done without his approval and whatever he decides will happen, happens. And he has decided that you will fight for him. Now Boss Tweed is willing to accept your apologies, recognizing that you did not know who you were dealing with."

John stepped up onto the porch and approached the big man. Tweed had full mutton chop sideburns and wavy thick hair. His breath smelt of whiskey. John stood toe to toe with the man.

"You are right. I had no idea who you were. I have heard of you, though. I also know I have nothing to apologize for. I have no desire to fight for you or anybody else."

As Tweed and John squared off on the porch, Rat Face moved into the street, quietly summoning four ruffians who appeared from both directions, each carrying a club. John stepped back and calculated the odds. They were not good. While Tweed and Rat Face were no problem and he doubted Jamal would fight, he was sure the other four were a problem. It was easy to tell they were experienced street fighters there for one reason. They were walking fast and John had only a minute or two to decide what to do.

He jumped off the porch and caught Rat Face by the back of his collar and the seat of the pants and started running toward the two men approaching from the east. He yelled "Hank!" as he tossed Rat Face into the oncoming men. They dodged him, which gave John an opening. He dove into the man on his left and they landed hard on the ground. John was on top of him punching when he felt a heavy blow across his back. It was the other man, using his club. John tried to ignore the pain but he had no breath. He head-butted the man on the ground hard enough to render him useless. The man blacked out and was no longer a problem.

The other was winding up to deliver another blow when Hank changed the equation. Running at full speed and flying the last few yards, one hundred and fifty pounds of angry Hank made no sound except a low growl as he caught the man full force in the chest, knocking him backward. Hank was on top of him with a mouth full of the man's chest. He was shaking the poor fellow like a terrier would shake a rat.

John got to his feet. He had the club now but what he didn't have was his breath. He knew his ribs were damaged. The other two men were almost upon them now as Rat Face gathered himself and went scampering back to the porch. Boss Tweed was standing on the porch watching but Jamal had entered the fight. He was coming up fast behind the other men. John didn't know at this point if Jamal was there to help him or his foes.

"Hank, get them."

John's voice was weak but Hank heard him and let go of the quarry, who was bleeding profusely. Hank spun around and dove toward the oncoming ruffians. They stopped and Jamal jumped one of the men while Hank attacked the other. Hank had his man under control in seconds with powerful jaws wrapped tightly around the man's throat. Jamal and his man were rolling around on the ground as John walked up and thumped the man on the head with the club. John told Hank to release the man before he killed him.

John, Jamal, and Hank left the attackers badly injured on the street and walked up to the porch. By now it was full of men watching the battle. John nodded in Tweed's direction as his breath began to return.

"I guess you got your fight after all."

He turned to Jamal.

"How much do they owe us for this fight?"

Jamal grinned.

"I figure about $250."

Before Tweed could answer, John looked at Hank and pointed at Rat Face. Hank growled as the man backed up to the house, hurriedly pulling a wad of cash from his coat pocket. Jamal took his time counting it out, then handed a few bills back.

"I was wrong, Jamal said. "Looks like our share is $375."

Tweed and Rat Face made what they hoped was a dignified retreat. A few other men had now appeared and were dragging the injured fighters off the street. Miss Irma sent for a doctor for John as Hank watched them leave. Hank remained on the front porch on guard the rest of the evening as Jamal and Miss Irma made John comfortable on the living room sofa. Miss Irma busied herself in the kitchen getting dinner ready. This untimely business was putting her schedule in jeopardy.

Meanwhile, Jamal and a few of the other boarders sat with John, awaiting the doctor. He was able to breathe now but his breaths were shallow. If he remained still the pain wasn't bad. One of the boarders, a young tailor named Vernon, was sent to the nearest bar to buy a bottle of whiskey. Jamal believed whiskey to be the best cure for whatever ails a man.

"You realize we both have to get out of New York fast, don't you?" he said. "My ship leaves in a couple of days so I can lay low on board until we pull out. I will be fine. But we must get you out of town, and the sooner the better."

"How much money do we have?" John asked.

"I told him $375 but I got a little over $400."

Jamal was pleased with himself. He put the money on the coffee table.

"Divide it by three," John said.

It took a few minutes but Jamal eventually had three piles of bills.

"I figure there were three of us in the fight. You, me, and Hank. I say we each get an equal share. Does that sound fair?"

"Yes, it does."

Jamal pocketed his share as the doctor arrived. The doctor took John's shirt off and checked him out as Jamal explained the nature of the impact wound. John thought he would pass out as the doctor raised his arms above his head. He felt along John's back, then sat down and opened his bag.

"It looks like you have a few cracked ribs—at least two, perhaps as many as five. It's hard to tell. Have you coughed up any blood?" the physician asked.

"No sir," John answered.

"I know it will hurt but I need you to take a deep breath," he said.

He listened as John did this.

"I don't think your lungs are punctured. That is good. I'm going to give you a little morphine. Then I'm going to talk Miss Irma out of a piece of pie. After the morphine does its work, I need to set the ribs. It's going to hurt but we need to do this so the ribs heal cleanly. It's a straightforward procedure we can do right here. I'll need your help, sir."

He looked at Jamal, then disappeared into the kitchen.

John sipped the whiskey as he felt the morphine kick in.

"Let's move him to the bed he'll be sleeping in," the doctor said when he returned.

They laid John flat on his back in his own bed. Jamal held his feet while the doctor grabbed his arms.

"On three you hold him firm, then let me do the work," he said.

"Wait!" shouted Miss Irma. "Let me make sure the door is shut tight and locked. Hank will kill us all if he thinks we are hurting John."

John screamed when the doctor set the bones. They heard a thud on the door and loud barking and they wondered if the door would hold Hank back. A few minutes later they heard a ruckus in the front room. He had gone around front and was weaving his way through the house, knocking over everything in his path. They were finished with John by the time Hank burst into the small room. Hank went straight to John, settled down, and started licking him. Miss Irma and the doctor made themselves scarce in case Hank changed his mind.

With a full dose of morphine onboard and a fair amount of whiskey, John dropped off to sleep almost immediately. Hank stayed by his side and so did Jamal. Jamal spent the night in the small chair, sipping whiskey and watching over his friend.

In the morning John awoke to the snoring of a one-eyed Turk clutching an empty bottle. John's head was clear. He had slept hard. Now it was time to assess his condition. He had just started to move when Hank sprang up, concerned. John rubbed Hank's head and managed a weary smile. Hank's tail began to wag for the first time since the fight. John sat up, gathered himself and walked into the kitchen, holding on to the wall for balance.

Breakfast had been over for hours. Miss Irma was busy with lunch preparations but she violated another of her rules and served him a cup of coffee and a biscuit.

"I sent word to Billy you would not be there today," she said as she set his coffee down.

"Thank you, Miss Irma. You have been like a second mother to me. I appreciate you so much."

She didn't turn around. She didn't want him to see the tear in her eye.

"I want you to know how much you mean to me. And that I'll be leaving today. I won't be back. I'm paying you for the rest of the month and I need you to get word to Billy. Thank him for me. Can you do that?"

"I can."

Her voice was husky with emotion.

"He owes me wages for the last week. I want you to have them," he said, daring a light peck on the old woman's cheek.

John got up and went outside to relieve himself. On his way back in he woke up Jamal. They went to the front porch to talk, accompanied by Hank. Miss Irma brought them coffee and cookies. Yet more rules were broken.

"I need you to help me pack my things," John said. "If you can, I need you to get me to St. Patrick's. I think they'll let me stay until I'm well enough to travel. Can you do that for me?"

"Of course. But I cannot go inside the church. I'm a Muslim."

"What is that?" John asked.

Jamal laughed and sipped his coffee.

The buggy ride was hard on John but they soon arrived at the church. Hank and Jamal waited outside since neither a dog nor a Muslim was welcome in St. Patrick's. John found Father Matthew. A few minutes later he came outside with the priest. Jamal walked off as soon as he saw the priest coming.

"Stop, Jamal. Can you wait here, Father?"

"I need to talk to you Jamal, wait."

His friend finally did stop, once he'd put some distance between himself and the church.

"Jamal, I just wanted to thank you."

"This is not goodbye my friend. Our destinies are entwined. We are meant for greatness and we will meet again soon. I saw it in the stars," Jamal said. "I will be here around the first of June. Please give me your word you will be here."

John thought about it, then put his hand out to shake.

"You have my word."

Jamal turned and walked away, not looking back.

John and Hank stayed at the church for a few days. An exception had been made for Hank since he was on guard duty. As John and Father Matthew loaded up and started out for the farm, John told the priest all about the fighting. He told it as if it had happened to someone else. Father Matthew showed no interest or delight in his fame. After they finished talking about it, John said he did not want to talk about it again.

It was a pretty spring day and John drove the wagon as Father Matthew read every letter from Nelly and David. John had kept them all. John enjoyed the letters more the second time. Hearing all about the Swanson boys and what Mildred was doing brought joy to John. He felt he was getting to know them more as he heard about them from the letters. John's ribs were still sore and the trip was hard but John was having a good time being with the kind priest who had become a good friend.

CHAPTER 8

South Texas

The children had been with the Kings for over three months. They were adjusting well and they loved their new life but they missed Mac. Josephina thought it odd that she missed him as much as she missed her father. She had only known him a short while but they had been through so much together. Mac cared for them when there was nobody else. She also missed Broken Wing. Mac had promised Henrietta that he and Broken Wing would stay close and come often to visit but they hadn't. Seeing Mac, Sally, and Chico leave had been hard.

Henrietta had big plans for a beautiful Spanish-style hacienda, a bunkhouse, a schoolhouse, and even a church. The King ranch would be its own little community someday, and Henrietta planned for Josephina, Felix, and Aldo to be a part of it. Her husband had also treated them well, though he was seldom there. He was always off on business. As Mac had told them months before, he had a steamboat company that ran freight up and down the Gulf Coast and he was buying land as fast as he could. What Mac didn't know is that King owned almost all the land from the Nueces River to the Rio Grande.

Life on the ranch was even better than the children could have hoped for but they still missed Mac. Felix was learning to ride and he was good with horses. Aldo spent most of his time with books. He read constantly and Henrietta was already talking about sending him to college. She said he had a career ahead of him. Josephina spent most of her time caring for the Kings' daughter. She was named after her mother but they called her Nettie. Nettie was almost two and was an active, curious child. Josephina didn't really have a set schedule of duties but she stayed busy all day every day, doing what Henrietta couldn't do herself. She was learning about everything and she had never been happier.

Things were not going nearly as well for Mac. As he left the ranch, a strange melancholy spirit had come over him. He thought at first it was just not being with the children. Their youthfulness had been like a tonic to him and he had grown to love them. They were good for him and they gave him purpose.

For most of his life, Mac had held positions of importance. Even with his physical deformity, he had been able to hold his head high and provide considerable value to his superiors. Then one day he had simply walked away.

Broken Wing had given him a purpose. Learning to live as she lived was what he had needed to get over his life change. She did not see him as a freak. She just saw him. He had grown to love her company and was happy with their life until the children came. Now he wondered if it would ever be the same. He just did not know. Broken Wing needed him and he needed her. The uneasy feeling grew as he continued to look for her. He was a good tracker but if Broken Wing didn't want to be found then neither he nor anyone else would find her. He had figured she would find him but she hadn't. He had already been to the place they had camped on the river. The shack was still there and it had been used by several travelers but not by Broken Wing. He spent several days there letting Chico and Sally rest, all the while hoping she would come to him.

It was several weeks before he decided he needed to find her.

They went northwest following the river. After three days, he found a place she had stayed a few days. He knew he would find her soon. And he did. He found her just in time. She was so weak she could barely walk and she was skin and bones.

Mac made camp and nursed her back to life but he feared her life would be short. She continued to lose weight and her skin had an unhealthy look to it. Her bowels didn't work properly and there was often blood in her stool. Mac knew it was cancer. It was too late for even her most powerful medicines to work. She was dying and all Mac could do was make her comfortable. So that is what he did. Day after day, Mac watched over her. She lived through the winter, a mild one that year, and she died during a hard rain in the middle of March. Mac tended to her burial with respect for her people's customs. He grieved for her. Then he, Sally, and Chico turned south and made their way to the King Ranch. He did not plan to stay but he felt a need to tell the children about Broken Wing. He also wanted to see for himself that they were thriving.

Mac arrived at the ranch in early April. He had taken his time on the journey. Getting over Broken Wing was harder than he could ever have imagined. He woke many nights thinking she would be there. But she wasn't. He kept watching the horizon, thinking that at any moment she would appear. She did not.

There were times when he thought he was losing his mind. His thoughts were full of doubt and his thoughts raced, traversing the same path over and over. How does one know he is slipping mentally? He had known men younger than he who had lost their wits. Maybe his caring for Broken Wing as much as he did was a sign that he was unstable. She was the most unsocial person he had ever met yet he found a certain peace when he was with her. They had somehow figured out how to communicate but maybe he had only thought they were connecting. Maybe it was his failing mental state that made him think they understood each other. Maybe seeing the children would help him decide if he were going mad. He found himself talking more to Sally than he usually did, and this worried him too, until he realized that maybe talking was good for him—maybe it was healthy. He decided he would watch Sally closely since she would be the first to know if he had lost his mind. She was always the first to sense trouble. This gave him a bit of solace.

Aldo had been reading the day Mac and the animals returned. In fact, he spent most of his time on reading assignments Henrietta gave him. He had a near-photographic memory and when he found a word he didn't know or a phrase that didn't make sense, he remembered where it was and could find the page and ask her to explain it to him. Henrietta was delighted at his curiosity. She was challenging him daily and Aldo thrived on the attention.

Henrietta and Josephina were inside the big house which was still under construction. Henrietta, who was now visibly pregnant with her second child, spent most of her time supervising every detail of the building and she had changed the plans several times. This was a challenge to the army of craftsmen they had working there but they were being paid well so they took it in stride. The plan had started out as a Spanish-style hacienda but it was beginning to look more like the southern mansions of Henrietta's childhood. She often asked Josephina what she thought about a certain feature of the house as if the girl would have had any idea. This worried Josephina. She wanted to give the right answer but she never knew what was right. Then Henrietta would patiently explain why it mattered. She was gradually teaching Josephina the things a proper lady should know. Etiquette was vital to Henrietta and soon it would be so to Josephina as well.

They heard Aldo's shouts as they were inspecting new carving on the banister of the large staircase and they ran outside to see what had happened. Aldo was running as fast as he could toward Mac. Felix, who was off with some ranch hands clearing brush from a meadow near the house had also seen Mac and he had hurried to the house to tell his sister and Henrietta. They sat on the big porch and watched as Mac approached. Josephina's heart was racing. She knew it would not be ladylike for her to go running out as Aldo had but she wanted to.

When Aldo reached him he threw himself into Mac's arms. They hugged each other for a long time. Then, without a word being said they broke into uncontrollable laughter. They were still laughing when, arm in arm, they reached the big house.

Mac spoke first. With a gentlemanly bow, he asked permission to approach, as if he were addressing a royal court. Josephina could hold back no longer. She ran from the porch and threw her arms around her dear friend's neck. Felix held back as long as he could but even he was overcome by emotion.

Soon all four of them were laughing. Sally was also trying to get in on some of the affection as she nuzzled her way into the tangle of hugs. It was a joyous reunion.

"Welcome to King Ranch," Henrietta said with a gleam in her eye. "It is so lovely to see you again."

Mac made a deep bow.

"With your kind permission, I would like to take care of my companions," he said, motioning toward Sally and Chico. Henrietta nodded and beckoned to a few hands near the house who led the animals to a nearby barn down a sloping hill.

"It is a blessing to see all of you," Mac said as they climbed the steps and made their way onto the porch.

Henrietta excused herself and went inside. A few minutes later she returned with a pitcher of cool water. Everyone was talking at once. Aldo was telling Mac all the books he'd read. Mac was familiar with almost every one of them. Josephina was telling him how wonderful life was on the ranch and all she was learning. She too was learning to read. Felix was full of tales of the life of a cowboy and he was enjoying Mac's acknowledgment that he was no longer a child but a man. When Aldo asked about Broken Wing, though, Mac fell silent. He had trouble mustering the words.

"So, to answer Aldo's question, I have something I must tell you. Broken Wing is gone."

"She is always gone," Felix said. "She'll be back just when we need her."

"No, son. She is dead," Mac said.

"She can't be."

Felix was choking on the lump in his throat.

"Broken Wing? Oh my, what happened?" said Josephina.

"I'm certain she had cancer of some sort. There is no telling how long she had had it. By the time I found her, she was too weak to fight any longer. I did the best I could and she made it through the winter. She was as tough as they come but it was her time to go."

Tears rolled down Mac's face as he told the children how he had nursed her, how she had died, and where she was buried. They were moved to tears at the loss of Broken Wing. She had been their savior. It was she who provided for their safe passage from sure death in the wilderness to a wonderful life on a ranch with kind people. Broken Wing was gone. They would see her no more.

"I wish I could have met this fine lady," said Henrietta. "Mac, would you permit me to give a feast tonight in her honor?"

"My dear Henrietta! What a wonderful idea!"

Mac brightened considerably at the thought of honoring his old friend.

Henrietta and Josephina went off to the kitchen to plan a special menu and Mac went to the bunkhouse to clean up after his long journey. Later, he found Aldo on the porch and they spent a few hours reviewing the books Aldo had read. Mac was pleased with the progress Aldo was making and Aldo was thrilled with Mac's praise. Felix stayed with Sally and Chico, making sure they were cared for properly.

When Henrietta rejoined them shortly before dinner, she clearly had something on her mind.

"Mac, if I may have a moment with you in private I have a matter I would like to discuss."

"After the kindness you have shown these dear ones, you may ask me anything you like," he said as he followed her into the parlor.

"Nonsense, Mac it is I who should be thanking you for introducing me to this fine family. Josephina has been a gift from God. Little Nettie loves her and Josephina is tending to her as I would myself, which frees me to take care of projects that have been delayed too long. And this brings me to what I'd like to propose.

Look out that window," she said, pointing toward a clearing down by a creek. "I will soon build a school there. I had planned to teach the children myself but the ranch is requiring too much of my time. Running a working ranch is a full-time job and Richard is not here enough to do it. And I admit it. I love ranching," she added.

Mac listened as she rose from her chair and began pacing back and forth.

"My children and all the children in the area must receive a proper education. It is vitally important to me and yet I have little time now to attend to all the details of establishing a school. I want it functional before Nettie is old enough to go to school and as you can see, I'll soon have another child. Finding time to put it all together will be difficult if not impossible. And this brings me to my point."

"Henrietta, I'd love to help in any way I can," Mac said before she could continue.

"Good. I had hoped you would say so. I have arranged to meet with a curator in New York. He has been assembling a collection of books for my library. I was scheduled to meet with him soon as he is returning from London with some of the latest novels as well a fine collection of history books, both ancient and modern. He has also assembled volumes on classic philosophy, science—even some medical books."

Mac could see her excitement as she warmed to the topic of the library she was assembling.

"I can't travel in my condition and I can't delay this any longer. I'd like for you to travel in my stead and coordinate the project with this gentleman. All the arrangements to transport the books here have been made. With Richard in the shipping business that is not a problem. I just need someone that can manage the process for me. I was praying over this earlier, just before I saw you coming. Then you appeared and suddenly, it seemed you might be the answer to my prayer."

Mac stood. Her energy was contagious, and he felt he needed to move about himself. He walked over to the window and looked out at the cleared spot where the school would be.

"This is an urgent matter and I hate to press you," she continued. "but I must get an answer soon. I would go so far as to say I believe God's hand is on this project as well as the work we are doing with the children. I believe God brought us all together for a purpose."

Mac smiled at her.

"I would be honored to help you in any way I can. Education is what this land needs. Texas has all the beauty and resources one could ask for. It simply needs educated stewards to make it all it should be," Mac said.

"Mac, I am delighted. I will prepare all the documents you need and will provide the means for this important task. In a few days, you will meet with a Russian tailor in Galveston. He will make you several suits appropriate for the business you will conduct on behalf of

Mr. King and me," she said, smiling as she rushed off to organize the evening's banquet.

The meal that night was fit for nobility, served on the Kings' finest china. Everyone on the ranch was invited. The highlight of the evening was Mac's tribute to Broken Wing. He was an eloquent speaker and even those who didn't know Broken Wing enjoyed it. After the meal, they gathered around a bonfire in an area behind the house. A few of the cowboys had guitars and they played and sang. The singing was mostly in Spanish, so the children loved it. The fitting sendoff for Broken Wing went a long way toward helping Mac get over the loss.

Mac left the ranch two days later for Galveston in a wagon driven by two of Mr. King's associates. The children gathered to see him off, waving to him long after he was out of sight. In Galveston Mac stayed at the finest hotel. While he awaited the delivery of the last of his new suits, he spent his time reviewing the instructions Mrs. King had given him. She was very specific on the topic of the type of literature the King School Library would have.

A knock on the door interrupted his reverie. A courier delivered a note asking him to meet one of King's associates for lunch at a nearby cafe. Mac did a little more studying, then dressed in a new suit, complete with a walking stick and a bowler hat. Though no suit could completely disguise his deformities, he looked every inch the gentleman. His mind was reeling. He was surprised at himself, at the degree to which he was enjoying this assignment. He had been responsible for large endeavors for much of his adult life. He had not thought he would do anything like this again, yet here he was.

Inside the restaurant, a dark-skinned man with a turban and an eye patch greeted him. Mac saw as he approached that the man had a weathered look that only years at sea could produce. The gentleman bowed slightly and offered his hand to Mac.

"Good afternoon. My name is Jamal Darvish. I'm First Mate on the *Hindi*. We have been commissioned to transport you to New York, to assist you while you are there, and to bring you back here as soon as possible."

"Happy to meet you, Mr. Darvish."

Mac was impressed that his new companion had looked him in the eye without taking note of his deformities. As they ordered their food and shared a meal, Mac told him about himself including a few visits he'd made to Jamal's part of the world. Jamal also shared stories about his personal adventures and informed him about the rich history of the *Hindi*.

"May I be frank with you sir," asked Jamal.

"Yes, of course."

"Who are you?"

Mac was both amused and curious.

"You knew my name when you invited me, so why ask now?"

"I don't mean your name, sir. Please excuse my question but it is a bit odd. I have never received such specific instructions concerning a passenger's safety and comfort as I have with you. You must be a very important man. Are you royalty or do you hold some vitally important office?"

"As a matter of fact, I do have royal Scottish nobility in my bloodline," Mac laughed, "but that has nothing to do with this. I simply am on a task for an important lady."

"Sir I will do all that is in my power to make your journey pleasant. A driver will collect you tomorrow morning at nine am at your hotel. We shall leave mid-morning," said Jamal. "It will be high tide and the weather should be good."

CHAPTER 9

New Jersey

The last few months on the Swenson farm had been like a beautiful dream. After his ribs healed, John spent most of his time with David, working on the new home he was building. It was a modest house but it was built well and on a beautiful spot of land David and Nelly had picked out.

Hank was happy to be home again. He was almost a year old now and he outweighed his mother by a good thirty pounds. Since the confrontation with Boss Tweed and his hooligans, Hank had changed. He would not let John out of sight and he was more cautious than ever of strangers, which meant Hank was there during most of the building of the house.

Nelly was happier than John had ever seen her. She had always been mature for her age but at sixteen she was now a grown woman. A grown lady would be more like it. Mildred had done wonders in helping her develop into a proper Catholic lady. Mildred considered herself an expert in this area. After all, she had raised a priest. Most days Nelly would bring a picnic lunch to John and David as they ate and laughed and talked about the future. At first, John had not been sure he had made a good decision to give his sister away. He was sure now. Father Matthew had been right. David would be good to her and she would make him a fine wife.

It was nice here. It was the perfect place for Nelly but not for John. Although he had enjoyed every moment, he knew he didn't belong here. After the wedding, he knew he would be released from the responsibility of his sister. Though he was ashamed of himself for being relieved, he was happy that he could leave without feeling guilty about leaving her.

He wanted to leave. He just did not know where he wanted to go. Perhaps he would know when he got there. He knew where he would not be. It would not be a city. And the farming life was too structured for him. Being raised by Michael Delaney had instilled a wanderer's spirit in John.

The wedding plans were complete. Mildred had taken care of it all. John had offered to pay for some of it but Mildred would not take his money. It was going to be a big wedding with lots of friends and family. She was planning to have the best wedding this community had ever seen. Of course, her son the Priest would officiate at the service. There would be plenty of food and dancing into the night as everybody was going to remember this wedding. Mildred was as sure of this as she was that David and Nelly would live happily ever after and have plenty of beautiful children for her to fawn over.

"May I ask you a question?" David asked John as they were finishing the roof. It was getting late and they would need to stop soon.

"You ask me questions all day. I spend most of my day swinging a hammer and answering your questions," John said.

"Good, since you are used to it, here goes. What do you plan to do with your life?" David asked again. This question had been posed several times over the past few weeks by almost every Swenson.

"I plan to finish this last board, then go to the house and get some supper," John replied.

"You know what I mean," David pressed the question.

"I suppose I do," John said.

"Then what? You have told me plenty of things you are not going to do—like house building, masonry, farming, boxing. You don't like life on the seas so what do you like?" David asked.

"You forgot a priest. I don't want to be a priest," John said.

"Then what?"

"I'm not sure, I think I'll know when I find it. Until then, Hank and I will keep looking."

"I suppose you will. I found what I wanted the minute I saw Nelly. Now let's clean up and get back to the house."

David seemed to really care what John did. This confused John. Why did it matter? They walked back to the house talking about all the different occupations John might try. John wondered if he would ever know what was right for him. Or would he keep doing things he did not like for the rest of his life?

The day of the wedding grew closer. John was ready for it all to be over. He was glad they were happy. He was sure it was a good thing. He was also sure he was ready to leave. There was a vast new country out there. The only place he didn't want to go was New York. But he had promised Jamal he would meet him. His father always said a man needed to do what he promised, even if he didn't want to. If he didn't want to, he should have never said he would. The memory of his father was important to him. His father was a great man and John needed to honor him by doing what was right. So he would go to New York one last time.

One morning John, Hank, and David took the wagon into Bedminster, a small town nearby, to get some supplies. Hank stayed by the wagon while David and John were in the general store. David had all the supplies on the counter and he was chatting with the clerk when John heard a low growl coming from Hank. John turned toward the door.

John knew Boss Tweed controlled New York City but he hadn't

known the man pulled strings this side of the Hudson River. It was obvious the men Hank saw were Tweed's men. Same bowler hats. Same hardened looks. David came out of the store with his hands full. He started to say something to John about not helping when he saw the hair standing up on Hank's back and his ears laid back.

"What's up, boy?" David said.

Hank took a couple of steps toward the men who still were a long way away.

"Stay," John said.

Hank stopped but he didn't take his eyes off the men and he didn't relax his vigilance. Every muscle in Hank's body was flexed and ready to go.

"Is it them? Have they seen you?" David asked.

"Hank is sure it's them. And I'm going to trust Hank on this one. Load up. We need to get out of here before they see us," John said as he took the goods from David.

"Up, Hank. In the wagon."

Hank jumped into the wagon bed, never taking his eyes off the men who still hadn't seen them. John was watching them too. One of the men saw Hank jump into the wagon. They may not have seen John but there was no mistaking Hank. The man pointed and they all watched as the wagon rolled away. As they were leaving, John recognized one of the men they had fought that day. He was a big man. Boss Tweed must have had men combing the areas around New York looking for John. Tweed was not going to take his defeat lightly. He had a score to pay.

Lucky was the leader of the gang Tweed had sent to find John. Tiny was the big man. The other two were Brady and Clem.

"That's them," Lucky said.

"Let's catch them," Brady said.

"Shut up and let me think," Lucky barked.

He was in charge, which meant that if it didn't go right, he would be answering to Tweed, who was already unhappy with them.

"Brady, you get saddled up and get back to the Boss as soon as you can. Tell him we have found Delaney and are keeping an eye on him until the Boss tells us what he wants to do. Clem, you stay here and keep asking around about them. Find out all you can. It's easy to get information about strangers in a town like this, even if you are a stranger yourself. Just ask and see what they say. Tiny and I will follow the wagon. Now get going."

John looked over his shoulder all the way back. As soon as they arrived at the farm, John locked Hank in the barn, then saddled their best horse and rode out to see if the men were coming. It's what his father would have done. *Never let yourself be taken by surprise if you can help it.* John rode hard but not on the road they came in on. He doubled around wide to the west. After a few hours, he found two of them headed toward the farm. It was obvious they were following the wagon tracks.

John watched as they moved slowly toward the farm. The two men found the property, then circled it a few times just looking. John watched without them knowing he was there. They made camp when it got dark not far from the farm. As soon as they settled in and were asleep, John walked the horse into the barn. David and Malcolm were there waiting for him. They both carried guns.

"What did you find?" David asked.

"Two men are camped out down by the creek. One of them I recognized. The other I don't know. They spent the day watching the farm. I don't like them being here."

"What are we going to do?" David asked.

"Hank and I are going to watch them. I want you to stay here. Don't tell the others and don't do anything out of your normal routine. I don't want them to know we know they are here."

"Too late," Malcolm said. "Everybody knows what's going on."

"Then act like you don't," John said.

"Keep the women in but don't do anything that will spook them," he added.

John let Hank out. They went into the kitchen and got a quick bite to eat.

"John, they will have guns. Do you need a gun?" David asked.

John stopped.

"Wait here."

David went in and came out with a long gun.

"It shoots true."

He handed him the gun and bullets, which John stuck in his pocket.

"Let's go, Hank."

John found a comfortable spot where he and Hank could watch undetected. Hank seemed to know what was going on. The two they were tracking slept until dawn. Then they made a fire. It was obvious they were not experienced trackers or woodsmen. You could spot the smoke for miles. After the dew was dried, the men circled the farm once more, then headed back to town. John and Hank followed at a distance. It was afternoon when John returned. The Swenson men had gathered on the porch to hear the report.

When Lucky and Tiny got back to town, they found that Brady had not returned yet but Clem had some good news. He told them the farm they found was the Swenson place. He knew how many people lived there and who they were kin to. He knew more than they did, and he hadn't even left town. Lucky told them all to stay close, and not to get drunk. It was all they could do until Brady got back.

Brady didn't show up until the next day around noon. He had two men with him, a thug named Blackie, who had orders to run the operation, and Simpson. Simpson was a fighter. He was simple-minded but he was tough.

"What did the boss say?" Lucky asked.

"He wants us to kill the dog and bring Delaney back to him hog-tied. He said he wants everybody to know what happens when you defy him," Blackie said. "And it's high time that lad learned a lesson. We'll take it easy today and in the morning, we'll go get him. I need to think about how best to do it."

Lucky went away sulking. He was annoyed about Blackie taking charge. He had never liked the man but Tweed was not to be crossed. So, he went to the bar with Tiny to get drunk. Tiny liked to drink and he did whatever Lucky wanted him to do.

"You know why Blackie wanted to be here, don't you?" Tiny asked after they had had a few drinks.

"I was wondering. That old loudmouth never leaves the city. Why now?" Lucky asked.

"I heard the boy we are after is the same Irish boy that beat Blackie up," Tiny said.

"Who told you that?"

"Some of those Irishmen who practically live at the bar Blackie hangs out at. I believe them," Tiny said.

"That's good to know," Lucky said and went right on drinking.

John and Hank were not working on the new house now. They were watching the road out of town night and day. Normally this kind of duty would not be fun but John had never felt more alive. With Hank by his side, John could sleep knowing nothing was going to escape the watch of his loyal friend. Finally, on the third day, they saw the riders leave town. No doubt about it, they were coming for him. Except now there were six men. He recognized several of them, especially the one leading them. It was his old enemy Blackie.

John pushed the horse as hard as he could. He knew what he needed to do after thinking about it for several days. Hank had no trouble keeping up. The big dog was turning out to be an exceptional animal. When John pulled the horse to a halt at the farm, all the family was on the porch as well as a few cousins and neighbors. They had been worried about John. John figured that David must have mustered the troops. All the men were carrying guns and they looked serious. John walked up to Mr. Swenson.

"Mr. Swenson, I'd like to thank you for your hospitality these last few months but I need to leave now. There are some bad men headed this way. I don't want them to find me here. They know I've been here so just tell them I've left. Tell them I headed west. And I'd like to buy a horse from you if I may."

"We will stand with you," David said.

"I know you would, and I appreciate that but no, you will not," John said sternly. "I know all about men like this. You do not want to have them as your enemies. It will never stop. Trust me. Back in Ireland, we dealt with this sort continually. They do not quit until you are destroyed and then they take all you have. This Boss Tweed seems to have some sort of authority in the government. You do not want to cross them. They do not want any trouble with you and I would like it to stay that way."

"He is right, son," Malcolm said. "What John is saying is wise. We will do as he asks. Now boys, let's hurry. David, you get Julie saddled, she is a fine mare. You cannot buy her, John, because I am giving her to you. She is a proper dowry for Nelly's hand."

"Nelly, can I have a word with you?" John said as they walked away from the others who were preparing for John's departure.

"I hate that I'm going to miss your wedding but if I come back you know they will see me. Revenge is what these men live for," John said. "Blackie is with them. I don't want him to know you are here."

A chill went down Nelly's spine when she heard the name Blackie. She never wanted to see him again.

"I know you are right, John. We watched men like this destroy our family. We can't let it happen here," Nelly said.

There was fear in her voice.

"I won't let it happen. Believe me."

He took her in his arms and whispered in her ear.

"You will be safe here. David will protect you. Nelly, I love you."

"I love you too," she said with tears in her eyes.

"Please keep writing me. Send them to Father Matthew. He'll know where I am. I promise you I am going to learn to read and write."

"Take care of yourself, John."

"Hank and I will be just fine."

The men had Julie ready to go. They gave John a sidearm and a long gun with plenty of ammunition. Mildred had packed enough food to last him for several weeks. He had all he needed. He said his goodbyes to everyone, checked his saddlebags to make sure his money was there and climbed onto Julie.

"Mr. Swenson, make sure you tell them which way I went. I need them to follow me. Tell them I left this morning. If they hurry, they can find me."

John rode away without looking back as Julie trotted at a comfortable gait. He didn't look back because he didn't want them to see the tears in his eyes. These were good people he was leaving.

Blackie and Lucky were not getting along well. Blackie kept giving arbitrary instructions just to prove he could. Lucky was the younger of the two and Blackie had been with Boss Tweed a long time. Since he hated Blackie, it made it hard to take.

"Simpson, ride up there and check out that waterway," Blackie ordered.

"No need for that," Lucky said. "Me and Tiny spent the night there. It ain't deep and it has a gravel bed."

"Simpson, do as I say." He glared at Lucky.

Simpson came back and reported exactly what Lucky said. Word for word. This made Blackie angry. When they arrived at the creek they let the horses rest a bit. They also rested themselves and drank from the cool brook.

"What are you going to do when we get that boy?" Lucky asked Blackie.

"You don't need to worry about that. I'll take care of things."

"I was just wondering. Do we hogtie him before he whips you again, or after?"

Lucky was taunting him. Tiny burst into laughter.

Tiny started telling the others about how Blackie had been beaten by the Irish lad in the bar. He knew the story well. The others joined in laughing.

"All of you shut up," Blackie barked. "Now mount up. We are going in."

As they mounted the horses, they saw a rider enter the creek opposite them. They had not noticed him before. The rider was an older man with a shotgun across his lap. He stopped about halfway into the creek.

"You gentlemen are about to enter my land, and I need to ask you what purpose you have here," Malcolm said.

It was then that they saw two more men ride up from downstream and another two from upstream. They were on their side of the creek and all were carrying guns.

"Whose land is this, may I ask?" said Blackie.

"My name is Malcolm Swenson."

Blackie looked at Clem. Clem nodded. That was the farm he'd heard about.

"You see, Mr. Swenson, we are here on a legal matter. It was brought to our attention that a fugitive was staying here. John Delaney is his name. We have orders to take him back to New York," Blackie said.

"I seen him here myself," Lucky said.

"I'm sure you do have orders. I'm also sure he is not here. He left this morning, headed west."

"Sir, if you are hiding him it won't go well for you," Blackie sneered.

Malcolm rode up to where Blackie was and got down off his horse. He walked up to Blackie and looked him in the eye. His sons were moving closer too, all with guns pointed at the men.

"Are you threatening me?" Malcolm asked.

"Is John Delaney here or not?" Blackie repeated.

"I told you he was gone. If you ride west, you'll find his trail."

Blackie took this as a victory.

"Come on boys, let's go."

They crossed the creek and headed west. Malcolm and his boys followed them until they were off his land. The posse picked up John's trail and lost interest in bothering the farm, just as John had planned.

He stayed just ahead of them for two days, taking them through some rough terrain. At night, when the men were camped, he and Hank would slip back and keep an eye on them, getting close enough to hear their conversation, which was mostly bickering and fussing about what they were doing. Blackie was losing control of the men. If things didn't change soon there was going to be a mutiny.

John was having the time of his life. He loved this. He and Hank were learning to communicate without words. John decided the best punishment for these ruffians was to have to go home and face Boss Tweed without anything to show but an expense bill.

The third night, John heard them making plans to return to New York. They still had his trail but they were out of food, out of ideas, and out of patience. The bickering had gotten worse. Just before daylight, John slipped into their camp and took two horses without being heard. The trip home was not going to be pleasant. Six men would have to share four horses.

John and Hank hurried back to New York. He sold the horses along the way to a farmhouse he passed. His money was building up. They arrived at the church and Father Matthew was eager to hear all about what John had done. John left out the part about stealing the horses. Father Mathew arranged for them to stay in the church.

"I am leaving New York soon but I need to see a man first. In the morning if he's here. Then we will be leaving," John said.

"Does the man have an eye patch?"

"Yes, he does."

"He has been here looking for you every day for the last few days. I suspect you'll be able to find him," the priest said.

Early the next morning, Hank and John left the church before dawn. They made it to Blackie's house before his mother was up. They waited until they heard her moving around, then John went to the door and knocked.

"Just a minute," John heard her say.

A few minutes later, the door opened.

"Good morning ma'am, do you remember me? I was here visiting your son," John said.

"Oh, course I remember you! Come in! I am about to put a pot of tea on. I sure wish you could join me. Jonas is out of town on some urgent business. Jonas is a very important man you know. He is such a good son."

They drank tea and she toasted some bread with a tasty jam of some sort. She was a kindly lady. How she could have raised a scoundrel like Blackie, John would never know. After a while, John got up and walked to the door.

"Can you give your son a message for me?" he asked.

"Yes, of course!"

"Tell him I am leaving town but he is not to worry. Tell him not to forget that I know where he lives," John said with a smile. "I am likely to show up here at any time."

"I will tell him."

John patted her on the shoulder and left. He needed to get back to the church.

CHAPTER 10

New York

The voyage from Galveston to New York took two months. It went as planned, with only brief stops for provisions. The crew aboard the *Hindi* was experienced and Jamal ran a tight ship as first mate. Captain Milton Bromley rarely came out of his cabin. Mac could hear him coughing day and night. He was dying of something but refused medical assistance. Except for occasional bites of salt tack, he lived on rum and cigars. The captain's wish was to die at sea and to be buried there. He had no family that anyone knew of. The only time they heard him barking orders was if they lingered too long in port. He was afraid he might die and be buried alongside regular land lovers. In recent days, as his mind was slipping, he had begun to imagine himself to be a bit of a pirate.

The *Hindi* had once been in the hands of some rather notable pirates and the captain associated himself more with them than with his current crew. The vessel had been used mostly as a cargo ship running rum. No war guns had been mounted on it when it was captured by the royal navy and sold at auction. Built in western India of the finest teak, it made the trip easily to New York. The current was strong and the winds favored them, and at the captain's behest, no time was wasted in any port.

Mac had a cabin next to the captain. It was comfortable and he

113

spent most of his time reading, getting ready for his appointed task. Jamal took his meals with Mac most days. They had become good friends and since both men were storytellers they found plenty to talk about. The two grew close during the few months they traveled together on the *Hindi*.

When they pulled into the New York harbor, it was obvious that Captain Bromley was not happy. The stay here was going to be longer than normal so his fear of dying on land haunted him. Jamal ran things and he had strict orders from the shipowner to stay in New York as long as Mac needed. He knew Bromley was not going to be happy so he made sure there was plenty of rum. Every sailor was instructed to tell the captain, when asked, "Sir, we are preparing to leave now."

Captain Bromley had once, not long before, tried to make a sailor walk the plank for not pulling up anchor when he wanted to leave, though there was no plank to walk. He also would brandish his whip from time to time, even though the men did not fear him. Still, it was a distraction.

While in port in New York, Jamal tended daily to the business of readying the ship to leave and keeping the sailors close. Then he would check in with Mac and visit the church to see if his friend John had kept his word. By now Jamal was ready to go. The men were getting too much shore leave and if they didn't depart soon he would have to bail a few out of jail. He had no real reason to think John would be there but there was something noble about this Irish boy that made Jamal believe in him. They had been in New York ten days and Jamal was more than ready to go.

Every day he would tell Captain Bromley, "It's only our second day in port and we are leaving in the morning." This kept the man satisfied. The day they were set to leave, Jamal picked up Mac in a wagon loaded with all his books. He then went one last time to the church. He was a few blocks away when he saw a huge blond dog that could only be Hank. When he pulled up to the church, John loaded his things in the wagon and told Jamal that he and Hank had to leave New York fast. John said he had money and would pay his passage. There was a twinkle in the one-eyed sailor's one good eye as he headed for the *Hindi*.

Jamal introduced John to Mac, and soon they were chatting like old friends, especially since Mac was familiar with the area in Ireland where John was from. When John finally got a chance to talk, he told Jamal about his recent visitors. Jamal knew why he was in a hurry to leave. Boss Tweed was a dangerous man with tentacles all up and down the New York area.

The ship was out of the harbor that afternoon. Most of the men were sober and the weather would hold. John and Hank were given a small compartment in the hull. It was usually used to store weather gear but Jamal had cleared it out to make room for his guests. Jamal would not take any money from John for the passage. Jamal asked only that they remain friends. It seemed to mean a lot to Jamal that John liked him.

Later that night, John reflected on this most recent turn of events, marveling that he and Hank would soon arrive in Texas with money enough to buy a good horse and enough supplies to do what they both enjoyed. He had heard about Texas even before he arrived in America. It was wild and free, just what John knew he needed.

Most of the men on the ship were afraid of Hank. It was rare to see a dog that size. Hank kept an eye on the whole crew. The only person on the ship besides Jamal that Hank trusted was Mac. If anyone else came too close to John, he would hear the deep-throated growl and know he was not welcome.

After a few days, Mac discovered that John had a desire to read and write, so he converted his cabin into a classroom and began teaching John. Here was a new student and he was excited about the challenge. Soon Mac and John were spending most of their time together.

All was well until the day Captain Bromley came up on deck and spotted Hank. Mac and John were in class and Jamal was on the bridge. Nobody knew exactly what Bromley thought he was seeing but it had apparently scared him. He started shouting orders for the men to capture the wild beast. When nobody approached Hank, the captain ran into his quarters to prepare for war. None of the men could handle the captain and none would go anywhere near Hank.

Bromley came out with his whip, a sword, and an ancient musket ready to slay the beast. He held the sword high in his left hand as he commanded his men to attack. Anyone remotely close to the area left quickly. The captain carried his unloaded musket and his whip was wound in a tight circle. He marched forward toward the monster that had somehow boarded his ship. Hank stood to face the attack. Captain Bromley was barking orders for the beast to surrender or die. Hank was watching, perplexed but refusing to give ground. As it happened, the captain was a little too well-equipped. He couldn't use all three weapons. He decided the whip was the proper weapon so he dropped the musket, put the sword in his belt, and held fast to the handle of the whip. As he unfurled it, he forgot where he had dropped the musket. He moved toward Hank and promptly tripped over the musket. As he stumbled forward, he thrust the whip backward which caused him to fall backward as well. The sword broke and he lost the whip in the fall. He was now completely disarmed, facing an unknown beast, and his crew had deserted him.

Hank walked over to the man and put his big paw on Bromley's chest. He closed his eyes, awaiting death. Mac and John had heard the thud as the captain landed and they hurried out to see what was happening.

"Hank, come here boy," John said and the big dog did as he was told.

"What is going on?" Mac asked one of the sailors.

The sailor told him the story. Word had gotten to the bridge about the ruckus, so Jamal showed up about the same time. The captain had not yet moved. Nobody knew if he was alive or had been killed in battle. Jamal and John carried him to his room, barely breathing. They nursed his wounds, then put him to bed. Jamal gathered up all the battle gear and stored it safely away.

"Is he going to die?" John asked.

"Yes, he surely will die soon," Jamal said. "But for now I think he's mostly drunk. I'll water down his rum."

The next day the captain was himself again, except for a few bruises. He had no recollection of his battle with the monster. In the meantime, John's reading skills were improving as Mac spent time with him, challenging him to learn as fast as he could. They used some primary readers but Mac would also read to him from the classics, hoping to instill a love for literature in the Irishman. It was working. John grew to love books. He still couldn't read the big books but he believed he would someday.

Having fully recovered from battle, the captain was back to smoking cigars and drinking undiluted rum. He and Hank were kept apart to ensure no resumption of hostilities. Order was restored and the ship was making excellent time until one morning, a few days after the battle, they found the captain dead in his quarters. Captain Bromley had accomplished his final goal. He had died at sea. They were in the Gulf of Mexico somewhere off the coast of Alabama when he died. Mac had found a book of prayers containing the proper liturgy for burying a sailor at sea. At dawn the next day, the service began. Mac conducted the service with the same reverence one might afford a head of state. Every man on board was instructed to wear his best clothes and all were required to attend the service. The sailors seemed to be listening, at least for a while. As the service grew longer, John saw a few men slip away and a few others doze off. Although it was fair to say that the captain's funeral had 100% attendance, John noted that the percentage to make it to the close was not as impressive a number.

Mac didn't care how long the funeral went on. The ship was headed in the right direction and he had nothing else to do so he continued, completing the entire service. After Mac said the final "Amen", they lowered a small skiff containing Captain Bromley, dressed in his best uniform, and they watched as he floated away.

Jamal was now officially captain. He had always wanted to have his own ship, even if it belonged to an English banking firm. He had been performing the role of captain for a long time so nothing had really changed. He supposed he would be getting a raise. Jamal asked Mac, whom he pronounced a noble man, to accompany him in inventorying the old pirate's treasures. The chest had a large lock on it and Jamal knew where to find the key. Word had gotten out about the treasure chest. Curiosity had captured the men, so they hung around the captain's quarters, hoping for a glimpse. A few of them tried to enter from time to time. Jamal kept order as best he could during the survey. Jamal finished up and had the wisdom to divide the booty before there was a mutiny. That night, Jamal broke open a keg of rum and they toasted the captain as they drank his rum and sang songs of his glory well into the night.

A few weeks later, they arrived in Galveston on schedule. Henrietta King was waiting for them as they pulled into the dock. She met Mac with great excitement. Mac tried to introduce her to John but she was too focused on getting Mac's report. John gathered his belongings and he and Hank took off to find a place that would accept both an Irishman and a mastiff. Both were rare in Galveston.

John was happy to be on land again. It was midsummer and hot, though the breeze off the gulf made the heat bearable. Mac made John promise he'd come to their hotel when he got settled. Jamal knew the town well and most port towns were the same. He helped John find a rooming house without a prohibition against dogs. Jamal had been trying to talk John into life at sea but John was clear. He did not want to be a sailor. After dark, he and Jamal sat near the water and talked as they listened to the waves roll in. John thought he might like Texas.

The next morning, John and Hank found the Kings' hotel. Then they found a bench nearby and watched the comings and the goings for most of the morning. John was in no hurry but he did hope to get in a little reading today if Mac had time. Mac spotted them when he came out of the hotel and he headed straight for them.

"Please join us for a late breakfast. We were up most of the night going over the inventory, so we slept in," Mac said as he looked at Hank. "Hank may be a problem though."

"He'll be fine. We ate earlier. Hank can wait for me out front," John said as they followed Mac to the hotel.

The Tremont Hotel was the finest hotel west of the Mississippi. Mac strode into the elegant lobby with complete confidence. He went into the dining room and made reservations for a party of eight. John washed up and waited for the guests to arrive. The first were three businessmen in fine suits. John wished he had worn his nice clothes but it was too late now. The men introduced themselves briefly, then went on talking. Richard and Henrietta King arrived next. They too introduced themselves. King took the seat at the head of the table and motioned for everybody to be seated.

"Mr. Brownlee will be joining us shortly. He is currently at the telegraph office taking care of an urgent piece of business. To my left here is George Mathis and next to him is Harvey Watson. Seated next to my wife is Leroy Story. Mac, would you please introduce yourself and your guest?"

Mac stood and bowed slightly, then introduced himself complete with titles and personal accomplishments, which were many. He then introduced John. John tried to act as though he were comfortable with the proceedings but he couldn't help feeling like a pig in a dress shop. Mac had John stand as he began telling story after story of John's noble character, how he had protected his sister, and how he had stood toe to toe with the most powerful man in New York because her honor was at stake. He talked about John's work ethic and how he had acquired a great sum of money through work and taking advantage of opportunities. John had no idea how Mac knew any of this.

As they ate, Mac continued to talk about John. He told about him defeating the best fighter on the East Coast in a fair contest. He then went into John's Irish heritage, talking about his brave countrymen. Mac knew a few stories that only locals should have known. John puzzled over Mac's knowledge of his life. He figured he learned some of it from Jamal but he knew things that John had never told Jamal. John also noticed Richard King taking a keen interest in the stories.

King, too, had been a young Irish boy who set out on his own with nothing and had been successful. His wife seemed drawn to John's character. Mac emphasized over and over his care for his family and his determination to acquire an education. Mac seemed to know exactly what to say to promote John to the Kings. Indeed, Mac was a master at marketing. He was touching all the right buttons at the right time. John thought that Mac would have been a successful politician.

Mac finally finished and sat down. The room was quiet for a moment. Mr. Brownlee showed up and handed a note to King, then took his place at the opposite end of the table. Several conversations commenced at once, as the businessmen talked about commerce and Mac and Henrietta talked about the library. John was more interested in the library than he was in the business.

After breakfast, Henrietta made a formal invitation to John to join their caravan to their ranch. She wanted him to complete his education which she planned to use to evaluate Mac's teaching abilities. She wanted to see how for herself how he taught.

John didn't know how to say no to Henrietta, or if it was even possible to say no to her. He thanked her and told her he would earn his keep. The old Scotsman was glowing. Once again Mac had accomplished his goal of orchestrating relationships and knitting uncommon lives together. At least for now.

Jamal left on his ship that afternoon. John gave him a letter Mac had written for him to give to the priest in New York. They said their goodbyes to Jamal. As was his custom, Jamal assured them they would all meet again.

John and Hank were in Galveston another two days as the caravan was readied for departure. King had procured a chestnut mare for John to ride. John had bought himself a rifle and a western-style holster for his pistol. He and Hank were ready for their new life, whatever that would be.

As they were loading the wagons to leave, John saw a pretty, dark-haired girl holding a baby and leading a two-year-old girl who was pleading to play under the wagon. He couldn't take his eyes off the girl. She had big brown eyes and a smile that lit up her face. Mac was standing with John and he saw him looking at her.

"Those are the Kings' children. The baby is named Richard, after his father. The girl they call Nettie, although her real name is Henrietta, like her mother."

Mac knew John was looking at Josephina but he was toying with him a bit.

"Fine children," John said, not taking his eyes off of the girl.

She looked up and saw him staring at her. She smiled at him and continued loading the babies on the wagon next to Henrietta. Then she took a seat behind them and made herself comfortable. She glanced at John again to see if he was still looking at her. He was.

"Come with me," Mac said as he and a big gray mule he called Sally led John toward the wagon.

"Josephina, I'd like you to meet John Delaney," said Mac.

"Pleased to meet you," she said.

"Ah, yes ma'am, I'm pleased too," John stammered.

Mac smiled at Josephina's effect on John and he and Sally walked away.

John kicked his mare and followed.

The group left Galveston behind that day. John didn't say another word to Josephina but he had a difficult time not looking at her. The caravan consisted of four wagons and Mac and Sally, followed by John and Hank. It fell into an order. Henrietta, along with the babies and Josephina were in the lead wagon, followed by Aldo driving a wagon filled with lumber. John thought he handled the wagon well even though he was a young boy. The other lumber wagon was driven by Chappo, an old Mexican man who had been with the Kings for years. He was an excellent cook. He had been a good ranch hand until he took a bad fall. Now he did light chores and helped around the house. Felix drove the last wagon, loaded with furniture.

John and Hank didn't stay with the group much. They would ride off, scouting the land, looking for the next camping spot. The Texas Gulf Coast was teeming with wildlife and Hank was having the time of his life chasing rabbits and digging out armadillos. John was learning to shoot his long gun and he had been able to keep the group supplied with fresh deer meat. John and Hank were loving Texas.

John would meet up with the caravan each afternoon to help them make camp. They had two tents, one for the women and children, and one for the men. After supper, Mac used the evenings to hold school.

Josephina, Felix, Aldo, and John were all at different skill levels, yet Mac kept them all moving on their own paths toward learning. They were eager students. Henrietta and Hank observed the process. She seemed pleased with Mac's techniques. She had been a fine teacher herself before she met Richard King.

C H A P T E R 11

Texas

The sun was sinking in the western sky and the wind sweeping over the South Texas landscape was doing nothing to cool things off.

"Now what are we going to do?" Herman whined.

"Shut up. I can't think with this toothache. And you drank all the whiskey," Jeb barked at his brother.

Zeke, their other brother, giggled.

"Zeke drank as much as me," Herman said.

The Rhodes brothers were out of coffee, tobacco, food, and whiskey. Things were not going well for them. They were lazy, mean, and without usable skills, unless you counted robbery as a skill. They were good thieves. They were raised that way by their Paw. He was the most cantankerous scoundrel in Arkansas. All he ever taught the boys was how to steal. Their mother had disappeared one day when they were young. Nobody knew whether she ran off to avoid the beatings or whether her husband killed her.

As soon as the three oldest boys were old enough to leave, they slipped off and never looked back. They left two sisters and a brother behind. They figured the youngsters would have to make it on their own. The older brothers had no regrets because compassion wasn't an emotion the Rhodes boys knew anything about. The evening they left,

124

they had been sent by Paw to steal some chickens. The owner of the chickens caught them. They got away but the man knew who they were. They didn't want to return home empty-handed. They were tired of the beatings so they headed south. They had heard the farther you go south the warmer it gets. And they didn't have coats.

Now they had been on their own for almost two years. As long as there were people to steal from, they didn't go hungry. Texas had an abundance of small towns full of good people, and good people are the easiest to rob. They would stay in a town until the people realized their chickens and assorted tools were missing, then they would move. They kept moving south in fear that their Paw would catch up with them. Each time they had just enough tack to make it to the next town. Then the boys would settle in and start the family business of stealing anything that wasn't tied down. They could take a goat or a young calf, have it butchered and the bones buried before dawn. It was a hard life but it was all they knew. Now they were somewhere in South Texas. They were having trouble finding anything to steal.

"What are we going to do when we run out of people that talk American?" Herman whined.

He was the oldest, the biggest, and the strongest. But he was not the smartest. Not by a long shot. He was what people would call simple-minded. Maybe he had been hit in the head too many times by his father, or maybe he'd just been born slow. They would never know. But he was loyal to his brothers and would do anything they said. Jeb was about a year younger and he was in charge. He was a capable man unless he had a toothache. His teeth seemed to be rotting faster than they should be. He had already lost a couple and he had a jaw tooth that was killing him. The youngest was Zeke, the meanest of the bunch. He was smaller than the other two but he was a wiry, tough kid, afraid of nothing. He was still a teenager, maybe 17 or 18. None of them knew exactly how old they were. Birthdays were not celebrated at the Rhodes house.

"Would you please shut up? I'll sell you to the first Mexican I see if you don't stop bothering me," Jeb ordered him. "We have to find some whiskey soon."

"And a whore," Zeke said. "I didn't get to be with a whore in Houston. You spent all the money on whiskey before I found a good whore."

"You should not be so particular," Herman said. "I found one."

This made Zeke angry, so he saddled up and rode off. He thought they should be looking for new opportunities rather than sitting around fussing at each other. Jeb was glad he was gone.

As they watched Zeke ride away, Herman's brow wrinkled.

"You won't really sell me to the Mexicans, will you?"

"No, now please, leave me alone. I need to think," said Jeb.

There was really nothing to think about. They were not in a good place. But the subject of thinking scared Herman since he didn't understand what thinking was. All he knew was to do what he was told. Jeb would take care of the thinking part. Herman rolled over and went to sleep. Jeb always marveled at how fast Herman could drop off to sleep. Day or night if he wanted to sleep, he slept.

Several hours later Zeke came riding up. He was excited.

"Don't kill that horse," Jeb said. "Herman's horse has already got the colic and this grass they are eating is no good."

"Well, it looks like our luck has just changed," Zeke said with a twinkle in his eye as he dismounted. "You will never guess what I found."

"I'm in no mood for guessing," Jeb said.

"I guess you found a house with chickens in the yard," said Herman.

"Better than that," Zeke replied.

"A house with a goat?" Herman asked. He was enjoying this game.

"Shut up and listen to me," Zeke said. "I found a bunch of wagons headed south. They are full of stuff."

"What kind of stuff?" Jeb asked.

"I don't know, the kind of stuff rich people have. I'm guessing they have whiskey. Anyway, here is the good thing, there are no able men with them, just women and children, an old Mexican and a hunchback."

"What's a hunchback?" Herman asked. "So can we ask them if they have whiskey?"

"Shut up Herman," Zeke said. "We need to figure this out and your stupid questions are not helping."

"We can slip in at night?" Jeb said.

He was interested now.

"We need to follow them and see what is best. I'll sneak up on them tonight and see what I can learn. Let's get saddled up. We ain't doing no good here," Zeke said.

"He's right," Jeb said. "Herman and I will circle around and get in front of them. You go in tonight and check it out. Then come find us.

"We are already out in front of them. And they are moving slow. My God, they have ten horses. If we can get their horses, we are set," Zeke said, more excited by the minute. "There's a creek a few miles from here. You two wait there for me. I'll find you in the morning."

"How?" Herman asked.

"I can hear you snoring for miles."

"Oh," Herman replied.

Zeke rode off on his recon duty and Herman and Jeb pushed on to make camp by the creek. Jeb's mind was working now. He forgot about the tooth. The thought of whiskey had eased the pain in his jaw.

While the travelers were setting up camp, Zeke did a complete survey. This time he saw his error. He hadn't seen the big man with the big dog earlier. Zeke wanted to get closer but he couldn't afford to alert the dog. The caravan seemed to have plenty of food, and he was sure the boxes contained things that would sell. He also realized that there would be no sneaking into their camp if the big dog was there, so he left to join his brothers. Just before dawn, he happened upon a young deer and he got off a lucky shot. They would at least have some food. The shot woke his brothers. They were sitting there when he rode in with their breakfast. Zeke was still convinced their luck had changed.

John had already found a spot for the caravan to camp the next night, so he decided he and Hank should head west for a few hours to see what they could find. Soon they began to see rolling hills and bigger trees. He was falling in love with Texas.

Meanwhile, the caravan moved south at a steady pace, just like every other day. Nothing unusual, just the steady clop-a-de-clop of the horses' hooves.

Nearby, the Rhodes boys had deer meat roasting and a solid plan for taking what they needed. In a few hours, they would ride straight toward their quarry, act like they were just passing by, then, when they had the advantage of surrounding them, they would pull their guns out. Jeb had warned them over and over that they were not to kill anybody. The guns were just to scare them. They would look through the wagons and take what they wanted. Then they would round up all the horses and ride west as fast as possible. They would sell the horses when they could.

Zeke liked the plan though he wanted to take the women, too. They fought about that while they ate the deer and saddled up. Herman didn't care. Jeb was sure it was a bad idea but he was also warming up to the thought. If they took them as far as San Antonio and left them there, maybe the law wouldn't care. He'd have to think about it some more. All the way there, Zeke talked about how he needed a woman. Jeb just tuned him out as he planned what he would say. His biggest fear was that one of the two idiots would give away their plan before they were ready. He realized once they were into it there was no going back. The truth was there was no going back anyway. They had to do something.

"Riders headed our way," Chappo shouted out.

He was the first to see them even though his wagon was not in the lead.

"I see them," Henrietta said. Mac stood up and looked. They didn't look dangerous. Just three drifters headed nowhere, he thought. When they got close enough, one of the men started waving in a friendly manner. Henrietta pulled her horses to a halt. Mac tied off his reins, jumped down, and walked toward the front of the caravan. Chappo did the same thing. Felix saw them headed toward Henrietta and he tied off his team and jumped down as well. Aldo stayed where he was. When the riders finally arrived, Mac, Felix, and Chappo were standing in front of Henrietta's wagon.

"Good day," the rider said.

"Hello," Henrietta said.

"We just left Houston. Hot day, huh?"

Chappo pointed due north.

"Houston is two days ride north of here. You came from the south."

Jeb had not thought of that. What else had he not thought of?

"Thank you," Jeb said, ignoring the correction but being as polite as he could.

By now the men were just a few yards from them. Mac wished he had his scattergun when he saw the little guy. The man looked like he was up to no good. Chappo and Felix both had pistols but there was no reason yet to pull a gun. The riders didn't move. They just sat there. The big man was grinning and Henrietta thought the other two seemed a little too interested in the wagons.

"May we help you?" she asked.

She was hoping they would get the message that they needed to go on about their business, whatever sordid business that might be.

"Yes ma'am," Jeb said. "As a matter of fact, you can be a big help."

He grinned, pulled his gun, and pointed it at her. The little man pulled his gun as well.

"Don't reach for the pistol, senor, or I shoot the lady."

Chappo didn't make a move. But Felix did. He pulled his gun and pointed it at Jeb. Zeke shot at Felix but missed. Felix pulled the trigger on his gun too, just as he heard the whistle of a bullet buzz past him. His shot went wide. The horses bucked a little but settled down soon. Not Sally though. She was pulling hard to get free from where she was tied to the back wagon.

"Stop shooting," Henrietta said sternly. "There are children here. Have you all lost your minds?"

Her order caused them all to pause and look at her. By now Herman had circled around and he had his gun out too.

"Drop your gun, boy," Jeb said, looking at Felix. "Just do as we say, and nobody gets hurt. Now drop it."

Henrietta motioned for Felix to drop his gun and he did.

"Now you too, senor," Zeke said. "Drop it."

Chappo did.

By now, both the babies were screaming and trying to get into their mother's lap. Josephina held them both but it was a struggle.

"Now everybody, get down from the wagons," Jeb ordered.

Herman gathered them as a group and walked them away from the wagons. Sally was still trying to get free. When the prisoners were safely at a distance, Jeb and Zeke started ransacking the wagons. After a while, Zeke lost interest in the wagons and turned his attention to the ladies. Mac, Chappo, and Felix all wanted to come to their rescue but there was nothing they could do.

That's when Jeb's plan seemed to go wrong. They had no idea one gray mule could cause so much trouble. Sally finally broke free and charged as hard as she could toward Mac's captors. She didn't stop until she saw Zeke. She lowered her head as she charged him, then threw her big neck backward, sending Zeke into the air. He hit hard on his back, the wind knocked out of him. His gun went flying. Herman laughed until he realized Felix had gotten Zeke's gun. Jeb tried to restore order but before he could move, Sally turned on him. He was not going to suffer the same fate as Zeke so began emptying his gun into the big mule. Mac yelled and took off to rescue Sally but Herman laid the barrel of his gun across Mac's skull. Mac dropped to the ground and didn't move. Felix pointed his gun at Herman and pulled the trigger. Once again, he hit nothing.

Jeb had finished shooting at the mule so he turned his gun on Felix. It clicked a few times because he was out of bullets. Felix then turned his gun on Jeb and pulled the trigger once more, only to miss again. The ladies, babies, and Aldo were clinging to each other while Chappo tried to get to Felix. He felt he could do a better job with the gun than Felix had. Zeke gathered himself and tackled Chappo. Jeb was loading his gun as he took cover behind the mule who was still kicking but only minutes away from death. Felix could not fire toward Sally. All he could do was watch Jeb reload. Herman walked over and snatched the gun from Felix and slapped him harder than he had to.

"All right, it's over now," Jeb said. "Everybody calm down. Herman go cut some rope off those wagons. Tie them all up. We can't trust them anymore."

Zeke was battered but he gathered himself and gave old Chappo a kick to the ribs. After they had them tied firm, the brothers went back to the wagons. Zeke found a case of wine. He and Jeb opened a bottle and had a few drinks. It wasn't whiskey but it would do. They then got busy. They piled the wine and anything else they thought they could sell into one of the wagons. They tied all the horses to the back of the wagon and prepared to leave. Zeke came over and cut Josephina loose, then walked her over to the wagon. He tied her down in the bed of the wagon, then did the same with Henrietta. Felix, Aldo, and the babies wept as they watched them ride off. Chappo was praying and swearing all at the same time. Mac was unconscious.

Herman drove the wagon while Jeb and Zeke drank wine.

"That didn't go so well," Jeb said.

"Never figured on a fighting mule, did you?" Zeke said.

He'd had a few ribs broken and it hurt to move.

"We need to keep moving. We have enough food now and we can't afford to be waiting around. They'll be looking for us. I'm thinking as soon as we can, we need to sell a few horses. We look like horse thieves," Jeb said.

"We are horse thieves. And mule killers."

Zeke smiled. He was drunk. So was Jeb. They were now on their third bottle.

"I don't want to be hung so we need to be careful," Jeb said as he dozed off.

Zeke was still awake, so he crawled over to the women and tried to untie them. Josephina kicked him in the stomach, letting him know it wasn't going to be easy. He slapped her then backed off. He was too hurt to bother with them now. It would have to wait until tomorrow. It was getting dark so he climbed up front and told Herman to sleep a bit while he drove.

"We've been riding all night. These horses are gonna drop dead and you can't sell dead horses," Zeke said.

He and Jeb were both on the buckboard and they were almost sober.

Zeke had also tried to have his way with Henrietta earlier in the night and that had not gone well. With broken ribs, he was no match for her, even with her hands tied. And Josephina joined in with another powerful kick to his sore ribs. When he figured it was not going to happen, Zeke just beat her with his fists and got back up on the buckboard. He sulked most of the night as the rain began to drench them.

"As soon as this rain lets up, we'll rest them a little. It's almost dawn."

Jeb paused a minute, looked at the sky, then sighed.

"We won't stay long. We have to keep moving."

"Good, I can't wait to get that bossy woman out of the wagon so I can show her who's boss," Zeke announced, loud enough for the women to hear.

"From what I saw, she showed you who was boss, and she was tied up," Jeb taunted him.

"She'll pay for that, I ain't forgot," Zeke mumbled.

"You know we are going to have to kill them both," Jeb said thoughtfully. "They're both too spirited. They'll talk."

Josephina's eyes widened as she heard this. Henrietta motioned for her to stay quiet.

"It don't bother me none killing them. I'll do it," Zeke said.

"Listen here Zeke, this whole mess is your doing, and I'm getting tired of it. From now on I don't want you to do anything unless I tell you. You hear me?"

"You ain't my Paw."

"I sure ain't. In fact, you are more like Paw than any of us. And if you don't start acting right we are going to leave you just like we did Paw. Then what will you do? Fighting with that crazy woman almost turned the wagon over. I mean for you to straighten up Zeke."

"How can that idiot sleep in all this rain?" Zeke said, looking back at Herman.

He wanted to change the subject and Jeb was always willing to talk about how stupid Herman was. So, the two brothers talked about

Herman for a while. The rain stopped just after it got light.

"Look yonder," Zeke said.

There was a creek bed with a sandy shelf that would do well to water the horses and let them rest.

CHAPTER 12

Texas

Mac thought he heard music. It was soft, pleasant, almost like chamber music. Then the music got louder and the notes turned harsher, not pleasant like before. It was like an orchestra warming up—just noisy loud instruments each playing a different song. His head began to pound. It was not music at all. The sound morphed into voices—voices that Mac didn't recognize, each speaking a different language.

Mac opened his eyes but could only see hazy shades of green. Everything was green—the ground and the sky were both green. He could not tell where the earth stopped and the sky started. He couldn't make sense of what he was seeing or hearing.

Then the voices all turned into one voice—a voice he knew. The voice was speaking a language that he almost understood but not quite. Then he recognized the voice. It was his old friend Broken Wing and she was speaking her native language. Mac could suddenly make out what she was saying. She was asking him where he had been. Why he had not come sooner. Then he saw her walking in the green field. She was walking with Sally. They were coming for him.

He tried to get up but he couldn't move. It was as if he were glued to the ground. His muscles wouldn't work. He tried to talk but he couldn't get the words out. Then she looked at him and smiled;

without saying a word she and Sally walked off. Then everything went from a soft, pleasant green to a harsh, dark shade of gray.

John had covered a lot of miles that day. He was tired but it had been a good day. They had seen a lot of beautiful country. He was as contented and satisfied as he had ever been. The rain was starting to come down just as he reached the spot where the caravan should have been stopped. They were not there. How could they have missed it? It was late enough now that they should have been here. Something was wrong. He hollered at Hank who was sniffing around an old log.

"Let's go, boy! We need to hurry."

He was able to get a good gallop out of his mare though she was tired and ready to call it a day. Three or four hours later, they found the wagons. It was a moonless night so John could see nothing. Hank barked to let John know he had them. As John rode up, he heard Aldo yell.

"John is that you?"

"Yes, I'm here."

He jumped off his horse and ran to them. He couldn't figure out what was going on. They were all tied to scrub oaks except Mac who was sitting by himself about thirty yards away just staring into the sky.

"Thank God it's you. We can't get loose. Bandits stole our horses and took Josephina and Henrietta. We tried to stop them but we couldn't. We thought they had killed Mac. He just lay there all day until it started raining, then he sat up. They hit him on the head so hard he may be crazy now. He keeps talking in that strange Indian language that he and Broken Wing used."

Felix could not get the words out fast enough and now the King babies, who had been asleep in Aldo's arms, were awake and crying. John untied them all, then checked on Mac.

"Is that you, John?" Mac said. His eyes were glazed.

"Yes sir, it's me," John assured him.

"My head's not clear but I think we are in trouble," Mac said.

"Yes, we sure are but I'm going to take care of it. Can you get up?"

"No, I'm too dizzy. I need to sit here a while longer," Mac said.

"Felix, I need your help," John said. "I need you to take care of my mare, brush her down, give her some oats and a little water."

Felix took care of her as Chappo told him the entire story. John was furious. He gave Hank a few bites to eat, made sure he had plenty of water, then asked Felix to saddle his mare again.

"Felix I'm going to get your sister and Henrietta."

"You need to hurry. Those are some mean men," Felix said.

"I'll catch them."

"Hurry, my boy," Chappo said.

"I will. Hank, let's go, boy," John said.

The trail was easy to follow, even in the rain. That many horses leave their mark. They rode hard all night. He hoped it didn't kill his horse but it didn't matter. He had to get to them before it was too late. It had been light about three hours when John found them. He and Hank didn't slow down. They charged into the camp as fast as they could. John saw one man tending the horses. He was the first to see John coming. He reached for his gun but Hank got to him first, attacking him from behind. John jumped off his horse and ran at the man who was kicking Hank. John hit him square in the nose and he went down. Just then, John heard Josephina yelling.

"Stop, please stop," she cried, terrified.

John and Hank took off on foot as fast as they could. They saw a wiry little man forcing himself on Josephina. Hank exploded as if he'd been shot out of a gun. A few feet away, Hank became airborne. The first thing Hank could grab was Zeke's right arm which was cocked to hit Josephina again. Hank's powerful jaws locked down on the upper part of the man's arm just under the shoulder. The momentum of 150 pounds of furious dog caught Zeke off guard. In one continuous motion, they both went flying, landing hard on the muddy ground some distance from Josephina.

A few seconds earlier, Zeke had been fighting with a girl. Now he was dealing with Hank. He no longer had the advantage. It was easier fighting a teenage girl than trying to fend off a protective mastiff. Although Josephina was holding her own, she would not have lasted long. Zeke squealed like a stuck pig and Josephina wasted no time crawling away from the fight as she headed toward Henrietta. Henrietta was still tied up, waiting her turn with one of the brothers. Josephina began working on the ropes as best she could to free her. She was out of breath so it was difficult.

Hank was dragging Zeke through the mud, shaking him like a rag doll. His right arm was out of its socket and he was yelling and cursing his brother Herman for not shooting the beast. John was running as fast as he could toward the fight. So was Herman, who had a rifle. He was aiming at the dog but he was afraid he'd hit Zeke. Herman had never been a good marksman. From where Herman was standing he could not get a clear shot. He started to circle around to improve the odds of hitting the dog rather than his brother.

Hank now had given up on the arm, which was completely ruined, and had taken a firm hold on Zeke's throat. John was still running toward them with his pistol pointed at Herman. Herman finally had a clear shot. The first shot rang out and spooked the horses. They started grouping together, stamping nervously. They were ready to bolt, stomping the ground and rearing up. Jeb finally got to his feet and aimed his rifle at the man running toward Herman. The first shot was from John's pistol, hitting Herman in the jaw a few inches from his right ear. The bullet came out just above his left ear, taking half of the skull with it. Herman dropped to his knees and toppled over. He was out of the fight.

Zeke was through yelling and cussing Herman for not shooting because now his throat was ripped open. Zeke was a bloody mess. John didn't stop until he got to the ladies. Just then the second shot exploded. It was from Jeb's rifle. It hit nothing but air. However, this shot had serious unintended results. With no idea where the shot had come from, John dove to the ground.

"Hank, come."

Hank dropped Zeke and trotted over to John.

"Sit boy," he said.

Hank obeyed immediately. John looked around to see where the shot had come from when he saw Jeb pointing the rifle at him. John had thought for sure Jeb was out of the fight. Then it happened. Jeb's second shot stampeded the horses. They started running toward the creek with Jeb in their path. He dropped the gun and started running but it was too late for that. The horses trampled him. They were still tied together so they could not have missed him if they'd tried.

"Were there just three of them?" John asked without looking at the ladies.

He was scanning the area looking for another player.

"Just three," Henrietta said.

John turned and looked at her, then at Josephina. It made his blood run cold to think a man could be so cruel. He reached down and started to touch Henrietta's face which was swollen badly. One eye was completely closed. Then he drew his hand back.

"How are you? I mean are you all right?"

He didn't know why he said that. They were not all right. He was just hoping he had gotten there in time. He was not sure he had.

"Son, you got here in time."

It was like she had read his mind. "Nothing happened. They slapped us around is all. God answered our prayers. He sent an angel to save us just in time."

She was free from the ropes now, hugging Josephina, rocking her like a baby.

"I'm no angel," John said as he got up and looked at his bloody dog. "Hank may be an angel though. He has saved me. He may be an angel but he fights like the devil."

John walked over to Zeke. The man was trying to breathe but having a tough time with multiple punctures in his throat. His right arm was useless. John bent down.

"How do you like being a horse thief now? If you try to get up my dog will finish what he started."

John walked over to make sure the shooter was dead. He was. Then he waded across the creek and gathered up the horses, who had not gone far. They were too worn down from the hard night. He untied them and led them to a patch of green grass to graze. They would not be ready to travel for a while. He called Hank and he and Hank cleaned up in the creek. Then he led the ladies down to the water, so they could clean up. John and Hank went back to the wagon and started going through the supplies to see what they had. He checked on Zeke who was barely alive and wasn't going to cause any problems. John found a shady spot and laid down with Hank by his side. They were both spent. They were fast asleep within a few minutes.

When John awoke, Henrietta and Josephina were sitting with them in the shade. Hank had his head on Josephina's lap. She was rubbing his ears.

"Are the babies safe?" Henrietta asked. She was almost afraid to hear what he had to say.

"They are fine. Aldo is taking good care of them," John said.

"I need to get to them," Henrietta said.

"We will but you both need to rest. You have been through a terrible thing. We will let the horses rest tonight and leave at first light."

"You remind me of Richard King. Always sure of yourself, with everything figured out," Henrietta said.

"I didn't figure on any of this. I'm just glad you are both safe."

"How is Mac?" Josephina asked. "He wasn't moving when we left. Just lying there. Is he alive?"

"When I left he was sitting up. Not talking much but he was mumbling strange things. He was talking about something with a broken wing."

"Broken Wing was his friend," Josephina said.

"What?"

"His friend was named Broken Wing. She was an Indian," she replied.

"I'll be honest with you. Mac had a bad head wound. You don't always come back from those. But he may survive. I just don't know. I had to get to you as fast as I could."

"We are happy you did, John," Henrietta said. Her eye was still swollen shut and she was as tired as he was.

"I don't have a tent but with that canvas, I can make you a dry place to sleep under the wagon. I'll fix us something to eat then we can all get some rest," John said.

Meanwhile, at what was left of the caravan, it was getting dark and the babies were not happy. None of them were happy. They were worried. The others should have been back by now. Felix wanted to go looking for them but without a horse it was hopeless. Chappo took charge and kept things in order. Mac was able to move around a little and he was starting to remember what had happened. He had spent most of the day just looking at Sally. The grieving and depression he had gone through with Broken Wing had now returned. Chappo set the tents in place and made a fire. It was going to be a long night. When they were all asleep, Felix slipped away from the group. He could not stay any longer. He had to go find his sister.

The next morning, Zeke was still alive. He couldn't do anything but gasp for every breath. And he was getting tired.

"I guess we can load him in the back with the others," John said.

"Let me look at him," Henrietta said.

"I can't believe you want to go near him," John said.

"I don't but it's the Christian thing to do."

She dressed Zeke's wound and somehow got his windpipe working. Then she gave him some water. He got it down without choking. His right arm hung limp. All the muscles and tendons had been ripped away from the bone. That arm would never be used again.

After they ate breakfast John loaded the wagon and tied the horses in a row. They pulled away minutes later—the three of them on the buckboard with Hank walking alongside them. The horses were in much better shape now and with an easy day walking, they would be fine. Zeke was still alive, piled on top of his dead brothers in the back of the wagon. He was barely breathing and his eyes were closed.

"Today there will be no talk about what has happened. Josephina and I lived through a horrible ordeal. By the grace of God, we got through it. Now it's time for us to put it behind us," Henrietta said. "Today we shall only talk of pleasant things. And everyone will talk," she said, looking straight at John.

"Yes ma'am."

"We have a long day ahead of us and we will spend the day getting to know one another better. We will tell stories about our lives. I will begin."

She began talking about the school in Brownsville she started. She talked about how she saw a need and put together the resources to educate the children. She talked about them one by one. She remembered their names and specific things about each child she mentioned. To her, education was important. No detail was too insignificant to mention. As she talked, she would muse about what they were doing now, wondering if they were using the things she had taught them.

Josephina went next. She talked about the little village in Mexico where she spent her early years and about how the entire town turned out for every occasion. She described it as a big family. John could tell she had been happy there. He remembered her screaming and hoped she would soon forget it. He didn't think she would, though.

Then it was his turn. He followed Josephina's example and told a few stories about his childhood in Ireland. He left out anything that might be unpleasant or violent. It seemed that much of John's life had contained violence.

Henrietta then talked about her college days in Mississippi. It seemed that every story Henrietta told had an element of religion in it. Josephina picked up on this and wove in a few stories about her church or a priest she knew. John didn't even try. They talked for several hours and were laughing together as they put the violence of the last day behind them. The last story John told was about fishing with David at the farm in New Jersey.

The sizzling summer sun was high in the sky. The afternoons could be brutal in South Texas this time of year. They needed to rest so John found an area where the horses could drink. While the ladies were cooling off, he tended to the horses. He looked in on Zeke who hadn't moved all day but was still clinging to life.

Not far away, Felix was wondering now if slipping off in the middle of the night had been such a good idea. He was hot, hungry, thirsty and his feet hurt. The boots he wore were designed for riding, not walking. It didn't matter now. He could not sit there helpless and wait for them to return. He had to do something. Aldo and Chappo had a purpose. They were taking care of Mac and the babies. Felix had nothing to do but sit and worry. If he'd used his gun sooner he could have saved them all. Why didn't he do it, he thought? Now he had to do something important. But he was afraid he had made another poor choice. He was miserable. The sun was straight up over his head so he figured he had been walking ten or eleven hours. Nothing to do now but keep moving.

Chappo woke just as the sun was rising in the east, painting the horizon in a beautiful soft golden glow that foretold a hot day ahead of them. The first thing he saw was Mac, sitting where he'd been when the sun went down. Aldo and the babies were cuddled together. He looked around. Everything was in place, except there was no Felix. Chappo knew where Felix was. He had talked about going after the bandits himself ever since John left. He must have set out on his own. Chappo got up and limped over to where Mac was sitting.

"Senor Mac."

Mac turned to him but did not look.

"I know you have been through some hard times but I need you to get up and get yourself together and help me. There is nobody else."

Mac looked at him, his eyes suddenly focused. The dead glare in his eyes was gone for the first time since Sally went down.

"Felix is missing. I need to go see about him. You need to take care of Aldo and the babies. They will be hungry when they get up. Start a fire and get breakfast going," Chappo said.

Mac stood up wobbly like a newborn calf. He gained his balance and stuck out his hand. Chappo looked puzzled then shook his hand. Maybe this was a mistake. Maybe Mac was not ready yet to move on. Maybe he would never be ready to move again.

"I am back, amigo. You can count on me," Mac said as he wobbled over and checked on the babies, then started a fire for coffee.

Chappo took off after Felix. There was no mystery about where he was. He tracked him for a couple of hours, then decided there was no use continuing. Felix was headed the right way. The trail was so wide a blind man could follow it. He turned around and went back to the others. He was curious about Mac. What if Mac went completely crazy and started killing the babies? A lump on the head like Mac has can make a man do strange things. He needed to get back.

Unbeknownst to Chappo, Felix had just reached Josephina.

"It's Felix, it's my brother Felix," she shouted with joy.

John had all the horses tied up and ready to travel. They had rested a few hours and needed to get moving if they were to make it back by dark. As he finished getting the horses hitched, he heard Josephina. Sure enough, Felix was walking their way. John could tell he was about to drop. He had walked such a long way. John went out to meet him but Josephina ran past him. She hugged and kissed Felix. They began speaking in Spanish to each other, smiling at each other as only a brother and sister can do. They walked back to the wagon together. Felix was worried about what Henrietta would say. It was John who spoke first.

"Good to see you, Felix," he said.

"How are my babies?" Henrietta asked.

"They are both doing fine. They miss you but they have a new mother in Aldo. He hasn't left their side the entire time. They love him. When I left last night, they were all three cuddled up like puppies."

When she smiled Felix had the answer he needed. He had come to her to report on the babies. This might work.

"How is Mac?" John asked.

"The same," Felix said sadly.

"We need to get you some water and something to eat. We need to get back on the road," John said.

The ladies took care of nursing Felix and John went to check on his mare. She looked better. He decided he would saddle up and ride ahead with Hank. The others were probably worried about them. It had been a long time since he left them, and he was worried about Mac. He put Felix in charge and told him not to let anything happen to the ladies. This is what Felix needed to hear. Henrietta winked at

John. She knew what he was doing. He and Hank hurried off to see about the others. By bedtime, they all should be together again.

A few hours later when John rode into camp, Chappo and Mac were sitting by the fire. The babies were playing a game with Aldo. Nettie was having a great time. Little Richard was just watching.

"Senor John, it is good to see you. I trust you found our Felix along the way," Chappo said.

"I did. He arrived just in time. I needed to get off that wagon," John said, grinning.

Mac got up and walked over to John. He hugged him and whispered in his ear.

"Were you in time?"

John was relieved because he knew Mac was back with them.

"Yes, I think so. I'll tell you all about it later. For now, it's safe to say both ladies are fine. They are looking forward to seeing you."

Aldo walked over then, leaving the babies alone a moment.

"Are they safe?"

"Yes, they are fine."

He smiled and returned to his duties caring for the children. A few hours later, just before the sun went down, Hank barked and ran toward the west. The wagon had arrived. They were all there safe and sound, except for Zeke. He had died shortly after John rode off.

CHAPTER 13

King's Ranch

John could not stop looking at the beautiful young girl he had learned so much about on the ride back. Her story was nothing like his but it seemed just as difficult. She had struggled as much to get here as he had. Thinking about this puzzled him as he watched her face glow with joy while she nurtured the little ones. A short time ago she had faced a horrible fate. Now she seemed so happy, so joyous. Seeing the babies, her brothers and Mac seemed to overcome what she had been through. Maybe it hadn't but John thought she had somehow passed through it all unmarked.

John hoped he had not said anything to make her not like him. He had never cared much what people thought of him but with her it was different. He didn't want her to think badly of him. John could also see Henrietta with the baby one on her hip, talking with Chappo. She was doing what every good leader does after a battle. She was making sure her people were well. John had seen his father do the same thing. Every man is different and the way each one deals with death is important. Even the deaths of the Rhodes boys.

After Henrietta was finished talking with Chappo, she gave him a big hug and found Mac, sitting by Sally.

"Mac," she said. "Let me look at your head."

It was still seeping blood. The thick curly hair was so matted with blood she could not see the wound well. She called for Aldo to take the baby and bring her the medical kit. She walked Mac over to a shady spot, holding his hand lovingly as they walked. It was an odd picture—the fine, cultured lady and a hunchback on wobbly legs making their way together. John watched as she tenderly cut a patch of hair from Mac's head, then cleaned and shaved the area and stitched the wound together. She and Mac chatted the entire time. John was moved by her compassion and her ability to render proper care.

Hank was taking a nap near where John and Felix had been working. He was exhausted. John looked at his noble dog, realizing again how valuable he was. No matter what the circumstances were, you could count on Hank. As John watched his dog sleep, he heard Henrietta call his name. Hank looked up, too. He sensed no danger so he put his head back down.

"Yes ma'am," John answered.

"We need to talk," she said. "Yesterday I told you we would not speak of our troubles then but now we should. I need to tell you a few things."

This alarmed John. Maybe she had not told him the full truth. Maybe she and Josephina had been violated after all.

"Was I too late?" John gasped.

"No. We couldn't have lasted much longer but you were in time to save us and I will be forever grateful. I hate to think how horrible it would have been had you not come when you did. They were planning to have their way with us, then kill us both. You saved our lives."

She reached out and held John's hand.

"I need for you to know how thankful I am."

"I should have been here. If Hank and I had been there this would never have happened."

"Stop that," she said firmly. "You had no idea what would happen.

You did more than enough. Now listen to me. Josephina and I must get through this, and we will. I have asked so much of you but I must ask one more thing. If you would, please stay close by until we reach the house. I would be forever grateful. I know you are getting the wanderlust. I have seen it in men and I know what it is. But I need you and Hank to stay close. We are not ready to go on without you."

"I would never leave you out here. Do we even know where we are?" He asked.

"Yes of course. This is our land but it is still rough and unsettled. We should reach the house tomorrow if we leave early and are not stopped."

John could not imagine anyone owning this much land. They must be very wealthy people.

"I want to say something else. Mr. King and I will never forget what you have done for us. We both will do everything in our power for you. I want you to know how much you mean to us, as well as to Josephina and her brothers. I can honestly say that you are our hero."

They left early the next day and made good time. Late in the day, three riders approached, all of them ranch hands. One of them rode hard back to the ranch to tell Mr. King. He had arrived earlier in the day and was worried about them. They should have been at the ranch several days already.

Just as the ranch was coming into view, they saw Mr. King ride up on a majestic black stallion. The horse held his head high, announcing to the world his noble lineage. Richard King was a striking figure on his fine mount. He spoke with his wife, then rode by all the wagons inspecting their contents and passengers. He took notice of the Rhodes brothers. They were stiff and starting to smell in the hot Texas sun. Then he circled back to the lead wagon and climbed up beside his wife. John could see them talking as they rode toward the ranch.

John was becoming more and more curious about the ranch.

Conversations with Mac and Felix had piqued his interest. He knew the big house was still under construction but that there was also a smaller Spanish-style house, a large barn, and a bunkhouse for the cowboys and ranch hands. As they drew closer, several ranch hands rode up, received instructions from Mr. King, then rode quickly back to perform the duties he had given them. It was dark by the time they arrived at the house. The wagons and horses were taken care of and the caravan passengers were greeted with a hearty meal.

Later, John and Hank were sitting on the porch of the bunkhouse. John was surprised when Mr. King approached with a bottle of whiskey and a couple of glasses. He sat beside John and he poured two glasses, then lifted his glass in an unspoken toast to the young man and his dog. Without saying a word, they clicked glasses and drank.

"My wife has told me everything of the events of these last few days," King said.

His face showed no expression and Mac had warned John that he was not a man to be taken lightly. So John listened, then nodded his head without comment.

"I was right about you. You are a man to be counted on. Mrs. King speaks highly of your valor as well as your manners."

Another nod from John. He still wasn't sure what to say.

"If you don't mind, I'd like to talk business with you," King said as he took another long drink from his glass.

John also sipped another swallow of the amber liquid. He welcomed a drink after many long days on the trail.

"Yes sir. We can talk about whatever you'd like," John replied at last.

"This part of Texas is still very dangerous. Both Mexico and America claim this land is their own. No matter how it turns out, I plan to hold on to my property. We have no reliable authority that I can count on, which means that I am the law. I don't say this in a ruthless way. If I do not provide security, there will be none. My men know how to handle themselves, and they are all able but they have their hands full taking care of the ranch.

I need a man whose only duties involve providing security and protection for my holdings. I need a ranger who can ride my property, detect threats and deal with them. I believe you are that man.

Mrs. King has told me how you handled the bandits. What I need you to do is patrol my property to ensure the ranch can run properly without threats. I will pay you well and provide you with everything you need."

"Tell me what I would be doing," John said, already excited by the prospect of this new adventure.

"You will report only to me. My men will be instructed to help you in every way. I want you to know my land like a ship captain knows his vessel. That means nobody comes on this land that you do not approve. I told you I trust your judgment, and I meant it."

"I'll do it," John said, "but I'll need a good horse. May I buy the mare you've let me ride? She has a lot of heart and I would not have reached your wife in time had she not been such a fine horse. I call her Bonnie. I can pay for her. I have some money…"

"She is yours. Consider her as a part of your first month's payment. How much money do you have?" he asked, changing the subject abruptly as only a seasoned businessman can.

"I don't know. Enough I suppose."

John got up, took another sip of whiskey, then retrieved a leather satchel that he handed to his host.

"It is all in there."

King pulled out a wad of bills, some gold coins, and a few old Spanish gold pieces. After dividing it and counting it he asked John if he knew how much he had. John shrugged.

"Almost a thousand dollars here," King said.

"Yes sir, I think that is right."

But John actually had no idea. He hadn't counted it since he left New York.

"What are you planning to do with this money?" King asked.

"Keep it I guess, or spend it. What else can you do with money?"

King laughed. He put the money back in the satchel and handed it to John. He then poured more whiskey. He looked over at John.

"You invest it. That's what you do."

"How do you do that?" John asked.

"My first investment was a… never mind. I said I trusted you. Do you trust me?"

"Yes sir, I do," John said quickly, because he did trust him, and he admired him.

"I know a banker who will open an account for you on my word. I'll put this money and what you have already earned into this account. Your first month includes a large bonus, by the way. You earned every penny of it when you saved my family. I'll also deposit your monthly wages. You won't need any money here. When I see an opportunity, I'll invest the money for you."

"We have a deal," John said as he offered Mr. King his hand.

John had heard enough. He had the job he wanted, the horse he wanted, a place to live, and now Mr. King would be looking after his money.

"Then you are my ranger, John. Bonnie is yours. You have the run of my place, and if you need anything at all, tell Henrietta. She will take care of it."

The next day, King gave John a new long rifle and a better pistol. They spent several hours together shooting and exploring the area near the house. The following day, John and Hank set out for his first day as a ranger for the King Ranch. As he rode off, Josephina waved from the porch and smiled. The world was suddenly beautiful to John.

King had given him a set of maps that laid out his holdings. John went west first, riding the boundary for a few days. Then he turned south and explored that area. He and Hank hunted when they were hungry and rested when were tired. After about a week, he returned to the ranch. King was away on business so John spent a couple of days getting to know his way around the ranch and talking with Josephina whenever he could. The following week, he rode due east to explore that area. He saw nothing that caused him any concern. He tracked a few drifters but they meant no harm.

One day, John was in the bunkhouse cleaning his rifle when he saw Josephina approaching. It was a beautiful spring day, the sky was clear and birds were singing as they searched for mates to begin the nesting season. Life was good and it got even better as he watched the beautiful Mexican girl. Her smile sent chills down his spine as he walked out to meet her.

"Good morning," John said.

"You need a haircut," she replied, with a smile.

John reached back and felt the hair down his collar. It was rather shaggy.

"No barber shop where I've been," he said.

"I can cut it," she said. "Get cleaned up and I'll meet you on the porch."

She turned and marched back to the big house. John raced into the bunkhouse and dug through his bag for some clean clothes. He grabbed a bar of soap and headed to the creek, Hank in tow. Hank loved to play in the water. After John had washed and dressed as nicely as he could, he hurried to the big house where Josephina waited for him. She had changed into a pretty dress and even had a flower in her long, black hair. She had watched Henrietta cut her husband's hair several times and had borrowed her shears and razor.

John had no idea this was an important part of the courting ritual but he sat obediently where he was told as she began the haircut. He could not have cared less how he looked. He was happy to be there as she lathered his face and gave him a shave with Mr. King's razor. Then she began to clip his hair, looking at him from every angle. As she was finishing, Nettie came running out onto the porch looking for her. Henrietta was not far behind her. She snatched her up and scolded her for running off.

"When we finish, we can have lunch together on the back porch, if you like," Josephina said, hoping he would agree.

"I would like that," John said, still in the dark over the carefully orchestrated haircut and lunch.

Josephina gave him a mirror and watched as he examined his face. For a moment she worried that he might not be pleased with her work.

"This is the best haircut I have ever had," John said.

And he meant it. No matter how it looked, he had never enjoyed anything more. And the smile on her face made it even better.

Henrietta had set a table with two chairs. On the table was a blue floral print tablecloth and her best china. A flower was in a vase at the center of the table. John began to wonder whether lunch had been Josephina's idea at all.

"It's so beautiful," he said.

It must have been the right reaction. Josephina turned and hugged him. It was a quick hug but it was thrilling to John to feel her soft body, smell her perfume, and see her face up close. She pulled away and hurried up to the porch. John tried to get there in time to hold her chair but he was too late. They sat down, John nervous and Josephina as red as a beet. With exquisite timing, Henrietta came out with a pitcher of tea and glasses. A few moments later, she brought a plate of sandwiches cut into various shapes—she called them tea sandwiches—and she also brought a plate of cookies. John felt his mother and sister would approve of this lunch.

After lunch, they walked down the hill and watched a young colt taking his first few steps. John had never had a better day.

The next day, John rode north. Early that afternoon, he shot a young buck and had just begun to skin him when he saw Hank look up. Hank had spotted something.

"Easy, Hank," John said as he watched with amazement.

A giant man in a buffalo skin cloak stepped out from behind an oak tree. He was the biggest man John had ever seen. He was carrying a saddle and a heavy pack.

"With your permission—and that of your dog—I'd like to join you for supper. I was tracking that little buck myself hoping for a nice meal," the man said in a friendly tone.

Hank seemed to calm down.

"You are more than welcome to join us but it will be a while," said John.

The man put down his heavy pack and took off his cloak. John was amazed again at the size of the man. He looked even bigger without the cloak. He had a muscular body with arms as thick as John's thighs. He was a light-skinned black man with sky blue eyes and John found it hard not to stare as Hank walked over to their guest and sniffed him. The big man patted Hank on the head and Hank's tail began to wag. John realized now he was friendly. He knew he could count on Hank's evaluation of the man.

"If you would allow me to finish the butchering, you can start a fire. My name is Henry Lloyd Walker."

"John Delaney."

"Pleased to meet you, Mr. Delaney."

"Call me John."

"I will," Henry Lloyd said as he pulled a long knife from his boot and began working on the deer. "What's your companion's name?"

"His name is Hank," John answered.

Henry Lloyd dug into the deer, sliced out the heart, and tossed it toward Hank.

"Here you go, Hank."

Hank caught the morsel and made short work of it. Then Henry Lloyd began the skillful carving of their dinner. John was working on the fire but he still could not stop looking at this big man who moved so gracefully. Hank was staying close too, in case he might be tossed another treat. Their new friend tossed him several more before he finished.

Henry Lloyd prepared a roast, then took the liver out and trimmed it. He sliced it into thin strips and laid them in a saucepan he had taken from his pack. By now, John had a nice fire going. Hank kept close to Henry Lloyd, not because he was worried but because they were friends.

"While dinner is cooking, we can swap our stories. I'm curious as to why a young Irishman is patrolling the area with such a fine dog."

"How did you know I'm Irish?" John asked.

Henry Lloyd just laughed. It was a jolly laugh—a laugh that invited others to join. Henry Lloyd started rearranging the fire. He divided it into two sections—one to slow roast the deer rump and a small hot flame he used to quick fry the liver. He dug through his pack and pulled out a couple of small potatoes and a turnip. He opened a bag that contained herbs and spices. He carefully sprinkled some on the meat.

When the liver was brown, he set it aside and made a sauce from the juices of the meat. He added herbs, then placed the liver back in the gravy and set it near the roast to continue cooking. John and Hank watched him with amazement. He cleaned the vegetables and put them into another pot to boil with spices from another bag.

Henry Lloyd soon had the dinner under control. He made a pot of coffee that they sipped as they watched their dinner cook. Henry Lloyd told his story. And it was a story worth telling.

He had been born a free man. His father was a wealthy businessman who took a light-skinned Island girl for his bride. Her heritage was mixed but she was classified as a Negro. His mother had died in an accident when he was very young. His father was too busy to raise a couple of boys so he and his brother Bootsey had been raised in an orphanage. They both received good educations. Henry Lloyd spoke fondly of the people that ran the orphanage. He was trained as a chef and he had worked in some of the finest hotels in New Orleans. He had even attended a culinary school in Paris for a year, where he was tutored by some of the most talented chefs in Europe. He had been married and had a son he raised by himself after his young wife took ill and died. Sometime later, when the boy was grown, Henry Lloyd stopped cooking and started preaching. John didn't understand this but he listened. Henry Lloyd went west and spent several years hunting buffalo and preaching the gospel to whomever he met.

During the storytelling, Henry Lloyd decided the food was ready and they ate. It was an excellent meal, though they were nowhere near a decent kitchen. John marveled that it had all been prepared on a campfire using only what the big man had in his pack.

They swapped stories until they were ready to sleep. John dropped off quickly but then woke up a few hours later, thinking about all he had heard. Henry Lloyd was a fine man and a special person. John was happy their paths had crossed.

CHAPTER 14

Texas

When John woke the next morning, the sun was already up. He was alone. The fire was blazing with a pot of coffee off to the side so Henry Lloyd must have gone somewhere. Hank was gone too. John looked for their tracks and found them both, a short distance from the camp. Hank was lying down and the big black preacher was kneeling. His head was bowed. John thought he must be praying. Hank saw John and came running over. The big man got up and walked over to John.

"It's a bit colder today. I think a front is moving in. It's going to get nasty before dark today," Henry Lloyd said.

"Let's get some breakfast, then we can head to the ranch. You will be welcome there," John said.

John walked with Henry Lloyd for a couple of hours, talking about whatever came up. The man was easy to talk to. Then John mounted Bonnie and he and Hank left Henry Lloyd to walk. The front had arrived by the time John and Hank reached the ranch. He went straight to the big house where he found the family sitting in the parlor, watching the girls play. Josephina announced his presence, then hung back a bit, not too far, because she wanted to hear what John had to say. Henrietta was enjoying Josephina's interest in John. She did not disapprove of her watching.

"Hello John, I didn't think you would be back so soon. May I get you something to drink?" Henrietta said.

"No thank you. I am in a hurry. I met a man while patrolling the north line. By the way, I found the shacks you had built for me. They are perfect," John said.

King had had his men build several small sheds for John to use. They were simple eight by eight wooden shelters but on a cold or rainy night, they would provide ample protection from the elements. Henrietta smiled and nodded.

"Anyway, he is on his way to New Orleans to see a grandson he has never met. His horse took lame and he had to put him down so he's walking. I told him he was welcome to stay at the ranch until the weather breaks. There's a front coming in."

"If you trust him then I do too. Richard said he trusts your judgment. And so do I."

"Hank and I trust him. I may not always know about character but Hank never misses. He is a good man and an interesting one. He is a buffalo hunter and a preacher," John said. "He hunts and traps while he preaches all over the plains. I have never heard of anything like that but that is what he does."

"Preacher?" Henrietta asked.

"Yes ma'am, I know what you're thinking but I believe him. He knows all kinds of Bible stories. In fact, almost everything we talked about was from a Bible story.

"By all means, John please bring him," she said.

"I will but I just want you to know he doesn't look much like a preacher," John said. "For one thing he is a huge man, the biggest man I have ever seen. He is gentle and polite. His clothes are made of animal skins so he doesn't look civilized at first but he speaks like a gentleman. He is a black man."

"Do you mean a Negro?" she asked.

"Yes, ma'am, I do. He says he is a free man and he has the papers to prove it."

"As I said before, John, if you trust him, so do I. He is welcome to stay here."

John excused himself. He found Aldo and had him take care of Bonnie while he and Chappo hooked up a team to pull a small wagon to fetch his new friend and his gear. It was raining hard when the wagon arrived at the ranch. Mr. King had just ridden in and he and Henrietta were both waiting for John to return with his guest.

John and Henry Lloyd went straight to the barn to care for the team. As John was finishing, he noticed Hank and Henry Lloyd both looking at the door. The big man either had mystical powers or he could hear as well as Hank. Either way, John knew someone was coming. A moment later, Richard King walked into the barn. King was just under six feet and muscular but he looked fragile next to Henry Lloyd. King stuck out his hand.

"Welcome to my ranch. My name is Richard King," he said.

"It is kind of you to have me, Mr. King. My name is Henry Lloyd Walker. Your gracious hospitality is much appreciated," he said.

"Our pleasure. However, if you don't mind, there is a bit of business that we must take care of first. I'd like to look at your papers. I don't wish to offend you but this is a slave state and I have business dealings with cotton people all over the area. I need to know I'm not harboring an illegal runaway."

"Not at all. I completely understand," said Henry Lloyd. "If you will excuse me a moment…"

The buffalo skin-clad giant opened his homemade bag and found a roll of documents. He thumbed through them until he found what he was looking for. He looked over it, then smiled at John as he handed the papers to King.

King was satisfied with the document. It was a legitimate court-certified document declaring that Henry Lloyd Walker, a 6" 11" light-skinned mulatto, born July 17, 1815, in Saint Bernard Parish, was a free man.

"John said you would be staying with us. Please make yourself at home. We will have breakfast around eight in the morning. Mrs. King and I would be delighted if you and John would join us."

"Thank you," he said.

It was not every day a black man was invited to eat with white people in Texas. These must be extraordinary people, Henry Lloyd thought. When King left, Henry Lloyd handed the papers to John.

"I don't need to see them. Your word is good enough for me," John said, not wanting to admit that he couldn't read very well yet.

"More blessed are those who believe without having seen," said the preacher.

John thought maybe Henry Lloyd was quoting from the Bible because it didn't exactly make sense to him.

"Let's get you cleaned up. I bet Chappo can find something you can wear."

Chappo had some oversized white cotton pants that were loose on him but they fit Henry Lloyd. The pants were too short for him but with a large woven serape, he was ready to dine in the big house the next morning.

None of the bunks fit Henry Lloyd so he made himself a pallet on the floor and slept with Hank. Before he dozed off, he read from the Bible, using the light from a candle he had in his bag.

The next morning, John woke to what seemed to him an unusual event. Over in the corner near the wood-burning stove, Henry Lloyd had a group of cowboys gathered. He was having some sort of church service with them. Hank was right there in the middle of it. John thought to himself that Hank would never have been allowed to attend church at St. Patrick's. He sat up in bed, watching as the big man lovingly shared Bible stories with the cowboys. Finally, Henry Lloyd had them all bow their heads and he prayed over each one of them. After the prayer time, he joined John out on the bunkhouse porch.

"The rain has stopped and I think we are going to have a fine day. Let's go in and make some coffee."

John followed his new friend inside. He watched as Henry Lloyd brewed strong, hot coffee in an unusual pot. It was unlike anything John had ever seen. Within moments they were enjoying a delicious brew.

"You look like you want to ask me something," Henry Lloyd said.

"No," John said but that was a lie.

He had so many questions for Henry Lloyd he didn't know where to start. They sat and talked until time for breakfast, then John told Hank to stay in the bunkhouse and he and the big preacher went to meet the Kings.

Breakfast was spent talking about various topics. Henrietta had heard a bit about Henry Lloyd's culinary skills. Now John told them all about the fine meal he had prepared with just the young buck and a few potatoes over an open fire. He told them how their guest had worked as a chef in several fine hotels and restaurants in New Orleans and that he had even attended culinary school in France. Henrietta made him promise that he would prepare several different dishes John had never heard of. Henry Lloyd spoke openly and honestly about anything and everything they wanted to discuss. Everyone found him charming.

After breakfast, the men went to the porch to enjoy cigars. With cigars and no women around, the conversation turned to politics. King, like every good businessman, was current on the events of the day. John had little idea what he was talking about. Earlier that month, John Brown, a staunch abolitionist, had been hung in Harpers

Ferry, Kansas, for raiding a federal armory and inciting a slave rebellion. King had strong opinions about the way it had been handled. He, like most southerners, was resentful of the northern states implementing laws that seemed to always favor the North.

The southerners in congress were always outvoted. The last two Presidents had both been democrats but they were northern democrats and they worked with the Whig party to weaken the South in many ways. According to King, if a southerner wasn't elected soon, the Union was going to fall apart. Henry Lloyd politely listened without comment. After the cigars, the men went down to look at a few of King's prized horses.

Later, at Henrietta's request, Henry Lloyd prepared dinner for them—beef in some sort of sauce that John couldn't pronounce. They all thought it delicious. He had also made a light dessert from figs. It, too, was pronounced a success. The conversation drifted to religion and went on late into the evening. John was even more lost in these discussions than he had been in the session on politics.

The next day, Richard King came to the bunkhouse and found Henry Lloyd reading his Bible.

"Mr. Walker, I have rearranged my schedule. I had planned a trip to New Orleans later in the spring but I think going now will benefit my purposes better. I know you have plans to visit family there, and If you would like, I can arrange for you to accompany me on my steamship to New Orleans. It will be faster than walking."

"I would appreciate that greatly," Henry Lloyd said.

"There is only one stipulation. Mrs. King says I am to make sure I bring you back. She wants to enjoy and learn a few of your recipes. And I'm sure she wants to talk more religion. There is nothing she likes better than talking religion."

"I can make no promises. This is not because I don't want to come. In fact, I would like nothing more than to return and spend time here but as a minister of God, I must go where he sends me. I never really know where I will end up. I believe He sends me where I can be used for His purpose. Seeing my grandson is a privilege the Lord is allowing me. After that, I don't really know what I'm doing. If I'm not called away, then I will be delighted to return with you."

"I think she will understand that," King said.

John was glad the Kings understood Henry Lloyd because he sure didn't. They spent the next few days hunting. The big man knew about tracking and he showed John some important things to look for. In the evening they would sit around a fire and talk about different things. He showed John how to tan the skins and how to fashion them into clothing and shoes.

After a few days, King, Henry Lloyd, and a group of several other men who often accompanied King set out for Galveston where they would take one of his steamships to New Orleans. As they were leaving, Henry Lloyd turned to John. John held out his hand to his friend. Henry Lloyd pushed his hand away and hugged John.

"I'm going to pray for you before I leave," he said as he put one of his big hands on John's head and began to speak.

The prayer was loud and long and everybody stopped what they were doing to listen. He asked for God's blessings and God's mercies, and for protection. John saw Henrietta watching as the big preacher prayed. John was becoming a little embarrassed because everything seemed to stop while the prayer was going on. When he finished, Henry Lloyd hugged John once more.

The next few days were hard for John. He had only known Henry Lloyd a little over a week but it felt as if he had known him his entire life. With Henry Lloyd gone, he felt like he had lost his best friend. He was getting ready to ride out again when Josephina found him loading his things onto Bonnie.

"Are you well?" she asked.

This was an odd question. He had not been sick. He had not talked to anyone about his feelings. *Why was she asking if he was well?*

"I'm fine. I'll only be gone a few days, I need to ride the western edge a piece, then maybe check on the southern border."

"I know how hard it was to see him leave," she said.

How did she know this?

"He'll be back, I think," John replied.

"John, may I ask you a question?"

"Of course."

"What did you see in him that was different?"

John looked at her, not sure how to answer.

"He is different, don't you think?" Josephina continued.

"He is different in quite a few ways," John agreed.

"That's not what I mean. Never mind. I suppose you don't know what I'm saying," she said.

"Yes, I do," John said. "He is different. I just don't know why. He is so open and honest. I like that. And he didn't want anything from me. He just wanted to spend time with me. I guess I'm used to people always wanting something. It was different with Henry Lloyd."

"Do you think I want something from you?" Josephina asked.

"That's not what I meant," John said, embarrassed.

"Why do you think I come and talk with you? Do you think that I want something?"

Josephina sounded hurt.

"No, it's different with us. When I'm with you I feel different," John said.

"What do you mean?" she pressed him.

"Different in a good way, that's all. The first time you touched me I felt tingles all over. After I'm with you I can't stop thinking about you. I don't know why. I just can't get you out of my mind," John confessed.

"I'm glad. Because I love you too," she said, with her big brown eyes set on his.

What was she saying? John thought he had not said he loved her. He thought quickly about what she'd said. Then he realized that yes, he did love her. He just didn't use the word. He had never thought about it but maybe it was love. Maybe he did care for her like that. Like his sister and David. But now what? He couldn't just ride off after talking this way. He needed to do or say something. But what?

"Do you think we can talk to Henrietta about this?" John asked.

"Why?" she asked.

"I do not want to do or say anything that is not appropriate. Henrietta will know what we should do," John said.

He was looking for help.

"Let's go see her now," Josephina said.

"Ah, maybe she is busy."

"She will make time for us. Come on."

She took him by the hand and the quivering sensation was back. But he liked it. They walked hand in hand to the house and he sat in a rocking chair on the porch, waiting for the ladies to come out. It felt like forever. John figured they were talking about it without him. Maybe this was good. Maybe he wouldn't have to say anything.

"John," Henrietta said when they finally came out with a pitcher of tea and some cookies. "Josephina said you had something you wanted to talk with me about."

"Yes, ma'am I do. If this is not convenient I can come back."

"This is fine. I have nothing pressing. What is it?" Henrietta asked.

"Josephina and I were talking."

He paused because he didn't have any idea what he would say.

"Yes, I've seen you both talking a lot lately."

"Since I found you both that night, I feel different toward her. I mean I always thought she was pretty. Please forgive me for being honest. The first time I saw her I thought she was the most beautiful girl I had ever seen."

Josephina blushed and hung her head.

"Since that night, I find myself thinking about her all the time. I thought it was just me. I figured I'd get over it until she said she had feelings for me," John said.

After another pause, Henrietta asked, "So what is it you want to say?"

"I want to do what is right but I don't know what is right," John said.

"I see," Henrietta said.

"I don't want you to think I'm trying to take advantage of her."

"I don't think that. It is obvious to everybody on the ranch, even Mr. King and he is hardly ever here, that you two like each other," Henrietta said.

"I guess what we are asking you is what should we do?"

"Since you asked, I'll tell you. You should ask her to marry you, or you should leave her alone. This poor girl has been through enough hardship for three lifetimes. I'm not going to sit here and watch her get hurt again."

Henrietta took her last sip of tea and got up from the chair. As she left, John saw her smile at Josephina. He sat there as Josephina looked at him with her big brown eyes and waited for him to say something.

"I love you. I want to be with you all the time but I also like being a ranger. I like what I'm doing," John hung his head. "But I think I like you more."

"I like you being a ranger. It makes me feel safe," Josephina said.

"You mean you think I can do both?"

"Both what?" she asked.

"Be married and be a ranger," John said.

"Of course you can. I can keep working with Henrietta as long as she'll have me. I couldn't stand to leave the children any more than you can't stand to stop being a Ranger," she said.

For once, John didn't need to think about what he was going to say next.

"Will you marry me?"

"Yes, I will," she answered, almost before he could get the words out.

Then she hugged him and ran to tell Henrietta the news. John sat a few minutes then went to the barn and he and Hank took off. He had a lot to think about.

CHAPTER 15

Laredo

As John left the ranch, an unusual peace settled over him. He was glad he had asked Josephina to marry him. Recalling events of the past few months made him realize that he did love her. He was glad she had taken the initiative to make it happen. He was afraid that if it had been left up to him, he would still be hanging around the barn watching her.

If Josephina had been purposeful in making it happen, the timing was perfect. He also wondered if this was just the first of many decisions that she would make for them. Then he realized he'd never really made the decision but he was still happy about it.

The weather was pleasant as John and Hank surveyed some land to the west they had never seen. It appeared to him that it had been a long time since anyone had seen this country. There were few trails or paths so they found themselves weaving in and out of mesquite trees growing as thick as he had ever seen. He didn't think cattle could make it through this brush.

It was early when he found a suitable clearing for them to camp for the night. He had not killed anything today and he had left without much food, so he and Hank chewed on a piece of dried jerky and then went to sleep early. John dreamed about Josephina.

The next morning, they continued moving westward. By the end of the day, they had come to the border of King's property. They would go due south in the morning. They had seen no one since they left the ranch. John shot an old doe, so they had meat. He found himself wishing Henry Lloyd were there. The man could probably even make this tough old doe taste good. He was wondering if Henry Lloyd had seen his grandson yet.

Two days later they were riding into Laredo. Laredo was a good distance from King's land, however, John needed supplies. He realized he would need to be better at planning in the future. Hank hadn't complained about John's shortcomings, though. Hank was the perfect traveling partner.

Laredo currently had a population of roughly 250. Ten years before, there had been twice that many people there. Times were hard on the border. The people didn't know if they were Texans or Mexicans. The politicians and lawmen bent whichever way they had to. If Mexican troops were in the area, then Laredo was a Mexican town. If a Texas Ranger came into town, then Laredo was 100% Texan. John had never been there but he had heard the men on the ranch talk about how wild it had become. He wanted to see for himself what Laredo was like.

Juan Martinez was walking home, passing familiar houses he'd seen his entire life. He was waving to neighbors as he strolled home. He had gone into Laredo to sell a few young goats. It had been a good year. Most of his nanny goats had produced twins and he'd only lost a few to predators. He was able to pay off his grocery bill with the money he made. It didn't leave him anything but in another few weeks, he'd sell a few more kids. Besides the goats, Juan had two milk cows, both with half-grown calves that would sell in the summer.

He was whistling to himself as he made his way home. He felt on top of the world. He and Maria had four children—two boys and two girls—with another little one on the way. The two oldest were now able to help with chores around the place, so life was getting better with each season. They made a living from about ten acres that had been in his family for generations. They were living in the house he'd been raised in.

Juan planned to stop and talk with his friend Pablo. They had known each other all their lives. Pablo, too, was living in the place where he had been raised. It was not as big as Juan's place. He had only about three acres. Pablo was coming to meet his friend when he heard Juan's oldest son Jessie yelling for him. Juan hurried toward his son. Something was wrong.

"They are back! They are back! Hurry Papa, they are back!"

Juan and Pablo knew what he was talking about. So did all the neighbors who were alerted by the shouting. Juan hurried home, followed by several neighbors. As he neared his house he could see Maria sitting in the front yard, crying as she held their youngest child.

"They took everything this time," she cried. "I couldn't stop them."

The yard was filling with neighbors who had seen it happening. Juan knew they could do nothing but watch. Everyone was talking at once, telling him about the raid. The man who lived nearest them had mounted his old gray horse and trotted into town to report it to the Sheriff. They all knew it would do no good but it had to be reported. The Sheriff would do what he always did—wait a few hours, then send one of his deputies out to look around and ask a few questions. It would all be forgotten in a few days. Laredo had no law, just a few lazy lawmen.

It was the Mexican soldiers who had taken his goats and his four head of cattle. All the Martinez family had now was a yard full of chickens. The Mexican soldiers were on patrol in the area and had camped on the south side of the Rio Grande, which was considered Mexican territory. There were about fifty of them. They patrolled the Rio Grande Valley from Brownsville to Laredo, which meant every few months they would be in the area. When they were around, nothing was safe from their looting. About six of them had ridden in to take the livestock they wanted. It was just that easy.

John saw a gathering of people as he reached the outskirts of Laredo. The road he was on passed right in front of them. He slowed up. It was obvious that something wasn't right. They were mostly speaking Spanish, so he couldn't tell what they were saying until a teenage boy who spoke English made his way over to him. He didn't get too close. John could see he was afraid of Hank. John got down from Bonny and told Hank to sit. He walked over to the boy.

"What has happened?" John asked.

"Federales," the boy said. "They took all Senor Martinez's goats and cows."

"Why?" John asked.

"That is what they do. They usually only take a few but today they take them all," the boy explained.

"In broad daylight? How can they do that?" John asked.

The boy just shrugged his shoulders.

"What about the law?"

"They are the law."

John watched the man in the yard holding his family as they grieved together. John knew he had to do something. It was not his business but he knew his father would not turn his back on these poor people. So rather than head into Laredo, he and Hank followed the trail of the goat thieves. If he was going to take a wife and become the man he should be, he knew he had to do something. That is what his father would do. His father would not leave these people without doing something. He could hear an indelible voice in his head. *This is what the Delaneys do.*

The trail lead to a shallow crossing of the river. He saw where it went in and then out the other side. He decided to cross as he realized that now he was not only beyond King's land, he was also in another country. He quickly found where the soldiers were camped. He didn't let them see him. He watched them a while, then turned around and went into Laredo.

John bought supplies, then found a saloon. Saloons were the best places to hear gossip. It didn't matter what town it was, a saloon was where you found out about all local events. It didn't take long for him to learn what had happened. While he was at the bar, he discovered that Laredo had a sheriff named Sampson and two deputies, one Hispanic and one Anglo. The sheriff rarely left his office except around election time. Sampson would ride around passing out money to ensure he won the election. If any crime took place, and plenty did, he would send one of the deputies out to make a report. Whatever that meant. John decided he wanted to meet this sheriff. He went to Sampson's office, which was next door to the jail. He didn't like the jail. It smelled bad, and it was full.

John knocked on the door. He was invited in by a gentleman with a deep voice. John opened the door and saw a skinny little man dressed in a fine suit sitting at a big desk.

"I'm looking for Sheriff Sampson," John said.

"I'm Sheriff Sampson," the little man with a big voice said. "May I help you?"

"Yes, you may. Earlier today I came upon a crime. I arrived right after it happened," John reported.

John could tell the sheriff did not want to hear about this. He had deputies who could handle such things. But they were both out doing something else. One was getting the sheriff's supper and the other was checking into a knife fight that had taken place behind a cantina on the south side of town.

"Some men stole cattle and goats from a family that lives on the northeast road coming into Laredo," John told him.

"Yes, I know about that. We have a report," the sheriff said.

Then he went back to looking at some papers on his desk. He obviously wanted John to leave.

"I followed the trail of the thieves."

John was using language that should have aroused any lawman to action. But it didn't.

"I found out where they are. If you go there you will see for yourself. You can arrest them and restore the property to the rightful owners," John said.

"So where are they?" Sampson asked, with little interest.

The door opened and a big man carrying a tray of food came in.

"Deputy Miller, I'd like you to meet... what did you say your name was young man?"

"John Delaney."

"Deputy Miller, if you would get out the Martinez file, John Delaney wants to add some information to it. Take Mr. Delaney next door and take the information. Close the door behind you. Good day, sir."

John just stood there. The big man sat the tray down and opened the door, inviting John to leave. After a long uncomfortable pause, John turned and followed the deputy.

"If you will follow me," the deputy said.

"I already told the sheriff. I think I'm finished talking with you both," John said.

"Suit yourself," the deputy said, then turned and went back to report to the sheriff.

John had been tempted to lecture him about blindly following a man like Sampson but he figured it would do no good. He wondered what made some people follow men like that when he remembered what his father told him. He compared them to sheep. Sheep will follow a leader, even to their own slaughter. It gave him an idea.

John went to the stable where he had left Bonny and Hank. He paid the man extra and asked if he could sleep there with his animals since he'd be leaving early. It was not yet dark but John lay down and slept until about one a.m. Then he saddled Bonnie and they went back across the river. There was a homemade corral of rope confining the stolen animals. John left Hank and Bonnie near the river and slipped into the camp. It was easier than he thought it would be. The soldiers were guarding the horses on the other side of the camp but no one was watching their stolen food supply. First, he took down the rope, making it look like the goats might have done it, which he knew they could have if they'd wanted to. If a goat wants to escape, he will figure out a way to do it. Then he found the biggest billy goat and prayed he was used to people. He fed him a few of the sugar cubes he kept in his pocket for Bonnie, pitching a couple of cubes to the other goats to get their attention. The billy followed John and so did all the other goats. To his surprise, the cows came too. Not just four cows. In the dark, it looked like there were about seven or eight of them.

Crossing the river was a bit of a problem but by dawn, he had the livestock across the river and back in Texas, thanks to Hank. Somehow Hank knew how to herd goats. John was continually surprised and pleased with Hank's abilities.

Just before noon, John had the goats and the cows back in Laredo. As John and Hank drove them down the street toward the Martinez house, all the neighbors came out and followed the parade. Juan Martinez owned all the goats, two cows, and one calf. The other calf had probably been last night's supper for the Mexican troops. Several extra goats and the rest of the cows were claimed by different neighbors.

All afternoon the place was like a fiesta. The women were cooking while the men were sorting out the animals. John tried to keep up with what was going on by talking with the English-speaking boy.

John decided then that if he was going to be a ranger in South Texas, he needed to speak Spanish.

That evening, the entire community had a party at the Martinez house with plenty of food, music, dancing, tequila, and laughter. John was treated like a hero and the party lasted well into the night. John and Hank spent the night there on Martinez land, partly watching for the soldiers to return and partly because he was enjoying himself. The people were warm and friendly, even if he couldn't understand much of what they were saying.

The next morning, John was preparing to leave when he saw Sheriff Sampson and the other deputies ride up. John walked around the front of the house with Bonnie and Hank to see what was going on. Sampson was speaking to Juan in Spanish. The longer they talked, the angrier the little sheriff got. After he had what he thought was the story, he stared at John and rode over to him.

"Where did all the animals come from," Sampson demanded.

"I told you yesterday where they were," John said smiling. "I am sure it must be in your report."

"You can't just take the law into your own hands," Sampson said.

"I did what you should have done," John said.

"Who do you think you are?" he fumed, "telling me what I should do."

"I introduced myself yesterday. I work for Richard King. I keep cattle thieves and outlaws off his land," John said.

He could see the teenage boy telling Juan what was being said.

"There may be consequences for your actions. What are these people going to do if the army returns?" Sheriff Sampson asked.

"I suppose they will have to take care of it themselves since you are a lazy coward who won't do his job," John said as he nudged Bonnie closer to the sheriff.

After a minute, when the translation was completed, all the people in the yard started laughing at the sheriff.

"Who do you think you are talking to? I might just arrest you right now," Sheriff Sampson said.

"No, you won't."

"Deputy Sanchez," Sampson barked, "Arrest this man."

The deputy pulled out a pistol and pointed it at John. Before he could line up the shot, Hank leaped at him, grabbing his forearm in his mighty jaws. John hopped down from Bonnie, grabbed the skinny sheriff by the shirt, and jerked him off his horse. Hank had pulled Deputy Sanchez to the ground and was on top of him.

"Hank, stop," John said.

Hank got off the deputy but he didn't go far. The poor man's arm was bleeding badly. John had slung the sheriff to the ground and was standing over him. He reached down, took the sheriff's pistol, and pointed it at him. The man's eyes widened. John took the gun back and held it by the barrel. Then he tapped the sheriff on the forehead hard enough to make a knot.

"What are you going to do now?" asked John.

The sheriff said nothing.

"Since you don't know what to do, let me suggest you get your deputy to the doctor before he loses more blood. The last man Hank had to deal with didn't make it. We had to bury him."

John threw the gun across the road. The sheriff got up and looked around but nobody seemed to be afraid of him any longer. He helped his deputy onto his horse and they rode off.

John let him get a good head start into town. He talked with the people about how they should always keep a lookout for the soldiers and what to do if they showed up. John told them that if they stuck together, the soldiers would not bother them anymore. They had a few weapons and if they banded together and watched out for each other, they would be safe. Then he rode into town to finish his business with the sheriff.

Sheriff Sampson took his deputy to the local doctor to get patched up. Then he went to his office. When he walked through the door, he saw Deputy Miller sitting in a corner chair with his pants off. Hank was sitting next to him. Behind his desk sat John.

"Come in, Sheriff," John said.

"Now you've done it," Sampson said.

"Sit down and shut up. Here is your gun," John said and put it on the desk with the chamber emptied. "What I should do is lock you in your own jail and send for the Texas Rangers to deal with you. But I don't have time for that. So I'm going to give you one chance. Only one chance. If you don't start acting like a real lawman and protecting the people, then I'll be back. And I will not be alone."

"I'm duly elected. You have no right to…"

"Only one chance," John repeated, interrupting him.

"I hear you," Sampson snarled.

"I will be back in a few weeks. If I find things have not changed you will regret it. Do you hear me?"

Sampson nodded yes.

"Let's go, Hank."

They rode back to the Martinez house and had lunch with them. He told them through the teenage translator that if they had any trouble with the sheriff or the soldiers to come and get him. He took out a map and showed them where the ranch was.

After lunch, he left for the ranch. He would finish the southern patrol later. He wanted to see Josephina again. He wanted to gaze into those beautiful brown eyes.

CHAPTER 16

King Ranch

John and Josephina were to be married on May 23, 1860. Somehow all the wedding arrangements had been finalized in his absence. John found himself somewhat superfluous to the planning and details but he looked forward to having Josephina as his wife. John had also found a letter from Nelly waiting at the ranch. She had given birth to a little girl they named Molly Elizabeth, after his mother and his baby sister. John wept as Mac read the letter to him. His heart was so full and for the first time, he could look into the future and see himself there.

Over the next few months, John stayed close to the ranch. He and Josephina spent a lot of time talking, laughing, and holding hands. The church building was completed, though they were still without a pastor. Henrietta also had the carpenters building a small house for John and Josephina. She said the house would be kept a surprise until their wedding day. Josephina was on pins and needles wondering what her new home would look like.

A few weeks before the wedding, Mr. King sent word to the ranch that Henry Lloyd was on his way home. He had had some trouble in Liberty, a small town in Texas. He had been arrested by a local sheriff who couldn't read. The man could not fathom that a Negro—even a light-skinned Negro—could be free, regardless of what he said. King had happened to be in Houston on business when he heard about Henry Lloyd. The Liberty sheriff had sent a dispatch to every town in the area asking about a runaway slave. King knew from the description that it must be Henry Lloyd so he and a few of his friends, one being a state senator and another being a lawyer, went to Liberty. Henry Lloyd was a free man an hour after King arrived.

Three days later, Henry Lloyd came riding in on a big white horse. He was not dressed in buffalo skins now. He wore a black tailored suit and a broad-brimmed hat. John was out on patrol when he arrived but Henry Lloyd did not stay in the bunkhouse this time. Henrietta had invited him to stay in the guest room in the big house. By the time John returned to the ranch, Henry Lloyd had already prepared several meals for her.

Felix was out looking for strays when he saw John coming. He rode out to meet him. After almost a year on the ranch, Felix had learned to be a cowboy. He liked it and was good at it.

"Josephina thought you had left for good," Felix teased.

"I've only been gone a week," John said.

"That's a long time for you two love birds."

"You know I'm going to be your brother-in-law, don't you? We will be family," John said.

"Yes."

"And you know I'm older than you right?"

"So, that don't make you my boss," Felix said.

Felix loved to tease John but he also looked up to the big Irish ranger. John's heroics were rapidly becoming the stuff of legend in the area and Felix was looking forward to being known as his brother.

"Where did that big white horse come from?" John asked, pointing at Henry Lloyd's horse grazing in the front pasture.

"Napoleon rode a horse like that," Felix said.

"It's not Napoleon," John said with a smile.

"How do you know? Mr. King knows many important people," Felix said.

"Napoleon has been dead almost thirty years," John said.

"Then it must belong to Henry Lloyd Walker," Felix said, grinning at John.

John took his hat off and swatted at Felix as they laughed and kicked their horses to a gallop. John rode up to the house and saw Josephina with the children, having a tea party under a shade tree. When she saw John riding up, she ran to meet them.

"It's John, he's back," she shouted.

He got off Bonnie and ran to hug Josephina. She was even prettier than he had remembered.

"Where is he? Felix said he's staying in the big house," John said.

"He is probably in the kitchen. Henrietta has been having him cook for her every night."

They walked arm in arm back to the kitchen, a small building just beyond the back door. The room was dominated by a huge oven Henrietta had imported from France. It had an indoor water pump, a root cellar below, and shelves full of spices. Henry Lloyd was cleaning a duck when John and Josephina stepped into the room. He dropped the bird and washed his hands. Then he hugged John.

"I am so glad you came back," John said.

"Do you think I would miss the wedding of the prettiest girl in Texas?" Henry Lloyd said as Josephina blushed.

"It sure is good to see you," John said. "Did you get to see your grandson?"

"Yes, I did. He is as fine a young man as you could ever hope to see," said Henry Lloyd. "It was hard for me to leave him but I felt the Holy Spirit urging me to go west."

"I don't understand that but I'm glad you came," John said. "I'm going to go wash this trail dust off. I've been out for over a week.

You'd better get back to those ducks," he laughed.

"I must do that, and I also need to get my sauce started. The dew-berries are in season so I made a cobbler for dessert. I think you will like it," Henry Lloyd said.

John and Josephina left the kitchen holding hands. She walked him to the bunkhouse. He cleaned up and took a nap. When he woke up, he put on his best clothes. He wanted to look nice tonight.

Henrietta met him at the front door.

"Now don't you look handsome?" she said. "If I weren't already married, I'd see to it that you were courting me instead of Josephina."

John heard Josephina giggling from behind the door. She stepped out and John saw she was also dressed in her best. She wore a new dress John had not seen before. Her hair was different and she was wearing some of Henrietta's perfume. John wanted to take her in his arms and never let her go. But he just smiled when he saw her.

"I was hoping to be invited to dinner. Henry Lloyd said he made a cobbler," John said.

"I bless the day you brought that wonderful man here," Henrietta said. "He has prepared some of the finest meals I've ever had. Since I will not be doing as much work around here I'm so glad he is back."

The child in Henrietta's belly was becoming more apparent with every passing day.

"I told you he could cook. I saw that right off," John said.

John and Josephina sat next to each other on the sofa. She looked and smelled wonderful. They didn't talk. They just looked at each other and smiled. They knew they were in love. It was the first time for them both so maybe they shouldn't have been so sure but they were. A few minutes later they could hear Henry Lloyd's laugh as he and Henrietta came into the parlor.

"Don't they make a handsome couple?" Henry Lloyd asked Henrietta.

"Yes, they certainly do. I thought he would never get up the nerve to court her," she said. "He is a brave man when dealing with outlaws but rather timid when it comes to the ladies."

John blushed.

"Well, he sure picked a pretty one," Henry Lloyd said.

He was holding a bottle of red wine.

"Let me suggest this as a before dinner drink. It is light on the palate and it should be the perfect prelude to the duck."

As the conversation waned, John's attention drifted. He had been back to the Martinez family home earlier in the week and he was thinking about them. Their baby would arrive any day now. The sheriff had left them alone so far but the rumor was that he had reverted to his old ways. The only difference was that he had now hired a couple of deputies. Both were more prepared to tangle with the citizens than the two he currently had. Smitty was a big man he had hired more as a bodyguard than as a lawman. He went with the sheriff everywhere he went. Lonny claimed to be a gunfighter but nobody had ever heard of him.

The Mexican Army was spending most of its time in Brownsville and had not been back. The neighbors all around the Martinez house had taken John's advice and were prepared to defend one another if needed. John was proud of them. As of yet, he had not shared this with anyone at the ranch.

"Shall we go into the dining room now?" Henrietta suggested, interrupting his reverie.

Mac was waiting for them. He had been in the kitchen helping Henry Lloyd. Dinner was served on fine china. They continued talking as they ate the duck with orange sauce and sweet potatoes. They had coffee with Henry Lloyd's sumptuous cobbler. After dinner, they went out to the porch where the conversation turned to the scriptures. Both Henrietta and Henry Lloyd were eloquent on the subject. Mac,

Josephina, and John listened. John was as happy as he had ever been, sitting with his girl, listening to his friend teach them things he knew nothing about.

In the course of the conversation, John learned that the first service in the new church was scheduled to coincide with Mr. King's return in a few weeks. Henry Lloyd was going to be the preacher. They had yet to determine what brand of church it would be. Henrietta was the daughter of a Presbyterian minister and Henry Lloyd was an ordained Methodist. Most of the ranch hands were Catholic. This was worrying Henrietta as she tried to figure out the name of her church. Henry Lloyd didn't seem to care what it was called. She, however, was convinced it needed a name before they held their first service.

"I've been thinking about tomorrow's menu," she said as the night drew to a close.

"I was thinking of riding out with John tomorrow. We have some things to talk about if you don't mind, Mrs. King," Henry Lloyd said. "But before we leave, John and I will butcher a couple of hogs and let them smoke for a few days. When we get back I'll show you how they cure hams in Spain. They have some of the finest ham you have ever tasted there, and if I do say so myself, I've perfected the art."

Early the next day, John, Aldo, and Henry Lloyd went to work on the hogs. Aldo was to be in charge of the smokehouse while they were away, so he received extra training from the preacher/chef. It was late in the day before they were ready to leave. John sat on the porch with Josephina while Henry Lloyd read his Bible. Both were doing what they loved, so time got away from them and they didn't leave until the next morning.

"I'd like for you to go with me to Laredo," John said as they rode off.

"Why?" his friend asked.

John told him the story. He didn't leave out anything. He also told him why he wanted to go back. He wanted to talk with the sheriff again. Henry Lloyd listened carefully, occasionally interrupting for clarification.

"Let me ask you, why do you want to go back? It's not your business."

"That's a good question. I asked myself that. I also ask myself what my father would do. I find myself asking that question more often as I get older. Let me tell you something else I ask. I ask myself what Henry Lloyd would do."

"What would your father do?" Henry Lloyd asked.

"He did not like people being mistreated. We spent a lot of time fighting for those who couldn't fight for themselves," John said thoughtfully.

"And what do you think I would do?" Henry Lloyd asked.

"I guess I'll find out," John said.

"Then I'll tell you. It's a noble thing you did. I'm proud of you. I'm not quite sure confronting the sheriff is wise. Let me pray about it. However, I'd love to meet the Martinez family."

"They don't speak English," John said. "I'm learning Spanish but I'm not very good at it yet."

The big preacher just smiled. They made camp early that night by a small creek. Henry Lloyd rigged up a fishing line and caught and cooked a couple of fish for dinner. The two men talked most of the night about the west.

"Why do you want to go all the way to California?" John asked.

"It's a free state."

"You are free here," John said.

"Not completely. You see, it's not easy for a black man in a slave state. My skin color doesn't bother you but most white men don't look at it that way. I could tell from reading the papers in New Orleans there is a change in the air. This nation is pulling apart. I don't want to be on the wrong side when it does."

"I don't understand what you are talking about," John said.

"I know you don't. I've seen enough ugliness in my life to not want to be in it anymore. California will not be perfect but I think it will be better for me. The Lord has me traveling from place to place preaching. I could never do that in Texas."

"What do you mean when you say the country is pulling apart?" John asked.

"You see, there are really two very different economies in America. The one in the North depends on skilled workers. In the South what they need are people who can pick cotton or tobacco, so they need slaves. If they had to pay white men to do this work, they wouldn't be able to make a profit. At least that is what they say. I'm not sure that's right but it doesn't matter. It is what they think. For the last few years, nothing the government has tried to do has solved the problem. I'm afraid there is going to be trouble. I need to be as far away from it as I can. My son and daughter-in-law are going north. I was thinking about going with them but after I prayed about it I think the west is where God can use me best."

This conversation was troubling for John. He let it die without further questions, though he had plenty of them. His sister was up north. He hoped Henry Lloyd was wrong. They went to sleep early that night and John had strange dreams that made him uncomfortable. In his dreams, he was riding by himself and his saddle horn came off. Then the stirrups fell off. He got off Bonnie and his entire saddle fell apart. Then he looked around and limbs were falling off trees. It didn't matter where he looked, things were coming apart. He woke up before dawn, well ahead of Henry Lloyd, and he started the fire.

Later in the day, it rained. It wasn't a hard, windy Texas storm, just a steady rain, so they kept moving. It stopped raining and started getting hot. In South Texas, it could get hot in a hurry, even in early

May, and it did. As they approached Laredo, Henry Lloyd opened his heart to John.

"I've been thinking and praying about you visiting the sheriff and I don't think it is wise. Your behavior thus far has been righteous but you don't need to go looking for trouble. Trouble has its own legs and it will find you soon enough. You are a grown man and you can do as you like but I suggest you not go stir up a hornet's nest."

John nodded and said nothing. It was probably good advice. His father probably would have said something similar.

"But if you decide to go, I'll be right there with you," his friend said.

John felt a lump in his throat. Henry Lloyd would stand with him. For a black man in a southern state to volunteer to confront authority for a friend was not a small thing.

"Thank you," John managed to say, his voice almost cracking with emotion.

They would not make it to Laredo before dark so they decided to pitch camp. They had to look hard for a spot that wasn't covered in cactus. Henry Lloyd rode off looking for game while John made camp. He was still troubled about the conversation of the previous night. Henry Lloyd knew it. He seemed to know more than he should and this also troubled John. How could the man know so many things? John heard a gunshot, which meant they would be having fresh meat. Then he heard another. After a couple of more, John was about to saddle up and see if Henry Lloyd needed help. It was not like him to miss. It wasn't long before his friend returned with four rattlesnakes hanging from his saddle.

"Have you ever eaten rattlesnake?" Henry Lloyd asked.

John just looked puzzled. His friend was laughing.

"Well, then, tonight will be a first," he said.

He roasted the snakes and John was intrigued. The meat reminded him of poultry, though there was something wild about it. The conversation that night was light and easy as they talked about adventures they had had and places they had been. By noon the following day, they were at the Martinez house. Maria had recently given birth to a healthy girl baby. Juan wasn't there. He was helping a neighbor build a fence. One of the children ran to get him while Henry Lloyd and Maria conversed in Spanish. At first, John was amazed that his friend spoke Spanish but when he thought more about it, he decided he would have been surprised if he didn't.

Juan arrived a short time later. He was glad to see John, though at first, he was afraid of Henry Lloyd. John figured he had never seen a man so big and powerful. John could tell that Juan had something on his mind. He would eventually come out with it. John was learning that this culture approached things differently. It took these people time to get to the point. They would just have to wait until Juan was ready to share with them.

It was after dinner before he said what he wanted to say. Henry Lloyd translated. He shared that the soldiers were back. The first thing their captain had done was go straight to the sheriff and lodge a complaint about the livestock. He'd thought they escaped but he later learned from talk in town that they had been stolen from his camp.

He could overlook that this once but if the sheriff couldn't control his citizens, his men would need to step in. It was widely known that the sheriff was on the payroll of the Mexican army and this Mexican captain expected a better return on his investment.

John looked at Henry Lloyd. John didn't want to confront the sheriff but he might have to. He was not going to let the authorities abuse these people. It reminded him of how the English had ruined his family.

"Let's go talk a walk," Henry Lloyd said.

The three men and the big blond dog walked through the streets of Laredo talking.

"Henry Lloyd, I want you to head back in the morning. Hank and I can handle this," John said.

"I know you can," Henry Lloyd said.

"You don't need to get involved in this," John said, remembering how quickly they had jailed Henry Lloyd in Liberty for no reason. Given a reason, John was certain things would not go well for his friend.

Ignoring what John said, Henry Lloyd thought for a moment.

"It seems like we have a few choices here. We wait for the sheriff to do what he is going to do, then we react to that. At that point, we do not choose, he does. Or we can take some action now and perhaps we can get ahead of this."

"What are you thinking?" John asked.

The conversation went slowly because Henry Lloyd was translating for Juan.

"First we need to decide if we would rather deal with the sheriff or the soldiers," Henry Lloyd said.

"There are only four lawmen, so that would be my choice," John said.

Juan agreed with him.

"Don't be persuaded by numbers. The sheriff might be more evil than the soldiers. Here are our options as I see it. One is to keep the Mexicans on the south side of the border. There are a couple of things we can do to accomplish that. The other option would be to take the sheriff and his men out of the picture. And there are a couple of ways to do that."

John was once again amazed. Henry Lloyd was no longer a preacher or a chef or a buffalo hunter. He was a general, planning a strategy to win a battle.

"Let's talk through all these options," John said.

"We should go back to Juan's house. I don't think us hanging around here in the dark is the best idea," Henry Lloyd suggested.

They went back to Juan's house and sat in chairs on the front lawn. They talked strategies late into the night, finally settling on a plan. After going through it a few times, John was convinced it could work. The plan was simple and safe yet brilliant if it worked. If it went wrong, then people could get hurt. He knew every battle plan had a degree of risk. This plan hinged on Juan's ability to act. Juan was sure he could sell it. John hoped he was right. If he was successful, the Mexican Army would pack up and leave. If they didn't buy his act then he was on his own, in the middle of a hornet's nest.

Juan was dispatched to recruit two more men they could depend on. He did not want family men because this could be dangerous. The two he selected were Beto and Alfredo. Beto was a young man without a family. He was bold and courageous and Juan knew he could count on him. The other fellow was older. His family was gone. He was a loyal friend and Juan knew him to be a man you could trust. After talking with them both, Henry Lloyd was happy with Juan's selection.

They went over the plan several more times to make sure everyone was on board, then they went to bed early. It would be a big day tomorrow.

CHAPTER 17

South of the Border

A few hours before dawn, five riders and a big dog left Laredo. The entire village watched them head northwest, following the Rio Grande. Just before noon, they crossed into Mexico and headed south. It took them most of the day to reach their destination. They were now south of the soldiers and far enough away that military scouting parties would not find them. While they made camp, John and Hank set out on foot toward the soldiers' encampment.

It was late when they arrived. The camp was asleep and they eluded the guards easily. John was able to find what he needed and to slip out without anyone ever knowing he was there. It took him the rest of the night and part of the next morning to walk back to camp.

He now had a private's uniform with all the accoutrements, including a rifle, a sword, a Mexican saddle, a bedroll, and one of the leather pouches they all carried for their ammunition. Juan put on the uniform. He looked the part. Henry Lloyd had been working with him all day rehearsing his assignment. He had also created a document that could pass for military orders.

He rehearsed a few more times in full uniform for John to see. John thought it might just work. When Henry Lloyd thought he was ready, Juan mounted one of their horses with the military saddle John had stolen and rode toward the Mexican army's camp. The rest of them took their places.

Beto was a young man but he was tall and sturdy. He was bright so he had learned fast. Henry Lloyd was sure he would do fine. His job was to circle to the east and get as near as he could to the camp without being seen. If things went as planned, he would have little to do. If things didn't go well, he was going to be busy. He had several guns and most of the ammunition. His job would be to impersonate a band of fighters.

Alfredo was another neighbor, a man whose wife had died a few years before. His children were all grown. He volunteered for the adventure because he had no real responsibilities and he had no love for the Mexican army. He had been fifteen years old in 1835 when he was forced into duty as a foot soldier under General Antonio Lopez de Santa Anna, who was moving his army north toward San Antonio. Along the way, Santa Anna conscripted every able-bodied young man he could find. Alfredo was assigned to General Martin Perfecto de Cos. He saw the slaughter of Fannin's men in Goliad. Later that month, they arrived in San Antonio. He was in the third wave of soldiers to storm the northwest wall of the Alamo. After that, General Cos took his men east, following Sam Houston. They joined up with Santa Anna's army on a swampy peninsula on the Buffalo Bayou known as San Jacinto. By then, just about every solder he knew was ready to quit. Being driven as they were without proper rations or supplies had defeated the army. The Texans were just there to finish them off.

Alfredo managed to avoid getting killed or captured. He and a few others walked south. He got as far as Laredo and met his wife, settled down, and raised a family. Now, over thirty years later, he found himself once again entangled with the Mexican army.

He and Henry Lloyd would double back to the Texas side of the river and be ready to duplicate Beto's mission from that point. John and Hank would come in from the west. The only difference was that John had to get close enough to see what was happening. He would start the firing if it was needed. It was almost dark when Juan rode into camp.

"I have orders for your captain from General Ignacio Seguin Zaragoza," Juan said to the sergeant who met him.

Juan was wearing the private's uniform, so addressing a sergeant in manner was a bold move.

"Let me look at what you have," the sergeant said.

"My orders are to hand-deliver them to the captain," Juan said, without looking at the sergeant.

He stayed on his horse, looking for the biggest tent, then kicked his horse in that direction.

"Please tell him I have his orders."

His horse walked past the sergeant who sent another soldier running to get the captain. Juan pulled his horse to a halt outside the tent and waited. He didn't look around. He just fixed his eyes on the tent.

John could see it all. Henry Lloyd was right. He had said when Juan arrived all the commotion would make it easier for John. The two guards watching the camp where John came in were both occupied with an unknown private outside their captain's tent. John and Hank entered the corral where their horses were and walked among them without being seen. Most of the camp was watching too, waiting for the captain to emerge from his tent.

To prove his importance, the man kept Juan waiting as he finished his meal. When he was ready, he marched from his tent, then stuck out his hand for the orders. Juan dismounted and reached in his bag to pull out the papers, rolled and tied with a ribbon. He saluted the captain as Henry Lloyd had instructed, then bowed his head and held out the papers.

From where John sat it all seemed to be going according to plan.

"What do we have here?" Captain Garza asked.

"I have no idea, sir. The General told me to deliver six of these to various selected troops. You are my last. When I finish here, I am to hurry back to Monterrey. The General will need every man he has," Juan said.

Captain Garza opened the orders and read them. He then motioned for his officers to return to his tent.

"With your permission, sir, I'd like to be on my way," Juan said.

"Wait right here," said Garza.

This was the moment of truth. If Juan was a good enough actor and Henry Lloyd's forgery was believable, then they might succeed. Juan stood there a few minutes then walked over and started talking with a few soldiers. He told them that Benito Juarez's army was in the mountains, threatening to take the city, and that General Zaragoza was not going to leave. General Zaragoza was prepared to defend it to the death. As this might be the definitive battle, he wanted to be there.

This kind of talk usually excited soldiers. What he said spread throughout the camp within minutes. By the time the captain emerged from his tent, there was no need to tell the troops what was up. As the officers were getting the men in line to hear from their leader, Juan got back on his horse. A spontaneous chant rose from the troops. "Viva la Mexico! Viva la Mexico!"

"Gentlemen," Captain Garza started, "our notoriety as an exemplary fighting force has reached as far north as Monterrey. General Ignacio Seguin Zaragoza has requested we join him in the most noble cause for any soldier: the defense of our homeland. We have been selected to be aligned with his most trusted troops."

The men let out a huge cheer and the chant started again.

"Soldier," Captain Garza shouted at Juan.

Juan turned his horse and stepped down.

"I have a message for you to get to the General. Wait here."

The captain turned and went back into his tent. The soldiers were now breaking ranks as they continued to celebrate. A few minutes later, the captain came out with a note, rolled up and tied with the same ribbon.

"Please deliver this to General Zaragoza for me. You are welcome to stay the night in camp if you and your horse need rest.

"Thank you, sir but I must go. All I ask is provisions for my horse and myself for my journey. I must travel swiftly," Juan said.

"What is your name, soldier?" the captain asked.

"Juan Miguel Martinez," Juan said. He used his own name since the captain would never know the difference. "I am from Veracruz."

The captain and Juan chatted about Veracruz. Juan, of course, had never been there. A few minutes later, the sergeant returned with oats for his horse and enough food and water for several days. As Juan saluted Captain Garza and rode off, John and Hank hurried back to their horses.

They made their way back across the Rio Grande into Texas that night. The Mexican Army was on the move first thing the following morning. Beto stayed to watch them leave, then he too headed back across the Rio Grande. Later that day, John, Henry Lloyd, and Hank were making preparations to return to the ranch when the sheriff and his two new deputies rode up. Laredo was not a big town and word had gotten out that John was back. The sheriff had a score to settle. He had lost a degree of respect during their last encounter and he was ready to reclaim his rightful place as the sole authority for the town.

Henry Lloyd saw them coming and he slipped off without being seen. He doubled back around behind them. Only John and Juan were visible in front of the house. Hank crouched at John's feet, ready to spring as necessary.

"What business do you have here?" Sampson said.

His deputies were ready to draw their guns and fire if they saw the dog move.

"Sit, Hank," John said. "I've come to see their new baby," he continued.

"What if I say you are a liar," Sampson said. "I happen to know you have been here for several days."

"That doesn't make me a liar. I like to look at babies a long time," John said as he sized up the two new deputies.

"Where have you been for the past few days?" Sampson asked.

"Have you been watching me?" John inquired.

"I watch many things. What if I have?" the man said.

"Then I'd say you didn't have much to do and maybe they are paying you too much," John taunted him.

"Arrest him," Sampson said as he pulled out his gun.

A second or two later, a rock hit the rump of his horse. The horse reared up and the sheriff took a hard fall on his back. The other two horses, each with a deputy aboard, were bucking too.

"Go, Hank," John said as he grabbed the bridle of one of the horses.

The horse jerked back as the rider tumbled off the left side. Hank landed in the lap of the other man—the big one. They both came off the horse. John picked up the sheriff and tossed him on top of the deputy on the ground.

"That's enough Hank," John said before Hank had time to tear the big man into pieces.

Henry Lloyd was there now and he picked the big fellow up and sat him down by the other two. Henry Lloyd then took all their weapons, sidearms, and a knife the big man had in his boot.

"I was hoping not to have to deal with you," John said. "You leave me no other option. We are going to have a trial."

John looked around to see most of the neighbors were in their front yards watching.

"Juan, would you please bring me some rope?"

John tied the three men up to a tree in front of the house. After they were secured, he told Hank to watch them. He asked Henry Lloyd to tell the people in Spanish that Sheriff Sampson would undergo trial in a few hours. Anyone with a grievance was asked to be there.

"Who do you…?" was all Sampson could get out before Hank stood, showed his teeth, and growled. The sheriff said nothing more.

John and Henry Lloyd rode into town. They asked around until they found the mayor. Laredo had no judge. Henry Lloyd escorted the man back to the Martinez place while John went to the sheriff's office. He found the other two deputies cowering there. Neither wanted to tangle with John so they left their weapons behind and followed him obediently to the Martinez house. By the time they got back, the yard was full of people.

"Henry Lloyd. would you mind asking the ladies to fix us all a meal? I think we should celebrate. No drinking until after the trial, though. Everyone is invited."

John spoke the last few words in Spanish.

Henry Lloyd laughed out loud.

"Very good," the preacher said in English and then again in Spanish.

As the food was being prepared, John divided the group of plaintiffs into two groups: those the sheriff had harmed directly and those he had refused to help when they needed him. Both groups were well represented. The numbers grew throughout the day as word got out about the trial. John and Henry Lloyd and the mayor went from person to person, listening to each complaint.

After dinner, John decided the trial crowd had grown too large for Juan's house. They loaded the prisoners onto a wagon, then drove into town. The people followed. Juan John and Henry Lloyd were at the end of the parade, riding their horses. They planned to leave as soon as justice was done. John was eager to get back to Josephina and Henry Lloyd knew Henrietta was ready for him to return to her kitchen.

The mayor said they would set up the court on a plot of land that would someday be the courthouse. The mayor would serve as judge and John would represent the people. When everything was in place, the mayor/judge called the court to order.

"Mr. Delaney, we will hear from the people directly. But I would like to hear your opening statement," he said.

The man seemed familiar with proper court procedure and protocol.

"All I have to say is these people have been putting up with poor service from Sheriff Sampson for a long time. It is time that it should stop," John said.

"You are not even a citizen here," Sampson interrupted. "When I get free from these bonds, I'll show you who is in charge."

"May I?" John asked the mayor.

The man nodded his approval. John pulled out a big knife and walked over to Sampson, whose eyes widened.

"You can't..." he sputtered.

John leaned down and cut the ropes that bound the sheriff's hands.

"Now you are free," John said as he stood over the man.

When Sampson said nothing, the judge continued.

"You may continue, Mr. Delaney. Mr. Sampson, you will not speak until I ask you to. Is that clear?"

"You old swindler," Sampson said to the mayor. "I'll tell everyone how you acquired that land down by the river."

John slapped Sampson hard across the face.

"The judge said to hold your tongue. Every time you speak out of turn the blows will get harder."

The crowd laughed. Sampson was seething but he was also afraid.

"That's all I have. I yield to the people," John said.

"Mr. Sampson, we will hear from you now," the mayor said.

"I would appreciate it if you addressed me as Sheriff Sampson," the man said, in a vain attempt to regain his dignity. "I first met this man," he pointed at John, "when he came to my office with a complaint. Upon investigation, I discovered he was a liar and a thief. He went into Mexico and stole property from the Mexican army. I was going to arrest him when he and that beast of his assaulted me and my deputy. I couldn't arrest him then because I had to get medical assistance for my deputy."

A new wave of laughter broke out among the crowd, some of whom had seen what happened and the rest who had heard the story many times.

"Please be quiet everybody. You may continue, Sheriff Sampson."

"We are fortunate that I have maintained a good relationship with our neighbors to the south," the sheriff continued. "If not, we might have suffered an international incident."

"You mean you take their money!" shouted someone from the crowd, triggering another round of laughter.

This was not going well for the sheriff. After the laughter stopped, the judge nodded for him to continue.

"I received word that Delaney had returned to Laredo just the other day. I went to arrest him and learned that he was gone. Upon further investigation, I discovered he had again crossed into Mexico. I was investigating this when once again, he assaulted me, falsely imprisoning me and my deputies, and creating this sham you are calling a trial, with no legal authority."

"Are you finished?" the mayor asked.

"Yes."

"Mr. Delaney, you may call your first witness."

Since he didn't know all their names, John pointed to each in turn. As they told their stories of abuse by the sheriff and his men, John stayed close, in case Sampson needed to be subdued. Some testimonies were in Spanish and some were in English. The mayor seemed to understand them all. The testimonies took several hours, during which a clearly frightened Sampson and his men remained quiet. When everyone was seated, John stood up.

"Now I'd like to question the sheriff myself."

John took him by the arm and forcefully marched him in front of the crowd to a chair from the saloon.

"How do you answer these complaints?"

"A pack of lies," Sampson said.

John slapped him across the face again.

"I will not have you slander all these good people again, Sampson. I was hoping you might apologize for your behavior. Now I'll ask the question one more time. What do you have to say to your accusers—all of them citizens you are pledged to protect?"

"I am doing my job the best I can. If some of these people don't like it, maybe it's because they prefer a lawless town where they can do as they please. I can't answer for what every criminal says about me," Sampson sneered.

"So you say all of the people here are criminals?"

"As a matter of fact, yes. Everybody participating in this sham trial today is a criminal. Especially you."

He pointed at the mayor. John slapped him again. Blood came from his lower lip.

"You will show some respect for this court," John said as the people cheered. "I've given you multiple opportunities to ask forgiveness and my patience is at an end. I'll ask one more time."

"I have said what I have to say," mumbled Sampson. His lip was swelling and so was his left eye.

John jerked him up and marched him back to his seat. Then he spoke quietly to the mayor.

"You may do what you wish with this man. I suggest you lock him up and send for some real lawmen. Or you could just escort him out of town and forbid his return. My friend and I are leaving. Good luck with whatever you decide."

John motioned for Henry Lloyd and as they walked to their horses, John grabbed Sampson by the collar and lifted him off the ground.

"I don't know what these people will do with you but it is better than what I would choose. If I ever hear anything about you again from these fine citizens, I will take it personally."

He dropped the sheriff and his legs didn't hold him. The man crumpled to the ground. John had a few final words to the deputies of the disgraced Sampson.

"You should probably try to get out of town while you still can. I don't care where you go."

The crowd erupted in thunderous applause as the deputies took John's advice. John, Henry Lloyd, and Hank headed northeast. Later, word reached the ranch that the sheriff had fled. Some thought he went north toward Austin but he was not seen in Laredo again.

King Ranch

After the successful conclusion to the Laredo business, both John and Henry Lloyd were ready to be home. John had missed Josephina and he was longing for the day when she would be his wife at last. Henry Lloyd knew his time on the ranch was growing short and there was much he wanted to accomplish before his departure.

As they made their way north, they saw a familiar figure come over a ridge. Felix had been riding the southern part of the ranch, hoping to find them before they arrived. John could tell something was wrong.

"What is it?" he asked. "Is it Josephina? Is she safe?"

"Yes. She is fine. She misses you but she is fine," Felix answered.

"What has happened?" demanded John.

"Everything. I don't know how to say this."

Felix looked at Henry Lloyd.

"It's all right, son," Henry Lloyd said. "You can tell us. Don't hold back."

Felix was finally able to get the story out. Mr. King had arrived a few days prior and was upset that Henry Lloyd had been staying in the house. He was afraid his partners in the cotton business would not approve. He had just signed a large contract to ship cotton to Mexico and other ports on his steamers. The idea of a Negro living in a white man's home, even a free Negro, was taboo. Henrietta was furious with her husband over this but King didn't care what she thought. He was not budging on the issue. He said Henry Lloyd Walker was welcome to stay in the bunkhouse but he would not be welcome in their guest room. He ordered Henry Lloyd's belongings removed from the house.

All of this was happening just days before the first church service was to take place. When Henrietta informed her husband that she had asked Henry Lloyd to preach and she was not going to change, King sent for a Presbyterian minister, hoping that would appease her. It did not. The household was suddenly an armed camp and the Kings were not speaking to each other.

Henry Lloyd could see the fury on his young friend's face but he had dealt with such things many times before.

"John," he said, "I will ride on ahead and speak with the Kings. Please do not say anything to them on my behalf. I know you will want to defend me but please do not. The Lord and I will handle this. Just go to the bunkhouse, get cleaned up, and go see Josephina. Stay clear of the Kings for now. Will you do this for me?"

"I will not stand for anybody mistreating you. You have done nothing but be kind to everyone. You do not deserve this," John said bitterly.

"John, I know what you are saying. I love you for it. But do not, I repeat, do not speak to them for now. Can you please do that for me?"

"Yes," John said but he was not happy.

"Good. Now you and Felix take your time getting to the ranch. I need some time to pray, then I need to take care of this."

The big white horse galloped off toward the ranch. John said nothing to Felix. He had been so eager to get home. Now he didn't even want to see the ranch. But he did want to see Josephina. Maybe they should run off together and get married. Maybe it was time for him to move on. He did know that he would not go without her.

Henry Lloyd rode up to the big house, dusted himself off, and knocked on the front door. He asked to speak with Mr. King. While he waited, Josephina came to the door.

"Where is John?" she asked.

She looked worried.

"He will be here soon. He is fine. We hurried back because he missed you," Henry Lloyd said, with a gentle smile.

She looked off into the horizon, a frown creasing her forehead. When Richard King walked into the foyer, she vanished into the parlor.

"May I speak with you, sir?" Henry Lloyd asked.

"Yes, of course."

"Mr. King, I have something I must say. I need to ask for your forgiveness. You have been exceptionally kind to me. You arranged for me to get to see my grandson. Then, when I was in trouble, you stopped what you were doing and interceded on my behalf. You have been a good friend to me and I overstepped the courtesy you have shown me by staying in your house while you were gone."

"It is not your fault. You were invited by my wife," King said.

"Sir, if I may say so, it was I who should have had the proper manners to turn down her offer. She was simply being kind. I should have realized the position it put you in. She may not have understood at the time but I surely should have known. Please forgive me."

King put his hand on Henry Lloyd's shoulder and nodded.

"And what I hate most is that this has created an uncomfortable situation in your home," Henry Lloyd continued.

"She will get over it. We are both headstrong," King replied.

"Can you forgive me?" Henry Lloyd asked.

"Yes, of course," said King.

"Thank you. Now I would like to propose a solution to our dilemma."

King seemed puzzled.

"With your permission, I'd like to tell Mrs. King that you have invited me to stay in the guest room—and that I declined because I would rather stay in the bunkhouse. And if you make such a generous offer now, it will not be a lie."

"I have never been able to fool this woman," King said with a smile.

"That is the beauty of this. We are not deceiving her. You are no longer in trouble with her and I can spend more time with John before I leave," Henry Lloyd said.

"Nobody is asking you to leave. You may stay on the ranch as long as you like," King said.

"I understand, and I appreciate your hospitality but I feel the Lord leading me out west. I'd like to stay until John gets married, if I may. Now, with your permission, I'd like to go talk with Mrs. King before John gets home."

"Wait a minute. Aren't you forgetting something?" King asked.

"I beg your pardon?"

"Henry Lloyd, would you be a guest in our house for the next few days?" King asked with a grin.

"I would love to but I would rather sleep in the bunkhouse if it's all right with you, sir."

The two men laughed and shook hands again. Henry Lloyd turned and walked back to the big house. Mr. King walked on to the church.

"Mrs. King," Henry Lloyd said as they sat on the front porch. "Mr. King has invited me to stay in your guest room."

"No, he hasn't. He has moved your things out and I'm furious at him," she said.

"After we talked, Mr. King asked me to stay in the guest room. And as much as I would like that, I have decided to stay in the bunkhouse with John," he said.

Henrietta fixed him with a skeptical gaze. She did not wish to accuse a man of God of a falsehood but it was not like her husband to back down.

"You see, there are not many days left before the wedding. I'd like to spend time with John talking about what makes a good marriage work. And I suspect you will be talking with Josephina about how to be a godly wife."

"That is wise but let's get back to the subject of your staying in the bunkhouse."

"In the morning after we have had breakfast, I'd like to go over some scriptures with you that we can ensure they both understand. I'm afraid they are both somewhat lacking in their spiritual training but God will help us," Henry Lloyd said, smoothly changing the subject.

"Yes, He will," she agreed.

Henry Lloyd rose and excused himself. He wanted to leave while she was still pondering teaching rather than where he would be sleeping.

He was sitting on a bench in front of the bunkhouse reading his Bible when John and Felix arrived. He looked up and smiled.

"I think everything is going to be fine now."

"I'm not happy about this. This was no way to treat you," John said.

He was still angry with his employer.

"Sit down and I will tell you a story," Henry Lloyd said.

Felix took the horses and John sat on the bench beside his friend, glaring up at the big house. Before Henry Lloyd could begin, he saw Josephina heading their way.

"I suppose the story can wait," Henry Lloyd said, more to himself than to John.

The two young people hugged, looked deep into each others' eyes, and for the first time, John kissed Josephina. First, he kissed her on the forehead, then when she smiled, he kissed her on the mouth. She did not pull away from him. The kiss lasted only a few seconds but it was enough to send chills down his spine. Suddenly his anger was gone. He sat down with her on the bench. They were holding hands.

"Henry Lloyd was about to tell us a story," John said to his wife-to-be.

"I like Henry Lloyd's stories," she said.

"Once upon the time there was a man named Jacob," began Henry Lloyd, nodding to Josephina. "He had twelve sons. He loved all his sons but his favorite sons were two boys he had with his second wife Rachel. The boys' names were Joseph and Benjamin. Jacob gave his blessing to Joseph which meant that upon his death, Joseph would become the head of the tribe. When the older brothers learned of this, they became angry and resentful. They thought of killing him but instead, they sold him into slavery. He ended up in Egypt. Now Joseph didn't pout and cry because he had been mistreated. He worked hard and gained favor with the Pharaoh. Eventually, he became the second most powerful man in Egypt. Later, he had a chance to get even with his brothers but he didn't. Instead, he blessed them and took care of them."

"I don't understand how this has anything to do with what is going on," John said.

"Then I'll tell you. I am like Joseph. God has chosen me to be his spokesman. Among all the people in the world, God has chosen to bless me. The men who want to get rid of me are like Joseph's brothers. They don't really hate me, they just don't understand why God loves me so much. The truth is, though, God loves them as much as he does me. They just don't know it. I could pout and be angry about how people have mistreated me or about being sent to California or I could be thankful and make the best of it."

"So you are going to be the most powerful man in California?" Josephina asked.

"If God wants me to I will," Henry Lloyd laughed. "And if he wants me to be a trapper then that is enough too. We will just have to see. And now, I'm going down to the creek to clean up."

"He is the strangest man I've ever met," John said when he was gone. "I don't mean that in a bad way. He seems to have learned how not to make foolish mistakes. He always knows what to do or say. I will miss him."

"We all will, and I know what you mean. Mac is like that as well. He found us when we were in trouble and we would be dead now if not for him. He knew just what to say to the Kings to get them to take us in. Mac always seems to know what you are thinking by just looking at you."

"Mac has been great. Do you know he is teaching me Spanish?" John asked.

"Yes, I know. He said you are doing well."

Josephina looked so pleased that John felt proud.

"Oh, but John, do you know I still have not seen the house Henrietta is building for us and it is almost finished!"

"She has been so good to us," he said.

"She can be but when she is angry like she was with Mr. King, then she scares me," Josephina said. "I try to stay away from her when she is mad."

"Josephina, I wish we could just get married now," John said.

She grinned, then kissed him again before she when back to the house. There were the chills again, John thought. He shivered as he tried to imagine their wedding night.

The following morning, Henrietta and Henry Lloyd had their Bibles out on the porch discussing their appointed task. After they were satisfied with the scriptures they had chosen and the direction they should take their conversations, she looked at Henry Lloyd.

"We need to talk about Sunday's service," she said.

She did not want to have this conversation but she had promised her husband she would deal with it. She didn't realize Henry Lloyd already knew about the Presbyterian minister who was due to arrive later in the day. It was hard to keep things secret at the ranch.

"I am glad you brought that up," he said. "I am used to preaching to black folks and buffalo hunters. It's a different kind of preaching than preaching to white people."

Henry Lloyd had a gift for setting up a conversation.

"Mr. King has invited a Presbyterian minister to preach. He didn't know I had asked you. Now we have two preachers scheduled and I don't know what to do," she wailed.

"This is great news," Henry Lloyd said.

"No, it is not. I wanted to hear you preach," she said.

"Let me talk with this minister when he gets here. We will pray together and figure out what God wants. I'll be sure to thank Mr. King. He is a fine man."

Henry Lloyd nodded to her and walked away singing a hymn.

Later that day, the Reverend Marvin Shivers arrived. He was a small, neat man, almost bald. He wore glasses and he had a high, shrill voice. The planning meeting for the service was scheduled for after dinner. Reverend Shivers, Mac, Henry Lloyd Walker, and the Kings would attend.

King took charge of the meeting. He let it be known that several of his business partners would be in attendance. Everyone knew he meant they would not be comfortable with a Negro preaching to white people. He didn't have to say it. Regardless of this obvious slight to Henry Lloyd, though, things remained friendly and warm. Henry Lloyd made it clear that he understood and agreed with King. Henrietta let it pass, not wanting to start a squabble with two preachers in the meeting.

Everyone seemed to know what Henry Lloyd was doing except Shivers.

The passage rolling through Henrietta's mind was 'Blessed be the peacemakers for they shall be called the sons of God.' It made her want to make peace rather than get her way. After everything was discussed it was determined that Henry Lloyd would read the opening scripture and would then introduce Reverend Shivers. They decided on the hymns to be sung and the order of the service, which was to be a typical Presbyterian liturgy. Mac would be responsible for the Spanish translation since many of the hands that would attend did not speak English. They talked about a name for the church but came up with nothing, so they agreed to leave it nameless for the present.

When John found out the next day what had been decided, he was furious all over again. He could not believe that once again his friend has been slighted. He saddled Bonnie and rode off without saying a word to anyone. After all, he had a job to do. Henry Lloyd was busy tending the smoked pork with Aldo so he didn't see John leave.

John regretted not telling Josephina he was leaving. He was afraid to talk to anyone about it. He was afraid of what he would say. Henry Lloyd might be fine with the way things had turned out but John wasn't.

He had only been gone a few hours when he picked up the trail of cattle being moved. They were headed southeast. This seemed strange. When King's men took cattle to market, they went either northeast toward Corpus or west toward San Antonio. He could tell there were at least three horses and about a dozen head of cattle and he knew something was not right.

He and Hank picked up the pace, slowing as darkness fell. There was no moon and the area was rough. They kept moving, though. Hank had the scent and John followed.

By morning they were beyond the border of the ranch and they were close to their prey. Hank's ears perked up and John knew they had found them. They circled around so he could get ahead of them. In the distance, he could see the dust the livestock were kicking up. He found a place to ford the creek the rustlers would need to cross. Then he waited.

The cattle finally arrived at the creek. When John held up his hands and shouted, they held up and began drinking peacefully in the creek. Two men rode up behind them.

"Hello," John said.

"Why did you halt our cattle? We're in a hurry," one of the men said.

"I can see that. These cattle look like they could use a rest, though. Where are you off to in such a hurry?"

"That is none of your business," the other man said.

John could hear a rider coming up from behind him. The man must have been scouting the area. He was galloping now and would arrive soon. Then John spotted another man walking his horse up the creek in his direction. There were four of them, all armed, and they had him surrounded.

"Easy, Hank," John whispered.

"I think I'd like to start with your first question," he told the man.

"What?"

"You asked me why I halted the cattle. But you called them "our" cattle. That's the reason I stopped them. These are not yours. These cattle belong to Richard King. Unless you have a bill of sale, I'll be taking them back to where you got them."

The rider behind him was close. John turned to see that he had his gun drawn. The two men in front of him were enjoying their advantage.

"You are mistaken, young man. These are our cattle. If you ride off now then we won't have to shoot you," the first man said as he took his hat off.

John figured that was a signal for the others to make a move. John knew who was boss now. In the corner of his eye, he saw the man in the creek go for his gun.

"Go, Hank," John shouted, and Hank flew toward the man behind John. John drew his pistol and shot the man in charge. The man was still waving his hat and the bullet went straight through it, entering his chest. The man in the creek aimed at John but before he could pull the trigger he saw Hank leap onto the man behind John. He pointed his gun at the dog and fired. He missed. John turned and fired at the man in the creek. The horses were moving and he missed as well.

John took out his long gun and jumped off Bonnie. He ran a few steps toward the fourth man. He didn't fire because the man had his hands in the air. He was looking at the dead man on the ground and crying. John turned to the man in the water.

"Drop your gun," he said.

The man was frozen. He had watched Hank maul his partner. He dropped his gun.

"Hank, come," John commanded.

Hank did as he was told. He was covered with blood, none of it his.

"Get off your horse," John told the man in the creek.

The other man was already off his horse, leaning over the dead man. The man Hank had dealt with was not going anywhere. He looked around and counted sixteen cows and five calves. More than he'd thought. His tracking skills must not be as good as he'd thought they were. And there were four riders. Then it hit him. Maybe there are more. He pointed his gun at the nearest man.

"Are there any more of you?"

The man shook his head no.

"There'd better not be. If anyone else rides up, I'm shooting you."

John looked around. All he saw were the cattle.

"Go get your friend."

The man helped his bloody partner up and they crossed the water. John checked the man he had shot. He was dead, as John had figured.

The other fellow was mumbling to himself. It seemed he was the dead man's brother. John took his gun. The rest of the day was spent burying one man and doctoring another. They finally got his wounds to stop bleeding. Both forearms were damaged, and his face was a mess. John was sure he would live. The cattle rested that day and night.

In the morning they were ready to head back to the ranch. John wasn't sure how he was going to watch two prisoners, care for a wounded man, and move twenty-one head of cattle seventy miles.

As it turned out, the cattle did most of the work, following the same trail they had made a few days earlier. The man from the creek was named Harley Wilson. He was gentle enough and he was a talker. He was not a killer, just a thief. The wounded man was named Johnson, and the boy that had lost his brother was called Clem. Clem grieved his brother the entire way back. Johnson and Wilson spent the entire time watching Hank. They were terrified of him. When John crossed over onto King's land with the cattle, he found one of the ranch crews working some strays on the southern part of the ranch. He was glad to be rid of the cattle. Now all he had were his prisoners.

John found that word of his adventure had preceded him. Some of the cowhands had spread the word. King rode out to meet him on his black stallion. John had forgotten all about the church service. He was too busy being a ranger. He hoped it was over as he realized he didn't even know what day it was.

"I hear you've been busy," King said looking at the cattle rustlers.

Johnson was still in bad shape but the other two looked like regular working men.

"I didn't know if I could get them all back. Turns out these gentlemen were no trouble at all. We didn't lose a single head," John said. "Let me get these men put up in the bunkhouse and I'll tell you about it."

"You mean jailhouse," said King.

"If you wish. It's up to you. These men are not bad. They just followed the wrong man. If you give them a chance, I bet they will make you good cowhands."

"We don't tolerate thieves around here," King said.

"Your call. I have dealt with mean men my entire life. These men are not mean. They stole your cattle so it's up to you what you do with them. I think they have learned their lesson."

"We will talk about it later," King said.

He was pleased with his ranger.

As they rode back to the ranch they spoke of several things. The church service was not among them. John was no longer angry with his employer. He was disappointed in him but his anger was gone. It was like they were old friends. King asked his opinion on several business ventures he was starting. John had no idea if his answers were anywhere close to being right but he appreciated the fact that King had talked to him about it. At the barn Mr. King turned, appraising his ranger for a moment.

"I have decided to entrust the futures of these men to you. If you are going to amount to anything in business, you will have to learn to judge a man's character. This might be a good lesson for you. Let me know what you decide."

"Before I decide I'd like to think about it. I would like to talk to you about it further, and I'd like to get Henry Lloyd's and Mac's opinions as well."

"Good idea," King said with a smile, then pointed.

"Look who is coming."

Josephina had seen them and was running to meet her future husband.

"We can finish our talk later. I can see you will have other things on your mind now."

CHAPTER 19

The Wedding

King and John were enjoying a cigar on the porch after everyone else had gone to bed. It was a few days before the wedding and King had told John to take a break from his ranger duties. The days had been full. Henry Lloyd was teaching him how to be a good husband and Mac was teaching him Spanish. King was talking with him more and more about various business ventures. The rest of the time, Henrietta was instructing him on manners and hygiene. She was convinced that no marriage would work unless a man knew how to stay clean and civil at home.

Tonight, however, there was no lesson. They were just two men enjoying a little brandy and some good cigars. At some point, his employer asked John what he was going to do with the men who had rustled his cattle. Johnson was almost healed though his face was always going to be a mess. He and the other two ex-horse thieves were helping with light chores around the barn and had been behaving themselves as waited to hear whether they'd be staying or heading for prison.

"I've about decided they are not dangerous men," John said.

King agreed.

"They did commit a serious crime, though," John added.

"They did," said King.

"First of all, they need to make restitution. What are twenty-one head of cattle worth?" John asked. "I think they owe you at least that much. I know you didn't lose them but if I hadn't come across their trail you would have. I've been thinking about how they can pay you. The English made a man work off his debt. That seems fair to me."

"I'm listening," King said.

He had never heard John string that many sentences together, and he could tell his ranger had been thinking about this.

"I believe they should pay you twice what the cattle are worth, just to make certain they have learned their lesson," John said.

"I can live with that," King said hiding a smile.

"Don't worry about their behavior. As long Hank is around, they will be model citizens. After the debt has been paid, they can either leave or apply for work here at a fair wage," John continued.

"How did you come up with this?" King asked.

"I talked with Henry Lloyd about it. He told me a few Bible stories. Each story had a different lesson. After all the stories, I ran this idea past him and Mac and they liked it. Mac said he remembered a time when he was shown mercy and he said it helped to form his character. Henry Lloyd said Texas can always use a man whose character has been reformed.

"How much money do you have John?" King said changing the subject.

"I gave it to you to invest for me," John said. "Plus whatever my wages have been.

John was confused by the question.

"John, I know what you have. I am asking if you know."

"Mr. King, you trust me with the security of the ranch and I trust you with my finances. Am I doing well financially?"

"I like how you turned that around on me. A good negotiator will often ask a question when he either doesn't want to answer or has no answer."

"I am not a negotiator, I'm a ranger," John said.

"Yes, you are, and a fine one at that. You could also become a businessman if you chose to. I was thinking of increasing your wages just to ensure you don't go looking elsewhere for a better position," King said.

"Mr. King, I am as happy as I've ever been. Hank and I are not leaving."

"Good. So, you think Hank is happy with his situation?"

King reached down to pat Hank on the head.

"Yes sir, I do."

"Then I don't need to give him a raise," King said with a wide grin.

The wedding day finally arrived. It was Wednesday, May 23, 1860. Henrietta was satisfied that everything was in place. Henry Lloyd would perform the ceremony and Mac would walk Josephina down the aisle. They had practiced their lines and everyone knew what to do.

The church would be full of people, most of them from the ranch. After the wedding, a grand feast would follow. They had smoked a pork roast, a few dozen chickens, and a side of beef. Nobody would work that day except the kitchen crew.

The church was covered in flowers with lace draped over the windows and altar. Henry Lloyd wore a black suit. Standing to his left were John, Felix, and Aldo. Henrietta and Juanita, who worked in the house as a maid and had become good friends with Josephina, were standing on his left.

The service began with a band of Mexican guitar players playing and singing traditional Spanish love songs. When Mac walked Josephina down the aisle, John thought she was more beautiful than he had ever seen her.

Then Henry Lloyd spoke in a booming voice.

"Who gives this woman to be married?"

"Her brothers and I," Mac said with pride.

He leaned down and kissed her gently on the cheek. Henry Lloyd nodded and the musicians sang another song. When the song ended, Henry Lloyd preached about what a marriage should be. John had heard all of this over the past few weeks. Next, Henry Lloyd had them recite their vows out loud. Then he put his big hands on them, one on Josephina's shoulder and the other on John's head and he began to pray. He prayed for a long time, asking God to bless them in every sort of way. The wedding concluded with Henry Lloyd pronouncing them man and wife.

They were married. But before they could leave, Henry Lloyd motioned to Mac and the old Scotsman came to the front. Everyone stood and Mac cleared his throat and began the Irish Prayer.

"May the road rise to meet you.

May the wind be always at your back.

May the sun rise warm upon your face,

May the rain fall upon your fields,

And until we meet again, may God

Hold you in the palm of his hand."

The crowd broke into thunderous applause. The guests were in a fine mood as they left the church and headed back up to the main house where the wedding festivities would take place. Long tables had been set up out on the lawn and the party began with eating, drinking, singing, and dancing. The celebration would go on until the wee hours but Henrietta had arranged for Aldo to bring the buggy around to take the newlyweds to their new home long before then. Alone at last in their own little house, John couldn't find the words. He was overcome by everything that was happening.

"It looks like a fine house…" he began.

He looked over at his bride and saw that she was weeping.

"Is something wrong?"

He was exhausted and confused and overwhelmed by the love he felt for his beautiful Josephina.

"It is perfect."

Tears of joy streamed down her face. John was relieved, as he began to understand that this exquisite creature of his could cry with happiness.

"Let's take our time, Josephina. Let's look at our new house together. This is the place we will live and will raise our family, thanks to the kindness of the Kings."

She put her head on his shoulder, grateful to have this brave and sensitive man as her husband. She grabbed his hand and they began to discover their home together. The house consisted of two buildings covered by a single roof. Each building was an eighteen-foot square. A ten-foot dog run between them.

"It was designed by Henrietta," Josephina said. "I believe it is like the house she grew up in."

"Let's go inside," she said.

They began with the building on the left, which was the main living area. It was one spacious room with a fireplace big enough for cooking and for heating the room in the winter. A table and four chairs had been placed to the left of the fireplace. The other side of the room was designed for sitting, reading, and receiving guests.

Candles had been lit and a vase of flowers had been placed on the table. There were windows on each wall and a wide entrance door. Another door on the left side led to a pantry fully stocked from the King's house. The last door on the right led to the dog run. As Josephina looked around the house of which she was to be mistress, she became emotional again but also fiercely happy. She finally completed her inventory and they went into the other building. This contained their sleeping area, a sitting area, and a small room off to the side.

"I can not believe this is our home," she said. "I have never had anything like this."

She wanted to inspect every detail. John walked outside to check on Hank and to give her some time. Hank had already made himself at home and was lying near the door to the sleeping room, wagging his tail.

"There are three of us now, boy," said John. "I hope you don't mind."

Hank raised his head and thumped the hard-packed ground with his tail. John rubbed his head, and Hank licked his hand.

After a few minutes, John went back inside. Josephina was sitting on the bed, reading a letter from Henrietta. She read it to him. Now he, too, had tears in his eyes. She told them how she was pleased to have them in her life. She wrote about what fine people they were and that she hoped that their families would always be close.

Josephina put the letter in a drawer. John knew she would keep it always. Women were like that. When she sat down on the bed beside him, she leaned in and kissed him on the cheek. He could scarcely believe she was his, as he took her in his arms and held her close.

"Let me look at you for a moment," he said.

She smiled. She was nervous but she didn't flinch as he pulled her to him and kissed her again. This kiss they held longer. She was no longer hesitant but still, she walked over to the window to pull the curtains closed. John admired her beauty as she moved across the room. He took a few steps toward her.

"I love you," she said.

"I hope so since we are married now," John said.

"We really are married. My dreams have come true. Except this is more wonderful than I ever imagined it would be," she said.

"Mrs. Delaney, I love you too," John said.

Henry Lloyd had made much of the mystery of marriage in the

weeks before, talking about how a man and a woman could become "one flesh." John and Josephina were beginning to understand this. They were now a married couple. They lay together, talking about the wedding, the Kings, and just about everything. It had been a perfect day. They finally dropped off to sleep a few hours before dawn. They were fast asleep when they woke to a loud racket. John jumped up and ran to the window. The sun was just coming up. He could see a few drunk cowboys beating pots together and yelling. When the cowboys saw the curtains open, they rode off laughing. John turned around to see his beautiful wife sitting up in bed, smiling at him. He was overcome with emotion all over again but couldn't trust himself to speak. He felt tears of happiness welling up in his eyes but he couldn't let Josephina think him weak.

"I'll go make a fire. You must be hungry," John said.

They were now Mr. and Mrs. Delaney, John thought, as he worked on getting the fire lit. Perhaps I have found what I am supposed to be, he thought—a married man.

After breakfast, John walked around the back of the cabin to a small shed that held his gear. A corral had been built about fifty yards down the hill. Bonnie was grazing in a small fenced pasture. Hank was at his side. His wife was in the house. He had everything. What a beautiful life he had found. He walked down to see Bonnie.

He and Josephina spent the day talking about their new life. She showed him where she wanted a garden. He asked her if she would be comfortable when he had to leave for days at a time. They talked through everything as they fell into a comfortable routine as master and mistress of their new home but their joy would soon be marred.

It was almost dark when they heard a knock on the door. It had to be somebody Hank liked or he would have alerted them. It was Henry Lloyd and John knew instantly what was happening. Henry Lloyd was taking his leave of them.

His friend had packed all his belongings on Chico, who was tied behind his white horse. Chico had never really found a purpose at the ranch after Sally died, so Felix had offered the animal to Henry Lloyd for the trip to California.

For the second time in a day, John had tears in his eyes but these were not tears of happiness.

"John, what a blessed day it was when the Lord brought us together. I will miss you, my brother," the big man said tenderly.

"Do you really have to leave so soon?" John asked.

"The time is right. I was able to see you married and settled with your new wife."

"It's too late to start a journey. It's almost dark," John argued.

"It's a full moon. I'll make camp soon," Henry Lloyd said.

He hugged John, kissed Josephina on the forehead, then mounted his horse.

"I will write you when I get to a place that will post," Henry Lloyd promised over his shoulder as he waved goodbye.

Henry Lloyd's departure was a crushing blow for John. He told Josephina he needed to check on Bonnie, then he and Hank walked down to the corral. He stayed there until well after dark, looking up at the sky, remembering the times they had shared.

That evening he and Josephina didn't talk much. They went to bed early and slept through the night.

Soon everything was back to normal around the ranch. Josephina spent most of her days helping Henrietta, just as she had before. John found plenty of things to do around the ranch while she was busy. King had told him to stay close to home for a few weeks after the wedding but John didn't want to neglect his job. It was two weeks before he left again to ride the range. As the weeks passed, he found himself staying away only a few nights at a time, though. He wanted to be home with Josephina as much as possible.

As John looked out for the ranch, Josephina took care of the children and helped Henrietta. They were preparing to open the school and Henrietta once again had a purpose. She and Mac were putting in long hours in preparation for the first day.

The church had become a disappointment for her. Henry Lloyd had preached a few times and he was an inspiring minister. He sang beautifully too. Now he was gone, though. The building was sitting empty and this bothered Henrietta greatly. So the school had to be a success. She would not countenance another failure.

Summer was over and there was a chill in the air when Richard King arrived one day with a group of men. They stopped by the ranch for a few days in preparation for a trip they would make to Austin, the state's capital. The mood was solemn. John sat with them one evening on the porch as they drank brandy and smoked cigars. A new president, Abraham Lincoln, had been elected and none of these men were happy about it. In fact, most of the southern states were considering secession. They talked openly about how they would form a new government. Such talk was not new for the people of Texas. Every few years they had pledged allegiance to a different nation. First, there had been Spain. Then Mexico. Then they had been the Republic of Texas. Now they were part of the United States but they felt they had no voice.

John had nothing to say about any of this. He just listened. King was upset about the new leadership because he saw Lincoln as an obstacle to his business enterprises. The discussions were heated. The men were not upset with each other but were angry at the northern states. All John could think about was his sister in New Jersey.

King and his associates finally left for Austin but the dark cloud had not lifted. Until this rift among the states was settled, no one would be at ease. John understood that and yet it seemed a distant threat. He and Josephina were in a comfortable routine. They had their jobs, their home, and each other. And now they were going to have a child.

This latter news had come as a surprise to John. He had supposed that one day they would have children but it wasn't something he expected to happen right away. Still, what a fine thing to become a father! After thinking about it he was happy. His beautiful wife was carrying his child. He needed to write a letter to Nelly.

They had become faithful correspondents after John learned to read and write. He wanted to tell her about the new baby but he also wanted to know what she and David thought about this problem between the states. He was happy here and Nelly was happy there. If the country fell apart, what would that mean for their family?

Over the next few months, John and Nelly exchanged numerous letters. Nelly and David had had a second child, a boy they had named John Michael. Nelly expressed strong views about the political situation. She and David were certain the southern states were making a mistake. King, of course, was solidly on the other side of this issue. John read all he could about the problem. It was all from the point of view of the southern newspapers. Their perspective was mostly one of self-determination and the ability to self-govern. The South would not be told how to run their states.

President Lincoln, who had not even taken office yet, was painted as a villain in these articles. The cartoons in the papers would portray him as either the devil or as a puppet being controlled by fat cat businessmen from New York. John remembered a few of the New York politicians but he thought they could not all be like Boss Tweed. Or could they?

John also got a letter from Henry Lloyd. He was in a place called Taos, New Mexico, a new territory of the United States. He was living with the Tiwa Indians, preaching to them and learning their way of life. He described the land to John with wonder. He said it was beautiful but that he would not be there much longer. He told them Chico was too old to go any further. He had been a fine companion but would not be making the trip to California. Henry Lloyd had found a home for him among the Tiwa and Chico would live out his life near the Rio Grande del Norte. God had given him his marching orders and Henry Lloyd would be leaving for California as soon as the snow was gone.

John longed to join his friend in this beautiful territory but he had responsibilities now. He was a ranger and a husband and he had a baby coming.

CHAPTER 20

Austin

John was only staying away a day or two at a time now as Josephina's pregnancy advanced. He returned one day toward the end of February 1861 and found that even his home was different. There was now a cradle in their sleeping room and a smaller cabinet full of baby clothes. Henrietta and Josephina had spent the last few days preparing the little nursery and Josephina was so proud of how everything looked. The arrival of the first Delaney baby was now Henrietta's immediate priority. The baby coming and a possible war on the horizon kept John in a constant state of turmoil.

Most of the men who had accompanied Richard King were ready for war. They all figured it would last a few months and the North would learn its lesson. John's experience with the Irish fighting the British made him wonder. The pub talk in Ireland had always been about what poor fighters the British were. The British, however, with their superior numbers, won every time.

"You have another letter from Henry Lloyd," Josephina said.

She knew that would cheer him up. The letter was postmarked Taos. John sat down and pored over his friend's words. The snow was melting and Henry Lloyd was getting ready to leave for California. John looked out the window, gazing off into the distance. Josephina's voice brought him out of his reverie.

"John?"

"The room looks wonderful," he said.

He should have said it sooner.

"It really does. The baby is moving a lot more now," his wife told him.

John walked over and put his hand on her belly. He didn't feel anything.

"Are you hungry?" she asked.

"When you are ready to eat, I am," John answered.

He always looked forward to her cooking.

"Let's go see what we have," she said taking his hand and leading him out into the dog run. "You clean up, I'll start supper."

They ate early that evening and went to bed early too, though Josephina couldn't find a comfortable position for sleeping until the wee hours. Soon after the sun rose, King came riding up on Champion. He told John to saddle up. He wanted company on his trip to Austin. John was ready to ride in only a few minutes. Hank led the way as they galloped toward the state capital.

King and many other businessmen had meetings scheduled in Austin. Sam Houston would be leaving office in a few days. He had been asked to step down as governor because he refused to pledge allegiance to the Confederate States. All the other southern states were getting in line but old Sam was refusing to leave the Union. It was an embarrassment for Texas. Just about everybody with any political pull was going to Austin to ensure there was no trouble.

Sam Houston had mellowed in his old age but there were those who feared he had one more fight left in him. Edward Clark would soon take office. He had been born in New Orleans and he was a true southerner. King and John were to meet people along the way. As they did, the conversations were always about only one topic. By the time they arrived in Austin they were almost twenty strong. As they made their way to the capital, each man shared his thoughts. Everybody except John. Hank and John would listen for a while then they would slip off to explore in quiet.

All the men stayed at the same hotel in Austin and they continued to meet throughout the week to discuss how they would handle Houston. He was still a hero and he was beloved by most Texans, even if he was out of step with the times. One evening, as the politicians and businessmen gathered at the Capitol building, John and Hank sat out in front of the hotel watching the wagons go by. Sam Houston strolled up to them. He was by himself. John knew who it was. It could be no one else. He had big, bushy sideburns and a fancy carved walking stick as tall as he was. The governor was dressed in a long, Cherokee ceremonial coat that went all the way to the ground. On top of his long, curly hair sat a wide-brimmed hat. Sam Houston stopped and looked John and Hank over, then walked up and sat down beside John on the bench.

"That is a fine-looking dog you have. Why aren't you with the others plotting my demise?" the governor asked as he petted Hank.

"It's not my business," John said.

"I suppose it is not but neither is it the business of most of the mob gathered here. What, may I ask, is your business?"

"I'm a ranger," John said.

"Are you now? And what brings a ranger into the capital city. I was not aware we had bandits here at the hotel. All our bandits are busy down the street."

He pointed his walking stick toward the Capitol.

"Which group are you attached to?" the governor asked.

"I am not a Texas Ranger. I work for a private citizen," John reported.

"I have never heard of anything like that before. You must be quite the entrepreneur," Houston said.

"I'm not sure what that is. I work for a man named Richard King. You might know him," John said.

"Everybody in Texas knows Dick King. Tell me, what does a ranger for Captain King do?"

"Where we are there are no lawmen, so I make sure nobody steals his property," John said.

"I suppose that is a full-time job. I hear King has a sizable ranch," said the governor.

"My father told me if you have something valuable there will always be someone who will try to take it from you," John said. "Mr. King has a lot of cattle and cattle are easy to steal. They just walk off with whoever has a notion to try and get them."

"Tell me, son, what brings an Irish philosopher like you to Texas?"

"I couldn't live in the big cities. Texas suits me just fine," John said.

"I suppose there is little need for a ranger in the cities," Houston said.

John wanted to tell him he was wrong. New York needed an army of rangers to clean up the crime but he didn't say it.

"My name is Sam Houston," said the governor as he stuck out his hand.

"Yes, sir. I know who you are. I'm John Delaney and it's a pleasure meeting you."

They shook hands and Houston rose to his feet. He was an older man but still strong.

"I'm going to tell you something nobody but Mrs. Houston and I know. In the morning I'm going to the steps of the Capitol to resign. All their scheming and plotting has been a waste of time. I'm ready to retire. Nobody listens to me anymore," he said with no sorrow in his voice.

He nodded to John and walked away.

The next day at noon it was all over. Sam Houston graciously stepped down and went back to his home in Huntsville. The contingency that had traveled with King was relieved that Clark would take the oath and that Texas would soon join the other southern states. On March 4th, 1861, Edward Clark took office. Later that year, in November, he would be defeated in a close election but by then nobody would be watching politics in Texas. There would be a war going on. Clark's reign would be short but he, like the good soldier he was, would do what was expected of him.

Riding back toward the ranch, John had many questions. He wanted to ask King about the Confederate States but he did not. The trip back took longer because they stopped at every small village to tell people the news about Texas joining the Confederacy. Texas needed an army. Virginia, South Carolina, Mississippi, and Georgia already had troops in training. If Texas didn't hurry, the war would be over before they had troops ready to send.

A little over a month later, John and Josephina had a baby boy. They named him Henry Patrick Delaney. He was born April 12th, 1861. They would later learn that their son had arrived the same day Fort Sumter was fired upon by Union troops, touching off the war between the states.

Henrietta was proud of Josephina. Indeed, he was in awe of her. It had been a long and painful labor. John and Hank sat out in the dog run listening as they waited. Several times Hank tried to break into the room to rescue his mistress. John was able to stop him but Hank was not happy until he saw her for himself. When Henrietta finally let them in the house, Josephina was sitting up in bed nursing the child. Even though she looked tired, John thought she was beautiful. Hank approached carefully, then sniffed the baby. His tail began to wag. He seemed to understand now what the screaming had been about.

A few days after the baby was born, the Kings drove their buggy down to pay a visit to the new Delaney child. They had brought their children for Josephina to see. Josephina had missed getting to see them daily and they had missed her even more.

John and Mr. King walked down to see Bonnie.

"John, I have two things on my mind I'd like to talk to you about."

He began, not waiting for John's acknowledgment.

"First would you consider breeding Bonnie with my stallion Champion? She has turned into a great little saddle horse and I think she and Champion might produce a nice colt. I have a fine gelding you can ride."

"I'd never thought about it. I think I would like to see her have a colt. I like the idea," John replied.

"The next thing is, I need to know your plans," King said.

"What do you mean?"

"I have not heard you say a single word about the war. I think you and a few Indians on the Llano Estacado are the only men who have not expressed an opinion," King said watching John as he spoke.

"I suppose it is a little late to have an opinion. The war has started."

"Yes, it has, and what are you going to do about it?"

"What do you mean?"

John was becoming uncomfortable with this conversation.

"Do you plan to join? If you do, I can recommend you be given an officer's rank. You would be a fine soldier. Men would follow you and you know how to handle yourself when trouble comes."

John said nothing as he listened.

"The military is a fine way to make your mark. A good man will advance through the ranks and when it's over, find himself in a much better position."

"Or, I could get killed," John said.

Mr. King ignored the comment.

"Well, are you going to join?" King asked. "I need to know what my ranger is going to do. I will support any decision you make. You have earned that."

"I'd like to keep doing my job here, if I may," John said.

"I was hoping you would say that," King said breaking into a grin. "I have just signed a contract with Texas and Mexico. My steamships will be busy transporting cotton to Mexico. Guns and ammunition will be brought back to the states in exchange. The Union ships are all over the Gulf so it will be a bit risky. They are not a match for my steamers though and my people know all the local channels for hiding along the coast. Having said that I will need to stay personally involved. This means I will be away from the ranch quite a bit."

John shook his head in acknowledgment.

"War is often a dangerous time. Most of the good men will be away. This gives the bad element an opportunity to take advantage of the situation. I want you to find a couple of good men to help you watch the place. I also want you and Josephina to move into the house with Henrietta. I would feel better knowing you and Hank were there."

"Yes sir."

He knew Josephina would love nothing better than to be back with the children.

"Thank you, John. I am encouraged," King said.

A few days later, they moved back into the big house. John decided it was time for him to take a few days away so the women could get the routine down that suited them both. John had been thinking about what Mr. King had said about getting help. He knew who he wanted to hire. He saddled Bonnie for what might be her last trip with him for a while. He made Hank stay behind. Hank didn't like it but John would feel better with Hank watching the place while he was away. Sure, there were plenty of men around if something happened but John felt better knowing Hank was there.

He moved fast and was in Laredo by dinner the second day. He ate with the Martinez family. His Spanish was now good enough that he could converse with them. They were happy to see him. He told them all about his new baby and as much as he knew about the war. He listened to them talk about the local situation in Laredo. Sheriff Sampson had left and had not returned. The only deputy to stay behind was Lonnie, the big-talking gunfighter. He spent his time in the saloons not bothering anybody. The mayor had now hired a new sheriff, a sober-minded professional lawman. Laredo welcomed his support this close to the border.

That evening after dinner, John and Juan walked into town to look around. It was a quiet night and John enjoyed spending time with Juan. John asked his opinion on hiring Beto and Alfredo to help on the ranch. Juan thought it was a promising idea. Beto's family had been longtime residents in the area and Alfredo was a hard-working man. Juan said Alfredo missed his wife and was starting to drink a little too much but with something to do he would be fine. They decided Juan would accompany John the next morning as he met with them both.

They found Alfredo first. He was helping a neighbor butcher a goat.

"Good morning old friend," John said in Spanish.

Alfredo wiped his hands clean and hugged John.

"It is so good to see you. I have not heard of a problem? What brings you here? Am I getting so old that they don't tell me things?"

They laughed. Alfredo was barely fifty but that was old if you didn't have a wife.

"No problem," John said. "I have come here to offer you a job."

"Where is your dog? I hope he is fine. I tell everybody I see what a fine animal he is. I will never forget how he handled the sheriff's men," Alfredo said with a smile.

"He is fine. I left him at home to watch my family while I am away."

"God help the pistolero that tries to get your family," Alfredo said.

"I told you Alfredo was a talker," Juan said. "You better ask him fast before he talks our ears off."

"Do you want a job?" John asked.

"Yes, I do," Alfredo said. "I'm tired of skinning goats for lazy neighbors."

He said this loud enough for his friend to hear, grinning all the while.

"Let me tell you what it is before you say yes," John said.

"It doesn't matter what it is, or where it is. After what you did for this town I will follow you anywhere."

"I want you to be a ranger, like me."

"Ranger? I don't even have a horse. I'm guessing a foot ranger will do you little good."

"We can find you a horse. So, you will work for me?" John asked.

He stuck out his hand so they could shake on the deal. Alfredo pushed his hand aside and hugged him again.

"Let's go get you a horse," John said.

While John and Alfredo were packing his belongings, Juan went to find Beto. He was not as easy to locate. His sister seemed to know where he was yet she was reluctant to tell Juan. She agreed to find him and send him over to see them. Juan's wife Maria had heard a rumor that Beto was seeing a married woman on the south side of town. She told them it was dangerous business if true. John figured she knew it was true. A few hours later, Beto showed up at the Martinez house. As he stepped in, Maria gave him the evil eye. He knew what that was about. Beto just grinned.

"Beto, I would like to talk to you outside," John said.

The two of them went outside to get away from Maria, who was glaring at them both.

"Beto, I would like you to come and work with me on the ranch. I am looking for someone who can help me. I need a man like you who is not afraid to act when action is called for."

"You mean a full-time job?" Beto asked. "When do we leave?"

"I guess that means yes."

The men shook hands.

"Do you have a horse?" John asked.

"No, but I have a gun," Beto said.

"I suppose you need a gun close by if you are doing what Maria thinks you are," John grinned. "Go get your things packed up. I need to go buy a couple of horses."

John rode into town. He was able to negotiate for two horses and a couple of used saddles. He also bought a couple of rifles and some sidearms. He did not know the condition of Beto's weapon. It all cost more money than John had with him so the mayor stepped in. The town would pay for it all. The mayor said it was the least they could do for John.

The three rangers rode out that afternoon. Alfredo was handy at making camp and taking care of things. Beto was more interested in his new guns. The horse Beto was riding was about half-wild but the man did a good job handling him. John knew they both had a lot to learn but it would be good having them work with him.

After watching his new employees he decided they needed to learn to work as a team. He also knew that Alfredo would need to be in charge. He was hoping they would work well together. They would be one team and he and Hank would be the other. With two teams they could watch the ranch closely. On the way back to the ranch they practiced their shooting skills. Alfredo knew what he was doing and was a fair shot with the rifle and the pistol. Beto did not know how to use either one very well at first. John had Alfredo teach him. He wanted to see if Beto would submit to Alfredo. Beto did and under Alfredo's tutelage, he picked it up fast. They both seemed eager to please John.

When they were still a good distance away, John saw Hank running toward them. Hank had been watching for John's return since the moment he left. Josephina was also happy to see him and was eager to tell him all about the baby. After John introduced his new rangers to Henrietta, then got them settled into the bunkhouse, he was reunited with his family. The following day, John would start showing Beto and Alfredo what was expected of them. There were basic skills they would both need to learn.

The next few weeks, John spent almost all his time with his new rangers. He was glad to have something to do. With the war in full swing now, it seemed no one wanted to talk about anything else. John was not happy about the war. It isolated him from Nelly. He wanted to tell her all about his son and he wanted to hear how they were doing. He was afraid he would never see Jamal again. The Union ships were not allowing any traffic into Galveston or Corpus and he had not heard from Henry Lloyd in months.

John tried his best not to think about the war but it was impossible. King's steamers were able to dodge the big Union vessels easily. King was moving product and making money. For him, the war was good business.

After a few weeks, Alfredo and Beto were accustomed to their new life. They were learning the ropes and were happy with the money John was paying them but most of all they loved the freedom the ranger life afforded them. They were working well together so John felt comfortable letting them go out by themselves. Alfredo took the lead naturally without having to be appointed and Beto respected him. When John told them to do something they got right on it. King called this a testament to John's reputation, which was spreading throughout Texas.

The two new rangers were fitting in at the ranch as well. Just the threat of rangers kept most bandits away, as King had predicted it would. But there would always be exceptions. The very mean and the very stupid bandits would keep coming.

One day Beto and Alberto ran into some of the mean variety. John was holding the baby while Josephina helped Henrietta with the children when he saw a rider coming hard toward the ranch.

"Josephina," he yelled, "take Little Henry. Something is wrong."

He strapped on his gun, grabbed his rifle and a couple of boxes of shells, and ran to the barn.

"Come on, Hank," John said as he saddled the gelding.

He could make out that it was Beto, even from a distance. He rode out to meet him. They pulled up when they reached each other.

"We have trouble. Alfredo sent me to get you. We ran across the trail of some horse thieves. They were headed west. We were about an hour behind them when we came across a farmhouse they had just left. They killed the farmer and one of his boys. Two of his children hid from the bandits. They told us what happened."

Beto was out of breath.

"How far?"

"I've been riding about four hours."

"What about his wife?" John asked.

"I don't think he had a wife. I think it was just him and the three boys. The oldest boy is dead. Alfredo sent me to get you. He is finding somebody to take the boys. We couldn't just leave them. These are some very bad men."

"Yes, they are. Go get something to eat and a fresh horse. Then get back as soon as you can but don't wear the horse down."

John and Hank took off headed northwest.

CHAPTER 21

The Chase

Alfredo was at the farmer's house with a couple of local men. They had just finished burying the farmer and his son. John greeted the men then turned to Alfredo.

"What happened here?" he asked in Spanish.

"We followed their trail here. I know it is probably beyond Mr. King's land but I got a bad feeling."

John nodded. He knew that feeling.

"The bandits had been gone from here about two hours when we arrived. The two little boys were down at the creek fishing or they would be dead too. They heard gunshots and came home. They found their father and brother lying dead. They hid in those bushes. The bandits had taken their horses and whatever else they could steal. I sent Beto for you and I took the children to a neighbor's house about a mile up the creek."

"You did exactly right," John said.

"I hope they don't have too much of a head start," Alfredo said.

"My name is John Delaney and I work for Richard King," John said to the two men who had found the murdered farmer and his son.

John was speaking to the older gentleman he figured was the younger man's father.

"We have heard about you," the older man said. "My name is

Griffin—Bill Griffin—and this is my son Jim. We can ride with you."

"Thank you but that will not be necessary. I have another ranger on the way. We will find these men. If you can, I need you to take the boys. They will need to be cared for. It's not a good thing they saw."

"Sure, we can do that. The boys are with my wife," said Griffin.

"Alfredo, you and Hank get some rest. Take care of your horse. He has had that saddle on all day. If Beto gets back before I do, just wait for me. We will catch them."

John made the sign of the cross over the graves and climbed onto his horse. He needed to see the boys so he and the Griffins rode away together. The two boys were in varying degrees of shock. John was able to get some information from the oldest one. The younger child just kept sobbing about the blood. John discovered from talking with the older boy that there had been five or six men. Two of them appeared to be Indians and a couple of them wore Mexican apparel. They had a few dozen horses with them and the cattle they had stolen from King. They were headed north. John thanked the Griffins and he rode back to get Alfredo. He hoped Beto had arrived.

He found them both back at the settler's cabin. Alfredo was roasting a chicken, Beto was cleaning his gun and Hank was waiting patiently for the chicken. It was late so John decided they would get some sleep, let the horses rest, and then start out early in the morning. There would be no problem following the trail the rustlers had left.

The following morning at dawn, as they were packing to leave, they saw a single rider headed their way. John took his gun and he and Hank walked out to meet the man.

"He-he-he-hello," the man stuttered. "Ma-ma-ma name is Wilbur Fletcher."

"Hello, Mr. Fletcher. What brings you out this early," John asked.

The man appeared peaceful enough.

"I am fa-fa-fa-following some outlaws. Really ba-ba-ba-ba-bad men."

Alfredo and Beto walked up behind John.

"Are they horse thieves?" John asked.

"Yes, and a lot wa-wa-wa-worse than that," Wilbur said.

"They were here yesterday. Killed two people and stole just about everything here they could find. Do you know these men?" John asked.

"I have been chasing them all the wu-wu-way from La Salle," Wilbur said, "That's the Tom Bentley gang. They are real mean folks."

"What do you know about them?"

It took a while because of Wilbur's stuttering but he told them the story. The Bentley brothers—Tom, Marshall, and Walter—were from out west somewhere. They had come to Galveston to join the army. The army did a little checking on them and decided to pass. Then the Bentleys hooked up with a couple of Comanche Indians and some Mexican bandits who were on the run.

They had killed a man in La Salle who had tried to stop them from stealing his horses. Wilbur was in a posse tracking them. Everyone else had turned back but the man they killed was his friend. Wilbur was going to get them or die trying. The horse he was riding was just about dead—so lean you could count every rib on the poor animal.

"When is the last time you ate?" John asked him.

The man shrugged and didn't answer. John turned to Beto and told him to tend to the horse. He badly needed rest. A few more hours wouldn't hurt. Alfredo took care of getting Wilbur some food while Beto fed and watered the horse. He rubbed him down and let him rest a bit. John wanted to get as much information from Wilbur as he could while the man rested.

They finally left the farm about noon. John had no idea what kind of help Wilbur would be in a fight but he was impressed with the fact that the man wouldn't quit. That was always a good trait, especially in a fight. John knew there was going to be a fight. These men were bad.

All day they followed the trail. They were not gaining on them. The outlaws were moving fast to have as many horses and cattle as they did. It was a full moon so they kept moving into the night. Hank was on their trail so there was no chance of losing them, even in the dark. About midnight, they stopped at a creek to rest. They didn't make camp. They just let the horses rest. John managed to get a couple of hours sleep and so did Beto and Wilbur. Hank and Alberto stayed awake, listening and watching. They were getting closer.

At dawn, they saddled up and continued the pursuit. A few hours later, they found the outlaw camp. This meant the men were only a few hours ahead of them. The rangers picked up the pace. They were gaining on them now. John and Hank prepared to ride out ahead and John told his men to keep moving at the same pace.

Hank found them just after dark. They had made camp. John knew they would probably have a rider circling looking for visitors so he and Hank rode back to meet up with the others, who were not far behind. John had them make camp without a fire as they waited for first light. They rested some but not much.

Before dawn, John woke everyone. He, Hank, and Beto were going to follow the gang on foot. If they had Indians with them it would not be easy to stay undetected. Beto and John on foot was the best bet. Wilbur and Alberto would ease along behind them, bringing the horses at a slow pace.

"Don't move too fast," John told Alfredo. "Stay alert. There are eight of them and they are prepared to kill. If you come upon any of them don't hesitate. Shoot first and shoot straight."

It was dark when they found the outlaws. John watched from a high spot. He sent Beto to circle wide and scout out the land. He wanted him to find good cover to shoot from. John had been studying them and had discovered a pattern. Every two hours they changed guards. The guards didn't do much. Mostly they just kept the fire going. There was one big Indian and one smaller one. The Indians would wander around looking for signs of intruders.

Beto got back after a few hours and John was ready to go. They walked back toward the others who were not far off. John told them what he wanted them to do. The best spot was on the south side of the outlaw camp. It had the high ground. John had been there most of the night. It had a clear view and was about a hundred yards from the camp. Wilbur would take this spot since it was the best place and John didn't know how well he shot.

They left the horses tied up about fifty yards behind Wilbur. Alfredo was to go east. Just across a small creek was a tree large enough to support him and give him cover. It also gave him the advantage of shooting down. He was about seventy-five yards from the camp. John was also on the other side of the creek, north of the camp. He was able to find good cover in some brush down low. The shooting was going to be more difficult here but he was a lot closer to the camp. The running water helped to mask any noise he or Hank might make.

Beto worked his way around to the west of the camp and lay flat in some tall grass. He was closest to the camp. With everyone in place, they planned to wait until dawn.

John and Hank saw the big Indian take the watch. He looked all around then walked over toward Alfredo. John had his rifle aimed at the Indian just in case he spotted Alfredo. Alfredo was completely still and the big Indian never saw him. He then walked back up the creek toward John. John whispered in Hank's ear to stay down. The Indian looked their direction but didn't see them. He went back to the fire and stood for a while, looking around. John saw his head snap toward Beto. He must have heard something. The Indian watched the area intently. He took out a long knife and eased his way directly toward Beto. He was almost on top of him when a shot rang out. John saw the flash from Beto's rifle and saw the Indian topple backward.

This was not the plan. John wanted to wait until dawn, a good quarter-hour away. The eastern sky was just turning orange and it was not yet light enough but the fight was on. Beto had done what he had to. John hoped the others would know what to do.

"Let's go, Hank."

They jumped into the creek and waded across as fast as they could. It was only knee-deep. They made it to the other bank and he dropped to one knee and drew aim at the first man up. Before he could pull the trigger, Alfredo's gun reported and his shot was true. The top of that man's head flew off.

Before John could find another one to shoot, Wilbur shot a man who was just sitting up. No need to worry about Wilbur's marksmanship. The shot landed in the middle of the man's chest. Three down and five to go. John shot a man who was running toward the creek, trying to get away. Another man was running toward Beto, which was a mistake. Beto shot him in the stomach at close range.

The last two men standing had their hands up. Both were yelling.

"Hold your fire," John said.

He and Hank walked up to the men. Beto was walking in too. John looked around. Something was wrong. They had killed five. Two were still standing. That left one more. John made sure they didn't have any guns on them. Then he ran over and looked at the two dead men. The little Indian was not accounted for.

"Where is the other Indian?" John asked.

Both men looked around and shrugged. They had been sleeping hard. A few empty whiskey bottles lay at their feet.

"Beto look for him. Alfredo, Wilbur stay where you are until we find the Indian." John said. "Hank, find him, boy."

Hank looked confused, then ran around looking for the man.

"He's gone," said one of the two remaining outlaws. "He rode that little paint horse. It's gone."

"When did he leave?"

They shrugged again. They had no idea. After a few minutes, when neither Hank nor Beto could find him, John told Wilbur to get their horses. Alfredo came down from the tree and looked through their belongings. Hank watched the men while John and Beto drug the dead ones into the camp. They piled them all together. It worried John that the little Indian was still on the loose.

"Tie these two up," John said. "Hank and I are going to find the other one. Get things ready to move when I come back."

John and Hank walked around, looking for single hoof prints leaving the camp. When they did not find any he decided that the Indian must have used the creek to make his escape. It took a few hours but they found his trail.

"Alfredo," John said. "I need you to get some food together and feed everyone. They did an outstanding job today. Hank and I will find the other one. Beto, you and Wilbur keep an eye out. He may come back. Take care of the horses and get some rest. We'll be back soon, I hope."

The tracks came out of the creek on the northwest side of the camp. John also found a spot not far from where Beto had been. The man must have lain on the ground and watched the fight. John figured he must have gotten out before the rangers were in place. He probably spotted them and slipped off with his horse while they were getting into position. It was a good thing he'd decided not to join the fight. Things would have been different if he had. Beto would almost certainly be dead, and maybe a few others as well. John and Hank followed the trail. The man couldn't be too far ahead of them. The horse was still walking so he was not in a hurry. He was headed north. John and Hank were moving fast and would catch him soon. Soon John noticed his horse had begun to gallop. The tracks he left made it clear he knew he was being followed. This went on until the Indian found rocky ground. It would be harder to track him there. John and Hank turned back. The Indian was gone.

It was after dark when John and Hank got back. The two outlaws had just finished digging a common grave for their comrades. They were sitting together, listening to John tell the others about the Indian's escape. Total defeat was written across their faces. They had little hope now. They were beaten.

Beto pointed at one of the bodies.

"John come look what we have here."

John walked over. It was Lonnie, the deputy from Laredo.

"That is the one I shot running toward me. I didn't see who it was until it got light."

"Not much of a gunfighter after all, was he? I guess he's through causing trouble."

One of the two prisoners looked over at the dead man.

"He said his name was Lonnie."

"Where did you meet him?" John asked.

"In Houston, playing cards. He was not much of a card player. He said he was a gunfighter."

"Did he say where he was from?" John asked.

"He didn't say, and nobody cared where he was from. We never asked. He just started riding with us. I think he was going to Galveston before he hooked up with us."

"Why was he dressed in those clothes?" John asked.

The man started laughing.

"One night after a long drunk he had the runs. He went out to take care of business. Before he could squat good it was too late. He didn't know a skunk was right there digging for grub worms. As soon as Lonnie dropped his load the skunk sprayed him right back. That skunk won that stink contest.

We burned his clothes. Lopez had a pair of those white pants and

a white shirt. We burned his hat just for fun the next day. So he started wearing that big sombrero."

"Get them buried," John said trying not to laugh.

"How long have we been gone?" John asked his rangers as they
sat by the fire watching the outlaws work.

They started trying to count the days. They got into an argument
about how long it had been. Wilbur stopped the fight when he told
them, after a long stammering ordeal, that he had been gone over a
month.

"Wilbur, you did a real fine job," John said when Wilbur finally
finished. "That was a good shot."

He turned to Beto and said in Spanish, "Beto I am proud of you.
You kept your head and did well. Alfredo, I was afraid the big Indian
had found you. You did well. This is a fine company of rangers."

Then he said the same thing in English for Wilbur to hear.

"What do we do with these two?" Alfredo asked.

"I think the nearest town of any size is Seguin. It might have a jail,"
John said.

"That's not on our way home," Alfredo said.

"Look at this," Beto said.

He walked over and grabbed a saddlebag. He had collected all the
outlaws' money and valuables. John looked through it.

"Here is what I want to do," John said. "On our way home, we
swing by the farmhouse where this all started. If the Griffins are willing, we will give them this money to work the land of the dead farmer.
Just until the boys are big enough to take it on themselves."

Alfredo and Beto both nodded in agreement.

"We will split up the horses. Half will go to the ranch with us.
They should make good cow ponies, and the other half Wilbur can
take back to La Salle. I think we have most of the cattle," John added.

Early the next morning, they loaded up and rode west. They were not far from Seguin when the weather turned bad. John wanted to drop off the prisoners and get back. The storm forced them to stay a couple of days. The front blew in a nasty cold. They had to use some of the money they'd taken from the outlaws to buy coats.

John missed his family. Seguin was not a big place but they had a jail to hold the outlaws and a hotel for the rangers. The local folks said they would hold the killers until a Texas Ranger came by, or a lawman from San Antonio. The two left alive were Marshall Bentley and a Mexican named Lopez. John figured they would hang soon enough. He was through with them.

As soon as it was clear they left. The Griffins were good people and had planned to take care of the boys even before they were asked. They thought the idea of working the land and fixing up the little farmhouse for the boys was a great idea. They promised they would use the funds wisely to make the farm productive. They waved as the rangers and their cattle and thirty horses left for the King Ranch.

Josephina was worried. The rangers had been gone a long time. It was rough country and she couldn't stop thinking about all the things that could go wrong. It was cold and John didn't have his winter gear. He'd left in such a hurry. All he took were his guns and ammunition. She was relieved when she looked up one day and saw them riding in. They looked worn out. Even Hank had lost some weight.

It was two days later when John found Beto tending to some chores in the barn.

"Beto, how are you making it?"

Beto just looked at him. He had no idea what John was talking about. John waited for him to answer.

"Making what?" Beto asked.

"I mean how do you feel?" John asked.

"I feel fine," Beto answered.

"What I mean is how do you feel after having killed two men. I know they were outlaws and needed to be killed but needing to be killed and killing a man are two different things. It has a way of eating at you."

"I don't think about it," Beto said calmly.

"Well, you need to. It is only human to think about it. Even men like that have sisters and mothers that will miss them. If you haven't thought about it yet, you will," John said.

"I did what needed to be done. I did my job," Beto said.

"Yes, you did. You did everything right. That won't be any help when you finally start to deal with this. Trust me. You need to think about it or it will gnaw at you. Has Alfredo said anything about it?" John asked.

"Not to me," Beto said.

"Come with me. Alfredo is in the bunkhouse. We are going to talk about this," John said.

"Do we have to?" Beto asked.

"Yes, we do."

They found Alfredo sitting on his bunk.

"We need to talk," said John.

"Yes sir, what have you got for us now? I'm about ready to ride again," Alfredo said.

"I need to ask you a question. How many men have you killed?" John asked.

"What is this about?" Alfredo asked.

"It's about killing the outlaws. I need to know if you are all right after what we went through. It was the first time for Beto. I need to know about you," John said.

"When I was younger, I was in the war. I was there in Goliad when Fannin and all his men were killed. That was awful. I had nightmares about that for years. In the battle at San Antonio de Bexar, I was in the third wave. I killed a Texan who was trying hit me with

248

his long gun. He was not much older than me. We both were scared. I think about him all the time," Alberto said.

"Are you all right now?" John asked him, putting his hand on Alberto's shoulder.

"It has been good to take a few days off but I'm ready to go now."

"Beto will need you to help him get through this. He doesn't want to talk about it. That's fine for now but he needs to deal with it. Do you agree?"

"Yes," Alfredo said looking at his young friend.

"Then I'll leave it with you, Alfredo. I need my rangers in tip-top shape."

John slapped them both on the back and left them. He wanted to spend time with his wife and son.

CHAPTER 22

War Comes to the Ranch

It was early 1862 and the ranch was growing. More land had been added and the production of cattle had increased, which meant more cowboys. Henrietta, who was managing the ranch, had done a good job with both the cattle and the land. The war had meant an increased need for beef and King had contracts with the Confederate government to provide as much beef as he wanted to sell. Jefferson Davis and King had also become good friends.

The Delaneys were still living in the big house. The children were growing and Little Henry was walking now and playing with the older children. Mac had twelve regular students now, which included the Kings' oldest, Nettie.

In the beginning, the war had seemed far away. Though it had been rough for the Union army in the east, they were now stacking up victory after victory in the west. Lately, the news about the war was seldom as good as it had been in the beginning. After the battle of Shiloh, where Grant's army succeeded in getting a foothold in Tennessee despite large casualties, the South was having to rethink its strategy of sending all its resources to Lee in the east. More men were required to keep the Union army from moving further south down into Mississippi.

The list of Texans killed or missing was creating a somber mood all over the state. Ten days after the battle of Shiloh, Jefferson Davis signed the first Confederate Conscription Act. It required every man between 18 and 35 to enlist in the army. At first, Texas pushed back, stating they were not going to be dictated to by the collective states. That was no different than the Union making demands on them. But they finally gave in and enforced the conscription on all non-frontier areas. This left a large loophole that allowed the state to do as it wished since almost all of Texas was frontier land.

The war came directly to the King Ranch when a captain named Fuller showed up with orders from General Hebert. Hebert was, at that time, headquartered in Galveston. A former sugar cane plantation owner, he was a West Point graduate from New Orleans who had been in and out of the army several times. Hebert had charge of all the forces in Texas.

In March of 1862, Hebert led the infantry for General McCulloch at the Battle of Pea Ridge. He technically oversaw the entire army after McCulloch and McIntosh were both killed. While Hebert was bringing the armies together to make a stand, he was wounded and captured. Later, he recovered from his wound. He was exchanged in a prisoner swap and returned less than a hero. When he arrived in Texas to oversee protecting the coast, he was ready to show his worth and prove he could do more than get captured. His orders were to gather every able-bodied man who could fight for the cause and bring them to Sabine Pass where he would mobilize a force large enough to hold back the Yankee invaders.

The North was pushing south down the Mississippi and if they could get a foothold in Texas, they could operate on two fronts. The South needed men and Hebert needed a win. Captain Fuller had about a dozen men with him, none of whom were real soldiers. They had spent most of their time serving officers. They were little more than stewards who spent their time on common duties like bringing coffee to officers and preparing their meals. The Confederate Army was now in such bad shape that even they were being pressed into doing something besides making officers' beds.

Fuller rode up to the big house and asked to meet with Mrs. King. He was a gentleman from Mississippi. He was charming. Henrietta invited him in. He and two of his men were seated in the parlor along with John and Josephina. They were served coffee and sweet cakes. However, the tone of the meeting changed when he read his orders and announced he would be using the ranch as a headquarters while he recruited in the area. Henrietta King was not one to be ordered around. After hearing what he had to say, she told him he was welcome to make camp down by the stream behind the school but his men were not to interfere with classes.

Fuller looked disturbed by this. It was obvious he took it as an insult. He lectured her on her responsibilities to support the war effort. He also told her that he would be staying in her house. The conversation was becoming heated when Josephina suggested the officers stay in their house.

"If the Delaneys offer you their house, I'm happy with that, as long as you behave as proper guests. If that is not good enough you can find quarters somewhere else," Henrietta proclaimed.

The captain said nothing for a while as he glared at her. Before it got any worse, John got up and walked over to the man.

"We are through here. If you will follow me, I'll show you to the house where you will be staying," John said as he led them out.

"I will look at this place. If it is sufficient to meet our needs, we will use it. If not, I will send word back," said Captain Fuller. "If that occurs, you are to vacate this house before I return."

Henrietta stood. Her jaw was clenched and there was fire in her eyes. John held up his hand and nodded at her to let her know he would take care of it. The soldiers followed John outside.

"Mount up," the captain ordered.

His men did and fell into order with three men abreast as Fuller led the parade. John and Hank took them down the road past the church, then past the school, and finally to the little cabin that he and Josephina called home. He hated for them to step foot in it but he held his tongue. Nothing was spoken until they arrived. The captain held up his hand, ordering them to halt. This was unnecessary. Everyone knew they were there. John got off his horse and told Hank to go to his place. Hank obediently walked to the dog run and sat there, watching the men. The captain sneered at the cabin. Just for show, he got off his horse and walked to the house, looking into both buildings before he announced it unfit.

"Sergeant Duncan, get word to Mrs. King that we will be taking possession of the main house before sunset," Captain Fuller said.

"No need to do that," John said, "I am going there now. I'll relay the message."

"Very good. By the way, son, why are you not in the army?" Fuller asked.

"It's a long story," John said.

"I suspect you will be soon," Fuller said.

John found Henrietta on the porch with Mac, Josephina, and many of the ranch hands. John tied his horse to the rail and walked up to talk with Henrietta. His face must have said all she needed to hear.

"I have already sent a rider to find Richard. I also have sent riders out to find Alfredo and Beto for you," she said. "We need to be calm and not let this get out of hand. Richard is doing plenty of business with the Confederates and we need to be careful. If it were only up to me, I'd run them off."

"They said they were taking the house by sundown," John said.

This brought more fire to Henrietta's eyes. She turned and found a rocker she liked and sat down. After a few minutes of furious rocking, she turned to John.

"Please ride out there and invite the captain to dinner. Tell him he is welcome to spend the night in our guest room. His men can stay in the barracks. That should give us time to figure this out if Richard does not arrive."

"I will do that. This Fuller fellow seems mighty impressed with himself. I am not sure he will be willing to negotiate," John said as he got on his horse.

Henrietta nodded her agreement.

John found the soldiers watering their horses in the creek.

"Where is your captain?" he asked one of the soldiers.

The soldier pointed to a single rider loping across the valley. John kicked his horse and took out after him. When the man saw him coming he turned his horse and rode toward John.

"Did you deliver my message?"

"I did. And Mrs. King has invited you to dinner," John said. "She also said you are welcome to spend the night in their guest room. Your men will be comfortable in the bunkhouse until other arrangements can be made."

"That is not what I said," Fuller barked.

"I told her word for word what you said. You can accept her offer or ride out. Your choice," John said.

"You will not dictate the terms of my departure young man."

"I need your answer now," John said.

Fuller answered him by turning his horse toward his men and galloping away. John sat on the gelding watching him. When he reached his men, he began giving orders and they started scurrying around, getting their horses saddled. John rode back to the big house. There he found even more people in the yard. Beto and Alfredo were among them.

"I did my best," John said. "He is a stubborn man."

"What did he say?" Henrietta asked.

"He told me that I would not dictate any terms to him. Henrietta, you have done your best. Now you need to let me handle this," John said calmly.

"Do what you must. Just remember, we have children here," she said.

"Alfredo, are you ready to ride?" John said.

"We are," Alfredo replied.

"Get your horses. I need four men who know how to shoot."

Ten men came forward. John picked four of them.

"You four saddle up. All the rest of you, I need you to stand ready here near the house. Felix and Hank, I need you here to protect my family."

John rode off with six men. When they reached the area John had marked out, he pointed to a hill on his right.

"Alfredo, take two with you and find a good shooting spot on that hill. Beto, you take the others and do the same behind the school."

John turned to see Mac riding toward him.

"I am coming with you, John," Mac said.

Before the army was in sight, Alfredo took two men and galloped to the left while Beto did the same to the right. John and Mac sat in the middle of the road, waiting for everyone to get into position.

"I see them coming," John said.

"Your eyes are better than mine," Mac said. "John, when they get here, let me talk. Maybe I will have better luck."

"It is worth a try," John said. "I'm through talking to them."

"Don't worry about me. I can hold my own," Mac said.

"I know you can. I would have never let you come if I didn't know you were capable. Henry Lloyd told me if I ever needed a man to depend upon, that man would be you."

"Did he now? Well, I always knew he was a wise man."

They laughed. As the soldiers got closer, John could see Alfredo's men easing in at the same pace as the soldiers. Just a slow walk. They were fanned out twenty yards apart. Their weapons were out and ready.

"Don't look at our boys," John warned.

"I am too busy watching the ones in front of us," Mac said.

"Halt," Captain Fuller said.

The soldiers did as commanded. They were in the same three abreast parade formation. If the shooting started, they would be easy to dispatch.

"Captain, I'd like to introduce you to Bartholomew McGentry," John said.

John bowed his head toward Mac as if he were a dignitary. Fuller watched Mac climb down from his horse and waddle over to the soldiers. Though the soldiers laughed, Mac held his head high. As he began to speak, the soldiers laughed even harder. The captain held up his hand again and the laughter died out.

"I am not sure who you are, or why you are here. I have no time for a hunchback fool," Fuller announced.

"I would like you to reconsider your proposed intention to occupy the main house," said Mac. "The time is not right but if you will kindly accept our invitation for dinner we can deal with this situation like gentlemen."

One of the men in the back started mocking Mac's accent, which triggered another round of laughter.

"We need for you both to get out of the way," Fuller ordered.

"Mac, get back on your horse," John said. "Now who is second in command here?"

No one answered. They smirked as Mac struggled to get back on his horse.

"Lieutenant, my guess is it is you," John said looking at the man behind Fuller.

"Our command structure is not your business," Fuller said, "Now step aside."

"Lieutenant, what do you intend to do about this?" John asked.

"He will do as I say," Captain Fuller said.

"The reason I ask you this, lieutenant, is that if you look to your right, that man with the long rifle is about to blow the head off your captain's shoulders. He never misses. Then you will be in charge."

John leaned forward on his saddle as if to whisper.

"I need to know your plans, because the man on the left, who is also an excellent shot, will be watching you," John said.

The soldiers were now aware of the six men pointing rifles at them. The laughter died away.

"I am through talking with this monkey," John said pointing at Fuller. "What do you think you should do, men?"

Fuller drew his saber as if he were about to lead a charge. John fixed his eyes on him and sat back in his saddle. John looked relaxed but he was ready to react.

"Lieutenant, what is it going to be? I'll not ask you again," John said.

"I would ride away," he answered.

"And we would let you and all your men ride away after you buried your captain but if I hear one more chuckle out of any of you, I'll beat you to death myself with my bare hands. I have held my temper as long as I can. I will not allow any more insults to my dear friend."

"Mr. McGentry," Fuller said, sheathing his saber. "I am most pleased to accept your kind invitation to dinner."

"Very well," Mac said. "I look forward to it."

John motioned and his men walked their horses slowly toward the soldiers. John got off his horse and walked over to Fuller. He reached up and jerked him off his mount. He held the man by the collar.

"You have no idea how close you came to taking your last breath," John said, releasing him with a push that landed him on his back.

"You'd better spend the rest of your life thanking your lieutenant here because he saved your life," John said, stepping over him. "Well, say thank you."

"Thank you," Fuller said at last.

"Not good enough," John said as he kicked the man in the leg.

"Say it like you mean it."

"Thank you, Lieutenant Sanders," Fuller said.

John kicked him again.

"I'll see you at dinner and there will be ladies there. I'd better not have to correct your manners again," John warned.

They rode to the ranch in silence. John and his men escorted the soldiers to the barracks as Mac and Fuller went to the big house to clean up. He asked the lieutenant to have the men take care of their mounts then said he wanted to speak with them. John went to see Josephina and Little Henry while the soldiers settled in.

When John got back, the men were all out front waiting for him.

"I know you are doing as you were ordered. I accept that. However, I am deeply disappointed in you for making fun of a man you know nothing about. He is one of the most decent men you will ever meet. He cannot help how he was born any more than any of you can help how you were born. If I hear any of you laughing at him again, I will string you up and horsewhip you. Now, I will appreciate it if each of you takes the time to ask his forgiveness," he said.

John then went to each man and shook his hand. He asked them their names and where they were from. He stayed with them, making small talk until dinner was ready.

Dinner was pleasant. They did not talk business. Captain Fuller was a perfect gentleman. After dinner, he again made the case for the use of the house. Henrietta offered the church building instead, and he accepted.

Over the next few days, Fuller conducted his interviews from the church as his men milled around, causing no problems. John kept a close eye on them. He witnessed several of the men apologizing to Mac.

Fuller was pleased with himself, even if his production was not as good as he had hoped. The majority of King's ranch hands were his Los Kinenos boys. That was a name they had given themselves. It meant King's boys. Years earlier, Richard King had bought an entire herd of cattle from several ranchers. They had gone through a few bad years due to drought and needed to sell. This loss of employment devastated a few small villages. King found out about it and went back and hired all the men who had lost their jobs. They and their families relocated to South Texas. Los Kinenos were fiercely loyal to Mr. King. He had been good to them. They agreed to talk to the soldiers but they would never leave Mr. King.

Fuller and his men were closing up shop and preparing to leave when Richard King returned. He had been worried when he first arrived but after hearing about what had happened, he was convinced it could not have gone better. He had been prepared to go straight to Jefferson Davis if need be. He also had a letter from the governor declaring the King land as frontier due to the continual border issues.

"I hear Bonnie is ready to deliver any day now," King said as he and John walked down to the corral.

John knew King was satisfied with the situation. He was not a man for small talk if there were issues to be resolved.

"I think so. I had no idea it would take so long for she and Champion to get their schedules to match," John said.

"I see they are leaving. How many men did I lose?" King asked as he watched the soldiers preparing for their departure.

"Seven I think but your Los Kinenos folks sent word to their families that you might be hiring. I hear about a dozen or so should show up soon. You should be able to find a few good hands in the bunch. Mrs. King thinks we made out well in the deal. She thinks those who left would probably have quit soon anyway."

"Little Henry is growing. He is as big as Richard Junior now." King said.

"They are both growing. They are together all the time. They think they are brothers," John said.

"They just about are," King replied.

King looked over to see Captain Fuller walking their way.

"This should be interesting," he said under his breath.

"Mr. King, I am honored to finally meet you," Fuller said, offering his hand.

King shook his hand but remained silent.

"May I have a word with you in private?" asked Fuller.

"No."

"Excuse me," he asked as if he hadn't heard correctly.

"You may not, I said. Anything you have to say to me you can say in front of John. In fact, I would like Mr. Delaney to hear what you say. I trust his judgment in all matters."

"This is a matter of confidentiality."

"Say what you have to say to me or ride off. John is not leaving," King said, his impatience palpable.

"Very well. It is about my official report," Fuller said, trying to maintain his courage like a good soldier.

He could not look at John or Hank. Since the first day, whenever he saw either of them, he got weak in the knees, felt faint, and sometimes had to throw up.

"Yes, I'd like to hear what you have to say. I was about to respond to Jefferson Davis about a matter we are working on and I might need to mention to him what has gone on here," said King.

"This man…"

Fuller pointed at John which made Hank growl. Fuller's hand went down immediately.

"He threatened my life and the lives of several of my men. He hampered me in the conduct of my official duties."

"I know what happened here," King interrupted. "Let me tell you something. You are fortunate to still be alive. John here works for me and he was doing what I instructed him to do. I trust his judgment in all matters and if he had killed you, I would have supported his actions completely. You may get away with bullying other people around because you have a uniform but that won't work here. The only reason I don't arrest you and turn you over to the authorities is because my wife asked me not to."

Fuller's knees were becoming wobbly and his lunch was about to come up. King knew it and he leaned in as he continued.

"But I don't always do as my wife asks."

"There will be no report," Fuller said as he backed away.

Now he had to add Richard King to the list of those he couldn't look at. He stumbled his way back to his men, who were watching with interest as he climbed on his mount.

"I am only going to take them up the road a little way. I don't think we will have any more trouble with them," John said.

"I agree," King said.

Two days later, Bonnie gave birth to a beautiful little filly. She was marked much like her mother but she had her father's black coat. She was not fully black though. She had three white socks and a white marking on her forehead. John named her Star.

CHAPTER 23

Staying Alive with Cotton

By the summer of 1862, New England and New York congressmen were pushing President Lincoln to invade East Texas and seize the great cotton lands. Even as Lincoln resisted the textile industry's pleas in favor of securing the Mississippi River, Texas cotton was pouring into the Mexican port of Matamoros just across the border from the Texas town of Brownsville. It wasn't long before the Union decided to invade Texas.

Richard King had shared with John that the South would lose the war. Few people were talking about it but it was inevitable. The North was losing more men than the South was but they just kept coming. The southern states were running out of steam while the Union was equipped with a seemingly unending supply of men and munitions.

King was worried because he knew that after war, there was always a period of lawless confusion until order was restored. For this reason, he was pleased that John had selected two more men to join his troop of rangers. From the four men who had stepped up to help settle the dispute with the Confederate Army, John had chosen two.

Alfredo was assigned the duty to train and work with a young man from San Antonio named Diego. Diego was a quiet man who took his job seriously. He was eager to learn. He and Alfredo made a good team.

The other man, Paco, was anything but serious. He found humor in everything and loved to laugh. Having a good time, no matter what he was doing, was an inextricable thread that wound through his personality. Despite this, he and Beto both thought Paco was well-suited to the ranger life. Paco had a quality that John admired. He was utterly fearless. Paired with Beto, another ranger who knew no fear, any outlaw would need to think twice before they crossed either man.

With three teams patrolling the range, John felt they had a better chance of maintaining order. The Delaneys were still living in the big house. During this period, Henrietta had added a room on the back of their cabin for young Henry. John spent much of his free time working with the carpenters, learning to construct a sturdy building. He knew that someday he might leave the ranch and he wanted to know how to put together a building that would be solid. He had already moved Bonnie and Star back to his corral

John was ready for this war to end. He had liked his life better before the war. He and Josephina had been happy in their little cabin. He wanted that again. He was working on the house, thinking about how life would be after the war when word arrived that Galveston was being evacuated.

The Union Commodore William B. Renshaw had sailed into Galveston harbor and demanded the surrender of the island city. When he landed in Galveston, the only occupants were its citizens. The soldiers were elsewhere. The Rebels were caught completely off guard. With virtually no defense force, the Confederate commander on the island, Colonel Joseph J. Cook, had little choice but to comply. The Union army could use Galveston as a dropping-off spot for more troops. Texas was now seriously in the picture. Most of the citizens were relocated to Houston but Houston was not able to take them all. Some were headed for Austin and San Antonio and others were going south toward the border.

Sabine Pass had been attacked a month earlier so going north was not a good option. Henrietta King was worried about her husband. At the beginning of the war, she had been upset because he was gone so much but now she worried about his physical safety.

King was using the easternmost part of his land as a collection point to gather cotton and transport it across the border to Mexico, either by land or by boat. The Confederates were finding it difficult to pay for what they needed. Selling cotton to Europe via Mexico was the only steady income the South had. The operation on the eastern part of King Ranch was not near the house. It had started in a small warehouse but it had grown to a rather large operation. It was only a matter of time before the Yankees found it.

John and Hank were watching the area when they discovered a small band of Union scouts sent from Galveston. They had seen more than they should have. John knew they had located the hidden warehouse and the land route to Brownsville.

King now needed to move the operation farther south, closer to Brownsville. There was no standing Union army in Texas yet but the Texas coastline was littered with small expeditionary groups. The area was too large for the Confederate forces to maintain a defense to prevent this. From that day forward he made sure that he or his men were watching the east.

In January of 1863, the Confederates took back Galveston. The battle lasted only a day. This victory did little good for the southern cause absent a civilian population, and with the Union naval blockade, the south could not get the port going again. It seemed to make the Texans feel better knowing the Yankees were gone but everyone feared it was a matter of time before they returned.

With most of the Union ships busy around the southern coast of Carolina, Mobile, Alabama, and New Orleans, there were few resources available for the southern Texas coast until September 1863, when a Union warship off the Rio Grande stopped and boarded the British-owned vessel *Sir William Peel*. Yankee intelligence reports confirmed the Confederates planned to turn this merchant ship into an armed Rebel privateer. Alarm bells going off in Washington were heard all the way to Lincoln's office.

The North wondered if Confederate warships disguised as merchant vessels were about to swarm out of Mexican waters and lift the blockade. If so, something had to be done about that. The "back door" had to be shut. Two months later, the invasion fleet steamed through Brazos Santiago Pass and anchored in Laguna Madre. Union troops took Brazos Santiago Island and established a base there. They unloaded massive artillery in preparation for a major battle. Other bluecoats occupied Point Isabel. This closed the main port the blockade runners were using.

Union regiments soon marched to Brownsville where panic-stricken residents were crossing the Rio Grande with their cotton bales and other worldly goods. Outnumbered, the local Confederate troops withdrew to San Antonio. Unwilling to leave Fort Brown to the Union, the Rebels set fire to the wooden buildings. The flames spread to nearby Brownsville and soon reached a merchant's supply of gunpowder. It blew up with a deafening roar that scattered burning debris and ignited much of the business district.

King was now out of business. He fled north with a small band of militia fighters. The Yankees wanted him. They sent a company of cavalry soldiers to find and destroy the cotton supply line. They were not far behind him.

King did not have enough men to stand his ground and fight the fifty mounted soldiers that were headed to the ranch. John's rangers were keeping watch as the bluecoats progressed. King sent word for John to meet him there.

"How much time do we have?" King asked.

"Two days at the most," John reported. "They wasted some time looking around the area where the cotton was being held but they are moving swiftly now."

"I am sending the women and children to San Antonio. The bluecoats are after me, so I will head northeast. If my plan works, they will follow me into a trap. I am not sure that two days gives us enough time. Henrietta is expecting another baby and I am worried about what this trip will do to her."

"What do you need me to do?" John asked.

"Make sure they get there safely," King said.

"We need more time—and I have an idea," John said.

"I'm listening," said King.

"Felix, Aldo, and Mac can take a few good men with them and make certain our families get to San Antonio. The western area is clear of any soldiers. If I take a couple of good fighters, I can hold them back a few days."

"Too dangerous," King said.

"Not really. I will not confront them. I know how to do this. My father and brothers were experts at harassing the British soldiers and from what I can see, the Union forces behave just like they did. Trust me. We will be fine. Our horses are better than theirs and we know the land. It's our land they are on."

"Let me hear your plan," King said, smiling.

John convinced him it was the correct path to take.

On October 4, 1863, Los Kinenos moved all the cattle and horses west as far as they could. Richard King and his men rode north toward Houston while Henrietta, Josephina, Mac, Felix, Aldo, and a few other men went west to San Antonio.

John had selected three more men to join his rangers. All of them had been with King protecting the cotton transport. They knew how to shoot and follow orders. That was all John needed. They rode toward the advancing army.

The San Antonio group took time to assemble. Henrietta insisted that there be three wagons to transport her group. One wagon was to be filled with the contents of her school library and two modified wagons were to be fitted out for transporting the family. Mac supervised taking a buggy apart and used the springs to fashion a bed for Henrietta in the wagon he drove. The other wagon was driven by Aldo and it was a traveling playroom for the children. Felix rode alongside the three wagons. He was capable and could be depended upon, and he loved his family. They were safe with him. He was the trail boss. They took three days to leave the house since they had faith in John and his rangers to hinder the soldiers' advance.

Mr. King had left two days earlier. He was zigzagging from settlement to settlement, gathering every able-bodied man he could find. If there was going to be a fight, he was going to be ready for them. He was furious that the Yankees were on his land.

The first engagement with the enemy came at night. John and Hank slipped in and killed two guards with a knife so there was no alarm, then they stole some of the horses. They took fire as they left but were not hit. They drove the horses off, scattered them, then made their way back to the other rangers. Beto and Paco kept watch over the operation, ready to fire from the other side if they needed to.

The soldiers were on notice that the battle was on. It took them most of the next day to gather their horses and put things in order. They had scouts out all day looking for the rangers but found no trace of them. John and Hank's tracks were mixed with those of the wandering horses.

John's biggest challenge was the lack of natural cover. The South Texas terrain featured scrub oaks, mesquite trees, and cactus. A rocky canyon would be ideal for what John had planned but there were none. He would have to use the Neches River. The river had areas that were easy to ford and others that were almost impossible to cross. John had to lead the army where he needed them to be. If they were in hot pursuit of the rangers they would be less cautious.

The plan was for Beto, Paco, and two other recruits to engage the Union soldiers in a fight, then retreat, leading the soldiers to the point where the rangers wanted them to cross. It was late in the day when Paco took the first shot, killing a scout who had found them. A few minutes later, several soldiers rode in fast. They took fire from the rangers, who killed two more of them, sending the others back for help. Beto sent the other rangers to join John. He stayed to make sure the Yankees were coming. And come they did. The entire company was fanned out over about a hundred yards. Beto fired at them a few times, then rode off just a short distance. He found another place to shoot from and waited. It was almost dark but they were still coming. They were ready to avenge the loss of their comrades. Beto fired again, killing a rider with the first shot. He fired a second time, hitting a horse that fell, injuring his rider. The Yankees fired back and quickly gathered into ranks awaiting orders to charge. Beto fired a few more shots but failed to hit anything.

The Yankee gunfire now was rapid enough to drown out the horse's hooves as Beto retreated. They were close enough for John and his rangers to hear them. He told Hank to stay and he rode out to find Beto. It was just getting dark when he found him, walking his horse.

"She pulled up lame," Beto said. "I think she took too many cactus needles."

"You are not far from the river," John said. "Take her in and take care of her. I'll see about our guests."

"They are not far behind us. I don't know if they are moving or if they have made camp."

"When you get there tell Hank 'find John, Hank, find John'—just like that. I may need him."

John rode to find the Union Army. He located them a few miles from where Beto had confronted them. He found a good spot in a gully where he could hide his horse, then took his gun and went on foot toward the soldiers who were settling in for the night. To move an entire military company through this kind of terrain takes time and planning. Just before John reached his position, Hank walked up beside him, wagging his tail.

"Let's wait here, boy," John said, ruffling his ears.

He was close enough to see what they were doing now. Hank would let him know if anyone came by—a likely event since they would still be on alert.

The soldiers had a fire going in no time and their horses were secured. It was a couple of hours before Hank looked to his right and growled.

"Shhhh," John whispered.

Hank was quiet but alert. Two soldiers were walking up behind them. John and Hank stayed still as the sentries walked by. They remained undetected. An hour later, two more soldiers came from the opposite direction. These two were headed straight for them.

"Shhhhh, Hank. Be still," John said.

When the men were only steps away John said. "Go, Hank!"

The big mastiff lunged and tackled the soldier on the left, knocking him down. Hank was on top of him with a mouth full of the man's right arm. John got to the other soldier a few seconds later and thrust his knife deep into his side, just below his ribs. Hank looked up to make sure John was safe, then went back to work on his soldier.

The man John had stabbed pulled out his pistol. He dropped the gun when John's fist struck his jaw. John slit his throat before he could yell.

He did the same thing to Hank's man.

"Sit, Hank," John said as he listened to see if anyone had heard them.

After a few minutes, he was certain they had not. He figured it would be a few hours before the men were missed and maybe dawn before they found the bodies hidden in the brush. They walked back quietly, listening as they returned to his horse. Just before they got there, Hank's ears perked up. He smelled something.

"Shhh," John said.

He stopped and listened. He knew what had happened. They had found his horse and were waiting for him to return. There might be several of them. The best thing to do was to leave the horse and let them watch for him until dawn. He and Hank looped around clear of the area and walked back to the river. They came upon Alfredo before they got there.

"Are you okay?" Alfredo asked. "Where is your gelding?"

"It looks like he might have joined the Yankees," John said.

He told Alfredo what had happened as they walked back to the river. The rangers had rested but not slept. It was about an hour before dawn when John and Paco crossed the river to watch while the others waited in the places they would fight from. Paco and John returned to the others about an hour after first light.

"They are coming," John reported. "Only about ten or twelve of them. The rest will not be far behind. Beto, you and Paco wade back across. One of you go upstream, the other one ease down the river. When they get close to the river, open fire. Be careful and don't shoot each other. Kill as many as you can. It should bring the others running. As soon as you can, come back across. Be careful. boys. I'll be here in the middle, behind that log. I'll take as many as I can."

The dozen or so soldiers followed the trail up to the river. They paused to look around when Paco fired first, missing everything. Beto shot the man closest to him and John dropped another. There was a moment of chaos as the horses were spooked and the soldiers were drawing their guns, looking to find where the shots were coming from.

John shot again, taking down another rider. Beto and Paco both fired again, each one hitting a target. The soldiers decided a retreat was their best option. As soon as they turned their horses to leave, Paco and Beto waded back across with John, still shooting at the retreating few. He managed to hit one more. He didn't know how serious it was.

The rangers took their places and waited. About an hour later, two riders came forward holding a white flag. They came to the bank of the river and waited.

"What is it you want?" John yelled.

"We wish to talk with your commander," the soldier said.

"You may cross. Hold your fire, men," John said.

The two soldiers nudged their horses into the river and crossed to the north bank. After they were across, John walked out from behind a tree.

"May I help you?"

Both soldiers dismounted.

"We are offering you the opportunity to escape. If you and your men leave now, we will not pursue you. Our business is not with you. My captain has sent for more troops so if you don't take advantage of this one chance we will have to defeat you completely," the soldier said.

"What do you mean our business is not with us? You are on our land," John said calmly.

"Are you Richard King?" the man asked.

"No."

"Then we are not on your land."

"So, what you are saying is that you are after Richard King?" John asked.

"I have said nothing to that effect. I asked if you were King."

"Do you think you have the advantage?"

"I am sure you know we have a full company," the soldier said. "We are prepared to defeat you if you continue."

"How many more men did you leave Fort Brown with than you have now?" John asked.

The man didn't answer.

"My count is ten. You have lost ten good men. For what?"

"We have orders," the soldier said.

John suddenly knew why the man was there. He was there to waste time.

"We are in no hurry," he said. "At this rate, you will be out of men in another week, and we have plenty of bullets."

He could hear his men laughing as he said this.

"So, am I to report to my captain that you refused his generous offer?" the soldier said as he climbed back on his horse.

"No, tell him we countered. If you leave now, we will stop killing you. If you keep moving forward, we have no other option than to kill you all, one by one. Not much fun burying your buddies is it?"

The men rode back across the river, looking around to see what they were facing. They saw nothing.

"Alfredo, they did this to waste time while they flanked us. Ride north to see if they crossed there. Diego, you ride south. Hurry."

They both returned shortly, reporting troops crossing from both ways, about two dozen in each group.

"Mount up. We need to ride."

The rangers were gone in minutes. They were down two horses, so they had doubled up on the mounts they had left. John scribbled a note and tacked it to a log near where they had met with the Yankees.

About an hour later, a bugle sounded and the cavalry charged the river. One group was riding hard from the east, the other from the west. The attack was planned well because they all arrived at the same time. The only problem was that there was no one to attack. Captain Leon Whitney was on his horse looking around when a soldier retrieved the note.

"Sorry we could not stay. Had urgent business elsewhere. Leave now while you still can."

Captain Whitney was furious. Another day had been wasted and they had only moved a few miles. He ordered them to make camp. He sent his best scout out to determine the direction the scoundrels were headed and how many were with them. The scout returned saying there were only six horses and a dog. They were moving fast, headed due east.

"They want us to follow them. Well, I don't have time for their rebel games. We'll set our course to the ranch and watch our flanks. We leave in the morning."

The following morning, the rangers were sitting around the fire after breakfast. Being a ranger is much like being a soldier. There were brief periods of chaos and intense action followed by long periods of waiting.

Alfredo had left at dawn to find more horses. He soon returned with their old friend Wilbur, who lived nearby. Wilbur helped them buy a few mounts and rode back with Alfredo, glad of the chance to once again help John and his rangers. Paco was entertaining them with stories when Diego came riding up. He had stayed behind to keep an eye on the army. Diego reported that the soldiers had left just after dawn, headed to the ranch. Eight of them had stayed behind to track the rangers. The eight had found their trail and were in hot pursuit.

"How far back are they?" John asked.

"Maybe four hours, maybe less. They are moving pretty fast."

John got up and walked away, thinking about what to do. The rangers packed and saddled their horses. They knew something was going to happen. They just didn't know what it was. They found out a few minutes later when John told them his plan.

Paco was to ride as hard as he could to the ranch and make sure the women and children had left safely. The others were to move northwest, staying ahead of the Yankees while John and Hank would need to slow the eight Yankees pursuing them. Things were getting out of control. He hoped Paco could make it before the Union army did.

It was just over an hour later when Hank found the soldiers. They were moving faster than John had expected. John moved around to their flank and found a good place to shoot from. He left his horse tied to a mesquite bush and he and Hank waited until they were in range. One shot dropped a soldier in the middle of the bunch. John watched as they circled their horse in a tight ring. Each man was looking in a different direction. No panic, no wild shots, they were ready to fight within minutes. This was a well-trained unit. John and Hank walked their horse off a good distance from the soldiers before he mounted. He figured the loss of a man might slow them down.

John knew they would be thinking they needed to be more careful now. This was a good bunch of fighters. He would prefer not to deal with them. But he had no choice. These soldiers would catch up to them soon.

CHAPTER 24

The Prey

Paco watched the soldiers ride up to the empty ranch house. He had arrived ahead of the Yankees, swapped horses, and was ready to return when he saw them coming. He decided to stay and watch them from a distance. John would want to know what the army was doing. They didn't appear to be in a hurry. Paco watched them for several hours, then rode to where he thought the rangers might be. They would need him if there was to be a fight.

Captain Whitney was furious to find the ranch abandoned. He had left Fort Brown with sixty-seven of the best cavalrymen they had. He was now down to forty-eight weary, depressed, confused men, low on supplies. He had pushed them hard for no reason. He'd been defeated by a few civilians and he could not wait to leave this hellish Texas terrain.

He gathered what he could from the ranch so the return ride back to the fort would be better provisioned. Perhaps his next assignment would be worthwhile. This one had turned out to be nothing but a wild goose chase. His men found only a few horses and a dozen head of cattle had been left behind. He stayed the night in the house, then they headed south.

John was proud of his rangers. They were all quality men. He found a little creek and they gave their tired horses a rest. John did not know how far back the soldiers were and this was beginning to worry him, though he knew the odds were better now with Wilbur and fresh horses. He knew the soldiers following them were capable fighters so another steady gun was what they needed. It was time to prepare for battle. John told them what he had seen. They continued to rest but kept an eye open for the Union soldiers.

John left Hank to rest. He rode off to find the best place he could to stage an ambush. This was not easy in South Texas. A stand of thick scrub oaks would have to suffice for cover. They could hide the horses on the back side with an easy escape route if things went wrong. If things went as planned, which they rarely did, it would be over in only a few minutes.

Within a few hours, they were set. They waited but nothing happened. Night fell and there was still no enemy. He didn't want to come out now when the soldiers might be waiting to ambush them. After several hours of darkness, John moved through the brush telling them all to go to their horses one at a time.

"Make no noise. We need to slip out of here," John told them.

What had been a good plan suddenly felt like a trap. John's stomach was turning. When they were clear of the woods they headed due west. The rangers were going home. They walked their horses single file all night without talking. When it was light, they rested by a little pond they had found that had good water for the horses. While the horses were drinking, Hank perked up, letting them know they had company. It was Paco. He too had traveled by night. He reported that the women and children had been gone before the army arrived. They were all safe.

This was good news. King had escaped, their families were safe and his men were all still alive. He did not know where the pursuing soldiers were, however. Were he and his men still the prey? After a few hours, John had had enough.

"This may be over with or it might be just starting. We must find out because we can't keep looking over our shoulders. So here is what we do. Wilbur are you ready for a fight?"

Wilbur grinned and nodded. John knew he was a good man and he was fresher than the exhausted rangers.

"Wilbur, Hank and I will find them. If we need you, we will come and get you. Be ready to come running. The rest of you, get to the ranch. Wilbur and I will do what we need to do and meet you there," John said.

John sat down and wrote a note to Henrietta, requesting that she pay the rangers two months' wages. He asked Alfredo to hold the note and give it to her when she returned to the ranch.

"You will return," Alfredo said.

"I plan to. Just hold the note," John said.

The rangers were preparing Wilbur and John's gear. Soon they were ready to go their separate ways.

"I would like to go with you," Alfredo said.

"No, I need you to take care of these youngsters for me," John said, with a grin. "Make sure you keep Beto away from all the married women."

The laughter broke the tension.

"Let's go hunting, Wilbur," John said.

They rode hard to where John had last seen the soldiers circle their mounts. It had not rained so their trail was easy to find. They followed the trail and, as John had suspected, the soldiers were tracking them. John knew where they were going so that made it easier. The soldiers had picked up the rangers' trail and were not far behind them. John was worried that his circling around was a mistake. It looked like the soldiers were moving fast. John and Wilbur rode through the night, resting only a few hours just before dawn. They were moving again when they heard gunfire. The soldiers had caught up with his men. They kicked their horses and hurried to the fight.

It didn't take them long to get there. The rangers were pinned down in a dry creek bed. Their horses had scattered. The soldiers had the high ground. The Yankees were flanking the rangers. It was a classic attack. Three soldiers were firing at them from behind good cover. Two had taken the left flank in the creek bed and were getting closer. The other two were doing the same from the right flank. John could not see any others. He knew there might be more. His best guess was that several more were behind the rangers. They got off their horses and tied them to a tree. Wilbur found a place to shoot from.

"Kill as many as you can. Don't hit our boys," John said. "Hank, go."

John pointed to the left and Hank took off as if shot from a cannon. John was afraid they would see him before he got there but there was nothing else to do. These soldiers had to be stopped before they accomplished their mission. John took off running toward the creek bed on the right where they were getting very close. The gunfire was covering the noise they made so the Yankees had no idea they were in the fight.

Wilbur's first shot was true. He killed the only man he had a good shot at. This caused a bit of a stir with the other soldiers. They didn't know where the shot had come from. They stopped shooting and began looking around. They decided they were being attacked from the rear and adjusted their position. Wilbur no longer had a clear shot. He moved quietly to his left to improve his chances as Hank leapt into the creek bed between the rangers and the Union soldiers. He rushed headlong into the advancing soldiers. They froze at the sight of this four-legged monster flying at them. Hank chose the closest man to attack. The man took a few steps backward so Hank was unable to get him off his feet. He was sparring with the man when a bullet flew his way. Fur flew everywhere as Hank felt the sting. John chose to enter the creek bed behind his quarry. He could see Wilbur moving. John saw a soldier he had not noticed before taking aim at Wilbur. The soldier fired and missed. Wilbur had reached his spot safely. But one of them knew where he was. John aimed and fired at the man just before he fired again. John missed but it startled the soldier enough that his shot went wide. John took better aim at the Yankee and squeezed the trigger. His shot landed in the shooter's right shoulder blade. He was out of the fight. Wilbur began firing again. Beto, seeing what was happening, charged the men in front of them, dove to the ground, aimed, and hit a soldier who had turned toward Wilbur. John heard horses come from behind his men. He could not see through the trees. He hurried toward his men, pistol in one hand and his rifle in the other.

Hank was bleeding. It was not a direct hit but the bullet had taken a hunk of meat from his right thigh. He left his quarry and attacked the shooter. He was able to take this man to the ground. The first man Hank had attacked was bleeding badly from his arms and chest. He was also in a state of terror, only able to watch as Hank mauled his buddy. Hank was able to get to this man's throat where he took a huge chunk of it. The man was dead in minutes as blood gushed from his jugular vein.

When the man was dead, Hank went back to the first man who immediately started running. Hank was hobbled with his hind leg wounded but he caught the soldier and the fight was on again.

Wilbur was firing at the Yankee nearest to him. He couldn't hit him but he kept him pinned down. He saw Beto crawling toward the soldier so he scanned the area to see if anyone popped up to fire at him. He saw another ranger running to join Beto. The rangers were the aggressors now.

John ran up on a couple of soldiers. He was on top of them before they knew it. He shot one man with his pistol from just a few feet away while he swung his rifle at the other man. The man he had shot kept moving and he was pointing his gun at John. The man John hit with his rifle took the gun stock across his jaw. He went down.

The first man John had shot now fired his pistol. John felt a burn in his right arm and he dropped the rifle. He had lost his grip but he still had the pistol in his left hand. He pointed it at the man's face and fired. The bullet entered his left cheek and pink spray flew out of his right ear. At the same time, John heard guns popping at a furious pace. The riders had arrived and his rangers were battling them. He was hit just above the elbow. He left his rifle and walked toward his men.

John yelled at them as he approached, letting them know it was him. He kept calling their names as he approached. The gunfire stopped before John got there. He could see them now.

"It's me. I am coming in," John said.

"Come ahead," Alfredo said.

John was bleeding badly now. They wrapped his arm to staunch the flow.

"Glad to see you," Beto said.

"Is everybody safe?" John asked.

"Sanchez is dead, and we haven't seen Paco. He was scouting ahead when the Yankees found us. Nobody has seen him. He may have been caught by the soldiers. We don't know," Alfredo said.

About that time, they heard Wilbur stuttering something. He was walking in with two prisoners. John learned that three Union soldiers had ridden in and were met with a flurry of gunfire. They had died before they could get off a shot.

"Where is Hank?" John asked.

"We haven't seen him but we heard him down the creek."

Beto pointed as he walked up with Wilbur and Francisco, escorting the two bluecoats.

"Stay here, I'll go see," Alfredo said as he went to find Hank.

Hank was sitting down, licking his wound. It had almost stopped bleeding but it was a bad gash. Alfredo checked the two dead soldiers, then knelt to see about Hank. John did not stay behind.

"Are you all right, boy?" John asked.

Hank's big brown eyes were filled with pain but he managed to wag his tail when he saw John. He hobbled over to greet his master. John sat, pressing a bloody rag to his arm, and checked Hank's wound.

"I should have never sent you," John said with tears in his eyes.

"The bullet went through cleanly. He will be fine. I can sew him up if he will let me," Alfredo said.

While the rangers were busy gathering horses and dragging up dead Yankees, Alfredo made a fire and boiled water. He sharpened his knife. The two prisoners sat peacefully watching all that was going on. They were not bound. The fight was gone from them.

The water was hot and Alfredo shaved the hair from Hank's leg while John held his head, talking softly in his ear. Alfredo took a needle he used to sew leather and some string from his cotton shirt and stitched Hank's wound. Hank watched him in obvious pain but he did not snap at Alfredo.

When he was finished with Hank, Alfredo cleaned the knife and the needle and went to work on John. He laid the knife blade in the fire until it was white-hot. He gave John a strap to bite on, then walked Hank over to where several rangers were sitting. They put a rope around him. John told him to stay. He sat watching as Alfredo put the hot knife to the wound. They smelled the flesh burn as he cauterized the injury. Then he sewed it up. John had to keep telling Hank to be easy. As soon as it was over, Hank limped over and sat at his master's side.

"What do we do with the soldiers?" Alfredo asked John after everything was settled for the evening.

"I don't want to do anything with them. They were following orders. I don't hold any grudge against them, do you?"

"No but I'm still worried we haven't seen Paco," Alfredo said.

"Me too. He should have been back by now," John said.

He paused, looking down at Hank.

"Bring the Yankees over here, if you don't mind. I don't want Hank to move for a while and I'm sure he won't leave my side."

The two men strolled over and sat on the other side of John, a safe distance away from Hank.

"What is your name?" he asked the first one.

"Jeffery Johnson," the man said.

"Where are you from, Jeffery?"

"Ohio. We all are from Ohio. I'm from Columbus."

"What did you do in Columbus?" John asked.

"I worked on my uncle's dairy farm," Jeffery answered.

"How about you?" John asked the other man.

"Thomas Duncan. I'm from Cleveland. I worked on the docks."

John talked with the men for a while about what it was like in Ohio, how they had joined the army, and where they had been. They gladly shared their stories with him. They wanted to know about John and his men. John told them about life on the ranch.

"In the morning we are riding west. What are your plans?" John asked.

They looked at each other strangely.

"We are your prisoners," Thomas said.

"No, you're not. If you leave us alone I have nothing against you. If you can help us bury all these men, you are welcome to take what supplies you need and leave. I suggest you head back to Fort Brown. You don't want to run across any Confederate troops. Stay west and you should miss them. They are patrolling the coastline regularly."

It was agreed after the bodies were buried the following morning that the two Union soldiers would go south and the rangers would go west. They were finishing up the common grave when Beto saw Paco approaching. Alfredo was more at ease now. The rangers buried their friend Sanchez with the soldiers from Ohio. They all had something good to say about him and Thomas and Jeffery said that the Union soldiers were mostly good men. Afterward, the two shook hands with the rangers and mounted their horses.

"Wait, you might need these," John said.

He motioned and Beto brought them their guns. They quickly put them away.

"Thank you," they said.

"Be careful," John said as the rangers waved goodbye to what was left of the Union army.

A few hours later, the rangers left. They had made a carriage sling out of two poles tied to a horse with a blanket secured between them. Hank would be riding. He didn't want to but John made him. John's arm was swelling some and he hoped it wasn't infected. Alfredo thought a small bone might have broken. causing the swelling. He fashioned a sling for it. John would need help for a few days.

After a while, Hank got used to the carriage and relaxed. John did not like having to be helped. It would be a long ride to San Antonio. The rangers took their time and enjoyed the leisurely pace. They hunted along the way and stayed on the main roads. When they finally arrived in San Antonio, they were ready for a vacation. They deserved the rest. Hank was doing better and so was John. They would both heal fine.

The rangers took their bonus pay and lived it up for a while in San Antonio, which was booming at the time. Most of the Texas coast had temporarily moved inland. Over the past few weeks, the rangers had become very close. John wanted to figure out a way to keep them all. Wilbur also wanted to become a full-time ranger. He was good at everything except talking. Since talking was not a big part of being a ranger, John figured the ranger life might be just what he needed. He decided to keep the group together through the end of the war. He would work things out with Richard King later. John couldn't stop thinking about how long the Irish had fought the British, though. Maybe this civil war, as they were starting to call it, would last a long time. If it did last, he might take his family and try to find Henry Lloyd in California.

Josephina had never been happier to see John. She fretted about his arm and made him see a real doctor. The doctor said Alfredo had done a superb job of field surgery. Though John would have a scar, he would regain full use of his arm.

They stayed in San Antonio until the spring of 1864. By then the war had taken most able-bodied young men. The army was starting to enlist boys as young as fifteen as well as older men up to fifty. If the war lasted any longer, there might not be a country left. Texas needed their men. They were dying at an alarming rate. The public seemed to be getting numb to it. Unless it was your child or your husband, it was just another poor soul who would not return. Lists of names were read regularly from the courthouse steps. John went a few times because he was curious. It was unsettling to hear the names of all the young boys who were dead or missing.

They packed up their wagons and started back to the ranch in mid-April, 1864. Henrietta had given birth to her fifth child, a little boy they named Robert. Josephina was pregnant with their second child but she was not due for several months.

They found the ranch in good shape. It didn't take long for everything to return to normal. The Kings were still making a profit, even with the Union blockade. With five children to raise, Henrietta was spending less time managing the ranch but it didn't seem to slow things down.

The Delaneys moved back into their cabin. With more rangers around, John was confident that the main house was safe. His men had proven they could handle an emergency. The additional room was almost finished and ready for Little Henry and the new baby. Bonnie's filly was grown now and was being trained as a workhorse. She was an excellent mare. As Richard King and John watched her one day, King offered to buy her.

"Buy her? She is yours," John said.

"No, she is yours. I'd like to have her, though. She is perfect for what I am looking for. I plan to produce a line of cattle horses that will bring top dollar at auction."

"Take her. I lost one of your horses to the Yankees. I think we are even. You have been more than generous with me," John said. "She is yours."

"What kind of negotiation was that? If you are going to be a businessman you need to learn to value something as fine as this horse."

King was smiling at him.

"How much money do you have John?"

"I don't know. You have been keeping up with it for me," John replied.

"You are doing quite well. What are your plans?" asked King.

"One day I want to have a place of my own. Maybe raise cattle like you and have something for my family. I am not in any hurry to do that, though. I want to see how this war plays out," John said.

"It can't last much longer. The South is broke. Wars, like everything else, require money. The South has no money. They have also run out of places to borrow it," King said sadly.

"I would like to keep all the men I have until the war is over. I will need trained fighters if we have to do this again," John said.

"You can have what you need John. I am pleased with what you did. You and your men held off a company of well-trained cavalry soldiers. I have never heard of anything like that before. If you were in the service you would be getting all kinds of medals," King said.

"I have all I need," John said.

"She is a fine young mare. Look at her prance," King said, watching Star go through the drills.

"Yes sir, she is going to be a fine horse. With her father's looks and her mother's heart she will make a fine addition to your stable," John said.

"Bonnie is a pretty mare but I think Star might be something special," King replied. "Tell your men they have jobs as long as they need them. And give them all a raise."

A few weeks after Mr. King returned to his office in Galveston, John received a letter from him detailing his financial holdings. John had become a wealthy man over the past few years and Mr. King had invested wisely for him. The investments plus his salary and bonuses had added up. John kept this information to himself.

Two days later, their second child was born. It was November 15, 1864. Josephina gave birth to a little girl they name Katherine. She would be known as Katy. She was born the same day General Sherman began his march of death. This campaign broke the will of the South to resist. Not long after his campaign ended on December 21, 1864, the war was over.

"I need to tell you something," John told his wife.

"What is it, darling?"

She was smiling at her husband, holding their baby while Little Henry lay on top of Hank. He and Hank had become close. John was afraid that Hank was now Henry's dog.

"I got a letter," he said.

"I didn't think you could get letters from your sister," she said.

"I can't. I miss her. I hope she is all right," John said. "The letter was from Captain King. He sent me an annual report of my holdings."

"What does that mean?" Josephina asked.

"It means we are rich," John said.

"What do you mean?"

"It means we can buy anything we need."

"We don't need anything. We have everything we could ever want," Josephina said.

"I know we do but this land and this house belong to the Kings," John said.

She just looked at him. She had never owned anything. She had never even considered owning anything.

"What do you think about us having our own ranch?" John continued.

"I have never thought about it."

"Well, I want you to think about it. A place where we can raise our children and have a life of our own," John said.

"We already have a good life," she whispered.

She had tears in her eyes.

"I have everything I want right here. My brothers, my babies, my…"

She couldn't say any more. John was silent too. After a few minutes, she spoke.

"May I talk to Henrietta about this?"

"Yes, please do."

They left it there.

CHAPTER 25

The Return

A few weeks later, Alfredo found John playing with Little Henry as Hank watched. Alfredo looked stern.

"I need to speak with you," he said.

John turned Little Henry over to Hank, who began wrestling with the toddler.

"You have treated me so well. I don't know how to tell you this but I have to quit," said Alfredo.

"Why?" John asked.

"In San Antonio, I met a lady. I didn't plan to like her but I do."

Alfredo was hanging his head.

"I thought I would get over her but since I left I cannot stop thinking about her."

"I expected that from Beto but not you. What is her name?" John asked, smiling.

"Camilla. She has three young boys—Mateo, Tomas, and Lucas. Her husband died and left her with the boys. She needs help raising them and I know how to raise boys. She likes me even though I'm an old man. I will be leaving in the morning. Do you think Mr. King will sell me my horse? I have saved some money."

"Wait a minute. I need you. Let's think about this," John said.

"Think all you want. I can't live without her. I'll be leaving in the morning," Alfredo said as he turned and walked back to the bunk-house.

John told Josephina he was going to the King's house. He saddled Bonnie and passed Alfredo on the way to the house. He found Henrietta at the school talking with Mac. John had a plan.

"Henrietta?"

John interrupted the educational planning meeting.

"What is it?" she asked.

"We need to talk. Alfredo is in love and wants to leave."

Henrietta was grinning. Nothing made her happier than a couple of people in love, even if one of them was an old man.

"Tell me about this," she said.

"He just told me about it. I had no idea. He says he can't live without her."

"Yes, I can remember when you and Josephina were courting."

"I need him. The men look up to him. He is a leader," John said.

"So his love is stronger than his need to ride around with a bunch of rangers?"

She was enjoying this.

"I have an idea," John said.

"I'm listening."

They could see Alfredo walking toward them. John needed to hurry.

"If you can let Josephina and the children move back in with you for a while, I can let Alfredo have my house until we can build him one. He can move his new family here. Then he doesn't have to leave."

She cocked her head to the side and thought for a minute. She usually did all the planning, so this was new. She liked the idea, however.

"The boys need a father," John continued. "That is the main thing. Alfredo is a good-hearted man."

By now Alfredo was close enough for her to call to him.

"Alfredo," she called. "What are the boys' names and how old are they?"

He looked puzzled but he answered her.

"Mateo is ten I think, Tomas maybe about seven, and Lucas is five or six," he said, looking to John for answers.

"And the young lady's name?"

"Camila."

There was a sparkle in his eye when he said her name.

"First thing in the morning I want you to get a wagon ready. Go to San Antonio and bring them back here. John needs you, the school could use a few more students, and I am moving Josephina and the little ones back into the house with me. I need her. John can come too if he wants. You and your new family will live in John's house," she said as if it had been her plan all along.

"Yes, ma'am."

Nobody wasted time arguing with Henrietta King.

"Then it's decided."

She turned and went back to her meeting with Mac, then stopped, as if with an afterthought.

"We will have the wedding as soon as you get back here. I know you want to do the right thing and marry her as soon as you can."

John walked Bonnie as he and Alfredo strolled to the bunkhouse. He knew Josephina would be fine with this since it was Henrietta's plan.

On March 15, 1965, a letter arrived from Henry Lloyd. It was posted from Santa Fe, New Mexico. He had never made it to California and now he had a new bride and baby. He planned to return to Texas but he had been delayed. He gave no details except that he was somewhere between Santa Fe and Taos.

John thought something was wrong. Henry Lloyd had not asked for help but John knew he needed it. He knew he needed to go find his friend.

John made all the necessary arrangements to be gone for a while, leaving Alfredo in charge of scheduling the rangers. He made sure Aldo was available to help Josephina. He shared his apprehensions with Henrietta. She gave him her blessing and told him to hurry.

The next morning, he kissed his wife and children, made sure he had plenty of supplies and an extra horse, then he and Hank struck out toward El Paso. He knew it was 700 miles but had no idea what the conditions would be or how long it would take. Mac helped him with a map he found in an old book. Mac calculated it would be about a two-week ride. After he left San Antonio, he knew the settlements would be few and far between. It didn't matter. Henry Lloyd didn't ask for help. He never would. But his friend needed him.

The first few days were easy. The weather was nice and the roads were wide and easy to travel. They found plenty of game and water was plentiful. Beyond San Antonio, he knew he would need to start planning more carefully since there were fewer rivers. He got a room in San Antonio for one night. It might be the last bed he would see for a while. West of San Antonio, the land became rockier and the travel slower. They ran into severe weather on the second day out of town. It was not enough to hold them up but they weren't covering as many miles.

John and Hank had been gone eight days when they reached Fort Stockton. It had once housed up to 300 soldiers but most had gone north, fighting the Comanches. Now the Comanches were raiding again. There were fewer than a hundred men left there. John and Hank were made to feel at home. Most of the soldiers had been from Texas and they had heard of John. John hadn't realized he was becoming famous around the state as the private ranger who had rescued Laredo, sent the Mexican Army away without firing a shot, and taken on multiple gangs of outlaws. He was also the ranger who had defeated the Union army. John refused to talk about any of this, which only made the legend grow.

Not many people passed through Fort Stockton so John wondered how all the stories had gotten this far. He and Hank rested a day to let the horses recover, then left for El Paso. They made it there without incident, though the map Mac had given him was of no use now. He had been able to find a map of the New Mexico Territory, however. There was a road that followed the Rio Grande all the way. They stayed only one day in El Paso. John was in a hurry.

The next morning, Hank spotted something across the grassy plain, toward the mountains to the south. Hank wanted to go get it. John made him stay. John took out his field glasses and saw it was a black mama bear and two cubs. She was a magnificent creature, just sitting, watching her cubs roll and play in the grass.

This country was wonderful, too, like Texas. The hunting was the best he'd ever seen. They ate like kings, with fresh meat almost every night. They had bought supplies in El Paso so the traveling was easy.

A few days out, John realized they were being followed. Hank had noticed their fellow traveler first and John had learned to trust Hank on these matters. The man following them stayed back. After a while, John decided to wait on him. When he got closer, John could see he was a young man riding a big brown mule. He had no visible weapons and he appeared to be no threat.

"Nice weather we're having," the man said when he was close enough to speak. It was obvious he was not comfortable.

"Yes, it is," John answered.

After a few awkward moments, the man spoke again.

"I sure hope this weather holds. The higher we get into the mountains the quicker the weather can turn nasty."

John just looked at him. The mule was stopped now and the young man was looking down at John and Hank. His behavior was not aggressive.

"My name is Chester Anderson."

Still nothing from John. Normally, John would ride along with this man, just to have company but he didn't want anything to delay him in reaching his friend. John could not help being anxious. He did not want to be too late to find Henry Lloyd.

"Is there anything else? If not, I need to be on my way," John said, climbing back on Bonnie.

"Yes, there is something. I don't quite know how to ask you this, Mr. Delaney," he said as he kept an eye on Hank.

"How did you know my name?" John asked.

"That is what I wanted to say. I was sent here to find you. I was afraid I had missed you. I was prepared to go all the way to King Ranch to find you. Then, a few days ago, word came that you were in El Paso. That you were actually coming."

"Who sent you to find me?" John asked.

"A friend of mine," he replied.

"Does your friend have a name?"

John was getting impatient.

"Walker. Henry Lloyd Walker," Chester said. "He said you'd be riding a pretty chestnut-colored mare with white stockings and would probably have a big blond dog with a black face. So, I was sure I had found you. Clyde has only one speed and it's slow. But he keeps going so I figured I'd catch you eventually."

John was excited now, though Chester's roundabout way of talking was making him more impatient.

"What is wrong? Is Henry Lloyd all right?" John asked.

"Well, Mr. Delaney, about everything that could go wrong has gone wrong. As to your second question, Henry Lloyd is well. If you don't mind me tagging along, I'll tell you all about it. It's a long story and we need to keep moving," Chester said.

John climbed onto Bonnie and looked intently at Chester as he began the saga which had started over two years before. John figured the best thing was to let him tell his story. Chester did that for the rest of that day and into the next. He was a well-mannered young man and listening to his story made the journey more interesting, though John was hoping he got to the point before they reached Santa Fe.

For the longest time, the story just seemed to be about Chester. Early in the war, when he had been just a teenager, Chester had worked for the Union forces in Colorado. He was an aide to Major Chivington. The Major was attached to the 3rd Cavalry regiment under Col. John P. Slough's command. They were on their way south to confront rebel forces marching north to capture and control the Santa Fe Trail. If the South could expand their territory to include the Santa Fe Trail, they would have access to the Pacific Coast. The Union blockade had closed all the ports on the Atlantic and the Gulf Coast. The South needed a new passage to sell cotton and obtain supplies.

The southern parts of New Mexico and Arizona were sympathetic to the Confederacy, so if they could gain control of the Santa Fe Trail, the Union Army would be out of the game. These were under the command of Brigadier General Henry Sibley. Their ranks were filled mostly with Texans and frontier fighters. They were a solid fighting force.

The two armies had reached Glorieta Pass on the Santa Fe Trail about the same time in late March of 1862. The evenly matched forces fought over several days. Ultimately the Union prevailed. They won the battle with superior fighting and solid tactics but at the close of the battle, an Indian scout named Anastasio Duran made the difference. His assistance to the Union forces led to the turning point in the western campaign.

Duran knew the area well. He had located the southern supply train that was currently passing through Johnson Ranch and was moving toward a more secure location nearer to the Confederate troops. Chivington's cavalry riders were circling, hoping to split the southern attack by attacking and exposing a rear flank. They were cut off from their intended attack by a troop of rebel soldiers with fresh mounts. They could not get through to enter the battle. As they were weaving their way through, trying to find a path to get back in the fight, they ran into Duran, who had found the supply train. He led them to a ridge where they could see the train moving toward the covered destination. They watched for over an hour before descending the ridge to attack the few forces guarding the South's train. The fighting was fierce for a while but the Yankees won. While the main forces were fighting a bloody stand-off to the east on the Santa Fe Trail, Chivington's men captured and looted the supply train. They burned 80 supply wagons, killing or driving off over 500 horses and mules before they returned to find that the Union army had retreated just before dark. Duran was able to get them around the southern army using another little-known trail through the mountains. They found the defeated Union troops licking their wounds.

General Slough, who was preparing to send a dispatch reporting his defeat, was now able to claim victory. He could hold the pass with the men he had. His career was saved. Sibley, the rebel general, was forced to return to Santa Fe which was only the first leg of a long road home to Texas. The South would never again have a chance to control the west.

All this history was interesting but it seemed to offer no connection to the present. After hours of listening John finally had to stop his young companion.

"What does any of this have to do with Henry Lloyd?"

"It has everything to do with him. I was getting to that," Chester said.

"I saw some game off to the left in those hills. Hank and I will see what we can find. Can you make camp over under those trees? We can pick up the story after we have eaten. And please get to the part about what kind of trouble Henry Lloyd is in," John said.

He was hungry but mostly he just wanted a few minutes of quiet.

"Good idea," Chester said as he went about taking care of John's packhorse and mule while Hank and John rode into the hills.

John shot what he thought was a spike buck but when he reached the animal, he knew it wasn't a deer. He had no idea what it was. It had a long thick body with a long snout. The antlers were thick and short. It was markedly different from any deer he had ever seen. When he got back to camp, Chester had a fire going. He told John he had shot a Pronghorn. Chester said they were better tasting than deer and he was right.

Chester continued his story as they ate. When the Confederate army moved south, they left a company of horse soldiers behind. Their job was to harass the Union troops in Santa Fe. They quickly became a band of raiders more interested in harassing the citizens than the soldiers. North of Santa Fe was the town of Espanola. It had no organized lawmen there so the rebels became the law. They were led by a Texan named Walter Riggins. He had forty-five hand-picked men that he knew were ready to fight or steal. They ruled the region with a heavy hand. Meanwhile, Henry Lloyd had been working with the Pueblo Indians alongside a missionary named Floyd Peters, from Pennsylvania. Henry Lloyd fell in love with an Indian girl and married her. They were preparing to go to California when Major Riggins arrived. Henry Lloyd could not abandon the people with Riggins' raiders in the area.

John listened intently, relieved that the story had finally progressed to the point of including his friend.

"What happened then?" he asked.

Chester continued the tale of Henry Lloyd's assumption of the noble task of protecting the citizens who were suffering under the heavy hand of the rebels. Winters in northern New Mexico can be harsh. There were scores of displaced people who needed his help. Chester had many stories to tell about the cruelty of the soldiers and how Henry Lloyd had saved many of the citizens by moving them from place to place. The soldiers called him the Yellow Ghost and they spent most of their time hunting him. They hated him. Henry Lloyd had trained a few men to help him harass the soldiers. This kept them busy. The rebels lived in fear of this one-man army. It made them furious that they were being humiliated by a Negro.

Santa Fe was now controlled by the Union militia under the command of Kit Carson. Carson was too busy to be bothered with Riggins' rebels. As long as the Confederates stayed away from Santa Fe, the Union Army was happy to leave them in the care of Henry Lloyd Walker.

"Chester, what is your part in all of this? How did you get involved? You seem to know quite a bit about everything."

Chester was silent as a tear trickled down his cheek.

"Mr. Walker saved my life," he said.

Chester choked back a few utterances, then he gathered himself and continued.

"Most of the Union army had gone back to Fort Union. Others were sent west to be a presence in the Indian territories and the rest of us remained to guard the pass. One day about two years ago, I was with two friends of mine, both privates. They were good boys. We were moving some horses from one end of the canyon to the other when some of Riggins' raiders rode up on us. They killed my friends and made me help them move the horses back north. After a while, they decided they could handle the horses without me and decided to shoot me. A big man with a bushy beard was pointing his pistol at me when he suddenly dropped. I heard the shot a split-second later, echoing through the canyon. Then another shot killed a rebel who was relieving himself. I got to my feet and ran for cover. Shots were fired continually for a few minutes, then it all got quiet. I crawled out from behind a rock and saw dead rebels everywhere.

Then, riding toward me with the evening sun at his back, I saw the biggest man I had ever seen. At first, I thought I was dead—that he was an angel sent to get me."

"Henry Lloyd," John whispered.

"Yes, sir. He was by himself. He killed all eight of them before they could figure out where he was. He had been following the rebels all the way from Espanola. They never knew he was there. I would be dead—I should be dead—except for this man. He took me back with him and I've been with him since. He is like a ghost. He never stays in one place too long. He is close enough to his family to protect them but he is never with them long."

"How many men does he have?" John asked.

"He only rides with a couple at a time but never the same ones. He is more concerned with their safety than anything else. Just about any man in the area, white or Indian, will gladly ride with him."

"Where will we find him?" John asked.

"He will find us," Chester said.

Soon, Henry Lloyd did find them, just south of Santa Fe.

"John, my boy! I knew I could count on the best ranger in Texas," Henry Lloyd shouted at them as he rode up from the west a few hours later.

John jumped off Bonnie and ran to meet his friend. Hank beat him to it. Hank and Henry Lloyd did an awkward dance as they greeted each other. Then John and Henry Lloyd embraced for a long while with Hank wrestling with them both. Chester made camp while Henry Lloyd and John talked. John told him about his son and daughter and about the Kings and their children. Henry Lloyd told John about his wife and daughter. The conversation grew serious when John wanted to know about Riggins' men.

"How many are there?" John asked.

"There are only a few of them left. They started out with forty-five. I think there are about eighteen now," said Henry Lloyd.

"He knows exactly how many there are," Chester added.

"It varies. They try to recruit as many as they can but lately, the locals have lost interest in their cause," Henry Lloyd said.

"Where are they?" John asked.

"In Espanola. They run that town. They think they are safe there." Henry Lloyd grinned.

"Tomorrow I want you to take Chester and Hank while I ride in to meet this Riggins fellow," John said.

Henry Lloyd listened.

"He doesn't know me," John said. "I want to see him for myself."

Henry Lloyd nodded. Then he wandered off to pray.

"He prays about everything," Chester said.

"I know he does. Let's get some sleep. He may be praying for a while."

In the morning, John rode northwest while the others continued into Santa Fe. The closer they got to Santa Fe, the more people they saw. Both Chester and Henry Lloyd thought there were many more people than usual. They began to hear people talking. There were rumors that the war was over. Nobody trusted the news, since for the past few months rumors had run rampant. Some were saying Lee had surrendered while others were saying the rebels had taken Washington and killed Lincoln. When they reached the Plaza, Henry Lloyd went to the courthouse and read the posted news for himself. It seemed that both rumors had an element of truth. Lee had surrendered his sword and a few days later, President Lincoln was shot and killed, not by an invading army but by an assassin's bullet in a theater.

A parade was being planned by the Union soldiers in town. The war had been a far worse affair than anyone had expected and it was a relief that the whole thing was over. Maybe this was less so for the southern boys but Santa Fe was ready to celebrate, then get back to life. On the frontier, life was hard enough without all the strife caused by politicians back east.

John had a very different experience as he entered Espanola. With Riggins' men still in control, the news had not yet reached the town. Riggins claimed he was waiting to hear from his superiors, believing this might be another Yankee misinformation campaign but he knew it was over. The rogue wasn't actually waiting for orders to return. He had come to enjoy the life of a raider. He and his men were able to take what they wanted whenever they wanted. He was in no hurry to leave. His men were happy enough here. Nobody bothered them except a light-skinned Negro they planned to kill soon. However, that goal at times seemed unreachable since they had hunted him for months and had almost given up looking for him. Every time they went out to find him, they came back with fewer men and they rarely ever saw their nemesis.

John found a good livery stable for Bonnie. He paid the man extra and asked him to give her a good rubdown. Then he checked into a hotel in the middle of town. He cleaned up, got something to eat, then went to Clifford's Saloon. It had a large sign proclaiming in bold print "THE BEST WHISKEY IN THE TERRITORY." Under the bold letters, in smaller print, the sign read "No Credit Come in Only if You Have Cash."

John had cash, so he went in, not so much for the best whiskey in the territory but to hear all the local gossip. He sat at the bar and paid for a glass of whiskey which was not the best he'd ever had but it was good enough. He chatted with a few men, some in Spanish and some in English. It was there he learned that the war was over. Nobody had any details but they all thought the North had won. A few Confederate soldiers were at a table in the corner playing cards. John walked over and ask if he could join the game. They were playing five-card draw. John played a few hands with the men, thinking they would ask him questions about who he was and why he was there. He was wrong. They didn't care who he was. They were only interested in their card game and drinking the best whiskey in the territory. John decided he had seen enough so he went back to his room. Tomorrow he would find Riggins.

Riggins, however, had not wanted to wait until morning. When John opened the door to his room, he saw the man sitting on his bed, going through his papers. Two of his men were pointing their pistols at John and Riggins was holding a profit and loss statement from one of the companies John had an interest in.

"Mr. Delaney," Riggins grinned as he looked up from the paper. "Come in."

Riggins was a middle-aged man with a full head of gray, curly hair. He was not a big man but he had the look of a fellow who liked to be in control. It took John a split second to know what was going on. His first instinct was to run but he knew it was too late. He was mad at himself for walking into an ambush. He should have known better. He focused quickly on what needed to happen. He had to take control before Riggins did. His advantage was that the room was small. The two soldiers were not going to do anything without a direct order—yet another advantage in John's favor. The third and final advantage was that Riggins was so interested in what he was reading he was not as prepared as he should have been.

John made eye contact with one of the soldiers and took a quick step toward the bed where Riggins was sitting. John was drawing his pistol, watching the soldier's every move. Before Riggins could register what was happening, the barrel of John's gun was on the bridge of his nose. The hammer was cocked ready to release a bullet into the major's brains. His eyes grew wide and he dropped the paper he was reading.

"Now we get to see how well these two like you," John said calmly. "If either of them makes the slightest twitch, you are a dead man. Then we will see what happens next."

Before the men could think about their options, John took command.

"Drop your weapons, easy."

They did as they were told.

"Now both of you get against that wall. Sit down."

John looked at Riggins, who had not moved a muscle. His grin was gone.

"Sir, you are in my room, uninvited, sitting on my bed, looking at something that is none of your business. Do you have an explanation for this rude behavior?" John asked.

Riggins made no response at first, then he began to speak.

"My name is Major Walter Riggins. I am the most senior officer in this part of the territory. I have orders to maintain the peace. What business do you have here Mr. Delaney? I have a responsibility to protect this town."

"What do you know about me?" John asked.

"I know you are some sort of self-appointed ranger. But you have no authority here," Riggins said.

"What else do you know?"

Riggins was quiet.

"Do you know that I'm not afraid to deal with the likes of you? Do you know I have killed men for pointing guns at me?"

John said this as he looked at the two soldiers, sitting passively across the room. John put his gun away and picked Riggins up by his coat. He pulled him in so close they were just inches apart when he next spoke.

"How long have you known the war is over. Be careful what you say. I can't stand a liar."

"A week, maybe two," Riggins said.

John could see the two soldiers looking at each other.

"When were you going to tell your men?"

"That is my business," said the major.

John hit him in the jaw so hard and fast that he lost consciousness. Riggins collapsed on the floor.

"Get him out of here," John said. "When he wakes up, tell him he has exactly forty-eight hours to get every rebel soldier in the area out of here or I'll kill every one of you myself."

John took the bullets out of their guns and escorted them down the stairs as they carried their major away.

John had been looking forward to sleeping in a bed but he knew he couldn't afford the luxury. As soon as they were gone, he and Bonnie left Espanola.

C HAPTER 26

The Battle

The weather was nice and John found a comfortable location on the river to spend the night. The running water created a soothing sound that made sleeping under the stars pleasant. He made a pallet of leaves almost as comfortable as a bed, though he missed sleeping next to Josephina. John was already homesick.

He woke to find Hank and Henry Lloyd sitting nearby. Henry Lloyd was reading his Bible while Hank watched for any movement from John. When John sat up, Hank ran to greet him. Henry Lloyd put away his Bible and strolled over to them.

"How long have you been here?" John asked.

"Not long," Henry Lloyd said.

"How did you find me in all these rocks?"

He had been careful not to leave any tracks.

"Hank found you. I could have used his help several times over the past few years," Henry Lloyd said. "Tell me about Espanola."

"I had a talk with Riggins," John said. "We didn't part in a friendly manner. In fact, we didn't meet in a friendly manner. He let himself into my room and I found him going through my papers."

"He is a take-charge sort of fellow, I hear," Henry Lloyd said.

"I gave him an ultimatum. I said since the war was over, he and his outlaws were to be out of the territory within forty-eight hours. It

304

appears he hadn't told his men about the war," John said as he rubbed Hank's belly.

"What did he say to that?"

"Not anything. He was not conscious when I decided he needed to leave. I believe his men will have told him what I said," John said.

Henry Lloyd was enjoying this.

"Where is Chester?" John asked.

"I sent him to check on the women and children," said Henry Lloyd. We have been moving them around every few days to make sure the rebels don't know where they are. They are used to it. The rebels don't look very long. They have learned it's dangerous to spend much time away from town. They usually lose a few men when they go on a hunting trip."

"Let's get loaded up. I'd like you to meet my wife Pojoaque," Henry Lloyd said, "and our daughter Jasmine."

Major Riggins started the day with a bad headache. He hadn't rested well at all. He had regained consciousness while they were carrying him to his quarters. He was furious when he heard about John Delaney's ultimatum. He was also worried that his men had learned about the war ending. By morning they all knew. The grumbling was reaching a level that made the major uncomfortable. Half the men wanted to get back to their families. The other half would just as soon stay and enjoy life as raiders. The one thing they all agreed on was that they didn't like it that Riggins had not told them the news.

After a few cups of strong black coffee, the major sent his lieutenant to survey the troops. Riggins had a spent the night preparing himself for battle. It would probably be his last and he had no intention of losing. The lieutenant returned with the following results: Of the twenty-one men, eight wanted to stay, ten wanted to go home and three of them didn't care. At noon he had them all standing at attention as he read the official proclamation. Then he shared his final strategy.

Pojoaque was standing in front of an adobe hut watching their daughter crawl around on the hard dirt. Jasmine was seven months old. Pojoaque had been expecting them. She was taking loaves of fresh bread out of a traditional outdoor oven. They gathered under a shade tree to enjoy the warm bread with honey.

"John, I'd like you to meet Pojoaque," Henry Lloyd said.

She nodded.

"Pleased to meet you," John said.

"I've heard so much about you," she said.

Her English was perfect.

"When can you be ready to leave?" John asked Henry Lloyd.

"We are always ready to leave when God tells us," Henry Lloyd said.

This was not the answer John was hoping for. Talk like that had landed him in this mess in the first place.

"Henry Lloyd, I'd like to make you a business offer," John said.

He could wait no longer. He had been thinking about this ever since he received his friend's letter.

"I am thinking about starting a ranch and I'd like you to help me. I have enough money to purchase some land and some starter cattle. On the way out here I saw some very pretty land."

"Of course, I can help you though I do not have the funds right now. This war has been hard on us all," Henry Lloyd said.

"You don't need funds, I have enough."

"What you have is yours."

"I need you, Henry Lloyd. We can do this. I know we can."

"I have never managed a ranch," said his friend.

"Just think about it," John said.

He knew it was going to be a lengthy process to persuade Henry Lloyd and he knew in the end it would be prayer that decided it. They spent the rest of the day visiting as John was getting to know

Pojoaque. She was easy to like. She smiled at everything. After a long trip, it was nice to be able to relax. But John knew these moments were illusory. They had plenty still to do.

Major Riggins had his men ready to leave. They had packed enough supplies to last them on a road trip to Florida if need be. The locals were more than ready for the Confederate army to leave so they could rebuild their town but Riggins still had a score to settle. He had shared part of his plan with his men but as usual, he didn't tell them everything. He had hired a Comanche scout named Limping Wolf to find Henry Lloyd. The man had reported that John Delaney was with the Yellow Ghost. Riggins had sent some of his men back home to Texas earlier in the day but he had kept a dozen of his best soldiers for their final battle. That score he had to settle now included John. His pride would not allow him to return home to Texas after being outsmarted for years by a sneaky Negro who refused to fight like a man. Nor would he forgive being sucker-punched by an Irish hooligan.

Josephina was concerned as she hung the laundry on the line. She was watching the back of the schoolyard. The children had been outside playing a long time. Too long, in fact. Mac was always so precise about the children's studies that she knew something was wrong. She decided she needed to look in on Mac. She picked up little Katy and walked over.

She froze when she saw him slumped over his desk. She hurried to him. His skin was clammy. He had a faraway look in his eyes and his breathing was shallow. She ran to the door and call for Nettie.

"Run as fast as you can and get your mama. Mr. Mac needs help. Hurry baby, run as fast as you can."

Nettie took off running and Josephina went back inside. She held his hand.

"Help is coming, Mac. Just hold on. Don't leave me."

Henrietta arrived a few minutes later with a couple of ranch hands. They gently loaded Mac in the back of a wagon. He 'looked at them without saying a word. It would be a long ride into town to see the doctor.

Several maids had collected the children and taken them back to the big house. Aldo had ridden ahead to tell the doctor they were coming. As they rode, Mac drifted in and out of consciousness. Henrietta was afraid they were losing him but each time they were able to wake him up. Josephina kept whispering in his ear to keep fighting. It was dark when they arrived at the young doctor's house. He had recently arrived in the area and he seemed to know what to do. He immediately determined that Mac had suffered a stroke. They made him comfortable and the doctor gave him some pills to take. Henrietta and Josephina spent the night with Mac but Henrietta could not sleep. She was not a person who could sit around waiting for things to change. In the middle of the night, she sent one of her men to Galveston to fetch the best doctor here. Henrietta then sat down and opened one of the doctor's medical books and started reading everything she could find about strokes.

While Josephina and Henrietta were busy caring for Mac in Texas, John and Henry Lloyd were just as busy getting the Pueblo Indians settled back into their own homes—places they had lived for generations. They were eager to return. That part of New Mexico was a network of canyons and natural caves. It had been easy for Henry Lloyd to move the people around, keeping them from harm. Though they were appreciative they were ready to get back to normal life. John was satisfied that Riggins and his men had left Espanola but he would remain vigilant until he was sure it was over.

John went into Santa Fe to post a few letters before their departure. One was to his wife and one was to his sister. He hoped the letters would be delivered. In his letter, he told Nelly about most of the happenings since the war. He now was a father. He was sure his sister would want to know about that. A third letter he sent to Richard King asking him what he thought about John becoming a rancher in his own right. He didn't know how King would take the news but he knew he would get an honest opinion from a man he respected. Everything in Santa Fe seemed to be returning to normal. It would be time to leave soon. John was ready to return to Texas.

Limping Wolf was an excellent tracker. He had been doing it most of his life. He was not as well known as some but his skills were just as solid. As a small boy, his right foot had been crushed when a horse stepped on him. The ankle healed badly and was stiff. His walk was not pretty but there was nothing he could not do. He had worked for just about anybody who needed a scout. He knew the mountains as well as anyone. These days, he was working for Riggins, who was not popular among the natives but he cared little what they thought. Riggins had paid him with a new rifle and plenty of whiskey. Working for Riggins was easy. He only had to watch Henry Lloyd, then report to the white man occasionally, telling him whatever he wanted to hear. The information he gave them didn't need to be accurate. The white man never knew the difference.

Currently, Limping Wolf was watching a canyon just north of Santa Fe where a group of native people had gathered. The group was getting smaller by the day. All that was left now were a few dozen women and children with three men. The big man and the man with the dog were there. That was all Riggins cared about. Limping Wolf had no idea why Riggins was interested in their whereabouts but he was paying him well to keep tabs on them. Riggins and his men were now camped near the Rio Grande, just a few hours' ride from where Limping Wolf was watching the quarry.

All the displaced Indians had returned home. Two young girls who had been orphaned remained. Pojoaque had taken them as her own. They would also make the trip to Texas.

They used Chester's mule and another army horse as pack animals. Pojoaque rode with the baby wrapped in a blanket around her. The two young girls rode together on a gentle mare. They moved at a comfortable pace. John and Henry Lloyd took turns scouting ahead to find the next place to camp and to provide fresh game.

On the second day, John heard a shot ring out and a bullet hit the ground to his left. It took him less than a second to realize they were being attacked. They were at the bottom of a steep canyon with high rocky walls on both sides. Henry Lloyd looked in every direction trying to find the best place to take cover. He spotted a pile of rocks on their left side.

"John," he yelled. "Get everybody to those rocks. Don't worry about the horses."

More shots rang out. John knew they needed to move fast. He escorted Pojoaque and the girls into the rocks for cover. They were almost there when the mare the girls were riding took a bullet in the neck. She wobbled to the side but somehow stayed on her feet. Chester had already grabbed his gun, jumped off his horse, and made it to the mare before she collapsed. He ran with the girls as fast as he could. John had gotten Pojoaque and the baby to safety in a little cove.

"Hank, stay," John barked, as he positioned himself to return fire.

He saw Henry Lloyd riding in circles, firing into the rocks in both directions. He was drawing most of the fire. It was obvious they had ridden into an ambush.

"Henry Lloyd, all clear," John yelled, as soon as Chester made it to safety with the girls.

Chester had found a small cave. With the girls safely behind him, he began looking for targets. They were easy to find since the party was being fired at repeatedly. Chester was about thirty yards from where John was dug in.

Henry Lloyd turned his mount to the opposite side and rode full bore into the canyon wall. His horse pulled to a halt and he jumped off. He swatted the horse's rump and it ran away hard from the fight.

John didn't like Henry Lloyd being alone. He could be low on ammunition and his cover was not nearly as good as theirs. However, he trusted his friend's judgment. The gunfire continued, with bullets ricocheting all around them. He watched as Chester carefully took aim and fired. He saw a man drop from above Henry Lloyd's location. Chester knew what he was doing. This encouraged John, who felt that for now, they were safe. He scanned the area looking for a target. He could see the flare off their guns but he had yet to see anything he could shoot.

Henry Lloyd found a target and dropped another one. The man yelled and cursed as he tumbled down the slope. The shooting seemed to slow up. That's when they heard it.

"You are trapped," a voice rang out.

John recognized Riggins' voice.

"I am offering you a chance to surrender."

The voice was coming from just above Chester's location.

"No thank you," John replied immediately. "We are pretty comfortable where we are."

"Hahaha," Riggins laughed. "This is your last chance. I'll not ask again."

A shot rang out from Henry Lloyd's gun and another one of their shooters went down.

"There is your answer," John said.

The shots began again with twice the volley of bullets. John saw a man move from one spot to another. He took aim. When the man knelt to shoot, John had a clear view. Just before he pulled the trigger, a bullet landed near his head, sending rock fragments into his face. He blinked and cleared his eyes. Blood was running down his forehead into his eyes. He focused again and pulled the trigger. The soldier toppled backward.

John heard a rumbling above him as rocks began to slide, moving down the slope. He looked at Hank and knew from his eyes that the mastiff was focused on an attacker.

"Go, Hank. Get him, boy."

Hank was waiting for the command. The muscular animal leapt from rock to rock climbing the cliff. He found his prey and tackled him, unleashing deadly fury on the rebel soldier. John moved to his left and watched as another man came into view just above Henry Lloyd. Before he could get his gun up, Henry Lloyd killed him. Chester was still shooting at another man in the craggy formation above Henry Lloyd when they heard rapid horse hooves coming from the entrance to the canyon. John counted four riders. He drew aim and dropped one. The men were getting closer. John needed to focus on the riders. He kept shooting but was not able to hit the moving targets. There were now three of them. Hank and the man he had by the throat tumbled to the ground between John and Chester. The rebel had stopped moving on his own but Hank was still dragging him around like a rag doll. John saw that Henry Lloyd was focused on something above Hank.

"Hank, come," he shouted.

The mastiff dropped the dead man and ran to John's side. John did not want him to be shot again. Just then, the three riders decided their efforts were not going to succeed and they rode away. The plan had been for them to arrive just as the men above were reaching the bottom. It was a solid plan, though it had failed to consider that Hank would be able to detect their movements and foil the timing.

The riders were out of range before he or Chester could make another shot count. John figured there were no more than two or three men left above him, and he was almost certain only one man above Henry Lloyd was still in the fight. After the riders left, the canyon fell silent. John could see that Henry Lloyd and Chester were still looking for shooters. When neither one of them showed any sign of detecting a clear target, John figured the rebel army was in full retreat. He laid his rifle down and tended to his head wound. It was still bleeding profusely but he could tell it was not a deep cut. He walked back into the cave to check on the girls. They were huddled deep into the rocks. Pojoaque was much calmer than she had any right to be as she held her baby. She smiled when she saw John, then got up and looked at his wound. He assured her he was fine, then went back to his position.

John saw Henry Lloyd in the middle of the canyon walking in their direction. He was moving fast, scanning the horizon for any movement. John stood up and waved at him. He nodded at John, then went to check on Chester, whom he found inside the cave, trying to comfort the two scared little girls. Henry Lloyd reached down and picked up the girls and hugged them. He whispered in their ears. He told them in their native tongue that it was over, that everyone was safe. He stayed a few minutes with them, then set them down and hugged Chester. He told him how proud he was of him. Chester had demonstrated courage and skill in the face of chaos and he wanted to acknowledge that bravery. He also admonished Chester to keep watch because the rebels might return.

"How is everyone?" Henry Lloyd asked as he approached John and Pojoaque.

"We are fine. How are the girls?"

John had been worried about them.

"I'm hoping they'll be fine but they have had quite a scare," he said.

Henry Lloyd did a quick inspection of John's wounds, then turned to embrace his wife and child.

"Chester's area offers better cover. Let's go," he said.

They made their way over to the cave and began to settle in. The little girls clung to Pojoaque, who began making the place more comfortable by moving rocks and fashioning places for the children to sit out of range of any potential threat.

Riggins had only four men left besides himself and he had no idea where that worthless Indian scout had wandered off to. With all the guns he had given the man, one would think he might have helped a bit more in the fight. It had angered Riggins when he saw the Comanche riding calmly away as the shooting began. Now he was nowhere to be found. It would be dark soon and they had no idea how to get out of this maze of canyons. They all looked the same to him. At least they had their horses. They rode toward where he thought they might pick up the Rio Grande.

"This is without a doubt the finest dog I have ever seen," Henry Lloyd said, rubbing the mastiff's ears.

It had been a couple of hours since the rebels' departure.

"I have seen some good coon dogs in my life but nothing like Hank. How old is he now?"

"Let's see. This is 1865, he must be about six. No, seven," John said. He was sad to realize he had not seen his sister in seven years. And because of the war, he had not heard from her in over five years. Henry Lloyd could read that John was suddenly saddened by his thoughts.

"John, here is what we need to do. I need to go see where they are."

"I'll go with you," said John.

"No, I need you and Chester to stay here. I'd like Hank to go with me though."

John nodded his approval.

"Hank and I should have no trouble finding their trail. You and Chester might try and find a horse or two if you can."

Henry Lloyd and Hank climbed the canyon wall like a couple of mountain goats. John loaded his guns and went looking for their horses. They were probably not far off. Hank and Henry Lloyd looked around, reading the signs. They found two dead soldiers in addition to the one Hank had killed. They were lying at the bottom of the canyon. There were horse tracks leaving, going in different directions. Hank was more interested in one set for some reason, so they went after them. It was dark but the dark presented no problem for Hank. They walked almost three hours before they found a small fire with a man sitting near it. Henry Lloyd walked up and sat down beside him. Hank sat on the other side. The man looked at Henry Lloyd, calmly offering him a bite of a ground squirrel he was roasting. It was Limping Wolf. Henry Lloyd recognized the man and now knew why the rebels had been so successful with their ambush strategy.

"How many men do they have?" Henry Lloyd asked him.

The spy feigned ignorance. It was an old Indian trick. If he didn't want to answer he suddenly couldn't understand or speak English. But when bargaining for blankets, guns, or whiskey his English was just fine. So Henry Lloyd asked him the same question in Tiwa.

"They started out the day with eleven men. They have five now," Limping Wolf replied.

"How long have you been watching us?" Henry Lloyd asked him, again in Tiwa.

"Half moon," he said.

"Are you still watching us?"

"No, you are watching me," the Indian said.

"Where are the soldiers?"

Limping Wolf pointed to the west.

"In the red rocks near Quail Creek."

"Don't go near these men again," Henry Lloyd said. "I will not be happy if you take them to us again. I will find you and feed you to this dog."

Limping Wolf looked into the eyes of the blood-stained mastiff and decided he was finished working with Riggins. Henry Lloyd took the ground squirrel out of his hand and tossed it to Hank. Hank's massive jaws crunched the roasted animal, snapping the bones like twigs. Hank swallowed the man's supper and licked his lips. Henry Lloyd and Hank then left as quickly as they arrived. Limping Wolf decided it was time for him to go north.

Everybody was asleep except John when Hank bounded into the cave with his tail wagging. A few minutes later, Henry Lloyd walked up.

"I see you found some horses," he said.

"Bonnie, the packhorse, and the mule. Don't know what happened to that old nag you ride," John said.

"I saw him with the others," Henry Lloyd grinned, "and I see he was rubbed down good. Thank you."

"It must have been Chester. What did you find?" John asked.

"Enough to know what happened, and why. The what is that Limping Wolf was tracking us. The why is that I wasn't paying attention. I should have known. Let that be a lesson to us both. No matter how good you are—and we are both very good trackers—there is always somebody better. I have heard about Limping Wolf. Had I known he was in the area I would have been more cautious. Now I know. Lesson learned."

"What else?" John inquired.

"Riggins has four men left. Limping Wolf said he is lost in the red rocks. If he finds his way out, he will not see us again."

"Can you trust Limping Wolf?" John asked.

"No, you can never trust him. But he is telling me the truth this time. He may not fear me but he is deathly afraid of Hank. He thinks Hank is a powerful spirit. He wants nothing to do with us while Hank is around. As we walked away I heard him praying to his gods that Hank never sees him again."

Henry Lloyd looked over and saw Pojoaque standing at the entry to the cave. They hugged and exchanged a few words in Tiwa.

"How long has Chester been asleep?" he asked John.

"A few hours."

"I'll send him out to relieve you. I'm going to get some rest. You need to as well. We have a big day ahead of us tomorrow."

As John and Henry Lloyd headed to Texas the next day, the doctor from Galveston was just arriving at the King Ranch. Mac was doing better. He still had not said a word but his eyes were clear and he was on a regular eating schedule. Josephina fed him broth and soda crackers on a schedule that Henrietta and the young doctor had devised. Henrietta also had him drink a glass of red wine every few hours. This was to keep his blood thin. He was learning to communicate with them by pointing and nodding. The left side of his body was weak but he had full strength in his right side. The new doctor reviewed his progress and agreed with the diagnosis. He also said they were doing everything they could for him. He felt it was time to start getting him to try and walk. Henrietta soon worked out a schedule for this too.

CHAPTER 27

Texas

John and the others left the canyon with more horses and guns than they had before the battle. John still wanted to find Riggins and deal with him. Henry Lloyd was more concerned with getting his family away from the violence. Chester didn't care what they did. He was content doing whatever Henry Lloyd asked of him.

Each girl had her own horse. Henry Lloyd spent most of the morning making sure they were comfortable riding as John and Chester loaded the others.

"I think we should go home a different way," Henry Lloyd said to John. "If we head due east we can stay north of the desert. There are some Apaches in the area but we can stay clear of them if we have our heads up. It's pretty country. We might even see some buffalo although they are probably north of us by now. We need to make sure we have plenty of water before we hit the flatlands."

"That sounds fine," John said.

"When we get to Ft. Worth, we can follow the Trinity River for a while, then head south," Henry Lloyd added.

The ride back to Texas was without incident. Just north of a settlement called Buffalo Gap, they spotted a cloud of dust to their north. Henry Lloyd told John it was probably a small herd of buffalo migrating north. John, Hank, and Henry Lloyd left the women and children with Chester and rode out to see the herd. John was amazed to realize how many there were. It was a sea of brown fur, easing along at a leisurely pace. They got as close as they could without spooking the herd. The line of bison was almost a mile in length.

"This is a small herd?" John asked.

"Yes, it is. I've seen much larger," Henry Lloyd said.

"Are they good to eat?"

"You and Hank stay here until I call you," Henry Lloyd said.

He rode toward the herd, staying on their right flank, matching his speed to theirs. He gradually moved closer. John saw him get off his horse. He lay on the ground and picked the animal he wanted. John saw a puff of smoke from the gun but it was a second or two before the sound reached them.

John saw a buffalo cow go to its knees. The herd did not spook. They kept moving along at the same pace. Henry Lloyd mounted his big white horse and rode to the downed buffalo. By the time John and Chester arrived, the herd had passed them. They field-dressed the cow and butchered her. When they had all the meat they could carry, they returned to the group. That evening Henry Lloyd prepared a fine meal for them.

By the time they reached Fort Worth, they were almost out of supplies. They were able to sell a couple of horses and they rested there for two days. John posted a letter to Josephina and another letter to Nelly. There was plenty of talk about now that the war was over and the Yankees were in control but other than that, everything seemed back to normal, or at least as close to normal as Texas ever gets.

"Someone is following us," said Henry Lloyd.

It had been two days since they'd left Fort Worth.

"This road is well-traveled. They might not be following us," John said.

"I'll feel better if we take a look," Henry Lloyd said.

John nodded. He turned to Chester.

"Just keep following the river. We will be back before dark. If not, make camp and wait for us," John said.

John, Hank, and Henry Lloyd doubled back to see who it was. They found a single rider. It was obvious he was no threat to anybody. He wore clothes more suited to New York than Texas, with a black bowler hat. The man had a handlebar mustache, waxed and curled to a point. He was a real dandy. He was waving to them as they approached.

"Do I have the honor of speaking with John Delaney?" he asked.

"And how would you know that?" John asked as Henry Lloyd ginned.

"You are a famous man. Stories about the Irish Ranger and his war dog have made it all the way to Philadelphia. I have traveled over fifteen hundred miles to meet you," the man said.

He accompanied this speech with a smile that signaled a degree of accomplishment.

"You certainly do have the pleasure of speaking with John Delaney," Henry Lloyd said. "If you like, you are welcome to travel with us. I'm sure our friend Chester will have a comfortable camp started by the time we return. Since you know John already, let me introduce myself. I am Henry Lloyd Walker."

He tipped his hat.

"Good to know you, sir. I am Phineas Arnold. Perhaps you have heard of me?"

"No," John said.

"Then let me introduce myself. I am a writer for *Beadle*, the number one publisher of western novels," he said.

"Pleased to meet you, Mr. Phineas Arnold. May I call you Phineas?" Henry Lloyd asked, smiling at John. It was obvious he was enjoying this.

"I left Philadelphia as soon as the war ended in hopes of obtaining some first-hand accounts of real battles on the frontier. I also have a list of notorious gunfighters I'd like to meet. Mr. Delaney, you are at the top of that list."

"I am not a gunfighter," John snapped.

"Don't be so modest," Henry Lloyd said. "You handle a gun as well as anyone I have ever seen."

John said nothing more. They turned their horses and rode back.

As they rode together the talking never stopped. At least not from Phineas and Henry Lloyd. John had nothing to say. Chester had a fire going and he was heating up some deer meat from the night before. Henry Lloyd made onion gravy to go over it and a batch of biscuits. By the time they were ready to sleep, Phineas Arnold was an official member of their group. In the morning it was decided that Phineas would travel with them all the way to the ranch. Seeing a working ranch was another item he had on his list of things to see, and if he could meet Mr. King, then he'd be all the more grateful.

Henry Lloyd and Chester were enjoying their conversations. Phineas was an easy man to like. He was quick-witted, with an exceptional grasp of details. Even John could see no harm in him tagging along. It would break the monotony of the daily grind. Phineas would keep Chester and Henry Lloyd entertained while John and Hank slipped off on a few more hunting trips.

John was not yet ready to share any stories with this Philadelphia writer but Phineas was confident he would soon win him over.

When Phineas was ready to chronicle their stories, it was Chester who began. He had first-hand knowledge of the inner workings of the Union command which had maintained the Santa Fe Trail. In fact, Chester had been right in the middle of the decisive battle in the western campaign. His account was probably better than most because the officers seemed to always want to tell the story as if they made the difference. Most battles swing one way or the other due to odd occurrences rather than proper management, Chester explained. Phineas was delighted to hear his tale and he took notes and asked questions as they rode.

John had heard it before but he enjoyed hearing it again. It was better this time because he was no longer apprehensive about how Henry Lloyd had fared in the story. In Chester's version, the real hero was a Comanche scout who figured out how to defeat an army with only a few men. Most of the first day was taken up with Chester's army stories. The following day it was Henry Lloyd's turn. He talked about life as a buffalo hunter, adding a few stories about cooking at some of the finest restaurants in New Orleans. Henry Lloyd's stories all seemed to have a purpose or moral that wove in a Bible verse or two. Phineas was enjoying Henry Lloyd's storytelling.

The next morning, as they prepared to leave, Chester, who had been scouting and watching the area, came riding up fast. John knew something was not right.

"You will not believe what I saw," Chester said.

His voice told them he was more curious than afraid.

"What is it?" John asked.

"You will want to see this for yourself," said Chester.

Chester and Hank stayed with Pojoaque and the children while Henry Lloyd and John rode out to see. Phineas tried to keep up with them but he was not much of a horseman. When they reached the top of a hill they could see what Chester was talking about. A string of Union Soldiers was marching with a few dozen horse soldiers accompanying them. John was trying to count them when Henry Lloyd spoke.

"Over a hundred on foot."

"Wonder where they are going?" John asked.

"We will soon find out," Henry Lloyd said as he pointed at five riders headed their way.

Phineas had just caught up with them.

"What do we have here?" he asked with excitement in his voice.

"We will soon see," Henry Lloyd repeated.

"Good morning," said one of the soldiers.

"Yes, it is a fine morning thank you. Good morning to you as well," Henry Lloyd said.

"What is your business here?" another of the soldiers asked.

"Whatever it is, you were correct in saying that it is our business," John said.

"Well, we need to know," the first soldier said.

"We are going home," Henry Lloyd said in a non-threatening tone.

"Are you alone?" another soldier asked.

"That, too, sir, is our business," John said.

Phineas was getting more excited by the minute, thinking there might be trouble.

"As long as we are all asking questions, may I ask you your business?" John inquired.

"My business is to determine what I do with the three of you," said the soldier, putting his hand on his revolver.

"I wouldn't do that," Henry Lloyd warned.

Matters were becoming tense as they saw another rider coming up. He was an officer.

"At ease, men," he said as he rode up. "I am Lieutenant Simmons. May I ask who you are?"

"I am about tired of all the asking. I am John Delaney, this is my friend, Henry Lloyd Walker, and the dude is Phineas Arnold. He is a writer from Philadelphia. Now I suspect that is enough information."

"Yes, it certainly is. Men, I will take care of this. I want you all to go about your duties."

They mumbled agreement with a 'yes sir' or two under their breaths and rode off looking for their next confrontation.

"I fear we might have gotten off to a bad start," said Simmons. "May I apologize for my men's behavior?"

"We understand things are tense nowadays," Henry Lloyd said.

"Yes, they are," Simmons agreed. "We are coming from New Orleans on our way to Fort Worth."

"You are too far south. You need to follow this river northwest," Henry Lloyd said.

"Thank you but we have business in Austin first. We are also escorting Governor Hamilton to Austin," Simmons said.

"I've never heard of him. I thought the governor was Pendleton Murrah," John said.

"Last we heard he was on his way to Mexico. Andrew Jackson Hamilton was appointed by Lincoln before he was killed. Hamilton had been in New Orleans," said the lieutenant.

"I thought governors were elected, not appointed," John said.

"That will come with time," Simmons said calmly.

"You are not that far from Austin," John observed.

"Is there anything we can do for you?" Simmons asked.

"There is one thing," Phineas asked. "Do you think I could interview the governor?"

"I will ask him. If he is like most politicians he'll be more than happy to talk with you."

"Good. I will ride with you to see him now," Phineas said.

He had a way of taking over. Simmons was not offended.

He bade the Texans goodbye and he and Phineas rode toward the Governor.

"Maybe we are done with him," John said as they watched him ride away.

"I don't think so," Henry Lloyd said. "Let's go get the others. By the time we get back, the bluecoats will be out of our way.

Mac was slowly improving. He could now stand and take a few steps with help. He still had not said a word, though. Josephina had asked both doctors many times about his progress. They both thought he was doing as well as could be expected. He seemed contented being back at the ranch. He would sit on the front porch most days and read books.

Aldo had taken over the school. Every day he would stop by to report to Mac on the progress of each student. Mac would write what he needed to say. Aldo was patient with him. Mac had a wheelchair and his bed was altered so that he could get into it by himself.

During this period, it seemed Mac had been working on a confidential project. Weeks into his recuperation, he handed Josephina the result—a sealed envelope entitled *My Last Will and Testament*—with a note instructing her to keep it until the time was right. Josephina did not want to think about Mac leaving her. His body had always been a challenge and now it seemed to be giving up on him. All they could do was to make him comfortable and spend as much time with him as they could.

Meanwhile, Phineas was still missing when it was time to make camp. Henry Lloyd prepared a light dinner and they turned in early. The next morning, there was still no Phineas. They continued without him, thinking he had found another more interesting story. A few hours after they left the camp, a rider caught up with them. He carried a message from Richard King, who had business with the new governor and was traveling with the Union army. In response, they doubled back, heading west to rendezvous with the bluecoats. They caught up with the caravan of traveling dignitaries in the early afternoon. Mr. King rode his black stallion out to meet them.

"I didn't think I'd find you riding with the Union Army," John said as they shook hands.

"And I was equally surprised to find you traveling with Phineas Arnold," King said with a laugh. "Henry Lloyd, it is good to see you again."

He got off his horse to shake the big man's hand.

"Good to see you, sir," Henry Lloyd said.

"I hear you have a new family," King said.

"Yes. Please allow me to introduce my wife Pojoaque. In English her name means butterfly," Henry Lloyd said.

"Pleased to meet you, ma'am."

She nodded at him pleasantly.

"So what is going on?" John asked.

"Let's get you all settled at the camp and then we can talk. I have a lot to tell you. And I'm sure you have plenty to tell me. Or are you saving all your stories for Phineas?"

Henry Lloyd and King laughed as they mounted up and rode into the Union camp.

King was with the Union Army negotiating with the new Governor. It was going to be tricky keeping order in Texas. Almost all the Union soldiers would be needed out west to deal with hostile tribes. Most of the Texas Rangers had been in the rebel army so he didn't know what to expect from them. There was still a need for serious law enforcement all over Texas. The governor had heard about how King's rangers had kept things quiet before the war. Mr. King knew that John was looking to start his own ranch, so he brokered a deal that would solve the ranger problem and get John started as a rancher at the same time.

The governor had the power to grant land in places where order needed to be established. About sixty miles north of Austin was the town of Belton. Before the war, it had been a hotbed of Union support. It was the county seat of Bell County with about 300 residents, including several influential members of the old Whig party who operated a paper called *The Independent*. They had supported Sam Houston in trying to stop Texas from leaving the Union. They had sympathized with the North throughout the entire conflict and this was never appreciated by those who were loyal to Texas. Now that the war was over, there was bad blood among many of the citizens of Belton. Several of the local citizens had been the victims of harassment and the tension was escalating. The local law would do nothing about it and the Texas Rangers had no real desire to protect these Union sympathizers. Since the old governor had ignored it, the new one needed to take action.

Just west of town was land the Kiowas had occupied for years. They were mostly gone now and the few of them that were left had joined the Comanches to the northwest. The governor would grant this land to John if he committed to maintaining order in the area.

King also brokered a deal for the state to purchase some of his cattle for John. If John agreed, he was in business. The governor and King were finishing the contract when Phineas showed up. The governor took this as a sign from God that it was to be done.

"What do you think?" John asked Henry Lloyd later that day, as they were walking together after hearing the plan.

"If that is what you want to do I think it is a valuable opportunity."

"Not me, us. I need you to help me," John said.

"Of course, I'll help you," said his friend.

"I mean us to be partners. Fifty-fifty. It's the only way. We will be equal partners," John said.

"I'll need to pray about this," Henry Lloyd replied.

"You can pray while we are traveling home. It will be a good reason to keep Phineas from bothering us. We can tell him God needs all our attention."

They grinned at each other.

"Henry Lloyd, I want your children to grow up with mine."

John had Mr. King alter the contract to add Henry Lloyd as a partner in the new ranch. After the contract was adjusted and signed, they sat back and enjoyed a brandy.

"I need to tell you something," King said. "Mac had some sort of spell. They had to take him to a doctor. They had a specialist come down to see him. Right now he's holding his own but the effects are serious. His left side doesn't work right. It could have been caused by that bad hit to the head he took a few years back. He is not talking yet."

"What do you mean, not talking?" John asked.

"The brain is a funny thing. Sometimes people get over these things and sometimes they don't. I heard about a soldier that took a musket ball through his eye and it came out his ear. You would think that would kill a man for sure but except for losing that eye and hearing in one ear, he is fine."

"So, is he going to be fine?" John asked.

"He seemed to be recovering. But I must tell you, your wife is taking it hard," King said.

John sat in silence. He knew how much she loved Mac.

"I have to get back now, he said. "You know the way home, Henry Lloyd. Hank and I are leaving tonight. I'm taking an extra horse. I don't want to push Bonnie too hard."

CHAPTER 28

A New Start

Mac was sitting on the front porch with Aldo when John rode up. Aldo helped Mac to his feet and steadied him as he took a couple of steps toward John, who was coming up the walkway to the porch. He shook hands with John and smiled. His grip was firm but John couldn't help but notice how his left arm hung lifeless at his side.

"It's been a long time," Aldo said.

"Yes, it has been a long time, too long," John said as Henrietta greeted him. She sent Nettie to get Josephina, then walked over and hugged John.

"Welcome home," she said warmly.

"We ran into Richard and he told us about Mac," John said.

"I better," Mac mumbled in a strange voice that sounded nothing like him.

"He's just started saying a few words," Henrietta said. "Soon he will be giving eloquent speeches once again."

John could see his wife running up the trail from the schoolhouse. He jumped off the porch and ran to her. She was weeping with a combination of joy and fear. She was glad her man was back where he belonged.

"Mac—he's really in bad shape…"

That was all she could say before she buried her head in John's chest and wept.

"Richard told me. I got here as soon as I could," John said.

She sobbed, holding him closer.

"Henry Lloyd and his wife and baby are a couple of days ride behind me, my love."

Josephina knew this because he had written to her but he thought it might cheer her up to hear that they were close. It didn't. He gently pushed her head away so he could see her face. It was not the same face. This worried him.

"I'll go clean up in the bunkhouse. Then we can talk," he said.

She made no reply but she dried her eyes with her skirt as she walked over to Mac.

John had been at the ranch for almost two days before the rest of the party arrived. These seemed like the worst two days of his life. Josephina was in a deep depression. Nothing he could do or say made any difference. He was beginning to think he had lost his wife. She did not seem to care for him any longer. She spent all her time with Mac. John was fond of Mac, as everyone was but he needed his wife. He was starting to resent Mac. It was not Mac's fault but somehow John was still angry—not at Josephina, not at Mac, just angry. He was hoping that seeing Henry Lloyd, Pojoaque, and their baby would perk her up but even that hadn't worked.

Mac was happy to see Henry Lloyd and his family. The whole ranch was glad he was back. Henry Lloyd was beaming when he showed Henrietta his daughter. Chester seemed to feel at home, as did Phineas Arnold. Richard King had never been in a better mood. He was pleased with the deal he had cut.

Phineas was eager to look around the ranch. Felix was given the responsibility of conducting the tour. Everyone was happy but John. He had lost his wife. Even Hank was too busy with Little Henry to pay any attention to John. John wanted to ride off, to escape but that was the one thing he could not do.

The following day, Henry Lloyd found John sitting under a pecan tree near the creek. Henry Lloyd sat next to him, put his arm around him, and looked at John without saying a word. After a while, John grew tired of his friend just looking at him.

"What?" John asked.

Henry Lloyd smiled. More wordless time passed.

"I know you have something to say. You always have something to say."

John was now becoming angry with his friend.

"Your wife is hurting," Henry Lloyd said.

"What do you want me to do? She won't have anything to do with me," John replied.

"She has hit bottom. I'm worried about her," Henry Lloyd said softly.

John said nothing more. The truth was he had hit bottom too. After talking with the governor, John realized he finally had what he'd always wanted—hope for the future, a future he wanted. Now it was gone.

"May I talk to her?" Henry Lloyd asked.

"Of course, you can talk to her. Why ask me?" John said.

"Because she is your wife."

Henry Lloyd hugged John, then got up and went off to be alone. John watched him as he stood alone out in the pasture. John knew he was probably praying. It was what he always did. After a while, the big man marched up to the house. John could see him talking to Josephina and Mac. A few minutes later, Henry Lloyd and Josephina walked off together. John followed at a distance. They talked for hours. John had no idea what they were saying but he was hurt—and angry—that she would talk to his friend but not to him. John wanted to saddle up Bonnie and leave for good when he saw her walking back to the porch. Henry Lloyd walked over to John.

"I guess you know I've been watching you both," John said.

Henry Lloyd smiled.

"She is going to be fine. Just give her some time," Henry Lloyd said confidently.

"That is good," John said.

Henry Lloyd looked at John.

"What now?" John asked.

"She is going to be fine," he said again. "What about you?"

"What do you mean?"

"I mean she has found what she needed. Are you interested in what you need?" Henry Lloyd asked kindly.

John's anger was fading, replaced by confusion. *How can he know she is going to be fine? How can he know what I need?*

"I'm fine," John said.

"No, you are not fine. You are hurting—and just about as depressed as she was."

"I'm just hungry," John said. "Let's go get something to eat."

"Sure, but first I have to know if you are curious about what Josephina needed?"

John did not know if he wanted to talk about this anymore. He just looked at his friend.

"She needed Jesus. And she found Him," Henry Lloyd said.

"She already knew about Jesus. Being around Henrietta, you can't help but hear about religion," John said.

"I'm not talking about religion. I'm talking about a relationship."

John didn't know what to say so he didn't say anything.

"Let me know when you are ready to talk," Henry Lloyd said.

He walked away whistling to himself and for some reason John couldn't articulate, this made him mad.

Morning found John still out of sorts, though he was enjoying watching Little Henry and Hank playing. His son was riding Hank like a pony. When he fell off, Hank would lick his face until he giggled, then he would climb back on the big dog. When Richard King walked up, John could see he wanted to talk business.

"In a few weeks, we will be ready to brand. I want to cut out the cattle that are yours before we brand. I was thinking you should head up to Belton and find a good place to settle. By the first of June, you need to be ready to drive these cattle north. You don't want to wait till it gets hot," King said.

"Yes sir," John said.

He had been thinking the same thing.

"Can we talk about the rangers?"

"Good idea. What are you thinking?" King asked.

"I think they are all good men. Alfredo is ready to run the operation. The men respect him. Also, Aldo needs to stay here. He will want to go with his sister but he needs to stay with the school since Mac can't. Henrietta would not appreciate us taking her teacher. Besides, he is good at it. Mac will also need to stay. He could not handle the trip. Josephina would feel better knowing Aldo was with Mac," John said.

"You are right. Alfredo's proven to be a solid hand," King agreed.

"Besides my family and Henry Lloyd's, I would like to take Felix, Wilbur, and Chester. I plan to make Felix my cattle boss. Wilbur is a good hand with a gun and I think I may need him. Chester is going to go with Henry Lloyd no matter what. If you don't mind, I'd like Felix to pick out a couple of hands that he can work with to go with us," John said.

"That all sounds fair. I will also send a few of my carpenters with you. I have purchased some timber from a man who owes me money. He is delivering it to Belton by the first of July. What about Phineas?" King asked.

"He can stay with you," John said, grinning.

"No thanks, I'm ready for him to go."

They both laughed.

"He'll leave when I do," John said. "I'll get rid of him."

"Be careful how you treat him. I don't want him writing negative things about either of us," King said.

They shook hands.

"Also, I am transferring all your assets to a banker I know in Austin. You will need to begin dealing with him. I trust him," King said.

Two days later, Josephina was her old self again. Whatever Henry Lloyd had said worked. It was remarkable how she had changed. With Josephina back, John was ready to go scout his new property. He and Henry Lloyd were off to find their new home. As they were packing up to leave, Phineas rode up. He was also apparently ready to go. This tickled Henry Lloyd for some reason.

"You are not going with us," John said.

"It's a free country. I suppose I can go where I please," Phineas said, in a very pleasant tone.

It was hard to get mad at the man.

"If you wait here and stay out of everyone's way, I promise you I'll tell you my stories when I get back," John said.

He figured that was fair. He was looking forward to being on the road with Hank and Henry Lloyd like it was before, just the three of them.

"That sounds good. It gives me time to finish up some of the material I'm working on.

Phineas was satisfied with the arrangement.

"Phineas, make sure John tells you about the pack of raiding Comanches he fought off single-handedly," said Henry Lloyd.

Phineas smiled and nodded as they rode away.

"I never fought with Indians," John said as they kicked their horses into an easy gallop.

"I know but I want to see you talk him out of the story. By the time we get back, he'll be convinced you are a real Indian fighter."

Pojoaque and the girls were settled into a small house that had been converted from a tool shed into a very comfortable one-room cabin. She waved to them as they rode away. On the way, they stopped at the land office in Austin and finished signing the partnership papers. They also registered their brand. DW was the mark. The Delaney Walker ranch was official. As they were leaving, John received a telegram from King. He wanted them back in Austin in eight days. He had a meeting set up with the Governor.

"I guess they are going to grant you the rest of Texas," Henry Lloyd said.

John folded the note and they headed toward Belton.

They made camp the first night just north of Austin. John thought the land in this part of the state was beautiful. It reminded him of Ireland.

"What did you say to Josephina?" John finally asked as they set up camp.

"I told you," Henry Lloyd said.

"No, you didn't."

"I did too. And I told you when you were ready that we would talk. Are you ready?"

"I'm asking, aren't I?"

"Are you? Do you want to find Jesus or are you just happy your wife is better?"

"Both, I guess."

As they got dinner started, Henry Lloyd told him what he said to Josephina. He explained that God had created people so that he could have a personal relationship with them. Not like a king to a subject but more like a friend to a friend. The reason God could not have a relationship with them was because people were evil. So God came to earth as a man, lived a pure life, then died on a cross. John had heard most of this before but it was different the way Henry Lloyd told it. It seemed to make perfect sense.

"He gave up his life for us willingly. It was love that made him do it. His love for us. Then, after He was buried for three days, he came back to life. It is a historical fact that he came back to life. Hundreds of people saw him. By defeating death and sin he was able to ransom us. Do you know what a ransom is?"

"Yes, that is where you pay money to somebody for something you want."

"That is right. He paid for us. With his life. Now remember, His life is worth so much more than ours is. After all, He is God. He is alive because He wants to have an individual relationship with whoever wants it. That is why I ask you. Do you want it?"

"What do I need to do?" John asked.

"See that rock over there?"

He pointed to a boulder about fifty yards away.

"Walk over there. Sit down and close your eyes. You will find God there. Tell Him you want to be His friend. Then tell Him you are sorry for wasting so much time. Tell Him you will begin talking with Him all the time. He will fix you like he fixed me, like he fixed Josephina. Now go on over there."

John thought this seemed silly but he decided to do it.

"John, all you have to do to make this work is believe what I had said is true. Do you believe me?"

"I do," John said.

Henry Lloyd had always been a man you could believe. So why not now? John went to the rock, looked around, and saw nothing unusual. He closed his eyes and said exactly what his friend had told him to say. First, he said it to himself. He waited a few minutes, then he said it again, this time out loud. He waited a few seconds more, then he said it again, adding *If you are here…* But before he could attempt to bargain with God, he remembered the last thing Henry Lloyd said. Do you believe me? And suddenly a strange peace came over him and seemed to ease his troubled mind.

He also remembered how real God had seemed to his mother, how real God seemed to Father Matthew, how real God seemed to Henrietta King, and of course how real he was to Henry Lloyd. These were all people he admired. *I do believe him. I do believe God is real. I do want to be his friend,* he thought.

The peace he was feeling seemed real to him. He felt comfortable, relaxed, and calm. He was happy—the same kind of happiness he had felt when he first held Josephina's hand. He sat down by the rock and repeated the same thing. This time he started with *"I believe you want to be my friend. You want to fix me and you want to talk with me every day."*

John sat there for several hours as he talked with God for the first time. It was dark when he wandered back to find Hank and Henry Lloyd eating.

"Did you find God?"

"I did," John said.

Henry Lloyd smiled.

"Good, now sit down and have some of this rabbit. It's good. We will talk more about these things tomorrow."

They didn't say anything else that evening about God or John's new relationship with Him. The next morning, they were up early. John still had the strangely comfortable feeling. Before they left, John wanted to go back to the same rock. Henry Lloyd told him there was no need to do that. Jesus would be riding with them all day. He smiled as he told John that Jesus would never again be away from him. All he needed to do was believe.

By afternoon they were in Belton. They decided to scout out the land before they went to town. It was a beautiful place and John felt they would be happy here. He felt like he was finally where he should be but all he really wanted to do was ride back to the ranch and tell Josephina what had happened to him by the rock.

CHAPTER 29

Belton, Texas

Josephina and Pojoaque were becoming close friends as they worked together getting things ready for the move to Belton. Henrietta assured Josephina that between she and Aldo, Mac would be cared for properly. She also promised them that as soon as he was ready to travel she would bring him to Belton. Josephina was feeling more and more comfortable with the move and she was thrilled that she and Pojoaque had so much in common. They both loved their men, they both loved children and they were both pregnant. Their babies would be born about the same time.

Meanwhile, John had found the site where he wanted to build their home. It was on a high area overlooking the river. It reminded him of his home in Ireland. He, Henry Lloyd, and Hank camped one more night on the land, then decided to go into Belton, to clean up, find a room, and sleep in a bed. Later that day, John and Hank were at the livery stable boarding the horses while Henry Lloyd explored the town. John had just left the stable when he saw his friend walking rapidly toward him.

"Back inside," Henry Lloyd said. "Look what I found."

He handed John a handbill with shocking news in bold print. 'Your Own Local War Hero Has Returned', it proclaimed, adding that 'the town is fortunate that their returning hero has agreed to run for

Sheriff.' The poster had been professionally printed with a picture of Belton's returning hero. Walter Riggins would be running for Sheriff in October. There was no doubt that he was the same Walter Riggins John had punched—the same man who had staged an ambush that almost ended their lives.

"Can you believe that?" John asked.

"We need to get out of here before he knows we are in town," Henry Lloyd said.

"I have never run from a man in my life. I'm not about to have this man be the first."

"John, listen to me. We will need to deal with him, I know. However, we need to deal with him on our terms. He out-planned us last time. He won't do it again. It is far better if he doesn't know we are here."

John knew his friend was right. He talked briefly with the stable boy before they left, and learned that Walter Riggins had been raised in Belton. He came from a large, respected family that ran the local store and the cotton gin. Thus far, he was unopposed for the position. Other men had planned to run but had all dropped out. Everyone understood that the Riggins family always gets what it wants. They left immediately for Austin. King would be there soon.

Despite their efforts, Walter Riggins found out they had been in town. The description of a young Irishman with a big blond dog accompanied by a giant Negro was more than enough proof that the ranger had been there. Walter was not worried. He was pleased that he would now be able to settle the score. He had thought of little else on his long trip home from that canyon in New Mexico. He was not a man without resources. He would find out what these two were up to.

John and Henry Lloyd arrived in Austin early and tried to find a hotel that would allow Henry Lloyd to stay there. There were none. They located a small rooming house in the Mexican area of town near the river. It was run by a young Mexican couple and they said they would allow a Negro and a dog. John was upset about these arrangements but Henry Lloyd seemed contented. He told John he was not going to allow a few white people he did not know to make him unhappy. John knew it was more than just a few.

When it was time to meet with the governor, they loaded their belongings and rode over the river and down Brazos Street, right up to the capitol building. They were told that the governor's office was at his house a few blocks away. John was pleased that Hank chose to empty his bowels on the lawn of the capitol before they departed. He thought it left the perfect message for the uppity politicians.

They arrived to find Richard King and the governor having a cup of coffee on the porch.

"Come in gentlemen," said the Governor. "We have been waiting for you."

With King and the governor were several other men in suits. John and Henry Lloyd were introduced to them. Each man had a title—secretary of one thing or chairman of another—it all meant nothing to John. After the introductions, they went inside, except for Hank. John told him to wait on the porch. Hank complied though he never took his eyes off John, who was still visible through large windows as the men were seated in a room with several rows of chairs. Governor Hamilton gave a speech about law and order and the need for responsible people to begin healing the wounds of war. After the speech, John and Henry Lloyd stood in front of the group as they placed their hands on a Bible and swore an oath to protect Texas and its citizens from all harm. Then they were given badges and manuals containing rules and regulations of the Texas Rangers. John figured most rangers had never looked at the regulations.

John's badge read CAPTAIN. Henry Lloyd's did not. The governor saw John looking at the star and he explained that captain was the highest rank in the Rangers and that he would report only to the governor. They shook hands with each of the men, accepting their thanks and various bits of well-meaning advice. Most of this fell into the category of what John considered meaningless platitudes but he held his tongue.

Later that afternoon, John, Hank, and Henry Lloyd were sitting under a tree behind the boarding house. John was reading the Texas Rangers manual and Henry Lloyd was reading the Bible.

"Look at this," John said, "It says here that as captain I can advance any Ranger's grade using my own discretion."

"I'm sure there is a great deal more than that you can do as captain," Henry Lloyd said without looking up from his Bible.

"Then I'm raising your rank to captain, same as mine."

"If you want to do that, it's up to you, John, but I don't require it. In fact, I wouldn't mention it to anyone else if I were you. The great state of Texas is far from ready for a black captain in the Texas Rangers."

"Ready or not, I say you're a captain," John said, closing the manual.

The next morning, John went with King to San Antonio while Henry Lloyd and Hank left for the ranch. Hank was not happy about this and he made that clear. As always, though, he did as he was told. Henry Lloyd thought Hank should have been made a Ranger with a higher rank than either he or John. The faithful dog had earned it many times over.

Though John would have preferred to see his wife and children, he could not tell Richard King no. The most unusual thing about this trip was that it was just John and Richard without the usual cohort of finely-dressed gentlemen. Today they were just a man riding a fine black stallion and his friend on a pretty mare. They talked about the challenges of ranching, the art of managing money and assets, directing people properly, and about life in general. John realized his mentor was educating him on the fine points of running a large operation. Although John figured Henrietta knew more about ranching than King did, he didn't bring that up. When they arrived, they checked into the nicest hotel in the town. They made plans to meet in the lobby for dinner later that evening.

"We will be meeting someone," said King.

John nodded his approval. Meeting with people was common with Richard King.

"You know this man," said King. "We are meeting with Phineas Arnold."

"Phineas?" John was startled. The little man had an unusual ability to pop up in places you would never expect.

"John, a man's reputation is important. This war has damaged my name with some folks in the north that I do business with. If Phineas would write a few positive articles about me, it would help greatly," King said.

"How do you know he will?" John asked.

"I have ensured he will by paying for his train fare to Philadelphia. He was glad to do it but this alone wasn't enough. He said I needed to ensure he could conduct a proper interview with you. The other stories he has are good but it is your story he needs. He is going to write it whether you talk with him or not. For my sake, please be cordial to Mr. Arnold."

As King and John dined in San Antonio, Walter, Clyde, and Buford Riggins were finishing their meal and sipping coffee in the back room of the Clyde's diner. This was a regular planning meeting. If Belton was going to be the kind of town they wanted it to be, certain things had to happen.

First on the list was ridding the area of unwanted Union sympathizers. For some time they had been coordinating efforts to harass these people. Some had already left while the stubborn ones seemed to be digging in. Some were even sending letters to the governor. This had to stop. Next on the list of people who had to go was Delaney. The self-appointed ranger and his colored friend had to be taken care of.

"I don't see the problem. They can leave just like the Yankee lovers can," Clyde said.

"I agree but this kid has connections. We must be careful. The Texas Rangers so far have given us no problem. I want it to stay that way," Walter said.

"How important can he be, trotting around with a dog and a darkie. This is Texas," said Buford.

Walter put both hands on the table, looking from one brother to the other.

"I underestimated them both before and I'll not do it again. For now, all I need you two to do is ratchet up the pressure on the Yankee lovers to the point that they decide to leave. I'll deal with this Irish lad after the election. We must make sure nobody else decides to run against me and I must keep my nose clean until October. I'll be kissing babies and shaking hands. Until then, you two need to do the important things," Walter explained.

During the dinner with Phineas, John tried his best to be cordial and friendly. The men talked about everything under the sun. Phineas seemed to know something about everything. When they finished dinner they agreed to meet in the morning in John's room so his story could be told properly, without interruptions.

The next morning, Phineas was ready for the interview with John. John began his life story with tales of Ireland. He told how he and his brothers had fought alongside their father. Most of these stories had a sad ending. He shared his heart with Phineas for some reason and it felt good. Then he told the story of his mother's death and his troubles with Blackie. He did not leave out any detail as Phineas scribbled notes furiously. He included his feelings and thoughts as well as the details of his adventures, including the story of his brief prizefighting career. Phineas had already heard this tale but had not realized it was about John. John talked about how he defeated the schemes of Boss Tweed and about leaving his sister and catching a boat to Galveston, Texas, where he first met the Kings.

In story after story, he told Phineas the truth about how he was always searching for something but without any idea what it was. Every adventure seemed to enhance his fame and his knowledge but not his peace. Lunch arrived as he was telling about the New Mexico battle with Riggins. He left out the man's name.

After lunch, he concluded his story with his experience at the rock. He told Phineas that he had finally found what he was looking for. He also made him promise to not leave that part out. All the adventures were nothing compared to what he found. Phineas agreed and seemed pleased with all he had heard. As Phineas left, the two men hugged like they were old friends. This puzzled John at first but it felt right. John had kept his bargain with Richard King but had remained true to himself.

When Josephina saw Henry Lloyd and Hank ride up without John, she froze in place. In her mind, she saw John lying bloody on the ground, just like her Papa had looked after the horse trampled him to death. She was paralyzed with fear. Henry Lloyd was close enough to see something was not right. He kicked his horse to a gallop and he and Hank rushed to her. He jumped from his horse and put his big hands on her shoulders.

"John is fine. He and Mr. King went to San Antonio. He is fine."

"He is?" she mumbled.

"Yes, he is fine. Your John is well—very well, in fact."

She threw both arms around the big man's body and squeezed him with all her might. He laughed his big, happy laugh—the one that made it seem everything was right with the world.

When John rode up the next day, Josephina ran as fast as she could to meet him. Their reunion was as sweet as any they had ever experienced. There was so much to share and they almost couldn't get the words out quickly enough between hugs and kisses. She told him they were having another baby and she was excited about their new home in Belton. She showed him the drawing Henrietta had made of their new ranch and told him the woman was doing all she could to make sure their move was a success. Josephina wept and called Henrietta a "second mother".

John told her all about the place where they would live. She smiled as he described the land. Then he told her about his experience at the rock. She listened to him with a satisfied look on her face, nodding. She told him she knew that he would find God and that she had been praying for it. They visited with Mac together, thrilled that he was much improved. His left side was still not right but he was getting stronger. Even his speech was better though he still had a long way to go.

The next day, John found Alfredo and asked if he had talked with the men. Alfredo apologized but said he hadn't felt right talking to them without John. John asked him to get them all together so they could explain the changes that were coming.

When they were all gathered, John told them that he and his family were moving, and why. He told them about where they were going and when they would leave. When it was Alfredo's turn to speak, he looked at John, unsure. John spoke to him quietly.

"These are your men now. They have always done everything I asked of them. Now they are your men. Talk to your men."

Alfredo cleared his throat, then looked at each face. These were good men and he was proud to lead them. Though he was not comfortable speaking, he forged ahead.

"Men, I am not happy about Mr. John leaving but he and Mr. King want us all to keep doing what we are doing. It is important that this ranch stays safe and you are all a big part of that. Anyone that wants to leave can but if you want to stay, I will treat you fair, just as Mr. John has always done."

As a group they nodded their heads, signaling their willingness to stay.

"Wilbur, if you will, I'd like you to come with me," said John. I will need you where I'm going. The rest of the men will miss you but I hope you will agree to join me."

Wilbur grinned. He had never felt wanted before. A tear came to his eye. He didn't even try to speak. He would never have been able to get the words out. He nodded his head and hugged the men standing around him. That same night John arranged for a big fiesta to celebrate their new boss and to reminisce about their times together.

Everybody was ready to leave two days after the party. It was decided that Wilbur would go ahead with the women and children, leaving the rest of them to move the cattle. Aldo wanted to go with them, just to see the place but Josephina would not allow it. Mac would be needing his help. John had noticed that his wife was becoming more and more like Henrietta, her friend, mentor, and second mother.

After Wilbur and the women had a head start, Felix took charge of moving the cattle to their new home. He had selected four men he wanted to work with. These included a young man from Alabama called Shorty. His family farm had been destroyed in the war so he had moved west to start over. Felix had also chosen two brothers, Pablo and Julio, who were close to him. Finally, he chose a man they all called Pockets. Nobody knew why he was called this but he liked the name and referred to himself that way. Pockets was a talker. He was full of stories. Some were true and some were not but he told them as if they were fact and dared you to prove him wrong. He was a good worker and was fun to be around.

They lost no cattle, rare for a drive. When they were a few miles west of Austin, John told Henry Lloyd he needed to see the Governor about Riggins. He asked for Henry Lloyd's badge but didn't say why. His friend handed it over.

"I've lived my whole life without it. I guess I don't need it now," said Henry Lloyd.

He dug through his bags and handed the badge to John. John told Hank to stay and he rode east to Austin. He arrived before dark and got a room in the same place they had stayed before. Early the next morning, he cleaned up, put on a new suit of clothes, attached his badge to his shirt pocket, and went to see the governor. He was met at the door and informed that the soonest the governor could see him was two o'clock. While he waited, John found a place to get some food, then sent a wire to his sister. He had no idea if she would get it. He told her about his new ranch and their new baby on the way. After that, he wandered around until it was time to see the governor.

"Here is the problem," Hamilton said after John had shared his concerns about Riggins. "In Texas, it's not real clear who has jurisdiction over local matters like this. Currently, we try to let the local folks handle these things. They only call us in when they need our help. Since there is no sheriff until the election, it's best we don't interfere."

"Riggins is not a man you can trust to maintain order," John said.

"Then it is up to the people to elect someone trustworthy. I must accept the will of the people. Why don't you find somebody better suited to oppose Riggins?"

It was clear the governor was going to do nothing about it. He had hired John, granted him land and now he wanted to move on to other issues he could fix. John thanked him and left. The entire meeting had taken only a few minutes. From there, John went directly to Texas Ranger headquarters and showed them his credentials. He exchanged

Henry Lloyd's badge for a captain's badge. He left with a smile on his face. The Texas Rangers had its first black captain.

On his way to Belton, he had a talk with God. He figured if Henry Lloyd could talk to the Lord, then he could too. He told God he wanted to talk with him more often now.

He told God all about why Riggins was not the man to be sheriff. At first, he felt silly doing this but then he remembered how he had felt when he talked to God by the rock. He went on talking to Him about everything he could think of.

While he talked with God, he suddenly remembered what the governor had said about finding someone else to run for Sheriff. He did not know anyone in Belton—only the men he was bringing with him. Henry Lloyd would be the perfect Sheriff but Texas was not going to elect a black man. Not yet, at least. Then it occurred to John that he had asked God who was "next best" after Henry Lloyd. The "next" part seemed to stick in his head. Chester was always right there, "next" to Henry Lloyd. *That's it*, John told God. Chester Anderson would make a fine sheriff. He was a fair man with a good heart and could spin a yarn as good as any politician.

CHAPTER 30

Delaney Walker Ranch

John turned Bonnie around and galloped back to Austin. He wanted to get to the telegraph office before it closed. He made it in time and sent an urgent telegraph to Richard King. Then he and Bonnie started out for Belton again. He decided to go into town before rejoining the rest of his group.

What he found in Belton surprised him. There had been trouble. Not the usual harassment, though. Three Union sympathizers had been hanged. Everyone knew what had happened but there was no proof that the Riggins brothers had anything to do with it. Several families were packing to leave while others were planning to stay and fight.

John put on his badge, then spent some time trying to find out what had happened. He got nowhere with this. No one was talking and all three of the Riggins had alibis. When his inquiry proved useless, he rode out to the Delaney Walker Cattle Company. The first person he saw was Shorty. He asked Shorty to get a fresh horse and supplies and be ready to ride immediately to the King Ranch. While he waited, John wrote two letters—one to the Kings and the other to Mac. He was finishing the letters when Shorty, Henry Lloyd, and Hank arrived. John gave Shorty the letters and told him to ride to the ranch as soon as he could.

"I just came from town. They hung three men. It's not good," John said as he hugged Hank.

"What do we do?" Henry Lloyd asked.

John reached in his bag and handed Henry Lloyd his captain's badge.

"I don't know captain, what do you think?" John said.

"I'll need to pray about this," Henry Lloyd said.

"I already have," John said as Henry Lloyd smiled. "I mean, I was talking to God like you told me, I guess that is praying."

"It sure is. Go on," he said.

"While I was telling God all about the mess we are in, I remembered something the governor said. He is going to be no help, by the way. He refused to get involved so it is up to us."

"That's no surprise. He is a politician," volunteered Henry Lloyd.

"Anyway, he said if Riggins was not to be trusted, then the good people of Belton needed to elect a man they could trust."

"Nobody will run against him," Henry Lloyd reminded him.

"Listen to what came to me while I was talking to God. I thought one of us could run. I know the best man to be sheriff is you but I also know you could not get elected. Besides, you have a ranch to run and you are a captain in the Texas Rangers."

They laughed.

"I was asking God, okay who is next? I meant the next choice, and then it hit me. Who is next to you? Every time I look around, Chester is next to you. It was like God was telling me Chester is the one."

"Sounds like God to me," Henry Lloyd said.

"I didn't hear a voice or anything like that—the thought just popped in my head. And the more I thought about it the better it sounded. Chester Anderson is a man you can trust, he can talk as well as any politician and he will listen to wise counsel," John said.

"Now I don't need to pray about it," Henry Lloyd said. "We have already heard from God. Part of knowing the Lord's voice is having faith in who He might speak through. I can trust that you now know God's voice. That's good enough for me. Let's go. I'll show you where we made camp and where the cattle are," he said as the Texas Ranger captains mounted their horses.

In Belton, the three Riggins brothers were at the cafe, having their daily meeting. Things were proceeding as planned.

"I think all we need to do now is lay low," Buford said. "They are too scared to give us any trouble."

"I think we need to keep the pressure on," said Clyde.

"I think Buford is right," Walter said. "We just need to keep our heads down and make sure no one gets any ideas about running against me. I'd still like to see that Yankee newspaper burn down. After what happened, we might need to let that little project slide for a while. If we need to do it later, we can."

"Did you know those outsiders from the south are back? They are settling north of town on the old Indian land," Clyde said.

"And they've driven a herd of cattle there already. They plan to settle in there I hear," Buford added.

"I know our fine governor caused that little problem for us. But he won't be in office long. We can deal with them after the election," Walter said.

At the Delaney Walker Cattle Company, the former King Ranch cattle were adapting quickly to the new land. The grass was better than down south and there was plenty of water. The carpenters Henrietta had sent were already well into building the first house. Josephina and Pojoaque were busy making the camp comfortable and planning their new homes and both ladies' bellies were showing evidence that the population of Delaney Walker was growing. Five days after Shorty left, he returned with letters from Mac, Richard, and Henrietta.

John had explained to Henry Lloyd that there was not a more qualified man in Texas than Richard King to advise them on how to run the sheriff's campaign. Mac was an expert on finding meaningful qualities and promoting a man and Henrietta would have excellent advice on how to run the ranch while all of this was going on. Even a major war hadn't slowed her down much except for that brief exile in San Antonio.

A few days after the letters arrived, John gathered everyone together. They took a half day off from work. Henry Lloyd had made a pot of his beef stew and after lunch, the meeting began.

It was Sunday so Henry Lloyd took advantage of the captive audience and told a Bible story. The men sat on the grass watching as the preacher began. It was about a king named Hezekiah. This ruler was in a bad spot but rather than fight his way out of it he decided to ask God to fight for him. John didn't understand where this was going but Henry Lloyd was a good storyteller.

Everyone listened intently. In the story, there was a part about Hezekiah sending out singers to go before the army. When Henry Lloyd reached a stopping point, Shorty decided it was a good time to sing. Shorty was from a church-going family and he knew several hymns. As it turned out, Shorty had a fine voice. Henry Lloyd knew the songs too, and he joined along. It wasn't long before most of them were singing.

John had planned to give a little speech about the need for everyone to pitch in to help the cause. He decided he didn't need to since there was already a bond with these men. He handed the letters to Henry Lloyd to read since he was the best reader. Nobody really knew what was coming next except Chester. As Henry Lloyd read, it was clear to the men what must happen. They nodded in agreement when John stood to pass out assignments.

"Wilbur and Henry Lloyd will oversee the Riggins brothers. We need to make sure there is no more trouble. The people around here need to know they no longer have anything to fear. Our next Sheriff, Chester Anderson, and Pockets will spend all their time from dawn to dusk shaking hands and kissing babies. They will make sure everybody in Bell County is in love with Chester."

The men chuckled at this. Pockets was the right man for this job and they were sure he and Chester would be successful.

"Felix, Pablo, and Julio you will oversee the ranch. You will be responsible to ensure the women and children are safe and that the cattle are secure and well cared for. Shorty, you will be with me. I plan to work with the newspaper people to ensure Chester's name is in every edition they print. We will be responsible for knowing what everyone is doing and where they are. If anyone needs help, we have to know how to get there fast. Are there any questions?"

John looked around. He knew that his men were fully committed and would not let him, or each other, down.

"Let's pray," Henry Lloyd said as he bowed and talked to the Lord about what they were doing. He spoke as though what they were doing was God's work and this seemed to give them a purpose.

"We start first thing in the morning," John said.

The next morning, each member of the team went about his duties with energy and zeal. John made friends with Harold Gibson, the editor of the local newspaper. Gibson was glad someone was running against Riggins. He told John what he needed to do to get Chester on the official ballot and by sundown, Chester Anderson was a candidate for Sheriff. Gibson said he would print advertisements. The next day, he interviewed Chester, getting his story for an editorial he would run. Meanwhile, Pockets went door to door, visiting with people and gathering support—and votes—for Chester.

Henry Lloyd had had plenty of experience keeping up with Riggins and he spent the first few days training Wilbur on how to read the signs. Wilbur was a quick study.

A few days into the campaign, Henrietta arrived with her children, Alfredo, and Beto. She told them she had been there for the birth of both of Josephina's first two babies and she was not going to miss this one. She also wanted to oversee construction on the first house and assess the overall running of the ranch.

Later that day, John, Shorty, and Pockets were canvassing voters. They had sent Chester into town to buy a couple of new suits. He needed to start looking like a lawman.

"It sure is a shame those men got hung," Pockets said. "A few years from now nobody will even remember anything about it. And they seemed to be good folks."

"They will be remembered if they have a memorial—a plaque with their names on it. We did that in my hometown for the boys we lost in the war," Shorty said. "We had a memorial service and the whole town turned out."

John pulled Bonnie to a halt.

"That is exactly what we will do. We will have a memorial for them. Speeches and a plaque—everything. And we will do it in town in front of the Riggins cafe."

"We need to do it before the Jones family leaves. They've already begun packing up," Pockets said.

"You boys go see all the families planning on leaving and ask them to stay until we have the service to honor these men," John said. "I'll go find the local preacher and get it set up. Then I'll go to Austin and have a plaque made up. I'll get the governor to write a letter to declare it an official holiday. The paper will help get the word out. This should get Walter Riggins' attention. He's been laying low but I bet this will flush him out."

Chester was returning from Austin with new suits and a new hat when he ran into Walter Riggins a few miles out of town. Riggins had a couple of men with him who Chester had never seen.

"Well if it's not the latest entry in the race for Sheriff. I think it's about time we had a little talk," Walter said.

"What's on your mind?" Chester asked calmly.

He was not worried because he saw his guardian angel sitting on a big white horse behind Riggins and his men.

"I have no idea who you think you are but if you're smart you'll leave the county while you still can," Walter said, matter-of-factly.

"As a matter of fact, I am pretty smart. However, I have no intention of leaving Bell County, Riggins," said Chester, making eye contact with Walter's companions. "Excuse me, sir, I didn't get your name?" he said to the man on Walter's right.

Chester was leaning forward, resting his elbow on his saddle horn. With the other hand, he was patting his horse.

"Why do you need his name?" Walter demanded before the man could speak.

Chester could see Henry Lloyd noiselessly moving closer.

"Well, that's a good question. I want his name because as soon as I'm sheriff, I'll be questioning him about his involvement in the recent lynching. Since he's running with you that makes him a prime suspect, as well as his friend," Chester said, pointing a finger at the other man.

Both men looked at Riggins with fear in their eyes.

"That pretty much tells me all I need to know," Chester said.

Riggins had had enough. He reached down and put his hand on his pistol. He did not draw the weapon, though. Just before his hand touched the gun, he heard galloping hoof beats closing in on him. Henry Lloyd was coming fast. Riggins had turned to see who it was when he caught a glimpse of another man behind a tree with a rifle trained on him. Henry Lloyd was pulling his big white horse to a halt when Riggins looked again.

The man removed his hand from his gun.

"Relax everybody," he said though it was clear he was not relaxed.

"Were you about to shoot me?" Chester asked.

Walter said nothing.

"I'm beginning to think it would have been better for everybody if we'd killed you back in Red Rock Canyon," Chester said. "We could have, you know."

A fresh wave of anger came over Walter as he realized that Chester Anderson, the man running against him for Sheriff, had been in the group that devastated his company and left them lost in the canyons in New Mexico. He should have been a hero for all he did in the war but this last failure would haunt him forever.

"The best choice is to ride away and stop threatening people," Henry Lloyd said.

Wilbur was walking toward them with his rifle still aimed as Walter and his men left. When they were out of sight, Chester got off his horse and greeted his two friends.

"Well lo-lo-lo-lo-look at you," Wilbur said. "You are a real d-d-da-dandy in your new clothes."

Wilbur's comment broke the tension but no one was under any illusion they'd seen the last of Riggins or his crew. They were waiting for trouble and it finally arrived the next night. It was almost midnight when Wilbur noticed a couple of men circling town. He couldn't imagine that they had legitimate business there at that hour. He rode out to the ranch where he found Beto and Shorty patrolling and was able, without too much stammering, to tell them what was going on. Beto and Wilbur turned and rode back to town while Shorty went for help. Beto got there first as the two men were breaking the windows of the newspaper office. They had torches and they were mounted to ride. The first man's torch missed the window and he jumped off his horse to get it. He knew Riggins would not be happy if they failed. Just then, a shot rang out, spooking their horses. Beto was coming fast.

"Drop the torch," Beto yelled. "I won't miss again."

The man with the torch tossed it into the street. The other man picked up the torch on the ground in front of the window and tossed it harmlessly away from the building.

"Raise your hands slowly," Beto said as Wilbur pulled his horse to a halt.

Wilbur took their pistols and began tying them up. They were both secured to their saddles with their hands behind their backs when John and Hank arrived. A crowd of townspeople awakened by the gunshot had also joined them.

On their way back to the ranch, John questioned the men. James Miller did most of the talking. He seemed most afraid. The other man, Thomas Sanders, was also talkative when asked. They told them what they already knew. Riggins had paid them to burn the building down. They both denied that they had anything to do with the lynching. John believed them.

Walter Riggins was not happy when he heard there had been no fire at the local paper. Now he couldn't find those two idiots. Nobody in town was saying anything about the incident. He was also furious about the upcoming memorial service but if he didn't show up it would look bad.

The memorial was scheduled for two days later. The plaque was prominently displayed in the center of town, near the courthouse. The Baptist preacher was ready to eulogize the fallen local heroes. A crowd made up of just about everybody in the county filled the town square. The agenda had been carefully planned. The mayor would read a declaration from the governor. Then, the preacher would give a eulogy. There were to be two guest speakers whose identities had not been disclosed, followed by a friendly message from Chester Anderson. The last thing was food for everyone. Two steers had been slow-roasted and there were huge pots of beans and rice. Two Mexican women were making tortillas and the tantalizing aroma filled the area.

The ceremony began on time. John surveyed the crowd, noting that the Riggins brothers were standing near the front entrance to the cafe. The mayor unveiled the plaque, read the proclamation, then turned it over to the preacher, who highlighted the virtues of all three men. After that, the mayor announced the guest speakers. First to speak were two men who had been recent guests at the Delaney Walker ranch. When Thomas Sanders and James Miller stepped forward, John had to suppress his amusement at the expression on Walter Riggins' face. Miller and Sanders told how they had been paid by the Riggins brothers to burn the press to the ground. They even showed the crowd the money that Buford had given them. The crowd began to protest with enough noise that all three Riggins brothers left before the food was served. The final speaker, Chester Anderson, spoke for a few minutes on his commitment to be fair and just to every citizen. The applause of the crowd was deafening.

Buford and Clyde were gone by morning. Walter was too furious to slink away with his tail between his legs. He would leave but not before he evened the score with these two rangers who had ruined his life. They couldn't really prove anything. Though he would never be elected, he did not think they could arrest him. He was wrong. Two days later, John and Henry Lloyd arrested him and took him to Austin to stand trial for murder.

During all the excitement in Belton, Pojoaque delivered her child, a boy they named Elijah Walker. He was a big baby but Pojoaque had little trouble with the birth. Ten days later, Josephina had another little girl they named Martha Ann Delaney. Martha arrived about the time the first cold front hit the area. The house was almost completed and they were starting work on the bunkhouse. John had never been happier. The election was now just Chester running unopposed for Sheriff and to top it off, John had just received a package from

Philadelphia. The package contained a note from Phineas that the first book in a series entitled *The Irish Ranger* had been released and was selling out all over the Northeast. A first edition of the book was also included. Though everyone on the ranch wanted to read it, John handed the book to Josephina. He told them he knew his story. He did not need to read about it.

Henrietta was finally planning her trip back to the King Ranch since everything in Belton seemed to be in order. John was helping her load the wagon when a man rode up with a wire for John. It was from Nelly. She and David and their children were coming for a visit. They would arrive by the second week of December. John was shocked. Before he could speak, Henrietta confessed.

"I took the liberty of making all the arrangements."

"I had no…"

"I have been writing to her regularly. We have become close even though I have never met her. I plan to come back to visit while she is here," Henrietta said.

John wept at Henrietta's many years of kindness to him and to his family.

Later he explained to Josephina that one of the few good things about the war had been the expansion of the railroad in Texas from Houston north almost to Ft. Worth. This was needed to move the cotton. Small towns were popping up all along the route and the nearest one to the ranch was a little village called Hearne. Two 'weeks before Christmas, John, Josephina, their children, Henry Lloyd and Pojoaque with all their children, and of course Hank, were in Hearne waiting for the train to arrive. The first to step off was Nelly. When she saw her brother, she ran to him and flung herself into his arms. For perhaps the first time in her life, Nelly was speechless.

Nelly and her family stayed through the first of the year. The Kings left before Christmas but not before Henrietta had all the time she needed to bond with Nelly. The children played together and David, John, Hank, and Henry Lloyd were able to get by themselves for a few days hunting and exploring Texas. The women laughed and shared stories about the children. It was one big happy family.

When it was time for Nelly's family to leave, she saw John looking distraught. She knew that look.

"Let's go for a walk down to the river," Nelly suggested.

They strolled to the riverbank and Nelly sat down and patted the ground beside her. John sat by his sister.

"What is wrong?" Nelly asked.

"There is nothing wrong. Everything is good," John said with a forced smile.

"It's better than good, it is great. We both have wonderful families. We both live wonderful lives. We made it through the war," Nelly said.

"I said it was good, didn't I?" John was defensive.

"I'm your sister. I know you. I know how you hate to share your feelings but that doesn't matter. You are going to tell me what is wrong."

Nelly waited. They were not going to leave that spot until he shared his thoughts with her. John knew how stubborn she could be.

"I really can't explain how I'm feeling," John said.

"You're just going to have to try," said his sister.

She reached out and grabbed his hand and held it as she looked into his eyes.

"Nelly, these last few weeks have been great. The Delaneys are a family again. I mean, you have a great family in a beautiful place and so do I. It's what we both wanted. I didn't know what I wanted until I found it. It took me longer but I have a home now."

He paused wanting her to join in but she just kept looking at him. She was going to make him share his heart.

"It's what we came to America for," John continued.

Another long pause.

"Do you remember when the family moved back to Galway? How happy we all were? We were all together and it was going to be wonderful?"

"Yes, I remember."

"Then it all fell apart. We didn't see it coming. We lost our brothers. Two of them were murdered and two moved away. They killed our father. We had to leave Ireland and on the ship, we lost our baby sister."

Tears came to Nelly's eyes and she nodded agreement to everything he said.

"Before we could figure out what to do in America, we lost our mother. We were all alone, just you and me. And now I am just afraid we are going to lose it all again. It's happened before."

John's voice was starting to break up as emotions rushed to the forefront.

"You don't know we are going to lose it," she said.

"I can't help but feel it slipping away. My entire life I've seen the good just evaporate like the morning dew on a hot day. I don't want to lose you, or Josephina, or our children. But I'm afraid I will."

She hugged him for a long time.

"We are Delaneys and we can do this," she said.

"I don't know if I have what it takes to be a Delaney. Father was so smart. He always knew what to do. Mum was so caring. Michael was strong and brave. Sean was so fun to be around—everybody loved him—and Danny was so funny. Patrick had it all together. I don't have what they had."

"Are you kidding me?" she asked. "I read 'The Irish Ranger', you know. I read it several times. If anybody can hold it together you can. You are a man of faith, a man of strength, and a man of action. Mrs.

King has told me what kind of man you have become. I trust she knows what a caring, responsible man is all about and that is how she describes you."

John said nothing. She waited.

"What would father tell you?" she asked.

John thought about what his father would say. He also thought about what Henry Lloyd would say had he told him this. And what Richard King would say.

"He would tell me to just do what I know to be the right thing and whatever happens just happens. It's what he always told us," John said.

"Then that is what you will do," Nelly said.

They walked back to the house holding hands. John thought about the day at the rock. Gradually, he felt his sorrow lift as they walked back to where the children were playing. Looking at them, he felt a new resolve. Life was hard and John knew it. But he was home now, and what he had was worth holding onto.

ACKNOWLEDGMENTS

First, I must mention my loving wife of fifty years, Terry, who has supported me in every endeavor I have attempted. When the LORD first talked about a wife being a helpmate I'm sure he had Terry in his thoughts, because if there ever was a man who needed a helpmate it's me. I could never have accomplished a task like this without her loving care. I'd also like to thank my dear friend, Susan Chambers. She believed in me when I didn't believe in myself. Her encouragement, literary talents, editing skills, judgments, and leadership pushed me through this process. Next, I'd like to thank all the loved ones, too numerous to mention, who inspired me and believed in me. You know who you are. And finally, I thank the person to whom I owe it all to, Jesus Christ my LORD and savior.